THE
CANA
MYSTERY

David Beckett

TUSCANY
PRESS LLC

WELLESLEY, MASSACHUSETTS
www.TuscanyPress.com

Tuscany Press, LLC
Wellesley, Massachusetts
www.TuscanyPress.com

The characters and events in this book are fictitious. Any similarity to real persons, living or dead, is coincidental and not intended by the author.

Publisher's Cataloging-in-Publication Data
(Prepared by The Donohue Group, Inc.)

Beckett, David, 1972–
    The Cana mystery / David Beckett.

      p. ; cm.

    ISBN: 978-1-939627-11-7 (hardcover)
    ISBN: 978-1-939627-10-0 (pbk.)
    ISBN: 978-1-939627-09-4 (ebook)

    1. Turning water into wine at the wedding at Cana (Miracle)—Fiction. 2. Benedict XVI, Pope, 1927—Fiction. 3. Massachusetts Institute of Technology—Graduate students—Fiction. 4. Storage jars—Middle East—Fiction. 5. Conspiracy—Middle East--Fiction. 6. Mystery and detective stories. I. Title.

PS3602.E355 C36 2013
813/.6   2013939718

Printed and bound in the United State of America

10   9   8   7   6   5   4   3   2   1

Text design and layout by Peri Swan.
This book was typeset in Garamond Premier Pro with Shelley Andante Script as a display typeface.

For Catherine

THE
CANA
MYSTERY

In a time when error reigns—
bleak days the world doth mourn,
cries of anguish, great with pain,
children of the light forlorn.

Ava of Göttweig,
"Der Antichrist," Vorau Manuscript
(trans. author)

PROLOGUE

Daybreak. Pope Pius II watches a fiery orb crest the Tiber. His mind drifts. He recalls that Aristotle's student Callippus once computed the seasons' duration, measuring the sun's movement within its ethereal sphere. While the pontiff ruminates, his valet methodically extinguishes the candles that had illuminated a long, busy night. Pius smiles. An educated man, he'd known it would be difficult to glean the secret. Nevertheless, anticipation grows in him. On this blessed day they may unlock the great enigma, a message concealed for a millennium.

One artifact has remained hidden in the catacombs since the Vandals' attack in 455. He'd retrieved the second from Scotland twenty-five years ago. Now he prays the cryptic knowledge these objects contain would avail his church in its desperate campaign against the Turks, who are occupying Constantinople.

Pius turns away from the window and crosses through a cleverly masked portal. Emanating from his private library, wondrous voices speak incomprehensible words. Inside, a dexterous young acolyte transcribes the mysterious cipher. Pius watches the boy ink words onto a scroll. Gradually, words form into couplets; couplets become quatrains. "It must be the lost prophecy," the

1

pope thinks, "just as Bessarion and Regiomontanus described." Pius understands not a syllable.

"What language is that, Jacopo?" he asks his most trusted cardinal.

"An ancient tongue, Holiness. Few in Christendom speak it. It's beyond my ken, but my young scribe can translate."

The pope is not surprised. Cardinal Jacopo Piccolomini-Ammannati is ever surrounded by an entourage of brilliant students. Over the years, he'd guided countless priests' careers. The shrewd academician could be elected pope himself someday, supported by this army of admirers and protégés.

"Very well. What does it say?"

The Gallic child smiles. He is eager to win favor with the Holy Father—and he is secretly pleased he will be able to report the prophecy to his true master, the brilliant Spider King. Having transcribed several quatrains into Latin, he begins to read aloud.

1

The tiny archipelago had been inhabited since prehistoric times. Romans named it Ilva, then Fussa, and, later, Bucina. In medieval times it was called Bicinara. Pisa and Genoa disputed ownership throughout the twelfth century. Four hundred years later, Corsican shepherds rechristened it Santa Maria Magdalena. Now it concealed a secret U.S. submarine base.

Across the bay a dilapidated ferry's halogen floodlights pierced the gathering fog. On board, Roderigo leaned against the wet metal rail and smoked. He checked his watch: 11:20 P.M., plenty of time. Earlier that day, he had crossed the causeway from Caprera and piloted his van through Moneta's narrow streets. The Italian's movements betrayed no anxiety. His papers were legitimate, his registration was authentic, and his custom-tailored delivery uniform bore Francese-Trinita Catering's interlocked F-T logo. Don VeMeli had seen to every detail.

The lumbering boat docked. Roderigo started the van and drove to the base, where, just before midnight, a moderately intoxicated guard waved him through security. At the appointed spot, the Italian parked, killed the ignition, rolled down the window, and tapped his cigarettes.

Before long, he detected a diesel engine's tubercular mutter. He swung his long legs out of the vehicle, stood upon the rain-soaked asphalt, and stretched. A motorized forklift emerged from the gloom. Roderigo hailed its driver, who nodded in recognition.

Working in collusive silence, the men removed three heavy suitcases from the van and replaced them with a ponderous steel container. Business complete, Roderigo was preparing to depart when he felt a hand on his elbow. He turned.

"Your boss . . . he keeps his word, right? He'll use it only on Arabs?"

The Italian's eyes narrowed. He appraised this curious confederate: shaved head, pale skin, several fierce tattoos, but really just a frightened lad.

"Because if that," the speaker continued, gesturing to the van's cargo, "goes off in New York, D.C., anywhere else in the States . . ."

Roderigo's nostrils flared, emitting a curl of bemused smoke. "Relax, *paisan*. The Gruppo hates ragheads as much as you. My boss will do the right thing, like Truman did in forty-five."

The serviceman's posture eased, and if he suffered further pangs of conscience, Roderigo knew, the million-dollar bribe would dull them.

"Okay. I just needed to be sure."

"No problem."

As they shook hands, the lanky Italian smiled, knowing the young American soldier would be dead inside a week. Roderigo rammed the door shut and started the van. Just before leaving, he called out, "Merry Christmas!"

BOSTON, FEBRUARY 2013

Ava was roused by her phone vibrating. Who calls at three in the morning? Groggily, she traced a finger across the screen to answer.

"Hello?"

"Hi, Ava. What's happening?"

The man's voice was familiar, but she couldn't quite place it. "Listen, I need help on something," he said. "What's your schedule next week?"

Emerging from a drowsy fugue, Ava struggled to identify the caller. Not Gabe, not Dad, not her thesis adviser. Maybe the pushy guy from the bachelorette party? Hadn't she given him a fake number? Was he stalking her?

"Who is this?" She was fully awake now, and riled.

"This is Paul. Paul Grant. Can you come to Yemen? My boss will pay for everything. We found something important and we need your help to—"

"Paul?" It had been years, and, as she recalled, they'd parted under ambiguous circumstances. Now he was calling in the middle of the night expecting her to drop everything and fly to Yemen?

"Is this a joke? Who is your boss?"

"Oh, I thought you knew. I work for Simon DeMaj. You've heard of him?"

Of course she had. DeMaj was a global celebrity. Rising from the slums of Algiers, the half-French, half-Algerian polymath had flown helicopters for the French air force before attending Yale. Later, he made headlines when his high-tech start-up landed contracts to provide Jordan, Syria, Egypt, and Libya with state-of-the-art digital infrastructure. DeMaj had wired half of the Middle East, becoming one of the world's four hundred richest men in the process. He was equally famous for romantic liaisons with models and actresses—juicy affairs providing fodder for gossip columns and tabloid pictorials. DeMaj was as likely to be seen hosting an economic development forum at Davos as canoodling with best-supporting-actress nominees at the California Governor's Ball.

"I may have heard the name," Ava deadpanned. "What does he want?"

"We need an expert in ancient languages," Paul told her, "someone who can solve difficult puzzles. I can't explain by phone, but you'll be well compensated. How about two thousand dollars a day?"

Despite herself, Ava was intrigued. She couldn't resist an intellectual challenge and she could use the money, but that was insufficient justification to leave the country.

"Paul, I need more info."

He groaned. "You'll get me in trouble. I'm really not allowed to say. How about this: I'll give you a hint and you figure it out, just like the old days."

In college, Ava had been known for cracking riddles. Classmates tried to stump her at every cocktail party, but she'd amazed them all. It was a gift. Too bad it didn't pay well.

She accepted the challenge. "Lay it on me."

"I'll e-mail you."

He pecked keys. "Okay, it's sent. I'm going on Expedia now. I'll book you an open-ended ticket from Boston to Yemen. Simon's lawyers will set up your visa and handle the diplomatic details. If you decide not to come, text me back at this number. Otherwise, I'll meet you at the airport in Sana'a."

She scrolled down to a message that was sent from PGRANT@ SDEMAJ.ORG: "Something sought in a historic hat bag has been found."

For half an hour Ava lay on her back and stared at the ceiling. She pondered the clue, working to discern a hidden subtext or

6

pattern, but she made no progress. A different puzzle preoccupied her mind: After all this time, why did Paul still have her number? Before she reached a firm conclusion, she fell into a dream.

When the alarm rang, Ava rolled out of bed. She dressed, grabbed her backpack, trotted downstairs, and, it being an exceptionally sunny morning, began riding her bicycle toward Harvard. Ava was earning her doctorate from MIT, but she'd enrolled in one cross-registered history course. She didn't need the credit; it was mainly an excuse to see her friends Gabe and Jess and to visit her beloved alma mater. After an invigorating ride, Ava skidded to a stop and secured her bike outside Lowell House. As she cut across the interior courtyard, her eyes lingered on a favorite tree, a majestic giant growing directly in front of the main entrance. Its tallest branches reached three stories; its lowest swept the ground. Each October it turned a brilliant gold, as if touched by Midas. Smiling, Ava crossed Mt. Auburn, made for Dunster Street, turned right onto Mass. Ave., and ducked into Au Bon Pain, ending up in line behind a striking young woman in a sheer tunic and skinny jeans.

"Hello, darling!" said Jess. Several male customers turned, secretly hoping. With her alluring features and sexy British accent, sable-haired Jess stood out in any crowd. A gifted scholar, she might have been Ava's rival. Instead, Jess numbered among the kindest, most sincere people in their class. Unlike many Harvardians, who would bayonet their peers to obtain a better grade or job, Jess rose above the competitive, duplicitous environment. She'd become one of Ava's closest confidantes and most steadfast allies.

"Ready to be televised?" Jess asked.

"What?"

"Have you forgotten? We have the guest lecture today. Bagelton. It'll be on Book TV."

Ava groaned. "You've got to be kidding. I knew he'd speak today, but I didn't realize it would be a media event."

Dr. Ron Bagelton was a rising academic celebrity. His books sold well, but Ava considered him guilty of pandering. The type of scholar who appeared on the History Channel, MSNBC, or *The Daily Show with Jon Stewart,* his usual method was to posit spectacular hypotheses based on scant evidence. One of his best-sellers described a previously unpublished *Divine Comedy* that featured characters who were different from those in the well-known version. Bagelton alleged that, contrary to Dante's wishes, a revisionist conspiracy had populated the inferno with victims chosen to reinforce orthodox Church values.

"It'll be a nightmare," Ava said, paying for their chai lattes.

"Why?"

She rolled her eyes. "Bagelton's ego is titanic. He'll use us as props to establish his brilliance. Our classmates haven't read his latest book, so they'll be unable to refute his outlandish theses. To the TV audience, polite passivity will be indistinguishable from submissive acceptance. Viewers will think Bagelton must be legit if he lectures an auditorium full of Ivy Leaguers, never mind that his treatise is just ahistorical speculation tarted up with academic gobbledygook."

They entered Harvard Yard and walked by Wadsworth House, a clapboard structure in which Washington stayed during the Revolutionary War. They passed Widener Library and entered a redbrick building named Emerson Hall. Ava and Jess took two of the last available seats in room 105, an airy lecture hall with three hundred wooden chairs bolted to its floor. Five minutes later, Dr. Bagelton burst through the doors and strode to the rostrum. With a sinking feeling, Ava whispered, "Here we go."

It was worse than she'd imagined. Bagelton lectured for thirty-five minutes, then spent another fifteen reading passages from his latest work, *The Philosopher-Queens,* its cover displayed for the cameras at all times. Afterward, he opened the floor to questions. There were no microphones for students. All cameras remained focused on the author. Ava recognized this bit of media manipulation. No cogent question, correction, or critique would be broadcast. Viewers would see only the speaker's smiling, confident replies. Despite the rigged game, Ava couldn't help but play. She raised her hand. Predictably, given the speaker's interest in pretty college girls, he called on her right away.

"Dr. Bagelton," she began, "your conjecture seems terribly unlikely. You assert that because highly advanced Atlanteans didn't conquer the ancient world, Atlantis must have been a peace-loving matriarchy. The notion certainly appeals, especially to women, but you offer no verification that a place called Atlantis ever existed. Even if we suspend our disbelief on that point, no archaeological evidence supports your second premise: that Atlantis achieved an advanced technology. Furthermore, you provide zero proof that the supposed inhabitants were peaceful. Maybe they tried to conquer the region but failed. Or if they did conquer—"

"My dear," Bagelton interrupted, "your course work must have skipped over the fact that no historical records document an Atlantean conquest, attempted or otherwise. If brave female warriors from Atlantis attacked Greece and Egypt, wouldn't some evidence remain? Because none exists, we must conclude that the Atlanteans were pacifists."

"No! The only logical conclusion to draw from no evidence is no conclusion."

Bagelton's features settled into a patronizing smirk. "As you advance in your studies, young lady, you'll discover that much true history has been repressed and hidden by the establishment. The fact that the world's first and, arguably, greatest civilization was dominated by strong, independent women threatened the monopoly of political power held by the Catholic Church and the European monarchs. These fearful males eradicated all evidence of Atlantis and its philosopher-queens."

To her amazement, Ava noticed many audience members nodding. What a crock! Frustrated, she collapsed back into her chair. The bigger the lie, she thought, the more books you sell.

The speaker called on another student, who expressed his deep admiration for *The Philosopher-Queens* and asked Bagelton if he needed a research assistant. The audience groaned, offended by such blatant boot-licking.

"I'll be happy to consider your résumé when I return from the G8 Summit in Italy," the author replied smugly.

After the lecture, Ava and Jess walked to the Garage, a converted building that housed a variety of shops and restaurants. Ava's favorite served authentic Vietnamese cuisine. Inside, boisterous students dined, joked, and debated. While Ava visited the rest room, Jess ordered a bowl of pho large enough to share. Minutes later, Jess spotted Ava threading her way through the maze of busy tables. Suddenly, Ava stopped. The restaurant's TV had captured her attention. A CNN reporter spoke.

"Catholics around the world were shocked when Pope Benedict XVI announced that he will resign for the good of the Church . . ."

Ava commanded the room to hush as the report continued.

"Thousands gathered in St. Peter's Basilica to attend the pope's Ash Wednesday service. The crowd gave Benedict a standing ovation. Many in the throng had tears in their eyes. Some observers waved papal flags, others lifted a huge banner reading GRAZIE SANTITA. Speaking softly in Italian, Benedict asked that the faithful 'continue to pray for me, the Church, and the future pope.' A chorus of schoolchildren sang in German. Benedict, who is Bavarian, thanked them for singing a hymn 'particularly dear to me.' He is the first pope to resign since Gregory XII, in 1415 . . ."

Ava shook her head. She turned from the television, came to the table, slid into a chair, and whipped out her iPhone. Jess saw that her companion was annoyed.

"What is it?"

"It wasn't . . ." Ava inhaled deeply, paused for a beat, continued. "CNN just compared Benedict's resignation to that of Gregory XII. The comparison isn't valid. The circumstances are different. Gregory refused to resign unless the antipopes—"

"Antipopes?"

"After the Great Western Schism, three men claimed to head the Church: Gregory XII in Rome, Benedict XIII in Avignon, and John XXIII in Pisa. Five years of chaos convinced Church leaders to hold the Council of Constance, which strongly suggested that all three popes resign. When Benedict refused, the council excommunicated him. John and Gregory both stepped down to become cardinals, but it wasn't an entirely voluntary move."

Jess nodded. Ava was Googling. She found a more historically precise article and read it aloud.

"Italian newspapers have lauded Benedict's shocking, unprecedented decision. 'We've entered uncharted territory,' remarked *La*

Repubblica's editor in chief, Ezio Mauro. In March, cardinals will convene to elect a new pope. Regardless of who next wears the Piscatory Ring, Benedict will enjoy a life of quiet prayer in a monastery on the Vatican gardens' far northern edge. His final papal acts will be audiences with key world leaders. Benedict has already agreed to see prominent politicians from Romania, Guatemala, Slovakia, San Marino, Andorra, his native Bavaria, and Italy. Many more requests are expected. The influential G8 has invited His Holiness to address its annual conference.

"While most Catholics praised the pope's decision, others fear the unexpected news validates an ancient prophecy that Benedict XVI will be the last good pope, that 'the seven-hilled city will be destroyed,' and that these events signal the end of the world. Such dire forecasts are found in the *Prophecy of the Popes,* a collection of cryptic Latin phrases attributed to Máel Máedóc Ua Morgair . . ."

Ava rolled her eyes and closed her phone.

Jess laughed. "Wow. That last bit is something Bagelton would enjoy."

"I know. Can you believe that guy?"

"He really got under your skin, didn't he?"

"No. As much as I disagree with Bagelton, I'm really furious with our classmates. They should have laughed him out of the building. Why do we tolerate pseudoscholarship? Success eludes responsible, legitimate writers who never plagiarize, monkey with facts, or exaggerate findings. Meanwhile, garbage like Bagelton's book sells a million copies."

"Are you surprised? People love myths. We invest in fantasies to make existence feel—what's the right word? Richer? More rewarding? Humdrum lives of quiet desperation take on meaning when they're populated by exciting supernatural beings and apocalyptic events."

"Does that make it rational to believe in the Roswell aliens? In Bigfoot?"

"Maybe not rational, but comforting. Lonely, frightened individuals form a community around their creed—any creed. Accepting and defending the existence of flying saucers, ghosts, angels, or Sasquatch helps certain people get along. Call it rational irrationality."

"If people need an emotional crutch that's fine, but it's still a delusion. No logical person believes things without evidence. Jess, I'm not demanding irrefutable scientific proof. There's not even a scintilla of evidence. Nil! Do these credulous saps believe a mad fairy zips from pillow to pillow collecting teeth?"

"Some probably do."

Ava laughed. "Okay. Good point. What did Mencken say? 'You'll never go broke underestimating the public.' People were convinced the world would end in 2012, and in 1844, and in the year 1000. I'd like to think humanity has advanced since the medieval era, but given the prevalence of superstition and magical thinking, I should probably be grateful no one wants to burn us as witches."

Jess grinned. "So you don't buy any of that stuff? Never check your horoscope?"

"No. No astrology. No conspiracy theories. No mysticism. I believe in scientific fact. Humans apprehend truth through rigorous experiment and analysis. Suggestions to the contrary are soft-minded nonsense or snake-oil scams."

"That sounds like your father talking."

It did. Richard Fischer was a paragon of scientific integrity. An atmospheric chemist at NASA, he'd been pressured by two administrations to revise data on how chlorofluorocarbons—CFCs—destroy ozone in the presence of high-frequency ultraviolet light.

Both times he'd refused, obliterating his prospects for advancement. Yet he'd become a hero in Ava's eyes. She smiled, thinking of her father, and wondered how her parents would react if she went to Yemen.

Sipping a spoonful of savory broth, Ava had a brainstorm. "Hey, I'm going to read you a message. Tell me if you know what it means: 'Something sought in a historic hat bag has been found.'"

Jess frowned. She mouthed each word, reflected a moment, then replied, "I've no earthly idea. What is it?"

"I don't know. It came this morning—supposed to be a riddle."

"A guy sent it, right?"

"Yeah. Why?"

"Only a person who never shops would say 'hat bag.' Hats come in boxes."

Ava's eyes widened, and for a second she looked dazed. She fell back in her seat.

"Are you okay?"

"Yes, I'm perfect," Ava replied, tossing her napkin onto the table. "Could you cover a few of my classes next week?"

Back at Lowell House, Ava climbed the stairs and let herself inside with the key that Gabe insisted she have. Dropping onto the ratty couch, she borrowed Gabe's iPad and wrote H-A-T-B-A-G on the touchscreen. Then, she rearranged those six letters into "T-A-B-G-H-A." A search under that spelling revealed dozens of websites. She picked one at random.

> Historic Tabgha, a city lost for centuries, was the
> setting for Christ's calling of the disciples. Here
> Jesus walked the shore and hailed Simon, Peter, and
> Andrew, three fishermen casting nets into the lake.

Tabgha was rumored to be the hiding place of the
legendary lost jars of Cana.

"What are the lost jars of Cana?" asked Gabe, biting into an
Oreo.

"Just Google it," Ava said. "There's an entry on Wikipedia."

"Yeah, but you probably wrote it."

Ava sipped her chai and smiled. "No, although I suspect I
know who did. It contains a few historical errors and is confused
regarding—"

"Just tell me!"

"Tell you what? The legend?"

"No. Tell me how you can drink that foul brew. You added,
what, six Splendas?"

She grinned. "I like it that way."

"Gross," muttered Gabe. "I don't know how you stand it. Now
please relate the legend of the lost jars."

"I'll tell you what I remember. In undergrad I was studying for
Professor Cusanus's final. Her lectures referenced several biblical
legends, things like the Holy Grail, the Spear of Destiny—"

"The Nazi thing?"

"Yes and no."

"What do you mean?"

"The Nazis thought the spear would make them invincible, but
it predates them by centuries. Back in biblical times, a Roman cen-
turion, Longinus, used the spear to stab Jesus. Hundreds of years
later, Baldwin II sold it to Louis IX to be enshrined in Paris. It disappeared during the Revolution—supposedly taken by Napoleon—
and it's in the Vatican now. Anyway, you've diverted me."

"Sorry."

"Cusanus also mentioned the lost jars, so I looked them up.
The gospel of John says Jesus attended a wedding feast at Cana.

When the party ran out of wine, Jesus ordered the servants to fill empty stone jars with water. The host tasted the contents, and shazam! Water had become wine. John considered it Jesus's first miracle. Anyway, the jars were taken . . ."

"Hey, I remember that story. These are those jars?"

"Exactly. The various Bible translations call them jars, water vessels, waterpots, or jugs. You can see them in Giotto's *Marriage at Cana,* although that artwork might not be the most accurate depiction. The relics are the subject of several wild stories. Apparently, the Crusaders searched for the jars. St. Peter may have taken them to Rome. A few historians claim the jars are hidden under Jerusalem, others suspect that the Knights Templar stashed them at Rosslyn Chapel."

"Or maybe they came from Atlantis and were created by Martians."

Ava giggled. "My thoughts exactly."

"Are they supposed to be magic or something?"

"Yeah. I mean, no, not magic, but almost anything Jesus touched was considered a sacred relic that could protect you from evil or cure diseases. Some medieval Christians thought the Holy Grail bestowed eternal youth."

"I saw that in a movie. What do the jars do?"

"I'm not sure. They might predict the future. According to legend, Jesus related a secret prophecy to his disciples. They hid the message in the jars and concealed them at Tabgha or Nag Hammadi or someplace. No one really knows. One account says they were taken to Rome and hidden in the catacombs. Eventually, the pope found the jars and tried to read the message."

"That's why the Church is so rich! Because the pope knows all the right lottery numbers and who'll win the World Series!"

Ava laughed. "No. This was centuries ago. I'm blanking on

who was pope, and it's unclear if even he understood the message. One legend warns that no human can read it with mortal eyes. In another story, the pope decided the prophecy was demonic and ordered the jars destroyed. The version I like says the pope couldn't comprehend the message because some jars were still hidden in the desert and the prophecy is too complex to be understood piecemeal."

Gabe nodded. "Was the message encoded?" he asked.

She could see that the notion appealed to him. Gabe saw the universe in terms of code. There was probably a fascinating information-theory problem nestled somewhere in her story. She suspected his subconscious was processing brilliant, nonlinear solutions as they spoke. It occurred to Ava that she might need his help.

"Maybe so," she said, encouragingly. "You wouldn't want just anyone reading it. If they took the trouble to hide the jars, why not encrypt the text?"

"And that's why no one can understand it!" Gabe said. "The apostles intended it that way. They knew the message might fall into the hands of wicked Emperor Nero or whoever was in charge. They didn't want evil people to know the future. If Nero foresaw that Christianity would spread throughout Europe, he'd have thrown all Christians to the lions. So the apostles separated the code into mutually interdependent sequences . . ."

Gabe was a rabid cryptography fan. As he rattled off ideas about the relative value of compression algorithms, Ava's mind wandered back to the mysterious phone call. What had they discovered, and why had Paul called her?

Gabe stood at the window, gazing out. After a minute, he turned. "Yemen?" he asked. "Don't you need a special visa? Do we even have an embassy there? What if something freaky happens?"

Stiffening, Ava said, "I'm a strong, independent woman. I speak three dialects of Arabic, and I've had all the necessary inoculations. I'm not a helpless little girl in need of male protection."

He wilted. "I know. I know all that. That's not what I meant, but you hear crazy stories about women traveling alone. Remember what happened to that CBS reporter in Cairo?"

She looked into his worried eyes. "You want me to be safe. I appreciate that, but I'm going. It's important. Will you help me?"

Gabe sighed. "Yes. Of course I will. You know I always will, but if you end up a prisoner in some nasty Sultan's harem . . ."

"Then you'll hack into the DOD mainframe and send Delta Force commandos to rescue me."

Gabe laughed. "Mainframe?" He shook his head. "No, I wouldn't—"

"Anyway," Ava interjected, cutting off his digression into technobabble, "I'll call each day until I'm safely home." At this remark, Gabe's eyes flashed with an idea.

"Here, take this." He tossed her a chunky black mobile phone that looked years out of date. Ava regarded him quizzically.

"It's a satphone, LEO. Should be fully charged."

"LEO?"

"Low Earth Orbit," Gabe explained. "I hacked it. Free unlimited minutes."

She smiled, impressed. "It wasn't my hack," he said quickly. "I got the code from a guy online, but it works. You can download data into my system, send me video of you in the shower—"

"Ha, ha, ha."

"I installed some cool encryption, making it untraceable. It should keep our conversations confidential, except from ECHELON and the NSA," Gabe joked.

Ava wrapped him in a bear hug. Gabe was wonderful. She knew he'd help. In her mind, Gabe was the kind, protective big brother she'd always wanted. Of course, she kept this to herself. Gabe didn't think of her as a sister, and Ava couldn't stand to hurt his feelings. Better to leave the matter unspoken, postpone the conversation, indefinitely if possible.

2

The plane began to roll. Runway lights flickered past Ava's window. The jet lifted off, lurched, and then steadied. Ava grabbed her laptop and began reading about the lost jars and various related miracles and locales. As the captain's voice announced passengers' freedom to move about the cabin, Ava reviewed her research. The first article was from *CNN Online,* dated December 21, 2004, and titled "Water to Wine: Are These the Jars?"

> Among the roots of ancient olive trees, archaeologists
> have found pieces of large jars. . . . Experts believe
> these could be the same kind of vessels Jesus used
> in his first miracle, and the site where the jars were
> found could be the location of biblical Cana. . . .
> Christian theologians attach great significance to the
> water-to-wine miracle. It was not only Jesus's first, but
> it also came at a crucial point in his ministry. The
> shards were found during a salvage dig in modern-
> day Cana, between Nazareth and Capernaum. Israeli
> archaeologist Yardena Alexander believes the Arab
> town was built near the ancient village. The jars
> date to the Roman period, when Jesus traveled the
> Galilee. "Just the existence of stone vessels is not
> enough to prove this is a biblical site," Alexander said.

> Nevertheless, she believes the vessels are the same
> type of jars described in the Gospel of John.

"How could she know?" Ava wondered. There were probably thousands of similar jars in ancient Israel. What's more, Ava didn't believe modern Cana was located in the same place as historical Cana. This seemed too pat. Scanning her research, she found the heading "Cana, Location."

> A tradition dating back to the eighth century
> identifies Cana with the settlement of Kafr Kanna,
> eight kilometers from Nazareth. Scholars have
> suggested alternatives to Kafr Kanna, including
> Kenet-al-Jalil, Qana, and Ani Kana.

Ava scrolled down absently. She doubted that so-called experts would ever agree on historical Cana's true location. Then, something caught her attention.

> . . . led to speculation about the ultimate location
> of the historically significant lost jars of Cana. John
> 2:12 states that, after the wedding, Jesus "went down
> to Capernaum with his mother, his brothers, and
> his disciples; and they remained there a few days."
> During this period, Christ may have announced
> a prophecy, which his followers recorded and
> sealed in the jars. Archaeologists sought the jars in
> Capernaum, others dug near modern-day Cana, but
> most maintain the jars were hidden in Tabgha.

She clicked on the file for Tabgha and found an article illustrated with a picture of a Romanesque mosaic.

Tabgha was described by a contemporaneous source as "not far from Capernaum, facing the Sea of Galilee . . . a well-watered land where lush grasses grow, with numerous trees and palms. Seven springs provide abundant water." The Synoptics locate the city in "a desert place" near Bethsaida, but the Gospel of John describes it as lush and grassy. Today, scholars believe a newly discovered archaeological site is the lost city of Tabgha, where the Church of the Multiplication stands. Tabgha is derived from the Greek name Heptapegon, meaning "seven springs." According to legend, Tabgha was situated on the northwest shore of the Sea of Galilee. St. Jerome referred to Tabgha as *eremos,* meaning "the solitude."

Ava opened the next file: "Newly Discovered Archaeological Site."

Recent excavation, funded by the philanthropist Simon DeMaj, unearthed walls and mosaics of a fourth-century Byzantine church near the junction of Highways 90 and 87, about ten kilometers north of Tiberias. A mosaic depicting fish, loaves, and one of the legendary jars can be seen next to a large rock. Historians believe this location was revered in Byzantine culture.

She shook her head. Did they actually have the nerve to call Simon DeMaj a philanthropist? That word means "lover of mankind." If he loves humanity so much, she thought, why does he live in a secluded villa and travel by private helicopter?

Although many attribute Tabgha's annihilation to the Arab invasion, it was more likely destroyed in AD 614 by Persians. Regardless, the city was lost for centuries. German explorers claimed to have rediscovered Tabgha in 1932 while seeking the lost jars of Cana. Because no evidence of the jars has been found at Tabgha or Jerusalem, scholars believe the jars must have been removed to a secret location (probably in Egypt) to prevent their being stolen or destroyed by invaders.

An effete flight attendant with a purely professional smile brought Ava a tiny cup of tomato juice. She'd have preferred the whole can. Maybe she could get a decent Bloody Mary during her three-hour layover. Ava closed her computer, reclined her seat, and dozed until the captain announced they'd begun their descent into Atlanta.

As she waited for the connecting flight, Ava resumed her research. Indexed under "Lost Jars" and "Cana," she found an article by Professor Alan Millard.

Archaeologists have found several stone jars in the ruined houses of first-century Jerusalem. At least six jars stood in the basement kitchen of the Burnt House. They are 65–80 centimeters (2–2.5 feet) tall, were shaped and finished on a very big lathe, and were given a pedestal foot and simple decoration. Such stone jars would hold large quantities of water for washing and kitchen needs. Flat disks served as lids. The jars at Cana may have been similar to these.

These facts squared with information from a particularly well-researched 2002 piece by Yitzhak Magen.

> Barrel-shaped kratars appear in different sizes, from
> 76 centimeters up to 87 centimeters. These stone jars
> have a wide opening. Some feature simple patterns
> while others have elaborate ornamentation, modeled
> after decorated bronze calyx kratars. Examples found
> on the Temple Mount have a large hemispheric
> receptacle and a base composed of a plinth and a
> torus. Larger kallal-type vessels had circular stone
> lids ranging from 40 centimeters to 50 centimeters
> in diameter, with the top surface worked into a
> profiled molding. The lids' underside is typically flat,
> although some have a stepped rim to fit the jar.

Eventually it was time to board. Passengers pushed and jostled their way onto the Boeing 777. A nasal voice boomed over the PA, demanding that everyone follow instructions. After stowing her carry-on and fastening her seat belt, Ava resumed reading until interrupted by the singsong tones of mock courtesy: "Miss, you must be eighteen or older to sit in an exit row."

Ava looked up to behold a stern attendant whose countenance had been drained of beauty by decades of nagging. "Thanks for the update."

"Honey, maybe you don't understand. You can't sit here unless you're eighteen."

Several passengers turned. Blood rushed to Ava's face. Her eyes widened, then narrowed. "I'm twenty-six," she snapped. The attendant paused, dubious. Ava went on, "I graduated from Harvard four years ago. Next year I'll finish my Ph.D. I'm twenty-six. Do you need to see my passport?"

"No, that's fine," the woman murmured, wandering off to bother the next passenger.

Paul was bone weary. He felt sand in his shoes, in his hair, even under his fingernails. Strong body odor attested to the fact that he'd not showered for days. Still, the work was exciting. When he accepted this job, he never expected to participate in one of history's great discoveries. His phone rang. It was Simon, his mercurial boss.

"Get packed, and make sure the truck is ready. We're going back to HQ. We need to perform more extensive testing, and the field equipment is inadequate. You've an hour."

Grinning, Paul verbally acknowledged the instructions. He loved that Simon called his Yemen office "HQ." So military! Paul unzipped his bag and started tossing in dirty clothes, toothbrush, razor . . .

Then he heard angry shouting outside the tent. What now? Had Simon failed to pay sufficient baksheesh to some petty official? Were the diggers demanding overtime? He stepped outside, ready to smooth whatever feathers Simon had ruffled. Paul walked to the truck. A short distance ahead, Simon argued in Arabic with a group of seven locals. Two were very old men. The others were much younger—some looked just fifteen or sixteen. They were shouting and blocking Simon's progress. Paul couldn't understand a word, but the argument sounded intense. After a few minutes DeMaj reentered the command tent and gathered his security team. "Uh-oh," Paul whispered. The guards were tough customers. Technically off-duty police, they were actually thugs. Simon kept them on the payroll to placate Sheik Ahmed, the regional drug lord. They carried AK-47s everywhere they went.

Simon's security team waved their guns threateningly, but the seven brave Egyptians stood their ground. DeMaj was irate. He threw up his hands in frustration and shouted in Arabic.

Then the guards started firing. Each emptied a full clip into the unarmed men, mowing them down, riddling their bodies with holes. Blood sprayed into the air. Bullets whizzed by Paul's face; others slammed into the vehicle.

"No!" Paul shouted. He climbed quickly into the truck and punched the ignition. He could overlook bribery, but not murder. Not the murder of innocent civilians. Not the murder of children.

As he hit the gas, he shouted, "I quit! Do you hear me, Simon? I quit! You'll never get the jars, and you can go to hell!"

Furious, scared, and alone, Paul sped into the dark, empty desert.

Halfway across the Atlantic, Ava tired of solving sudokus and resumed her research. Cross-referencing "hidden meaning" with "gospels," "Jesus," and "Lost Jars of Cana," she found an article among her files.

> Much controversy exists over what (if anything)
> the sacred jars represent. One theory is that they
> stand for the early Christian geographic divisions,
> and the leftover wine represents the Temple. Thus,
> as the wine is sealed in the jars, so the ancient
> Temple is superseded by the Christian churches. The
> importance of the jars' number is clear. In the Old
> Testament, the number 7 signifies wholeness and
> completeness. A week has 7 days. On the 7th day,
> God rested because his work was finished. There are
> 6 jars because Jesus himself is the 7th. Christ placed
> significance on the leftovers from these miracles,
> whether collected in baskets or in jars. When asked

by his disciples what to do, he chides: "Having ears,
hear ye not? Do ye not remember? How is it that ye
do not understand?" (Mark 8:18–21)

Ava deleted that article. She had no tolerance for mysticism
or numerology. She refined her search terms. To her great amusement, under "legend + Cana + wedding + jars," she found a
2012 article cowritten by none other than Dr. Ron Bagelton. Ava
couldn't resist giving it a look.

> The first miracle occurred at a marriage feast,
> often considered the wedding of Mary and John
> the Apostle, but a suppressed, older version of the
> legend reveals that the wedding was between Mary
> Magdalene and Jesus himself.

She rolled her eyes. Naturally, the unscrupulous Bagelton
would exploit the supposed proof that Jesus had been married.
Ava recalled the buzz around Harvard when Professor Karen
King unveiled a business card–size papyrus fragment purport-
ing to quote Jesus mentioning a wife. The gullible U.S. media
went wild. Fortunately, sober-minded journals exercised more
caution. The *Harvard Theological Review* postponed publica-
tion of Dr. King's article, citing the need for further research.
In Italy, the Vatican's *L'Osservatore Romano* declared the fragment a "very modern forgery." Faced with the growing consensus
among scholars that she'd been victimized by a hoax, Dr. King
conceded the existence of doubts about the fragment's authenticity, accepted the need for additional testing, and agreed to revise
her paper. Bagelton's article, unencumbered by any mention of
the dispute, continued.

The Secret Gospel of Mark relates the story of Jesus
in Capernaum, where Jesus says: "Happy are those
invited to the wedding feast of the Lamb. Write
down the true words of God. The one alone shall be
chaste [fruitless]. Only two together behold [contain]
the truth." Later, Jesus explains why Romans cannot
yet comprehend his message: "They listen, but do not
understand, because their minds are dull. They have
stopped-up ears. If you have ears, listen to what the
Spirit says to the people!"

Ava skipped a few paragraphs, then read on.

In Revelation 5:2, St. John writes: "Who is worthy
to break the seals and unlock the message?" This
passage has never been deciphered. The interpretation
might be similar to cryptic writings of Greek
mysticism. There have been attempts throughout
history to decode a biblical instruction set for
creating a mystic diagram, taking the gematria of the
passage into account.

Gematria? Ava laughed out loud. "Give me a break," she
thought. "How does a man like Bagelton still have an academic
career?" She moved on to the next article. On the whole, it provided more history and less baloney, but it concluded:

Some scholars interpret these stories as factual events,
prodding fanatics and treasure hunters to seek the
relics mentioned in the biblical text. The legendary
lost jars of Cana, said by John to have been used
when Christ converted water to wine, are rumored

to contain an unreadable prophecy predicting the ultimate apocalypse and providing the subtext for the warnings in Revelation against the coming Antichrist.

"Great," thought Ava, closing her laptop. "The end of the world."

Simon sat in his tent and fumed. Savage winds jostled the tent posts, rocking a kerosene lantern to and fro. Each pendular swing cast fearsome shadows across the sandy floor, sometimes lighting and sometimes obscuring Simon's face. He cursed. Events had overtaken them. The recovery mission had devolved into disaster, and now the situation was spiraling out of control. He tried Paul's phone again. No answer. DeMaj fought to maintain his composure. Pouring another cup of coffee, he wondered: Where would the young American go? What would he think? And what of the girl, the ancient-languages expert? She must arrive in Sana'a soon. Did she know anything? Would she be difficult? As the sirocco clawed the taut canvas, Simon plotted his next move. Reluctantly, he unlocked his phone and dialed Sheik Ahmed's number.

3

Surrounded by dramatic mountains of basalt, Sana'a has been inhabited for at least twenty-five hundred years. According to legend, it was founded by Noah's son Shem after the Great Flood. Ava remembered Sana'a had been conquered by the Mamelukes in 1517 and again by the Ottomans under Sulieman the Magnificent. Fortunately, neither conquest resulted in the historic citadel's destruction.

The plane landed and Ava breezed through customs. Mildly disappointed to find no welcoming committee, she waited as fellow passengers greeted friends, family, and business associates. Eventually, only Ava and a man remained at the gate. She regarded him furtively. His features had a distinctively vulpine aspect. Ava didn't recognize him from the plane. He must be waiting for someone, but she was the only passenger left. Was he waiting for her? She tried to ask him, but when she approached, he retreated into the airport crowd. With a shrug, Ava hoisted her backpack and trekked to baggage claim.

Twenty minutes later she'd recovered her gigantic suitcase from the carousel. There was still no sign of Paul. She rested her bags on a bench of polished chrome and black vinyl and sat down to wait. After all, she reasoned, why should she hurry? They were paying her two thousand dollars a day. Almost ten minutes passed before her natural impatience gained the upper hand. Ava unlocked her phone and attempted to check her voice mail but she didn't get service in Yemen.

Then she remembered Gabe's satphone. It should work anywhere. Kneeling, she opened her suitcase and began searching through its contents. At that moment she caught a chilling reflection in the chrome of the bench. Ava froze. It was the man from the gate. Concealed behind a pillar, he was watching her.

As terror gripped her, Ava struggled to remain calm. She told herself there was nothing to fear. He was probably just a lonely guy who watched women in airports. She shut her suitcase, stood, and began dragging her bags toward the exit. As she neared the automatic glass doors, she again looked at her reflection. Was anyone behind her? She wasn't sure. Then she saw him. He was following her out of the building. Heart pounding, Ava started to sweat. She tried to hurry, but the heavy suitcase anchored her in place. With all her might, Ava jerked it onto her hip, somehow curled her fingers beneath it, and jogged out the door. Yelling apologies in Arabic, she pushed to the front of the taxi line and threw herself into a waiting cab.

"Hotel," she demanded. "Hurry!" The driver dropped his newspaper and turned the ignition. As the cab pulled away from the curb, Ava glanced back through the rear window. Her pursuer had disappeared.

The taxi deposited Ava at an expensive tourist lodging. She checked in, keeping the receipt for reimbursement. Lugging her heavy bags, a bellhop guided Ava to her room and left the key. She gave him a nice tip, mentally adding it to her travel-expense tally. Alone, Ava sat on the edge of the bed, heart still racing from the traumatic experience of being followed. She felt scared and vulnerable. Worse, she couldn't decide if she'd overreacted. Was she a stereotypical American, fearful that every foreigner posed a threat?

Using the hotel phone, she called home. The call went straight to voicemail. Ava's mother, Helen, never answered calls from unfamiliar numbers. After recording a brief message saying that she'd arrived safely, Ava hung up and wondered if that was true. Was she in danger? Maybe she was paranoid. Regardless, she'd make a poor first impression on Mr. DeMaj in this condition. She needed to decompress, and for Ava the best method was exercise. Whenever she stayed in a high-rise hotel she got a terrific workout sprinting up and down the stairs. Ava stripped off her floral dress and donned black running shorts, a white tank top, and pink Reeboks. She dropped her passport, room key, wallet, and Gabe's satphone into a mini backpack, which she tied across her torso. Then, stretching her arms high above her head, she jogged into the hall and went in search of the stairwell.

In Ava's opinion the exits were poorly marked. After two wrong turns, she was lost. Although she could read Arabic, no signs or arrows directed her to the stairs. "What should we do in case of fire?" she thought acidly to herself. As she neared the corner, the elevator's bell rang. Ava relaxed. She'd just ride down to the lobby and ask the concierge about gym facilities, but when she turned, her heart jumped into her throat. The man from the airport had just exited the elevator. He was faced away from Ava, scanning room numbers. This wasn't paranoia. He'd followed her here. As she watched, he began walking down the opposite hall. Ava counted three rapid heartbeats and—timing the automatic doors precisely—dashed into the elevator. She must have made a sound, because at the last instant the man turned. Dark eyes brimming with malice, he stared into her as the stainless-steel doors slid shut.

Several times Ava pounded the LOBBY button. Enduring the agonizingly slow descent, Ava curled her hands into fists and vowed to make the man pay dearly for anything he took. Finally, the bell rang and the doors opened. She peered out of the elevator. He wasn't there. Never one to test fate, she ran past the startled bellhop to the front door.

"Gabe," Ava shouted into the chunky black phone. "Gabe, please! I'm in trouble!" She didn't want to mention the man following her, but she needed to convince him this was urgent. A long pause ensued. Was it a technical impediment or was Gabe making up his mind?

"Okay, Ava. What do you need?"

She gave silent thanks that she knew someone as savvy and loyal as Gabe. They'd met her sophomore year. Gabe lived in the dorm room directly above Ava's. Her roommate had called the resident tutor to complain about a "psycho" upstairs who insisted on blasting electronica until five in the morning and apparently smoking clove cigarettes, in obvious violation of dorm rules. Gabe came down the next day to apologize. Ava answered the door in a damp sports bra and running shorts. Even now she grinned, remembering his geeky, endearing efforts to maintain eye contact. He stammered out his mea culpas and explained that he'd been up all night blogging (critiquing something called *carnivore*) and that whenever he got into his hacker zone he lost all concept of time, music volume, everything.

Except for the clove cigarettes, which he quit that year, and the fact that he'd risen to become a resident tutor himself, Gabe remained essentially the same sweet-natured guy. He was a little taller and heavier but just as bright, quirky, innocent, and lovable.

"My contact never showed at the airport. I need to find him and all I have is a phone number. I'm not even sure what continent he's on. Can you help?"

"When was the last time you spoke?"

"Right before I left Boston." When was that? It must have been at least twenty-four hours before, but she couldn't be sure with all the time-zone changes. To Ava it seemed that a week had passed.

"Give me the number. I'll work backward. Try to use GPS. You're probably within signal-intercept range of Agios Nikolaos."

"Of what?"

"Nothing. Forget I said it. You don't want to know. Maintain plausible deniability."

"Okay. Just try, Gabe. That's all I ask."

"I will, but if I can't find anything, will you take the next plane home?"

"Maybe," Ava replied, adding silently, "unless they're still watching the airport."

"I found him," Gabe announced a short time later.

"Brilliant!"

"Or at least I found his phone. I can't be certain he's there. I have a satellite image of the location and the coordinates. It's in Egypt, very remote. There appears to be some kind of settlement. Just a village, I guess, at the foot of Al-Qalzam Mountain. The closest town might be Al Zaafarana. Does any of that ring a bell?"

Ava ignored the question. "What's the best way to get there?"

"Just a sec." She knew his tone: frustrated. He thinks I should come home now, she thought. He's probably right.

"I can book you a flight from Sana'a to Cairo. From there, I'm sure I can find ground transportation to the coordinates. Do you want—"

"No," she said, remembering the close call at the airport. "I prefer not to fly. Egypt is just across the Red Sea. Can you find me a boat?"

"Call me back in thirty."

Ava had every confidence that somehow Gabe would come through. I'm really going to owe him, she thought. Relying on Gabe was becoming a habit. Once, in college, he worked all night helping Ava translate Rongorongo glyphs. She worried they might lose touch after graduation, so she was thrilled to learn he'd be staying in Boston for grad school. For the hundredth time Ava wondered if that had been a coincidence. She knew Gabe could hack into any university's admissions department, but with his credentials every top school wanted him anyway. Gabe had written a revolutionary program for her Ph.D. project on the Great Vowel Shift, a subject of interest to linguistics scholars and students of language evolution. Enthusiastic at first, lately she'd begun questioning if that subject would be her life's work. "I guess that's why I'm here," she mused, "to find my calling."

A half hour later, Gabe had a solution. "Hire a truck. Have the driver to take you to Al-Salif. It's a fishing village just a few hours to your west. Of course, getting there might not be cheap."

"No problem," Ava lied. She had only about eight hundred dollars in cash, and she assumed few Yemeni truckers for hire took credit.

"I found a contact running fishing boats off Kamaran Island." Where did he find these people? "He'll meet you at the Al-Salif harbor. Look for a boat with two moons on its prow."

"Two moons. Got it. You're an angel!"

"Aw, shucks."

"Oh, Gabe? Do the two-moons guys take plastic? I mean, can I pay with my AmEx?"

A pause, then: "It's already done. A substantial amount of euros was transferred to their German bank, to be held in escrow. They'll receive the access code after they deliver you safely to Egypt."

"How did you—"

"Plausible deniability, Ava. Maintain plausible deniability."

She arrived at the Red Sea port of Al-Salif just in time to witness a sunset of lyrical beauty. She paid her driver and walked to the harbor, seeking a boat with two moons on the prow. Were they full moons? Half moons? Crescent moons? Gabe hadn't specified. Ava feared she'd never find the proper watercraft. As it turned out, she needn't have worried. The mustached Yemeni captain spotted her easily. Few American tourists visited Al-Salif. Furthermore, Ava remained conspicuously garbed in her flimsy tank top, running shorts, and sneakers. She resolved to obtain culturally appropriate —and warmer—attire at the earliest opportunity.

The captain ferried her across the bay to Kamaran Island. Because they couldn't depart until morning, he offered her accommodations in a traditional Tihama hut, just steps from the seashore. Ava was charmed. Islanders played music and cooked on the beach. She met several Europeans who'd come to scuba-dive on the reefs and around historic shipwrecks. They were having a grand time and invited her to join them. As she mingled, a donkey wandered over and sniffed her neck. She wondered how she must smell. It had been awhile since she'd washed. An island boy, wearing a faded San Antonio Spurs jersey, gave her the thumbs-up sign and said: "America!"

Ava responded in fluent Arabic. *"Salaam aleikum,"* she said, and asked him if there was a clothing store nearby. Surprised, he pointed to the dive shop.

She attempted to purchase a change of clothes, but the shop sold only bathing suits and T-shirts. Ava shrugged and bought one of each. At least they were clean. She wandered back to the beach and accepted a plate of grilled fish. Sitting on a stone bench appointed with colorful, embroidered cushions, she watched dolphins splash happily in the bay. The food was succulent and delicious.

After dinner Ava hiked among the ruins of a Portuguese fort predating the island's sixteenth-century Ottoman conquest. She found a private spot, removed the satphone from her backpack, and called the hotel in Sana'a. Claiming a family emergency, she asked the receptionist if the staff could store her luggage until she returned.

"That won't be necessary," came the answer. "Your husband collected your belongings this afternoon."

"My husband?"

"Yes, ma'am. He sounded extremely concerned. Can you give me your location? Is there somewhere he can reach you?"

Ava hung up. Drained, she retired to her hut and crawled under the mosquito netting but couldn't stay asleep. Wild camels roamed the island's interior. Whenever one snorted or bucked, Ava snapped awake, certain that evil men had found her.

At dawn the captain was surprised to find his American passenger packed and ready. He and a crewman helped her cross the narrow gangplank. After they cast off, he showed Ava to a tiny cabin, then left. Ava yawned. The jet lag and stress were catching up with her. All morning she'd been making cognitive errors, speaking ungrammatically, misjudging distances. She closed the cabin door and turned the latch, locking herself in. The bunk was wedged against the gunwale and smelled of dried fish. Outside, she heard gulls' cries. Waves washed gently and regularly against the hull. As the boat entered the Red Sea, Ava nodded off.

When she woke up, the boat was in the Gulf of Suez. Ava went on deck to bask in the glorious afternoon sun. As they passed the ancient lighthouse at Ras Gharib, she watched the ship's wake trace a long, chalky path over the sapphire swells.

At dusk they docked at Al Zaafarana, on the Egyptian coast. The experienced crew snuck her ashore with little fanfare and no difficulty. After thanking them profusely, Ava called Gabe to confirm her arrival. She handed the phone to the captain, and Gabe transmitted the authorization code, releasing the funds held in escrow. The captain smiled.

Satisfied that Ava was safe, Gabe told her that he'd reserved a room for her at the Sahara Inn. "Thank you so much," she said warmly. In the hotel's gift shop, Ava exchanged a substantial portion of her dwindling cash for some conservative khaki shorts, a white T-shirt, and sunglasses. She found her room, bathed, and slept. The next morning, she rose early and hired a taxi for the ride inland.

"Ava? Ava! What are you doing here?"

"What do you think I'm doing? Going on safari? You invited me! You paid for my stupid plane ticket!"

"But why are you in Egypt? You're supposed to be in Yemen. How the hell did you find me?"

"I have friends in high places. Now you answer my questions. Why didn't you meet me at the airport? Why are you hiding in a monastery? And most important, why is someone following me?"

Paul's face clouded. "What man?" Ava saw that he was greatly disturbed by her questions, and Paul didn't scare easily. This wasn't good. She was becoming more and more frightened. It didn't feel like an adventure anymore. Ava dropped the tough act.

"A dangerous-looking man intercepted me in Sana'a. He must have known my flight number. He followed me to my hotel, but I lost him in the Salt Market."

Paul was stunned. "Ava," he said, "it's all gone to hell. I don't understand what's happening. People have been killed. I hoped that if I didn't show at the airport, you'd just turn around, fly home, and rack up a few thousand frequent-flyer miles. I don't want you to be in danger."

"Wait, did you say killed?"

"At least seven people are dead. Two were just kids. It's awful." Paul looked like he might cry. Ava was terrified now. He continued, "It's all about the damn jars. I had no idea he'd go so far. I mean, I thought we were friends. I knew he was ambitions, but this is beyond ambition. He's obsessed! I never—"

"Wait a second, Paul. Are you talking about the jars from the legend?"

"Yes," he said. "We found the lost jars of Cana. They exist. They're real."

4

"Tell me everything!" Ava's fears were overtaken by her curiosity. This might rank among the greatest historical, archaeological, even religious finds of the past two hundred years. The jars were, theoretically, a direct link to Jesus Christ. This could be the seminal moment of her academic career, the basis for an award-winning book, a professorship, even tenure. Hungry for details, she pressed Paul to relate the tale.

"I don't know much. I'm sorry, Ava. I don't know the history. I don't even know where Cana is."

"Just tell me what happened."

"At our excavation in Israel, the diggers found part of a mosaic beneath an ancient church floor. It contained a map."

She was intrigued. In a hoarse voice, she asked, "Can you describe it?"

"It was oriented east, toward the altar. Simon said it was dedicated in AD 540. The intact section shows the region between southern Lebanon and the Nile Delta, from Alexandria all the way to the Sinai."

Just then Paul noticed Ava wobbling. Taking her arm, he helped her into a chair and fetched a cup of water. Once she could breathe again, Ava couldn't contain her excitement, "That map is a major find," she said. "It predates the Persian conquest!"

Paul shrugged. "If you say so. Anyway, the mosaic depicts several historical sites—Jericho, Nablus, Ashkelon, Bethlehem—a bunch of names in Greek. There's also a peculiar location hidden deep in the Red Sea Mountains. It had no name, just an illustration of two jars. Simon was obsessed with it. He dispatched a full archaeological team to that location, about eighty kilometers from here. Last week they found something. I was with Simon when he got the call. He was ecstatic. He kept saying, 'Are they intact? Are they sealed? How many are present?' He went nuts when they couldn't answer his questions. He canceled all our meetings. We jumped into his helicopter and flew to Egypt. By the time we landed they'd cleared the entrance to an ancient fortress. Underneath the stone structure were some caves connected by a network of tunnels. Simon was so focused. The jars must be worth a staggering amount of cash."

"If genuine, they're priceless," Ava said. Then she frowned. She knew Simon was an unscrupulous businessman. A high-tech mogul, he had a reputation for dubious ethics, antitrust violations, bribery, and seven-figure court settlements. Arrogant and outspoken, he'd notoriously lobbied the SEC and the IRS to investigate his competition, but Ava was shocked that he'd stoop to smuggling antiquities. If the jars were found here, they were rightfully Egyptian property.

"How much could he get for them?" Paul asked.

Ava's brow furrowed. "Some collectors would pay millions in secret, but he'd have a lot of trouble selling the artifacts without getting caught. He'd risk becoming an international criminal." Ava deliberated for a moment and then announced, "He doesn't plan to sell."

"Huh? I don't understand."

"DeMaj is a billionaire. He wouldn't care about another few

million. He has too much to lose. He wants the prestige. If he's discovered the lost jars, his name will go down in the annals of archaeology. He'll be mentioned in the same sentences as Howard Carter, Hiram Bingham, and Heinrich Schliemann."

"Do you think?" From his tone, it was clear that Paul didn't quite buy it, but he knew Ava well enough to recall that her deductions were almost never wrong. People in her world learned not to contradict her without an extremely good reason.

Ava's eyes narrowed. It wasn't about money. That didn't fit the profile. Simon was no stranger to controversy. He denied that global warming was a serious problem, he moved thousands of high-paying American jobs offshore, and he consorted with all manner of unsavory people, but DeMaj was indisputably shrewd. Surely he'd performed a cost-benefit analysis. The potential profit from selling on the black market couldn't justify the risk of getting caught, losing his investment, and going to jail. "Do you disagree?" she asked, ready to dissect any counterargument.

"No, I . . . I'm sure you're right. I just didn't realize he was doing all this archaeology stuff to be famous. I mean, he's already famous. He's been on the cover of *Wired* and *Forbes*. He dates supermodels. He's talking about buying an NBA team."

"It's a different kind of fame. This discovery would garner respect from academics, museums, and universities. All the ivory-tower intellectuals who complain about his politically incorrect outlook would be forced to bow and scrape, to acknowledge his colossal contribution to our knowledge of the ancient world."

"You're probably right, as usual. I'm just shocked he'd be willing to kill for that."

She blanched. "You mean Simon killed those people? You got me mixed up with a murderer? Nice. I think you'd better tell me everything."

"Okay," said Paul. "But I didn't mean to get you in trouble. I didn't realize—"

"Just tell the story. You can apologize later."

"Fair enough. As I said, when we landed at the excavation site, Simon was thrilled. We went into the cave, and the diggers led us to where they'd found the jars. It looked like a natural cave, except the air was bone dry. We could see the tops of two jars poking out of the sand. Simon was going crazy, telling everyone to be super careful. He offered the workers triple wages not to damage the jars, and he took hundreds of pictures. He wanted them dug up just so and taken to a clean room. That's when he told me to call you."

"Wait," said Ava, puzzled. "Simon DeMaj asked for me?"

"Well, no, not specifically. Simon told me to hire the smartest person available, someone who knows everything about everything, who understands history and reads ancient languages. Someone who can solve an impossible riddle."

"And you called me?"

"Of course," he said. "You're the smartest person I've ever met."

Ava felt as though she would cry. She knew Paul wasn't flattering her. In his direct way, he'd just stated his opinion, but his words constituted one of the nicest compliments she'd ever received. Embarrassment compelled her to change the subject.

"Speaking of phone calls, have you considered that DeMaj might track your GPS signal?"

"Yeah. That's how you found me, isn't it?"

She nodded, and Paul continued: "Yesterday, I gave my phone to some westbound Ababda nomads. I told them to call anyone they wanted. Why not? Simon gets the damn bill anyway."

Ava chuckled. If they tried to find Paul that way, they'd end up tracking signals from all over the Aswan. She was ready to hear the rest of his narrative. "What happened after we talked?"

"I booked your ticket on my laptop and went back down into the cave. The workers and I spent the remainder of the evening digging with little brushes. We didn't even stop for meals. That's why I was so rushed when we spoke. Phones don't work in the caves, and Simon insisted I supervise the excavation. He suspected some diggers were planning to steal the jars."

"Were you using locals?"

"Hell, we didn't know who we were using. More and more workers kept showing up, drawn by all the *gineih* Simon was doling out. He just hired everybody and told me to watch them. Eventually we finished digging. Once both jars were disinterred, Simon and I inspected them under a magnifying glass. He told me to look for words, letters, symbols, codes, numbers, anything written or etched." Paul looked sharply at Ava. "What was he after?"

"I'll tell you later," she said. "Just finish the story."

"We scrutinized the jars but found only a few bumps and chips—no symbols, no codes. Obviously, Simon was dissatisfied. We hauled the jars into a private tent and he ordered all the workers to leave. Once we were alone, I helped him unseal the jars. We used surgical instruments to remove the thick clay lids. We were so careful that it took hours. Finally, we got them open—"

"What was inside?" Ava asked, her eyes flashing with excitement. "Were there scrolls? Copper codices? Was there a message?"

"Damn. That's exactly what Simon asked. You sound just like him. 'Where's the codex? Where's the message?' He was going ape."

"Why?" she asked. "Did you break something? Were the jars damaged?"

"He was furious because the jars were empty. They stank a little, like old vinegar, but both were a hundred percent empty.

There was no hidden message. Not inside a jar, not written on a jar. I guess somebody else found it first."

They shared a spartan dinner. Afterward, Paul told her the story of the murders. He could barely keep the rage out of his voice.

"Who do you think they were?" he asked Ava.

"I'm not sure. You said they were locals. The Beja? Bedouins maybe? It sounds like they objected to Simon removing priceless artifacts from their homeland. It's not uncommon. During the 2011 revolution students formed a human chain, using their bodies to protect artifacts displayed in the Egyptian Museum."

Paul nodded. He confessed that he was perplexed by the situation. He'd been hiding at the monastery, getting his head together and pondering his options. He still wasn't sure what to do, but he promised to keep her safe. After listening awhile, Ava spoke.

"Look, it's okay to be scared. You'll lose your job, maybe even be charged as an accomplice," she said, "but we must contact the authorities."

"Job? Oh, I'm not worried about my job," he said, smiling for the first time. "I'm pretty sure I communicated my resignation loud and clear."

Ava gave him a warm look. "I'm proud of you."

Working for DeMaj was a dream gig: six-figure salary, first-class travel to exotic lands, meetings with world leaders and scientists. Just how someone with Paul's modest academic credentials landed such a deluxe position mystified her.

"And I know you consider Simon a friend . . ."

"No," Paul corrected her. "Not anymore." He looked as serious as Ava had ever seen him. "Not after what happened to those boys."

"That's what I mean. We have to call the police."

"The police? I don't think that will help."

"It'll be okay, Paul. You can turn yourself in, testify against Simon. We'll hire a good lawyer—"

"Oh, no. It's not that. I'm not worried about getting arrested. I'm worried about getting shot! The cops all work for Simon. He's in cahoots with Sheik Ahmed, the heroin kingpin who controls the chief of police. We can't go to the cops, Ava. The cops did the killing."

The monks opened an unused guest room to which Ava could retire. She located a washbowl and rinsed the ubiquitous sand from her face and hair. She attempted to call Gabe, but the satphone's battery was dead. Sprawled on an ancient pallet, she tried to sleep, but her mind sizzled with the day's events. She was sad about those poor boys and disappointed about the missing scrolls. She knew the jars were a historic find. The artifacts' mere existence necessitated a major rewriting of history texts. Of course, she regarded tales of a sacred, unreadable prophecy as mere superstition, but, religious agnosticism notwithstanding, Ava couldn't deny harboring enormous curiosity about a secret message connected to the biblical apostles. Lost in such thoughts, she faded into a fitful sleep.

Simon waited at the rendezvous site. Irate, he began to pace. He glanced at his Swiss watch. The glowing hands indicated that it was close to midnight, meaning the sheik was more than an hour late. Finally, Simon heard an engine. A Range Rover approached with its lights off, navigating by dim moonlight. It parked and the driver exited. He'd come alone.

"It's about damn time," DeMaj growled. He was unaccustomed to waiting for anything or anyone. This man worked for him. Simon had paid the sheik handsomely to influence the local authorities. "Your goons made a mess of my operation. Where have you been?"

Sheik Ahmed Qasim Hasan ignored the question. He pulled a cigarette from his case, lit it, and regarded Simon coldly. "Where are the jars?"

DeMaj was disconcerted. What did Ahmed care about the jars? Was he trying to blackmail him? Make a play for more money?

"I don't have them," Simon answered honestly. "I don't know where they are now."

The sheik nodded and dragged on his cigarette before flicking it into the sand. He exhaled slowly. "Then you are no longer useful." He pulled a Ruger SR9 from his pocket, aimed, and shot Simon twice in the chest.

Ava woke to the sound of monks chanting in Coptic, as their predecessors had for fifteen centuries. She relished the rare opportunity to hear people speak the ancient tongue phonetically similar to that of the pharaohs. Minutes later, a novice delivered pita bread, dates, honeycomb, and a pot of delicious red tea. She savored the feast and, thoroughly rejuvenated, resolved to make the day productive. She and Paul would elude the crooked cops and report Simon's crimes to the legitimate authorities. As she washed and dressed, Ava found herself singing: "When Israel was in Egypt's land, let my people go . . ."

Later, she wandered up to the tower, invigorated by the cool air. It would grow warm in a few hours, but early mornings were lovely. She'd never been anywhere so quiet. In the traditional

Coptic monastery, televisions and radios were forbidden. Visitors were required to switch off mobile phones. Guest rooms provided no electricity, only oil lamps, woodstoves, and candles. Ava longed to check her e-mail and charge the satphone, but otherwise she enjoyed the rare peace and stillness.

For a silent hour she watched the sun rise over rugged mountains. It amazed her that humans had lived here for thousands of years, maybe tens of thousands. The Israelites might have passed through this region centuries before Jesus's birth. She visualized Charleton Heston as Moses, raising his arms to part the waters. From this high vantage point, Ava gazed into the distance and observed the vast Red Sea stretching from horizon to horizon, miles upon miles of water and waves. It seemed unthinkable that any force could divide it, but maybe someday Bob Ballard would find the pharaoh's chariots preserved on the seabed. Who could say? People thought the *Iliad* was fiction until Schliemann found Troy.

She returned to her room. As she was pouring a second cup of hot karkade tea, Ava heard Paul's voice echoing off the courtyard stones. She looked down from the balcony and saw him talking with a distinguished-looking monk. They were laughing and smiling like old pals. Paul might be a goofball, Ava thought, but he could charm anyone. He had an athlete's grace and the self-confidence of a man to whom life had always been generous. She envied the ease with which Paul recruited friends. He would probably be comfortable introducing himself to presidents and prime ministers. Too bad he'd have nothing intelligent to say.

"So, as you can see," Father Bessarion continued, gesturing expansively, "we have several beautiful gardens, a library with more than seventeen hundred handwritten manuscripts, a mill, a bakery, five historic churches . . ."

"Everything here looks pretty historic," remarked Paul, earning an eye-roll from Ava. Although appreciative of the private tour, she was anxious to leave the monastery as soon as possible. They'd be found eventually. If Gabe could track Paul's location, so could Simon DeMaj.

"Egypt's monasteries are the oldest in the world," the monk said. "It began with the Essenes, pious hermits who withdrew from society to pursue a contemplative life. You may know of them from the Dead Sea Scrolls. Many believe the Essenes influenced the development of early Christian monasteries in Egypt."

"Really?" asked Ava, momentarily intrigued. "I thought the monasteries were built to escape—"

"Roman oppression?" Bessarion finished her question. "Yes, that's also true." Turning to Paul, he explained: "Julian the Apostate revoked the religious freedom granted by Emperor Constantine. The Romans began persecuting Egyptian Christians, seizing their homes and land."

"*Cujus regio, ejus religio,*" Ava observed.

"Exactly. 'Whose rule, his religion,'" Bessarion said, looking at her with approval. "Many believers fled to monasteries for protection. That's why most resemble fortresses. As you can see, ours was surrounded by a fortified wall. We still have a defensive tower."

Ava studied the protective structures. She imagined the monastery under siege in ancient times.

"How long have you been here?" Paul asked.

"This monastery was founded by St. Anthony the Great in AD 356. In fact, his sacred tomb is very near here."

"Awesome. You mean *the* St. Anthony?" asked Paul.

"Yes. You know of him?"

"I do," Paul said, much to Ava's surprise.

"Excellent," said Father Bessarion. "Perhaps then you know that he founded monasticism, and that he was born here in Egypt, near Heracleopolis, in 251. He lived to be a hundred and five years old, perhaps even older."

"We should all be so lucky," Paul said.

"Be careful what you ask for. He was tormented his entire life by temptations from the devil," replied the kindly monk, glancing at Ava meaningfully.

Paul smiled. "You know, it's an odd coincidence. My mother taught me to pray to St. Anthony whenever something was lost. And now, just a few kilometers away from his grave, we found the lost—"

"Thank you, Father, for an interesting tour," interrupted Ava, glaring daggers at Paul. "I know you have many responsibilities, and we wouldn't want to monopolize your valuable time."

"Don't think of it, my child," the monk said. "I'm happy to explain the history of this beautiful, holy site. And Paul, the St. Anthony your mother petitions when she's lost something is a different St. Anthony, St. Anthony of Padua. Nevertheless," he said, "I'm glad he helped you find what you needed."

Simon had difficulty breathing under the desert sun. Blood flowed from his wounds. It dripped off his body and stained the ancient sand. DeMaj knew a lung was punctured. Delirious, he teetered on the brink of death. An hour passed. As he slipped into unconsciousness, shadows flickered across his field of vision. He saw his mother's face, beautiful and young, before the years of poverty and hashish took their toll. In the distance a gentle voice spoke a language he almost recognized. Someone touched his hand. An angel? Beyond pain, Simon managed a small smile. "Who would have guessed," he wondered, "that I would go to heaven?"

"Paul," Ava said, "don't mention the jars to anyone. You said yourself that DeMaj bribed the police. We don't know who else he may have corrupted."

"Oh, the monks are cool."

She arched an eyebrow.

"No, really. The cops already came here once looking for me. Father Bessarion refused to answer questions or let them inside. The monks are the only ones I trust. Except you, I mean."

"That's good. I'm glad we can trust the monks, but it sounds as though we're endangering them by staying. What's your exit plan?"

"I've given that some thought. We shouldn't take the truck. It's in terrible shape after my midnight drive. The suspension is shot, and I might have bent an axle. Plus, I bet Simon's men are watching for it."

Ava nodded.

"And obviously we can't go on foot."

"I agree."

"So I think we should take the bus."

"Pardon me?"

"Bessarion said a religious group will arrive this afternoon. They'll pray at the monastery for a few hours and then return via bus to Cairo. We could buy seats on that bus."

"Won't we be spotted?"

"Maybe, but this morning I borrowed some traditional garb for us. We'll get all wrapped up and cover our faces. They won't expect us to be dressed like Coptic pilgrims. We just might slip through."

Ava thought it over. "I guess it's worth a try," she conceded. "We can't stay here forever."

"Cool. We'll chance it." He grinned. "That leaves only one issue to resolve."

"Yes?"

"What we do about the jars."

"The moment we hit Cairo, I'll contact Dr. Zahi Hawass. He's someone I trust. We met at Harvard years ago, although I'm sure he won't remember. Anyway, we'll report DeMaj for trafficking in stolen artifacts, not to mention murder."

"No, I mean what do we do with the jars? Do you think they're safe here?"

Ava inhaled deeply. Then she closed her eyes, exhaled slowly, and with great discipline kept her tone steady. "Paul, listen very carefully. Are you telling me that, right now, you're in possession of the lost jars of Cana?"

"Yes. I suppose so. I sort of borrowed them . . . temporarily. It was either that, or let Simon take them. That's why I stole his truck. The jars were already loaded into super-high-tech, indestructible titanium canisters. When I saw those poor people get killed, I jumped in the truck and split."

"And you didn't think to mention this last night?"

"See, I didn't tell you because even though you were exhausted, I knew you'd freak. You history nuts get worked up when anyone mentions the jars. I saw the way your eyes bugged out when I described examining them. You looked a little, I don't know, hungry, but also excited—"

"Paul," Ava interrupted, "where are the jars now?"

"I hid them in a cave. It's less than three kilometers from here—"

Ava insisted they go immediately.

Sheik Ahmed sat in his bunker, thinking. He expected an important call. One of his bodyguards entered and handed him a special phone reserved for calls from the master. Ahmed then gestured for the guard to leave. He spoke into the phone and in a respectful voice he said in Arabic: "I am your servant, great one."

The master had no time for pleasantries. He required an update on the mission.

"The Frenchman lost the jars. He paid with his life. My soldiers say his American aide stole them. He's hiding with a woman. We will find them soon."

"Find them and kill them," said the master.

5

Paul took Ava up a rocky trail into the mountains. They climbed for an hour, following the course of a dry streambed until they came to a wide ravine. The cave's mouth adjoined the wadi, but two overhanging boulders shielded it from view, making the entrance almost invisible.

"A decent hiding place," Ava thought, although a careful search of the area would likely result in its detection. Paul hid the jars here three days ago. How long until Simon's minions found them? Ava wiped her brow and watched Paul descend into the gulch, seemingly unencumbered by the thirty-six kilos of gear in his backpack. Secretly, she was grateful he'd insisted on carrying her equipment. She'd argued and called him sexist, but he had remained firm. When he reached up to help her down from the rocks, Ava smiled. Paul could be an obnoxious, unreconstructed paternalist, she thought, but he was helpful on a hike.

He removed a gas lantern from his pack, lit it, and ventured into the cavern. Ava followed.

"Check this out," he said, playing the light over a smooth section of the cave's interior. Ancient graffiti became visible. Ava could see words painted and carved into the surface. "Can you decipher it?" Paul said.

She translated: "Here it overtook me . . . that I fell down for thirst. I was parched, my throat burned. I cried 'This is the taste of death.'"

"Creepy!"

"Don't joke, Paul. Someone might have died here."

"Nah. There's a spring only five hundred meters away. I'm sure he was fine. Here they are!"

He directed the light into the cave's deepest recess. It reflected off something metallic.

Ava gasped.

Within his island stronghold, the master was confident. Over the course of many years, he'd learned that no complex plan conforms perfectly to expectations. To succeed, a commander must adapt to circumstances. Hence, Ahmed's update presented no cause for alarm. Regardless of the unforeseen developments, the sheik would complete his mission soon, dashing the order's last hope. He smiled, knowing victory was within reach.

Roderigo noted his boss's expression. "News from Egypt?"

The master gestured ambivalently. "A few trivial inconveniences, but the plan continues as scheduled."

"Are you concerned about the woman? The translator?"

"Not at all. Our agents report that she's a bookish academic, mere prattle without practice. Ahmed will eliminate her, and our American cell will tie up the loose ends."

Hands on her hips, Ava circled the ultramodern titanium-and-acrylic canisters and scrutinized them from all angles. Paul helped Ava unpack her things and showed her how to release the artifacts from the protective canisters. He lifted the jars and described how he and Simon had carefully removed each lid and found the jars to be empty.

Her eyes never left the artifacts. "Of course, I've every confidence in Simon's mental acuity as well as that of his archaeological team," she said. "Lord knows, they're the best brains money can buy. Still, I'm not sure it adds up."

"What's wrong?"

"They look the way I expected them to look."

"And that's bad?" asked Paul.

"Yes, because they're too . . . listen, in archaeology things don't often turn out as expected. My mental picture of the jars comes from Tintoretto's famous *Wedding Feast at Cana*. Have you seen it?"

When Paul didn't reply, Ava glanced up.

"Surely you visited the Gardner Museum, back in Boston?"

He rubbed his neck. "No, I never . . . wait. I saw that on television. There was a big art heist, right? Didn't the crooks pretend to be cops?"

"Yes. In the early nineties, criminals disguised as Boston police stole a Rembrandt, a Vermeer, a Manet. Thankfully, they missed the Tintoretto. It's one of my favorites. Anyway, you said OSL testing proved that these jars have been buried under Egyptian sand for at least fourteen hundred years. If that's true, how would Tintoretto know what to paint? I admit they're not identical—these are closer to the barrel-shaped kratars from the Temple Mount—but Tintoretto's depiction is correct in several key details." She gestured toward the artifacts. "Notice the hollow trumpet bases and the simple rims. I'd say these jars were turned on a lathe and finished with a hammer and chisel."

She circled the jars again, crouched, then asked, "What would you estimate: thirty-two, thirty-four inches?"

Before Paul could answer she went on: "Less than three feet anyway. That's about how tall they look in the painting. But Tintoretto created *Wedding Feast at Cana* during the sixteenth century, long after these were buried. Was he incredibly lucky? Did he benefit from divine inspiration? No. It's more likely that the DeMaj group scoured the world for a set of ancient stone jars that resembled the artist's famous depiction and upon finding some incorrectly assumed that they'd found the lost jars of Cana. You follow?"

Paul nodded. "I hear you, but Simon's experts seemed awfully certain. Couldn't Tintoretto have obtained a valid description from some knowledgeable source? Maybe he found a good sketch preserved in an ancient manuscript. Maybe an older, historically accurate rendering was available in Renaissance Italy, one that has since been lost."

Ava's eyes widened. "Or maybe he actually saw a jar! The legend claims a jar came by sea to Rome, where it was kept hidden . . ."

She began her examination. For a while Paul watched her work; then he grew bored.

"We studied them for hours, Ava. We couldn't find anything."

Engrossed, she ignored him. Paul decided to do something useful.

"I'll be outside, okay? I want to see how badly I trashed the truck."

If she had heard, she gave no sign. Paul shrugged and rested the lantern on the rocky floor. He could find his way back without it. The cave wasn't very deep. Light filtered in from the entrance.

Paul exited the cavern, hopped down into the ravine, and found the truck. He'd concealed it under a camouflage tarp that looked to be Gulf War surplus. A methodical inspection revealed that the damage was less severe than he'd reckoned. Although he wouldn't trust the truck across one hundred fifty kilometers of mountainous terrain, with a few repairs he could drive it back to St. Anthony's.

Paul gazed up into the bright azure sky and observed a hawk's graceful patrol. He took a long pull from his canteen and splashed cool water on his neck. Then, opening his tool kit, he set to work.

Simon opened his eyes. He wasn't in heaven. He was in a tent. He remembered now. The Beja caravan had found him bleeding to death in the vast desert. The nomads brought him to a traditional healer who had blessed him and pulled two nine-millimeter slugs out of his body. One had embedded itself in his shoulder muscles, incapacitating his left arm; the other had broken a rib and damaged his right lung. Overall, he'd been lucky.

His mobile phone rang. Wincing, Simon answered it. "Mr. DeMaj, we got a hit on the American girl. She used a credit card on Kamaran Island. We don't know if she's still there. Should we send a team?"

"I'll go myself and track her. We can't afford more mistakes. Lock on to my GPS signal and send the big chopper." An hour later, Simon was streaking over the Red Sea. He refused to rest until he located the girl.

"If I find her," he thought, "I'll find Paul."

By mid-afternoon Paul had the truck running. He drained his canteen and went to fetch Ava from the cave. Sitting in the same position, she appeared not to have moved in two hours. Paul stood behind her. What was she looking at?

When he touched her shoulder, she jumped.

"Hey, it's just me. Time to head back."

"Okay," Ava said, coming out of her trance. She explained that when immersed in a particularly difficult problem she sometimes lost touch with external reality.

"You are so odd," said Paul, grinning. They returned the jars to the protective canisters and loaded both onto the truck. Paul hit the ignition, turned around, and ventured down the ravine.

As they drove, Ava told Paul the results of her analysis. "I'd swear the jars are from the correct historical period. The material is right. The style is right. They look about two thousand years old, give or take a century. I don't have the capability to determine an exact age myself. I want to try Professor Aitken's thermoluminescence technique, but we need a special lab for that. Of course, even if they're from the right era and region, that hardly proves these jars are the lost jars of Cana."

Paul nodded. "Yeah, I suppose we can't be a hundred percent sure. There must have been tons of similar jars bumping around back then, but for some reason, Simon's experts believed these were authentic. Why would they say that if it wasn't true?"

"Maybe they just wanted to please the boss, or maybe they really didn't want to make him mad. I guess we've learned what happens when DeMaj gets angry. Anyway, I agree with you about one thing: The jars lack identifying marks of any kind. No messages, no codes. In fact . . ."

Ava paused, thinking.

"What?" Paul sensed that she had an idea.

"I examined the clay seals. The lids appear to date from the same period, and there's a thick crust of residue on the undersides. Before you and Simon opened them, I'd say the jars were sealed for several hundred years, at least. I saw no evidence of repeated opening. Besides, who would open the jars, remove the contents, and then reseal the vessels? That feels wrong. No, the evidence supports the hypothesis that many, many years ago the jars were filled with wine, which evaporated very gradually."

"So?" asked Paul.

"So . . . not much," Ava answered. "I could be way off, but I don't think any scrolls or codices are missing. I don't think anyone looted them, because there weren't any to loot."

Back at the monastery they saw the pilgrims' bus parked near the front entrance. Paul pulled the damaged truck in beside it. He climbed into the back, used his knife to cut the canvas tarp in half, reversed it, and wrapped each canister thoroughly. He secured the canvas covers with bungee cords. Meanwhile, Ava began the interminable process of negotiating fares with the bus driver, a salty old bedouin.

While they haggled in Arabic, Ava caught the driver eyeing her tanned legs. At first she was embarrassed. She should be wearing something more modest. Then she grew angry. He had no right to ogle her. Finally, she decided to use the driver's interest to her advantage. She smiled at him and batted her eyelashes. She flipped her hair and stretched her arms above her head, giving him a nice view of her chest. He was putty in her hands. He settled for half his asking price, promised not to leave without her, and swore a holy oath to guard her canvas-covered souvenirs.

"Mission accomplished," thought Ava. She turned her back to the driver and went looking for Paul. She spied him sitting in the garden. He'd already packed their meager belongings and Coptic clothing. Now he was thanking Father Bessarion for his hospitality and protection.

The crowd of real pilgrims, clad in full-length white robes, had just finished praying. Silently, they filed out of the chapel and into the courtyard. Many were strolling about the square, admiring the gardens or filling water bottles from the cistern. Paul smiled when he saw Ava approaching. She seemed quite proud of herself. Clearly, she was aching to tell him a funny story. Then he spotted something odd: A uniformed man was on the roof of the ancient monastery, crouched behind the parapet. He looked like one of Simon's security guards. The man rammed a magazine into his assault rifle. Paul's smile vanished.

"Ava, run!" he roared, vaulting the low wall and racing toward her. The guard raised his rifle and took aim. Ava was a perfect target, standing dead center in the courtyard, motionless, staring at Paul with an expression of bewilderment. She knew something was wrong but couldn't see the danger. Sprinting, Paul flew across the cobblestones, legs fighting and straining for every last ounce of energy.

He'd played baseball all his life. He remembered his coach's words: "Run straight through the base, son. Do not dive. Do not jump. You're fastest if you run straight through the damn base. Trust me."

Paul trusted his coach. He did not dive. He did not jump. He ran directly at Ava, who gaped at him. He kicked with all his might, forcing his body to the limit, and just as he heard the rifle's report, he ran straight through, tackling her at full speed and wrapping his arms around her waist as he knocked her backward. The machine-gun burst missed by centimeters. Bullets pulverized the area where she'd stood a moment before. Paul felt something hot slice across his calf. It burned like a scorpion's sting.

They crashed into a crowd of pilgrims, sending many sprawling. Ava hit the turf hard. Paul could see he'd knocked the wind out of her. He prayed he hadn't broken any of her ribs, but there was no time to check. He gathered her in his arms and ran through the nearest doorway. Just behind him, a hail of bullets splintered the paving stones, spraying razor-edged shards in all directions. Pilgrims, wild with panic, rushed for the exits. A horrific blood-stain marred the ancient masonry, but Paul couldn't discern who'd been hit. Then he saw two more gunmen fighting to clear a path through the terrified crowd. Only seconds remained.

"Paul, hurry, this way!" It was Father Bessarion, motioning toward a hallway that led deep into the monastery. Paul followed. He had no choice. In a second, the gunmen would have a clear shot. Bessarion led Paul down the hall and around a corner. Paul stopped to catch his breath.

"Ava," he said, panting, "you okay?"

"Don't . . . worry . . . about . . . me." Ava struggled to speak. She was dazed, likely concussed, Paul thought, but she wasn't bleeding.

Bessarion led them around another corner. From his pocket he produced a key in the shape of a traditional Coptic cross. He slid it into a hidden aperture and gave it a sharp twist. Paul heard a heavy lock spring, then a section of the wall wedged open.

"Go through here," Bessarion commanded. "At the intersection, turn right. That path leads to the front entrance. I'll try to delay them, but once you leave the monastery, you must make your own way."

"I don't know how to thank you, Father."

"Go, quickly," Bessarion urged, pushing Paul into the passage, "and remember, my son, *Gardez bien*! Protect what you found!" Then the monk heaved his weight against the door. With a bang, it slammed shut, and the lock dropped heavily into place.

Paul didn't hesitate. Lifting the now unconscious Ava over his shoulder, he ran down the passage, turned right, and emerged from a concealed exit about a hundred meters from the front gate.

The bus was waiting. The bedouin had kept his promise. When the driver spotted them, he waved furiously, urging them to hurry. Paul shifted Ava's weight across his shoulders and broke into a sprint. His lower leg was bleeding copiously. Ignoring the pain, he drove himself faster and faster. In the distance he heard gunshots. One assailant had taken up a firing position in the tower. Bullets rained down into the gravel.

"If he has a sniper rifle," Paul thought, "we're dead." Luckily, the gunman didn't, and at long range an AK-47 isn't accurate. Paul threw himself inside the bus. The driver slammed the door shut as he stomped on the accelerator. The diesel engine rumbled to life. Slowly the monastery receded, but then Paul noticed two gunmen running toward a khaki-colored jeep.

"Damn! This overloaded old bus will never outrun that." He should surrender now and offer to exchange the jars for Ava's freedom.

The jeep remained immobile. It wouldn't start! Laughing aloud, the bedouin driver shifted into high gear. The bus rumbled and thundered across the desert road, leaving mountains of dust in its wake.

Atop the monastery wall Father Bessarion watched the Americans escape. He heard angry shouts from the men kicking the jeep's four flat tires and glanced at his grinning novices.

"You two have a sin to confess?"

"Forgive us, Father."

Smiling, Bessarion gazed out across the sand toward the ever more distant dust cloud. "Farewell," he whispered.

6

King Louis XI was pleased by the emissaries' report. His young spy in the Vatican had served France ably.

"How did he corrupt the prophecy?" Louis asked his minister.

"Sire, the scribe deleted several stanzas and altered others. The true prophecy predicts failure for the pope's crusade. It foretells that Pius shall fall in Ancona, bereft of allies, to rest in an unmarked grave. These fatal details we have, by our conspiracy, excluded."

A smile flickered across the monarch's features. "Was his Holiness deceived?"

"Yes, Majesty. We believe so. He ordered our version of the prophecy read aloud at Mantua. He dispatched couriers to the East and revised his strategy on the basis of the false predictions."

"Good." The king harbored much resentment against Pope Pius II. Upon taking the throne, Louis had withdrawn royal sanctions issued by his father, Charles VII. These sanctions had curtailed papal influence in France. In return, Louis had expected the pontiff to support French interests in Naples. "But I was betrayed," the monarch thought angrily. "And for that, the Church will pay!"

"What else has been done?"

"Highness, we altered several lines of translation to suggest that

64

if Pius II personally takes the cross, he can free Constantinople."

"But the prophecy does not presage success against the Turks?"

"Just the opposite, sire. The prophecy foretells that Mehmed will survive a night attack and never convert to the True Faith. It says the sultan's capital will not fall to Rome."

The king trusted the prophecy. He maintained a number of acclaimed astrologers at court and relied on their prognostications.

So, Louis thought, the pope's crusade is doomed. He will die in the East. Nothing, then, stands against me. I can break the power of the dukes and reunify France. A proud destiny! "Tell me," the king asked his ambassador, "what does this prophecy augur for my reign?"

"It's a mystery, Highness. It predicts you will expel the English from France not by force of arms, but with goose, deer, and grapes."

"Fascinating," the Spider King reflected. "What could this mean?" Then he offered his decree: "This prophecy is now a treasure of France. Let it be housed in our private library and defended against all enemies."

EGYPT, FEBRUARY 2013

Sheik Ahmed spat in disgust and shouted into the phone: "You impotent dogs let them escape?"

"The *nazarani* monks helped the Americans. They warned them and sabotaged our vehicle."

"Failure is unacceptable. You understand the penalty for incompetence."

"We may yet succeed, *insh'allah*. I repaired the jeep. We will follow. Perhaps we will overtake them. We know they travel to

Masr [Cairo]. I've alerted our people there. If we don't catch them before, they'll be intercepted the moment they arrive."

Paul collapsed into the seat, exhausted. Before he could pass out, a pilgrim tapped him on the shoulder. He presented a first-aid kit and pointed to Paul's leg, which was bleeding profusely. Together they examined the injury: A bullet had grazed his calf. It was messy and painful, but not serious. Gesturing for his patient to relax, the pilgrim cleaned and disinfected the wound, bandaged it with clean linen, and offered Paul a metal cup full of cold water. Paul drank it down and thanked the man, who never spoke, only smiled.

Ava regained consciousness on a crowded bus, surrounded by curious strangers. She looked around nervously until Paul eased in beside her. "How do you feel?" he asked.

"I'll live," she replied, "thanks to you."

"I thought maybe I broke your ribs."

Ava raised both arms overhead and rotated her torso to the left and to the right.

"Bruised, I think, but unbroken."

Relieved, Paul lifted two flowing white robes from his pack. "I think it's time we tried these." Ava nodded and they donned the disguises. From a distance the hooded robes would mask their identities. The pair wouldn't survive close inspection, but it was better than nothing.

For a time the bus continued north through the desert. Paul limped to the front and thanked the driver for not leaving them behind. Though they lacked a common language, the driver understood and nodded solemnly.

The bedouin kept a demanding pace, especially given the

road's condition. He seemed to enjoy his role as getaway driver. After one particularly severe jolt, he turned to grin at Ava. They reached a T-intersection, where he swung the bus around to the left, or west, and continued on Highway 26. Majestic mountains towered to their north; empty desert stretched to the southern horizon. Later, a dazzling sunset spread across the Egyptian sky. As darkness fell, they passed Al-Burumbul and came, at last, to the Nile.

Paul asked the driver to drop them in El Wasta, a town of perhaps forty thousand located on the banks of the great river. The bus entered a broad square adjoining the harbor, where an armada of feluccas were moored. Paul unloaded the canisters, safely concealed by canvas, as Ava bade their companions good-bye. The driver told her she was beautiful. He embraced Paul, gave him the first-aid kit, and wished him luck. The driver cried, "*Marhabtein!*" then closed the door, started the engine, and continued north toward Memphis and Cairo.

Father Bessarion sat stoically in his chair. He was prepared to endure torture. He would never willingly betray the confidence of anyone who sought sanctuary within the monastery, but he'd read of extreme methods used to extract information from unwilling captives. He wondered if his years of training and mental discipline would enable him to withstand the latest pharmacological techniques.

Simon entered the monk's cell and sat down. His shoulder stung where the bandages had been changed. He was in no mood to linger.

"Father," DeMaj began, "I require information. Let us concede what is already known. Two Americans, a man and a woman, were here. You gave them asylum and protection. Now they've gone, on a bus. The bus goes to Cairo. It will arrive there in a few hours, unless it's overtaken and intercepted by the men in the jeep, which you sabotaged to help the Americans escape. There is no need to deny this."

Bessarion said nothing. He stared at the floor. Simon continued.

"I must know their plan, Father. I must find them quickly. Their safety depends on it. In addition, I must know if you saw what they carried. Did they discuss this matter in your presence? Did they tell you their intentions?"

Bessarion raised his eyes to meet Simon's gaze. He took a breath and then said, "The men with rifles threatened to kill me, and still I told them nothing. I am not afraid to die."

Sheik Ahmed walked through the hidden warehouse that his organization used as a refinery. Inside, workers converted poppy plants grown in Afghanistan and Pakistan into raw opium, which workmen carefully dissolved in hot water. Gradually, by adding a powder to the soup, they rendered the mixture alkaline. After filtration, a chemist added sal ammoniac, then collected and dried the precipitate. Distillers heated the solution with acetic anhydride for six hours. Cooled, diluted, and combined with sodium carbonate, the mixture generated crude heroin. Once the product was purified and decolorized, Ahmed's soldiers stacked brick after brick into shipping crates for transport to the United States and western Europe via Turkey and Sicily.

Usually the sheik was pleased to observe the operation's military efficiency. It gave him pleasure to view the construction and deployment of his army's deadliest weapons in the war against the West, but today his heart was not cheered. For the first time since he was a boy, Ahmed felt fear. Just as he would never tolerate failure from his servants, the master would not tolerate it from him. If the Americans escaped with the jars, he would lose everything.

Ahmed entered his private office, poured himself a cognac, and waited. He massaged his right arm, a nervous habit. Before long the dreaded call came. The master's icy voice asked why the two Americans still lived.

"Master," Sheik Ahmed said, "we shall have them soon. The Americans are on a bus to Masr. I would have detonated a bomb to kill everyone aboard, but I could not risk damaging your treasures. My men pursue your quarries as we speak. Many more soldiers wait to intercept them at their destination. I have legions of informants in the capital. My spies hold key positions in government, the police, the media, and the military. Our eyes watch the airport and the train depot around the clock. They will not wriggle free from this net."

Ahmed waited to hear his doom.

"I will send someone to assist you," said the master. "An assassin."

Gabe was apoplectic. It had been three days since he'd spoken to Ava, and she was in danger.

His room was a mess. Not a proficient housekeeper under normal circumstances, for a week he'd ignored the rules of hygiene. Empty pizza boxes and Hot Pocket wrappers littered the floor. Soda cans overflowed the trash bin. The room was beginning to stink.

Gabe had an idea. He pushed himself away from the computer desk, gathered some garbage into a Hefty bag, and carried it down to the Dumpster. Then he hustled back upstairs and checked his voice mail. Nothing.

"Damn." Experience suggested that important calls came the moment he stepped outside.

"Well," he thought, "that leaves me only one option." He'd drop the thermonuclear bomb of telephone call–inducing behavior. For the first time all weekend he strode to the bathroom and turned on the shower. He knew it would take six minutes for the water to reach an appropriate temperature. In the meantime, he checked and rechecked his various e-mail accounts, one after another.

Several felucca captains sat on an ancient wall, drinking beer or coffee, gossiping and bartering with the townsfolk. Cloaked in her pilgrim's attire, Ava approached a sailor. In Arabic she asked him politely if he owned a boat.

"Yes," he answered, without looking up from his meal. "What do you want?"

"Passage to Cairo."

"How many?"

"Two."

He studied Ava as he picked gristle from his teeth. "One hundred American dollars each, cash. You pay in advance. You bring your own food. We leave tomorrow noon. Okay?"

"No, I'm afraid not. We must leave tonight."

The Egyptian shrugged. "I leave tomorrow."

Ava removed three hundred-dollar bills from her wallet. She stepped up onto the wall, held out the money, and announced to all present: "I'll pay four hundred dollars cash for passage to

Cairo, three hundred now and one hundred on arrival. We leave immediately."

"Okay, okay, we leave now. No problem," the captain said, grabbing the bills before one of his competitors could make a better offer. "My name is Akhmim. I take you to Cairo."

His felucca was eight meters long and single-masted with a lateen sail. Handmade and decorated with Egyptian eyes, it could hold ten passengers with ease. While Paul and Captain Akhmim brought the Americans' luggage on board, Ava bought a kilo of *melouha* (smoked fish), two *aish baladi* (pitalike rounds of whole-wheat bread), a paper bag of salted pumpkin seeds, several *warah'enab* (grape leaves stuffed with rice, lamb, and herbs), some oranges, Stella Artois beer, and lemonade. The Egyptian helped Ava onto the boat. Then he and Paul pushed it into the channel, jumped aboard, and navigated through the small, crowded harbor by light of the kerosene lantern.

Though the winds were against them, the strong current carried the felucca north at a reasonable speed. Before long the city's sounds and smells faded. Paul and Ava were glad to have an experienced pilot. By the lantern's modest glow, he adroitly dodged tiny islands, submerged rocks, sandbars, and possibly a crocodile. As Akhmim leaned against the tiller and smoked, the two Americans finally relaxed. Ravenous, they made quick work of the food, reserving only some bread, seeds, and oranges for breakfast. Paul enjoyed two large bottles of beer, then tied the others to the hull and dropped them overboard. He winked at Ava, and then nodded off.

After sunrise Ava was delighted to observe the sights and sounds of middle Egypt. Ancient temples and monuments became visible in the distance. She watched fishermen draw their nets, enjoying a full harvest. Women washed dishes and laundry in the Nile, as their ancestors had for scores of centuries. Transported, Ava sang, "See the pyramids along the Nile . . ."

They stopped at a picturesque island for a quick meal and restroom break. By way of apology for demanding that he work through the night, Paul offered the Egyptian some oranges and a river-chilled beer. A non-Muslim, he accepted both gratefully. During lunch the winds turned in their favor. The captain unfurled the sail, and soon they beheld the outskirts of Cairo.

Just before sunset, Akhmim guided the boat toward the eastern bank and put in near a bustling souk. He needed cigarettes, and Ava needed a telephone.

After Paul helped her ashore, Ava scouted the area warily. They'd docked on the edge of eastern Cairo, a conglomeration of ancient communities that extended seemingly forever into the fertile Nile Delta. Ava pulled down her hood and looked around until she spied a pay phone. She found Dr. Hawass's office number and dialed, but she was disappointed to discover that he was on location in the western desert and wouldn't return for several weeks. Deflated, she returned to the riverfront. Paul was making a valiant effort to buy supper, but his attempts at pronunciation brought only laughter from the street vendors. Ava took over and obtained spicy kebabs of lamb, chicken, and rabbit, along with two liters of bottled water.

Akhmim returned. Paul gave him the final hundred dollars, as promised, and invited him to share their meal. Between mouthfuls of kebab, Akhmim asked what they planned to do in Cairo.

"Good question," Ava answered, glancing about to ensure that no strangers were eavesdropping. "The man we're looking for is out of town, and there may be people here whom we'd rather not encounter."

Paul raised a hand to his brow, shaded his eyes from the setting sun, and looked off into the west. "How far to Giza?"

Sheik Ahmed paced across his private office. He telephoned his aide, who answered on the first ring.

"What is your report?" the sheik demanded.

"We intercepted the bus in Memphis."

"And the Americans?"

"They were not on it. They were dropped off somewhere."

Somewhere? Ahmed stopped pacing. His jaw clenched in anger. "Did you question the driver?"

"He refused to answer. He is a bedouin. He swore a sacred oath to protect them."

Sheik Ahmed had experience with obdurate bedouins. The driver would not crack easily, if at all, but there was no need to waste time breaking him. He had more expedient means at his disposal.

"Interrogate the infidel pilgrims," he commanded.

"We tried. None will talk. The driver says the pilgrims took a vow of silence."

Ahmed exhaled. Was this aide incompetent or corrupt? In truth, it made no difference. The penalty for each was the same. Ahmed would impose judgment soon. For now, he must continue to rely on the worthless dog, but he was unable to keep the tone of disgust out of his voice: "A vow of silence means they cannot speak, but they can still write. Begin executing pilgrims. Continue until someone breaks his vow or deigns to write you a note. Call me the moment you learn where the bus left them."

He clicked off and then dialed for his chauffeur: "Prepare the car."

It seemed he must direct this operation in person.

Captain Akhmim apologized that he could take them no farther. He must return to his family in the south, he explained, before his wife found a younger man. Nevertheless, he offered to negotiate passage for them by motorboat.

He hopped ashore and disappeared into the crowd of Cairenes. Less than fifteen minutes passed before he reappeared with a teenager. This boy, named Sefu, and his brother, Ammon, owned and operated a fine boat, Akhmim reported. Considerably faster than the blue-and-white water taxis, it was large enough to accommodate the Americans and their heavy baggage. For a reasonable fee the boys would be happy to transport the couple to Giza, Rosetta, or even as far as Alexandria. Paul thought the price sounded fair, though he was sure it included a fat kickback for Akhmim. He shook hands with Sefu, who departed to fetch his brother.

When Paul saw their boat, he knew instantly that the young Egyptians shared his love of big engines and custom hot rods. The hand-painted, cabinless, converted panga skiff had a semi-V hull and racing stripes. Its thunderous Evinrude V-6, 225 HP motor growled astern. Watching from the dock, Paul noted with approval the bow's hydrodynamic sheer and flare. He smiled when he saw a repurposed '65 Chevy intake, carb, and valve covers. The boys had improvised a supercharger! This sleek watercraft was built to run at full tilt.

While Ava went back to the souk to buy a change of clothes and toiletries, the teens helped Paul transfer the couple's things onto the speedboat. As they awaited her return, Paul asked the boys some basic mechanical questions. He was delighted to discover that they spoke fair English. Soon the three of them were engrossed in a lively discussion of hydrofoils, ISKY cams, radial engines, dual-point distributors, Indian motorcycles, and Formula One racing.

When Ava returned she was astonished to find the three joking and carrying on like long-lost buddies. She'd heard Paul's distinctive laughter from half a mile away and, naturally, he'd neglected to wear his hood. No lookout could miss his boisterous antics and handsome American face.

Ava sighed. "We're the world's worst smugglers."

When they spotted her the three new friends jumped up to help her onto the skiff. Once she was safely aboard, Sefu ignited the powerful engine and roared off toward Giza, leaving, Ava thought, a rather unnecessarily large wake.

The voyage to Giza was brief. Even so, as they approached University Bridge, Ava dropped fast asleep with her head on Paul's shoulder. She'd been awake for quite a while. Given his injuries, Paul thought, he could use some rest too. He directed Ammon to put in near the Giza Zoo, and he paid the boys for their time. They agreed to meet at that spot the following day. Slinging a backpack over each shoulder, Paul carried them and the still-dozing Ava to a luxury hotel, where he deposited her on a leather couch in the lobby. Explaining that his wife had sipped one too many mai tais, he requested a room for the night. The hotel had a vacancy. Paul checked them in as Mr. and Mrs. Jones from Indianapolis and paid cash.

As he helped Ava into the elevator, she snapped to consciousness and grabbed his arm in a panic. "Where are the jars?"

"It's cool. I told Ammon and Sefu to keep them for us."

"Those boys? We hardly know them!"

"I think I know them. They gave me their word. Besides, Simon's people are probably looking for an American couple traveling with two conspicuously big, heavy packages. If we brought them, we could be identified."

Ava admitted there was logic to his reasoning, though it terrified her to trust such recent acquaintances. Regardless, the deed was done, and she was too tired to argue.

Paul read her look. "Hey, if Ammon and Sefu steal the jars, it's my responsibility, okay? Maybe they'll sell them to a museum, where the jars probably belong anyway. Maybe they'll sell them to Simon or his drug-lord partner. It's a gamble, I admit, but life is a series of gambles. Tonight I'm betting those boys are honest." Then he added, grinning, "And I'm also betting you could use a hot shower."

"Ohhh," she moaned, "that sounds spectacular." She hadn't taken a real shower in days.

He unlocked the door and held it open for her. The palatial room offered a beautiful view of the Giza pyramids.

"Wow. How much was this?" she asked.

"Well," he said, "it wasn't cheap, and I'm running out of cash, but we might have been spotted haggling for a better deal. Besides, I haven't slept in an honest-to-goodness bed in weeks. It's been all tents and deserts and monasteries."

Ava wasn't listening. She'd just noticed that despite the fine artwork, flat-screen TV, brass fixtures, and marble bathroom tile, the suite had only one king-size bed.

"Ah, hell," Paul muttered when he realized what she was thinking. "My fault. I told them we were married. They didn't even ask how many beds. Sorry. Look, you take the bed, I'll crash on the floor. Just toss me some of those really soft pillows."

"No," she replied. "I'm not a helpless damsel in distress. We're both adults and equals. There's no logical reason why one gender should be forced to—"

"Ava," he interrupted, exasperated. "This is Africa. I'm not sure feminism applies. You're taking the bed, and that's the end of it." He departed for the bar, letting the door slam behind him.

Ava thought: "Fine. If he wants to be a chauvinist jerk, I'll certainly take the bed. In fact, I'll enjoy it." She located an A/C outlet and plugged in the satphone charger. With luck, she'd reach Gabe tonight or tomorrow.

After locking herself in the ritzy bathroom she undressed and cranked the shower to maximum, filling the room with steam. The hotel provided a variety of botanical soaps and shampoos, of which she took full advantage.

Two hours later Paul returned to find a squeaky-clean Ava perched on the corner of the bed, wearing nothing but a towel.

"Oops!" he said, flustered. "Sorry. I didn't know you were . . . I mean, I'll come back in a few—"

Ava raised her hand for silence, stopping him mid-stammer. She'd noticed a light blinking on the satphone. When she turned it on, the screen reported one new text message: "Just checking in. I met James. Everything's proceeding by the book. Text back when you get this."

Her brow furrowed. Something was up. She showed Paul the message.

"What is it?" he asked.

"A text from my friend, but it sounds off. I don't know any- one named James." Ava sensed there must be a hidden message. She didn't see it immediately, but some codes had to be broken the hard way. Her mind began crunching possibilities. She disassembled the sentences, shuffled the sequence of words, rearranged words into anagrams, counted letter frequency, substituted numbers for letters . . .

"Your communications are compromised," Paul said suddenly.

Ava looked up in surprise. "What?"

"*Star Trek II: The Wrath of Khan.*"

"Never saw it."

"You've never seen *Star Trek II*? It's the best of the whole series. Maybe that's your problem. Too much Thucydides, too little Kirk."

"Just explain the stupid reference."

"Captain Kirk is trapped on the Genesis planet with that lady scientist, Dr. Marcus or whatever. The one he impregnates."

Ava stared at him blankly.

"Anyway, Spock is on the *Enterprise* and needs to tell Kirk that Ricardo Montalbán is listening to their phone calls. Spock says he's doing everything by the book, like Kirstie Alley would do. Kirk knows that 'by the book' means 'to assume the enemy is listening.' So your friend's saying someone hacked into your communications."

That made sense. Gabe loved sci-fi movies. He'd assume she'd seen *Star Trek II*.

"If he says enemies are listening," Ava observed, "we can bank on it."

She could hear him breathing in the dark room. It didn't sound as though he was asleep.

"Paul?"

"Mmm?"

"What are we going to do?"

"You tell me."

"We can't stay here. We have to keep moving."

"No kidding. You should see what they charge for whiskey."

Ava giggled. "I mean we have to leave the city."

"I know. We will. We'll leave tomorrow, okay? I'll take care of it."

"How?" she asked, remembering Yemen. "Simon's henchmen will be watching the airport, the train station, maybe the buses. We can't even go to the police."

He sighed. "That's why we're leaving by boat."

"What do you mean? With those teenagers?"

"Ammon said they can get us all the way north to Rosetta by river, and from there down the coast to Alexandria."

"Is the Rasheed branch even navigable?"

"I don't know. I'm not intimately familiar with the western delta, but I know this: It's the boondocks. No one will look for us out there. We'll be off the grid, effectively invisible."

In the dark, Ava nodded. She recognized the value of invisibility.

"Besides, their speedboat takes a very shallow draft. Even with us and the jars, I bet it can ride cleanly in a meter of water. A panga is super light, very buoyant."

"How long would it take?"

"About one full day straight through. They've made the trip before. Ammon said it's a little tricky in places, but I told him that a hard-core warrior princess like you would personally tow the boat through the fetid swamp . . ."

"Paul?"

"Yes?"

"Shut up and go to sleep."

Moments later, a quiet snore indicated that he'd fallen asleep.

For Ava, despite the clean, luxurious sheets and soft down pillows, sleep did not come so easily. When she finally nodded off, she dozed fitfully, disturbed by vivid dreams. First she was back in Boston, late for an exam. Next, she was hitchhiking through the lush countryside, discussing Jericho with Clark Gable. Then the world froze. Gable vanished. The backdrop metamorphosed into a desolate ice shelf on a frigid, moonlit night. Ava sensed a subsurface threat. The monstrous orca rose, circling a tiny floe that sheltered two seal pups. Ava's pulse quickened. Though she longed to protect the vulnerable creatures, she felt powerless against the six-ton predator. She cried out, but the howling arctic wind obliterated her warning. Desperate, Ava's lips began forming words she'd memorized long ago: "Hail Mary, full of grace . . ." As she continued the prayer she felt herself grow warmer. Then a miraculous, heavenly glow illuminated the seals. Startled, the killer abandoned its pursuit and descended back into darkness.

Gabe's phone rang. He looked at the caller ID and his eyes widened in surprise as he recognized the number.

"Hello?"

"Hi, Gabe. This is Jess. I don't know if you remember me."

He certainly did. Jess was among the most beautiful and enticing women Gabe had ever met. In real life, at least.

"Of course. We met at the May Day party. We discussed *Harry Potter*."

Gabe had read all the books. Jess had been an extra in one of the films.

"Right. Nice speaking to you again. By chance, have you heard from Ava recently?"

"No," he said. "Why?"

"She hasn't answered her phone in days. Now her voice mail is full. Dr. Fischer called me several times looking for her, and this morning Professor Kostova from MIT said a government agent has been asking questions. She fears that Ava may be in trouble."

More than you can imagine, Gabe thought.

Just before dawn the private study, richly paneled in Circassian walnut, stood dark and empty. The heavy door of oak and iron swung ajar with a loud creak as a man, dressed all in black, entered. He walked to the desk, lifted his phone, and dialed a private number. When the Egyptian answered, the churchman spoke an ancient password.

"I am your servant, Father. What are my orders?"

"Time grows short. Pope Benedict's reign will end soon. You must act. Do whatever it takes to discover their secret."

"I will."

"But use stealth," he cautioned. "Never underestimate their cunning. If they discern your true allegiance—"

"I understand the risks, Father. I shall beguile them."

The churchman smiled. "Your faith makes you strong."

As he gave the Egyptian detailed instructions, he emerged from behind his desk, crossed the room, and stood before a large marble figure of a man contemplating a human skull.

7

Ava woke with a start. Paul was gone. The sun was already high in the sky. It had to be at least ten in the morning. She checked the clock: ten forty-five. "The idiots must have forgotten our wake-up call," she said out loud. Furious, Ava jumped out of bed and was packing when she heard a knock at the door.

"Room service."

She didn't believe that for a second. Beginning to panic, she scanned the room for an exit but saw no options. The door to the adjoining room was locked. Could she jump from the balcony?

"Room service, madam."

Could she tie sheets together and climb down to the balcony below? Ava started to strip the bed but immediately a key entered the lock. She froze. Hearing the cylinder click, she crouched behind the bed. Where was Paul's knife? In the drawer maybe? As the door opened, Ava poked up her head, barely over the edge. An Egyptian wearing tan slacks, a red coat, and a bow tie entered the room. He wheeled in a cart laden with tea, orange juice, rolls, muffins, fresh fruit, and what smelled like scrambled eggs and bacon.

"Madam?" he asked, eyeing her curiously. He lifted the silver cover from a hot plate. The aroma was divine.

"Mister Paul, he order breakfast. He say you want karkade tea. You want coffee too?"

Still poised to sprint for the door, Ava watched him like a hawk. She said nothing.

"Okay," said the confused waiter. "No coffee today. Enjoy!"

Forcing a polite smile, he backed out of the room as quickly as courtesy permitted.

Once he was gone Ava cautiously approached the breakfast platter. She sniffed the fruit cup. No hint of poison, but many were odorless.

Then she heard Paul's voice in the hall. Of course he was laughing about something. Ava fumed.

Clean-shaven and sporting new attire, Paul entered. "Hey, the waiter is really sorry he woke you. He said you looked a little—"

"Paul, you moron! Did you even set a wake-up call? Why are we still here? They could find the jars any second! What in God's name made you think we have the time or the money for room service? You remember that they have machine guns, right? Do you by any chance remember that they're trying to kill us?"

"You needed sleep! They don't know we're—"

"But how long will it take them to figure it out? A day? Gabe says they're monitoring our communications. They saw the bus. They probably stopped it. The driver might not talk, but surely one of the pilgrims will. If they know we got off in El Wasta, they may have already found Akhmim. He'll tell them we went to Giza. Do you think he'd die to keep that secret? He has a wife and kids!" Ava started crying. "Paul, if we slow down, we get caught. If we get caught, we die."

Ava refused to eat breakfast, and Paul refused to leave it behind. He packed the fruit and bread into plastic bags that he found in the hotel closet and stuffed them inside his backpack. An uncomfortable silence ensued as they waited for the elevator. With a carafe of orange juice in one hand, a pot of tea in the other, and a heaping plate of eggs and bacon wedged between his arm and his body, Paul looked and felt ridiculous.

The elevator opened. An elderly, well-dressed couple was inside. The man and woman smiled. Then their eyebrows arched as they noticed what Paul was carrying. "Picnic lunch?" the woman asked.

Paul tried not to grin. He glanced at Ava beseechingly.

"We're, um . . ." she tried to explain, as a smile crept across her face. "We're in a really big hurry to see the pyramids." Despite herself, she stifled a giggle. Paul was struggling to hold back laughter.

The woman replied, "Oh, you needn't hurry, lass. Been there for centuries, haven't they?"

"Longer!" Her husband boomed enthusiastically. "Ten thousand years, I say." Paul could take no more. His laughter erupted in the elevator. Ava laughed too. Maybe she'd been a little harsh. She knew she was right, but she didn't need to kick in his teeth.

They rode down to the lobby, said their good-byes, exited the hotel, and headed for the river. Behind them, the Englishwoman shook her head. "Newlyweds!"

A radiant African sun cooked the ancient city. Paul understood why Egyptians had worshipped the sun as a god. The Americans arrived at the waterfront. Despite Ava's concerns, Ammon and Sefu were waiting at the agreed location, and the two canvas-covered packages looked undisturbed.

After everyone exchanged greetings, Paul noticed the teens eyeing his food. Reserving the bacon and juice for himself, Paul handed over the tea, rolls, fruit, and eggs. The hungry boys wolfed them down in seconds. Breakfast complete, Ammon ceremoniously presented Paul with an envelope full of Egyptian banknotes. Ava shot him a questioning glance.

"He sold my watch. They knew a man who'd give a good price for it."

"TAG Heuer," said Sefu reverently. "Aquaracer."

As the teens unmoored the skiff and shoved away from the pier, Ava gave Paul a gentle look.

"Ah, what the hell?" he said, grinning. "It was a gift from Simon. I didn't want it anymore. Besides," he added, raising his voice as Ammon revved the engine and launched them into the channel, "we need the money."

The boys were showing off, keeping the throttle wide open and zigzagging between larger watercraft. Sailors yelled and cursed when they almost swamped an antique-looking dhow. Nervous at first, Ava soon adapted to the boys' frenetic navigation. She took a fatalistic approach. If it was her time, she'd rather leave behind an obituary that said "Graduate student dies in spectacular Cairo speedboat crash" than "Lonely, cautious woman dies of natural causes."

Paul had convinced her that, under the circumstances, woolen robes were superfluous. The strong breeze made it impossible to keep on a hood. Plus, they were hot and itchy. Ava was far more comfortable in her running shorts and her white T-shirt from Kamaran Island. She stretched out at the bow, enjoying the brilliant sun, the scenery, and the occasional refreshing splash of cool water. Paul noticed the boys admiring Ava's clothing and wondered how many splashes were accidental.

They cruised past Gezira Island. As she regarded the Zamalek District's swanky high-rises, Ava pondered what response to send Gabe. She took his warning that big brother was listening as a certainty. It went along with what Paul had explained about Simon's methods. Having installed network infrastructure for several Middle Eastern nations, Simon had access to all manner of data streams. Naturally, he employed a team of crypto experts in Yemen to keep his own communications secure and occasionally to snoop on the competition. She decided to keep it short, sweet, and false: "Got message. Thx. In Cairo. Driving south to Luxor 2nite. Say hi to James."

Ava sent the text and then turned off the phone to conserve its battery. The skiff crossed under the steel Imbaba Bridge. From this point, the Mediterranean coast was less than two hundred kilometers away, but because the river twisted and curved back on itself like a coiled cobra, the actual distance traveled would be greater. Once they were sixteen kilometers downstream, Ammon reduced speed to twenty knots, veered west, and headed for the Nile's Rasheed branch.

While the boys argued about drag racing, Ava meticulously applied SPF 25 to her arms, legs, and neck. She tanned easily, but a full afternoon of direct Egyptian sun, even in the cooler February air, was too much for any Anglo. Paul took the hint, accepted a thick dollop, and slathered his exposed areas. He added a filthy baseball cap to shade his face.

When Ava gave him a look he said: "It's my lucky cap."

"Superstitious nonsense," she muttered.

After three long hours on the water, Ammon cut the engine and docked near the farming village of Gezai. Paul gave the boys some Egyptian pounds and the teens jumped ashore to buy supplies. Meanwhile, Ava reclined, bathing in sunlight. Silence dominated, interrupted only by the sounds of the flowing river and regular creaks from the rope tethering them to the pier. Soon, Ammon and Sefu returned with ice, Cokes, beer, and gasoline. The cold drinks were delicious. Spirits renewed, the travelers continued across the vast delta. North of the Tamalay Bridge they entered a section of river overgrown with blue-green algae. Ammon cursed. Navigating here was a chore. The opaque algae grew thickest in the shallows, where underwater hazards lurked. Paul didn't care for the odor. Judging from Ava's expression, she was equally displeased. "I have a riddle," he said, thinking to distract her.

"Let's hear it."

Paul reached across the skiff and lifted his olive-drab backpack. "If I tossed this into the river, would the water level rise or fall?"

Ava examined the item: sturdy canvas, leather straps, and a brass buckle worn smooth by use. She closed her eyes, crossed her legs, and arched her back. Slowly, she rolled her head from shoulder to shoulder, stretching her tired neck.

"Do we care about the boat or the water level?"

"Water level," he said. "I'm asking: Will the water in the river go up or down?"

She concentrated for several seconds, then asked, "Does your backpack float?"

"I think so," he answered, regarding the alga-infested channel with distaste, "but let's not find out."

"Provided it floats, the river's level remains constant. If it sinks, the level drops."

He laughed. "You nailed it."

"Basic physics. When your backpack is tossed overboard—"

"Never mind. Want something harder?"

"Bring it."

"You're trapped in a castle. There are two doors. One goes to the exit, the other leads to a deadly tiger. Between the doors is a robot. Good robots always tell the truth. Bad robots always lie.

The robot will answer one question. What do you ask?"

"Should I assume good and bad robots are identical in appearance?"

"Yes. Sorry, I forgot to say that. All robots look the same."

Ava stretched both arms above her head, interlocking her fingers. She took a deep breath, held it, then slowly exhaled. She stared at the horizon for several minutes. Ammon had guided them out of the algal bloom. He was increasing speed. She turned to Paul and smiled before answering: "Pointing to either door, I'd say 'Mr. Robot, if I asked you whether this door leads to the exit, what would you answer?' A good robot would tell me the truth, meaning he'd say the exit was the exit and the tiger was the tiger. A bad robot would lie, but because bad robots always lie, he'd also lie about what he would say, rendering his meta-response truthful."

"Are you some kind of witch? Who thinks of that?"

"Is it the right answer?"

"Maybe," Paul muttered.

"Good. Now I get to ask one." Paul made a face, but she went on. "It's a classic. There's an island. Every man on it has cheated on his wife."

"Manhattan!"

Ava laughed. "No. Don't interrupt! There are fifty couples on the island. Each woman knows instantly if a man other than her husband cheats but no woman can tell if her own husband cheats. If a woman discovers that her husband has cheated, she kills him that very day. The pope (who is infallible) visits the island and tells the women that at least one husband has cheated. What happens?"

Paul thought for a moment. "Are any of the ladies, you know, domestic partners?"

"Ha, ha. You're hilarious."

"Okay. Sorry. Can I consult with my associates?"

Ava giggled. "Be my guest."

Paul crawled astern and repeated the riddle to the boys. The Egyptians discussed it privately, then Sefu whispered their conclusion to Paul. He nodded in agreement and gestured for Sefu to tell Ava. He approached her shyly.

"This might be wrong," he said nervously.

"Don't worry," Ava said gently, "just try."

"All men killed?" he ventured.

"Yes! Excellent!" said Ava, patting Sefu's shoulder. "But when are they killed?"

Sefu wasn't sure. He went to ask his brother. Ammon reduced speed and the boys huddled, debating. Eventually they agreed, and Sefu announced their conclusion.

"As soon as possible?"

Ava laughed. It was a delightful sound, Paul thought, and it was good to see her cheerful, even for just a little while. When she had caught her breath, she explained the answer: No man died for seven weeks because no woman could be sure her husband was the cheater, but after forty-nine days passed without a murder, the only possible conclusion was that all fifty had cheated, so all fifty were killed on that day.

From their expressions, the boys seemed lost.

"Do you understand?" Ava asked.

They looked to Paul for guidance.

"She's saying that if you ever cheat on your wife, she'll kill you."

"Oh!" said Sefu, eyes wide. "Okay."

"Yes, ma'am," said Ammon.

Near the village of Kwam Sharik, the delta was lush and green. Cows grazed in the fields and drank from the river. An orange sun slipped behind the row of tall palm trees lining the channel. Ava rose from her seat and opened the hold. She removed two icy bottles of beer, resealed the compartment, and sat down next to Paul. The boys shared a look.

"Are both beers for me?" In college, Ava never drank beer, preferring fruity wines or champagne.

"No. I enjoy a good lager from time to time."

"Really? I had no idea."

"There's a lot you don't know about me," said Ava. She gave the cap a firm twist, removed it, and took a swig.

Slowly, near the village of Basyun, darkness overtook them. Sefu lit a lantern, but soon it was too dangerous to navigate. Paul asked the boys where they could camp. According to Ammon, they were close to a community called Sais. When Ava remarked that she'd heard of it, Paul was impressed, but when they arrived, he was confused. It didn't look very important.

"It's just like all the other villages, maybe a little bigger," he observed as they motored closer. "Why is this place special?"

"It may seem insignificant now, but in ancient times this was an important center for pilgrimage. It contains the grave site of Osiris, the Egyptian god of the afterlife."

"This place?" asked Paul doubtfully, eyeing ramshackle buildings and heaps of debris. "Says who?"

"Says Herodotus. This was also the location of Neith's temple."

"Who's Neith?"

"Neith was a hunting goddess and a creator. That's unusual in the Egyptian pantheon because creation deities are generally male. Neith gave birth to Sobek, the crocodile god, who represents fertility, power, and the Nile. In the Late Period, Neith's temple was famous for exquisite linen cloth. Priestesses wove flax into fine fabric. In fact, royal linen was semitransparent."

Paul flashed a wide smile. "So, back in the day, this town was full of hot chicks in transparent clothing worshipping a fertility god?"

"Nice!" said Ammon.

"Sexy!" said Sefu.

Ava refused to dignify their behavior with a response.

The boys felt this area was a great place to camp. Cautiously, they pushed a bit farther upriver to a secluded island featuring row after row of espaliered fruit trees. Once the boat was secure, Sefu waded ashore and hiked inland for additional supplies. Ammon opened the skiff's hold and removed four bags of camping equipment. He tossed them onto the bank, where he and Paul began erecting tents. As they worked, Ava directed a flashlight about the orchard. She sought a private grove for a bathroom break. Watching carefully for crocodiles, asps, and other dangers, she excused herself. When she returned, she watched them complete the tent-raising and Ammon lit a campfire.

Sefu arrived with a basket of fresh fruit, *aish baladi* (a bread), and roasted chicken. The four travelers enjoyed a hearty feast. Subsequently, they retired to the tents, having agreed to rise at dawn.

After visiting the latrine, Paul walked back to camp under a canopy of brilliant stars. Backlit by firelight, Ava's silhouette moved within their tent. She crawled into her sleeping bag and pulled it up to her chin. Paul entered, and, after stripping to his undershorts, changed the bandage on his leg. He noted with amusement that Ava's eyes were squeezed shut. Grinning, Paul gathered their sweaty laundry, took it outside, and hung it close to the fire to dry. When he returned, he zipped the flap shut and locked the zipper. Paul wasn't worried about crocs, but his time working on archaeological digs had taught him that Africa offered many creepy invaders to disturb slumber. He flopped down on his side of the tent.

"Sorry if I snore."

"It didn't bother me in Giza."

"Okay. Goodnight then."

"Goodnight."

Paul lay in darkness, listening. Above the river's patient murmur, hosts of frogs, flies, and beetles pulsed, chirped, and trilled. The boys debated something in voices too muffled to understand while a distant cricket fiddled. Ava wriggled inside her sleeping bag. He thought she must be roasting in there. A quiet laugh passed his lips.

"What's so funny?"

"Nothing."

"Then why are you laughing?"

"I don't know. Look, can I ask you something?"

"Yes."

"You said Simon was after a secret message inside the jars. What if it's still hidden in them?"

"How do you mean?"

"I'm not sure. Could the message be hidden in the stone?"

Ava rolled onto her stomach. "Yeah, I wondered that too. That's why he had you examine them so carefully. Simon suspected there might be a coded message carved on the surface, but we didn't find anything."

"But what if it's literally in the jars?"

"Meaning?"

"Maybe written on the inside. Sealed into the material somehow."

"I don't think so."

Ava mulled over the possibilities. With her mirror and lantern, she'd examined the jars' interiors and found no evidence of writing, etching, or carving. She wasn't really surprised. An intelligent author would expect chemicals in the wine to ruin anything written on the inside. Furthermore, she doubted anything was embedded in the stone. That would have been quite difficult to accomplish without giving away the trick at a glance. Plus, she intuitively rejected the notion that shattering the jars was necessary to obtain the message. Would the apostles want such holy relics destroyed? No. There must be another solution. Pondering these questions, Ava dropped off to sleep.

Sheik Ahmed arrived in El Wasta just before ten at night. When they recognized his Brabus Mercedes, the uniformed guardsmen saluted and opened the gate. The car entered the police compound and circled to the main building, where Lieutenant Barakah waited. After parking, Ahmed's chauffeur jumped out and hurried to open the sheik's door, but Barakah beat him to it. Ahmed turned off his phone, emerged from the car, and strode purposefully into the building. As he walked, Barakah provided his important guest with a summary of the evening's progress.

Ahmed interrupted: "Bottom line, did he talk?"

"No, sir."

"He will."

The police lieutenant led Ahmed downstairs to the basement. He motioned to a guard, who pulled a string of keys from his pocket and unlocked the interrogation cell, or, as most guards called it, the confessional.

Strapped to a wooden chair and bleeding was Captain Akhmim. After enduring hours of torture, he was unrecognizable as the felucca captain who'd taken Paul and Ava to Cairo. His lips were split, his eyes were swollen shut, and he was missing teeth. Interrogators had shaved Akhmim's thick beard and broken several ribs.

The sheik grabbed an aluminum chair and sat down close to the prisoner. He lit a cigarette and offered one to Akhmim, who refused it.

"You are a proud man," said Ahmed. "You are strong, and you follow the ancient ways. I have great respect for you."

Akhmim made no reply.

"Yet by refusing to answer our questions, you protect my enemies. This will not be permitted."

Sheik Ahmed pulled his phone from his pocket. Involuntarily, Akhmim flinched, expecting a blow across the face.

Ahmed dialed a number. His call was answered on the first ring.

"Do you have them?"

"Yes, sir."

"Put the boy on."

He turned to his captive and asked, "Would you like to speak to your son?"

Akhmim shook with fear. "No!" he begged. "Please, no!"

Ahmed smiled. "We have your wife and children. If you don't tell me where to find the infidels, your children will die. I shall allow you to hear them die, one at a time, over this phone. Then, my men will entertain your wife. Do you understand?"

Akhmim hung his head, his will broken.

"I delivered the Americans to eastern Cairo," he said quietly.

"When?"

"Yesterday. Sunset."

"Where are they now?"

"I don't know."

Ahmed shook his head. He raised the phone to his lips and said, "Kill the baby."

"No!" Akhmim screamed. "I swear on my life, I don't know where they are. They took a speedboat to Giza. They mentioned going farther west, to Rasheed, maybe to Alexandria, but I don't know!"

"Speedboat?"

"Two smugglers, mere boys, with a fast little boat, a white skiff painted with racing stripes. They took the Americans to Giza, maybe farther. That's all I know. I swear on my family, that's all I know!"

Ahmed nodded thoughtfully, finished his cigarette, and said, "I believe you." He lifted the Ruger SR9 from his pocket, pointed it at the prisoner's head, and squeezed the trigger.

Over the phone, he could hear Akhmim's family screaming. Sheik Ahmed put the speaker close to his ear and listened to their terror.

"Kill the family," he told his aide. "All of them. Bury the bodies in the desert."

As he issued these orders, Lieutenant Barakah shrank back. Ahmed noticed but kept silent.

"As I suspected," Ahmed thought. "Barakah is weak. He lacks the strength for what must be done. He is unfit to serve the master."

In the predawn light, Ava woke from a nightmare. It took a few moments to recall where she was. Then she panicked, realizing the two ancient artifacts were sitting in the motorboat, concealed by nothing more than canvas. She couldn't believe the risks they'd taken. Wandering bandits could easily steal the jars. The boys hadn't obtained anyone's permission to camp here. What if a farmer reported them? She and Paul might be arrested for smuggling antiquities, and if Simon's hitmen found them . . .

She resolved to check on the jars. She sat up and reached for her clothes. They were gone. Nervous, she looked left and right but saw nothing. Ava glanced at Paul. He was snoring away in blissful ignorance. She gathered the sleeping bag around her and peered around the tent. Nothing!

Just then, Paul stirred. He saw that Ava was up and assumed he'd overslept.

"What time is it?" he said, yawning, and out of habit glanced at his wrist. "It doesn't look like the sun's up."

"Paul?"

"Yes?"

"Where are my clothes?"

"They were damp and nasty, so I hung them by the fire to dry."

"I'd like to get dressed."

"Cool."

"Will you get them for me, please?"

Paul was annoyed. He didn't want to get up from his warm sleeping bag. Why had she awakened him so early? He still had time to sleep.

"Get them yourself," he muttered, covering his head with a blanket. "They're right by the campfire."

Holding the sleeping bag tightly, Ava sat motionless, looked directly at him, and said nothing for several seconds.

Then it dawned on him. He started to laugh. "Wait, are you buck naked under there?"

Ava felt a wave of anger rise from her stomach. She suppressed the urge to punch him in the face.

"Paul," she said, slowly and deliberately, "Go . . . get . . . my . . . clothes."

He knew better than to argue. "I'll be right back."

The black Mercedes sped north on Highway 21 toward Cairo. For several minutes the passengers rode in silence. Ahmed lit a cigarette and said, "You objected when I had our men kill the prisoner's family, didn't you Barakah?"

"I follow your orders, sir. I always have."

"Indeed, but you avoid answering my question. Do you feel the decision to kill them was a mistake?"

"I obey you in all things, and I never question your judgment."

Ahmed grew frustrated by his subordinate's circumlocutions. He brightened the limo's interior lights and looked pointedly at his underling.

"Tell me, would you have killed them?"

Barakah knew better than to lie. "No. The prisoner gave us the information we needed. I would have freed the woman and her children."

Ahmed nodded, satisfied to hear the truth. On the surface, Barakah was a decorated Central Security Force officer assigned to the Egyptian National Police. Secretly, he'd joined Ahmed's organization and risen through the hierarchy. Intelligent, competent, and thorough, Barakah followed every order to the letter. But the sheik maintained reservations about this ostensibly dutiful soldier. Ahmed suspected that Barakah lacked the courage of his convictions. In the eternal struggle, a mind clouded by mercy and compassion was a severe liability.

"If we allowed those children to live, they would have sworn a blood oath of vengeance against us and our cause. As adults, they would have fought tirelessly to defeat and kill us. A blood enemy is a true enemy, Barakah. A blood enemy cannot be bribed or dissuaded. He must be killed, exterminated. I choose to exterminate my enemies now, while I still can."

"But the woman? We could have left her."

Ahmed laughed. "Women are far more dangerous than men. To defeat a woman I must defeat not only her but also all her family. A woman's father, husband, brothers, and sons will sacrifice their lives to avenge wrongs done to her. Her sisters and daughters will never forgive or forget. Women are cunning and patient, willing to achieve vengeance through stealth and treachery. Remember the story of Shamshoum [Sampson]. They can bewitch honest soldiers, fill our minds with poison and confusion. Women live to deceive. They will turn brother against brother, *musahib*. Never underestimate them."

At dawn the travelers packed up camp, refueled the skiff, and resumed their journey. Despite the uncomfortable robes, Paul and Ava were again disguised as pilgrims. As the boat navigated a bewildering variety of canals, forks, locks, and side streams, Ava wondered how the boys managed without getting lost. Could they possibly have the intricate route memorized? Then she noticed that from time to time Ammon consulted a small gray box mounted on the stern. Curious, she eased her way aft and found that it was a GPS navigation device, specifically a Lowrance LMS-520C, of which the boys were immensely proud. Sefu insisted on showing Ava all its functions. It featured a five-inch, 480-pixel display; could ascertain their exact position on a satellite map; could sound a channel's depth up to ninety meters; and was waterproof. Before they left Cairo, Ammon had plotted their course and saved it into the device's memory.

Ava was impressed, but she knew such high-tech gadgets were expensive. The GPS must have run several hundred dollars. Was ferrying tourists around Cairo really that lucrative?

Occasionally the boys reduced speed and traversed shallower zones invaded by the fetid species of alga they'd endured upriver. Near Shubra Khit they encountered a particularly thick bloom.

"It reeks," said Paul, disgusted. "This stuff is gross."

"Oh, it's worse than gross. It's ecotoxic," Ava said.

"It's poisonous?"

"To the planet. The Aswan Dam project, which formed Lake Nasser, caused all kinds of environmental damage. Not enough water flows down. Consequently, the valley soil gets too salty, requiring more artificial fertilizer. Fertilizer runoff creates huge algal blooms, which block sunlight, harbor bacteria, and kill the fish. Nutrient discharge into the Mediterranean has declined drastically, weakening offshore sardine and shrimp fisheries."

"So why don't they release more water?"

"It's not that simple. The Nile runs through seven countries, and its waters are almost fully utilized. In Egypt alone the population has doubled since 1978, so more and more freshwater is consumed by people, tourists, and farms. The High Dam is particularly harmful because it blocks silt from passing. Without replenishing silt, alluvial soil degrades, fish starve, and the whole delta suffers."

"Okay, okay," Paul said, holding up his hands to block the verbal onslaught. "I didn't mean to uncork the Earth First! genie."

"Don't trivialize this, Paul. People face a shortage of drinking water because plutocrats would rather irrigate golf courses. Egypt has an annual water deficit of twenty billion cubic meters. Myopic capitalists like your boss should be held responsible for the negative externalities their so-called investments create."

"Former boss," Paul corrected. "I'm now a proud member of the unemployed proletariat."

She grinned. "Welcome to the revolution."

During the next hour they sped by several agricultural towns, including Mahalat Diyay, Diminkan, and Kafr Magar. Each one, Paul admitted, did not appear to have benefited from a capitalist economic bonanza. Poor farmers lived in mud-brick buildings with few modern amenities or conveniences. On the other hand, everyone appeared well fed.

Around noon they passed under two major highway bridges. Ammon said the large urban center was called Disuq. Paul wondered aloud if any famous gods were buried there. Ava smiled and said that centuries ago Disuq was a capital of the Hyskos, an Asiatic people who invaded from the east.

As they continued north, Ava could tell they were nearing the sea. The indigenous flora and fauna began to take on a marine character. In the large settlements of Qabit, Fuwah, and Sandayoun, boatbuilding seemed to be an important industry. A tang of salty air carried the pungency of old pilings, rotting despite their creosote. She noted a variety of rusty seagoing vessels at anchor. This stage of the river was heavily involved with aquaculture, forcing the boys to navigate carefully lest they damage the hull on a subsurface fish farm. When they reached Mutabis, Ammon reduced speed.

"We stop here," Sefu said. "Ten minutes, okay?" He tied the skiff to a rickety pier. Ammon disembarked and disappeared into the crowd.

"Ava, this might be a good place for a bathroom break," Paul said. "Why don't you scope it out?"

Something about his manner made her wary. He'd been consistently overprotective. Now he was suggesting she go ashore alone? Nonchalantly, she hopped onto the pier and went into a restaurant. Then she doubled back to a window to surveil the boat. Her suspicion was confirmed when she spied Ammon toting a large cardboard box mummified in shipping tape. He stowed it in the skiff's hold and smiled roguishly at Paul. Ava had guessed they'd been keeping a secret from her. Now she knew it.

Furious, she stormed back to the pier. "What's in the box?" she demanded.

Paul's eyes met hers. He shook his head and said, "Don't get upset. Everything's fine. The boys just need to deliver something to Cairo. We'll be on our way in a minute."

Ava was less than satisfied by his explanation. Tears formed in her eyes. In a voice tight with anger and sadness, she announced:

"No. I'm sorry, Paul. I'm getting off."

"Huh? Wait, you don't understand!"

"No, I'm sure I don't. I don't understand a thing about trafficking drugs except that I'm not getting involved. So, good luck, and I hope you all make a huge profit," she said, now sobbing.

"It's not what you think!"

"Oh really? What's in the box then?"

He glanced at Ammon and Sefu. His look asked, "Can I?" They shrugged, clearly displeased by the situation. Paul beckoned Ava aboard. Reluctantly, she complied. Ava doubted Paul would actually kidnap her, but if he was mixed up in drugs, nothing was certain.

He crouched, removed the box from the hold, and, using his knife, cut through the thick transparent tape. With considerable effort, he ripped open a flap and dozens of *Victoria's Secret* catalogs spilled onto the deck, along with old issues of *Maxim, Vibe, Details,* and *Playboy.* The boys leaped down and began stuffing glossy magazines back into the hold, looking over their shoulders to ensure that no one had seen.

"What the hell?" Ava asked, baffled.

"Pornography is forbidden by the Qur'an and by Egyptian law. So naturally the black market for racy magazines, VHS tapes, DVDs, and whatever else is thriving. It's incredibly profitable to smuggle. Back home, people give away this stuff. In Cairo, dealers sell these magazines for six bucks apiece."

"Isn't it easier to download your filth from the Internet?"

"You'd think so, but since the Arab Spring, the authorities have cracked down. At Internet cafés users sign a form swearing they won't access or download pornography. Private accounts are monitored and spot-checked by government censors. They even tried to ban YouTube, and if you break the law, you go to jail. Egyptian jail! Plus, most Egyptians aren't hooked up to the Internet. They can't download images or watch streaming video."

"But, I mean, *Victoria's Secret*? That's illegal?"

"Have you seen the pictures? It would have been illegal in Boston in the fifties."

Simon dialed the number for his Yemen headquarters. The receptionist answered.

"Connect me to crypto," he ordered.

From his tone, she knew better than to speak. She directed his call to the computer center's cryptologic unit, where the twenty-three-year-old manager picked up.

"Hello?"

He sounded as though he had food in his mouth.

"Fritz, I have Mr. DeMaj holding for you."

"Huh! What does he want? I mean, put him through, please."

"Where are they?" Simon demanded.

"Sir?"

"Our fugitives. I told you to drop everything and find them. So, where are they?"

"We know they're in Egypt."

Simon took a deep breath. Silently, he counted to three, allowing his frustration to dissipate sufficiently for the conversation to continue. Even so, a measure of anger leaked into his voice.

"Fritz, I know they're in Egypt. I'm the one who told you they're in Egypt. It's a big country. I need you to be more specific."

"Yes, sir. We tracked Paul's phone. It was a dead end. Apparently, he gave it to a desert nomad. Ava's phone hasn't been used since she left Boston."

"Credit cards?"

"We're watching them. Bank accounts too. Nothing since the hit on Kamaran. They must be paying for everything in cash and using aliases."

Simon had expected as much. Paul was hardly a master spy, but he'd worked for DeMaj long enough to learn some basic espionage.

"Have we picked them up on security video?"

"No. I think we can safely conclude they're avoiding airports, train stations—any form of mass transit. We're listening to the Egyptian military and police. They don't have anything either."

"What about text messages, e-mail?"

"We can read their mail, but we're having trouble tracing the device. It might be piggybacking a signal over the national net, relayed off a LEO satellite. The transmitter doesn't use standard GPS, and the software is hardened against reverse-search protocols. It's actually a pretty cool hack—"

"Find them," Simon interrupted, "and call the moment you do."

8

At four o'clock they reached Rosetta, which Ava insisted on calling Rasheed. Near the harbor dilapidated brick buildings had been colonized by squatters and repurposed into a vibrant, openair market. While Ammon tended to the boat and Sefu went to purchase gasoline, Ava found a rest room and Paul found a payphone. Since ditching his mobile phone, he couldn't remember any numbers, so he attempted to call information. This proved an exercise in futility, because the operator couldn't understand a word he said. Eventually he relented and conscripted Ava. She pretended to be aggravated, but she was secretly pleased that he needed her help. It took her about ten seconds to obtain the number for the Hotel Salaam in Alexandria, plus the operator offered to connect her directly. She smiled at Paul. "For whom shall I ask?"

"Is it ringing? Just give me the damn phone."

"Hotel Salaam," the receptionist said.

"*Bonjour*," said Paul, with the worst French accent Ava had ever heard. "*Je voudrais parler à Monsieur Nick.*"

"*Qui?*"

"Nick. Mr. Nick. *Señor* Nico. *Il est Americain.*"

"*Ah, oui. Monsieur Nick*," the receptionist repeated. "*Un moment, s'il vous plaît.*"

Ava said, "I don't know what game you're playing, but no one will ever believe you're French. Not with that accent."

"True. My French is terrible, but I know the receptionist. She's Portuguese. I'm hoping that despite my awful French, she won't flag me as an American. I mean, sure, she'll know I'm not French, but I could be a moron from anywhere."

Ava laughed. Then a masculine voice spoke over the phone.

"This is Nick. How may I help you?"

Paul switched to English. "Hello. I'm a regular customer in town on a confidential matter. Can a room be arranged?"

"I'll be happy to check with reception, sir, but we have very few suites, and rooms are often reserved quite a bit in advance. May I ask who is calling, please?"

"I'm afraid I'd rather not say. You see, I'm traveling with a woman who's not my wife. She's a business associate."

"Of course," said Nick politely.

"And I don't want scurrilous rumors started. No stories in tomorrow's papers. You understand."

"Indeed, sir. Did you say you're a regular customer?"

"Yes, but I must insist my name not be used. Why don't I use the name of a friend we have in common: Mr. Francona. I believe an associate of yours introduced us some years ago in Boston."

There was a long pause. "I dined with Mr. Francona—"

"At the Parker House. You ordered your steak purple."

Another pause. "Okay, Mr. Francona. I'll see about your room. Are you here in town?"

"We expect to arrive tonight, Nick."

"I'll give you my direct number. Call me when you arrive."

Paul hung up and wrote down the number.

"What the hell was that?"

Paul explained. "An old teammate of mine works as a casino

manager in Alexandria. He's a huge Red Sox fan. Back in 2008, I introduced him to Terry Francona."

"Does he know it's you?"

"I think so. There were only three of us at dinner."

"Can he get us a room?"

"Sure. They always keep a few open for celebs. He'll sneak us in the back, no credit-card swipe, no passport checks."

Just then, Sefu came running. He looked terrified. "Paul, go now, okay? We go now!"

As they departed, Ava sought an explanation. Sefu would say only that friends suggested they leave immediately. She assumed these friends to be fellow smugglers. Through a labyrinth of alleyways and back passages, Sefu guided them toward the harbor. Before long they entered the busy town square, which surrounded a battery of cannons dating from the Napoleonic era.

Sefu froze. Across the courtyard, two obese policemen were staring at them. The cops drew their pistols. With fear in his voice, Sefu cried, "Follow! Hurry!" and broke into a sprint. Paul grabbed Ava's arm and took off after him, trying desperately to keep pace with the Egyptian. Their overweight pursuers struggled through the crowd, shouting *"Qeff! Qeff!"* and brandishing their guns. Sefu, hurdling a picnic table, demolished a chess game as he raced toward the riverfront. Paul followed, bulldozing through the astonished players, creating a path for Ava.

Running at top speed, they gained ground on the slower police. One had fallen far behind; the other had dropped from sight completely. The harbor was less than a kilometer distant. They'd reach the dock in moments. Paul felt sure Ammon would be ready with the engine running, but as they rounded the final corner, Paul realized what had become of the second policeman. He'd taken a shortcut and was now going to intercept them! He stood on the pier, blocking their escape. Just a few meters beyond, Ammon waited aboard the skiff. They were so close! Paul slowed, but Sefu did not: He intended to run for it.

"Wait!" Paul shouted a warning. Sefu didn't seem to hear.

The policeman raised his weapon, smiling. When Sefu closed to within a few feet, the cop fired twice. One bullet whizzed by the boy's ear. The second found its mark, blasting a fist-size hole into Sefu's chest.

Paul saw Sefu fall and was overcome with rage. Like a man possessed, he roared and charged directly at the butcher. For a millisecond, their eyes met. Then the policeman's face blanched with fear. In Paul he beheld a frenzied spirit. The cop hesitated, and an instant too late tried to bring his pistol to bear against the charging man. Paul launched himself through the air, driving his brawny shoulder into the fat man's gut. The cop gasped as his sternum fractured with an audible snap. He fell back against a stone column, and when he exhaled, a mist of blood sprayed from his mouth. Paul's left hook slammed into the cop's face, shattering his nose. Blinded by tears and blood, the policeman managed to get off one wild shot before Paul's colossal uppercut connected. The cop staggered farther backward. Momentum propelled him over the low wall, and he toppled into the river.

Paul turned to Ava. "Run!" he barked at her. She obeyed instantly. Behind her, Paul bent low and gathered the teenager's body into his arms. As gently as he could, he carried Sefu onto the boat. The moment they were aboard, Ammon kicked the throttle wide open. Ava could see tears dripping down Ammon's cheeks as he whispered a prayer for his baby brother's life. They shot away from the pier, just seconds ahead of the other policeman. Over the engine's whine, Ava heard three staccato cracks. Two shots flew wide to their left; the third struck the skiff amidships, just inches from her body.

Then the air erupted with the sound of a heavy machine gun. "Get down!" Paul yelled, gesturing for Ava to hide behind the canisters. He poked his head up, scanning the horizon. Charging toward them from the north was an Egyptian Coast Guard patrol vessel, with thick, bulletproof armor, a deep V-hull, a government insignia, and a fifty-caliber deck cannon. Instantly Ammon yanked the skiff into a tight hundred-and-eighty-degree turn. Surprised by the maneuver, Ava slipped and fell. Her backside slammed against the rail. Frantically she sought a handhold. By hooking her fingers under the seat's fiberglass lip, she somehow kept herself aboard until Ammon helped her regain equilibrium. The patrol boat had throttled up and was gaining. At top speed, Ammon rocketed them across the water, jumping the shallow-hulled skiff from wake to wake. As they passed Rasheed, he veered away from shore. They heard more gunshots. The remaining cop was firing away.

The panga raced upriver. Quickly Ammon ducked into a narrow channel that cut around an island. The government boat followed, still gaining. As the larger craft neared, Paul focused on the bow cannon. In seconds they'd be within its accurate range. He envisioned deadly fifty-caliber shells shredding the fragile skiff, destroying everything and everyone aboard. At that moment he detected a familiar stench. Ammon had driven them straight into an algal bloom! Their speed slowed dramatically, and Paul's heart sank. The supercharged Evinrude motor screamed as it fought through the thick, stinking muck. He reached for Ava and took her hand. Paul struggled to find the words to apologize, to show his feelings. If he hadn't wanted to see her again, she'd never be in this mess. It was so stupid. He should have known about Simon.

How could he have missed it? Instead, he'd made a horrific botch of things. Now he'd be responsible for Ava's death as well as the deaths of two innocent kids. He looked up at her. Voice cracking with shame, he said, "I'm so sorry."

Ava, however, was smiling. Confused, Paul followed her gaze astern, where he saw Ammon beaming in triumph. The patrol boat was fading into the distance. Rushing to follow them through the swampy shallows, the pursuer had run aground.

There was not a moment to lose. Paul knelt on the deck, eased open Sefu's shirt, and attempted to check his vitals. Over the engine's roar, Paul couldn't hear a heartbeat. He felt for a pulse, but his own still pounded too strongly. Finally, he put his cheek to Sefu's lips, forcing himself to remain perfectly still. He waited.

After what seemed a lifetime, Paul felt a shallow exhale. Despite the gushing blood and the sucking wound, Sefu's chest slowly expanded and contracted.

"He's alive!" Paul yelled. Ammon's head shot up. His face burst into a hopeful smile. Ava began to sob. "Get us to a doctor," Paul commanded. He no longer cared about the jars. He didn't care if he went to jail, or worse. He would not let this boy die.

As the sun set, they regained the main channel, and Ammon opened the throttle wide. Squinting in the dim light, Paul dug through the pilgrims' first-aid kit, found some gauze bandages, and tried to stanch Sefu's wounds. He was losing blood much too rapidly.

"Is the satphone charged?" he asked. Ava said yes, but reminded him that DeMaj might be monitoring the number.

"I don't give a damn. Without proper care, he'll be dead in two hours, maybe sooner."

He handed the phone to Ammon. "Call ahead to the next town. Make sure they have a decent hospital. Tell them to send an ambulance, paramedics, and whatever else they have to meet us on the docks. Tell them money is no object."

Ava shot Paul a questioning look. In response, he grabbed his wallet, flipped it open, and withdrew a handful of elite credit cards.

"Take them all. Simon won't have frozen my accounts. He'd hope to track us by our purchases. Just spend whatever it takes."

Ammon locked eyes with Paul. For a moment, neither moved or spoke. Something profound passed between them. Then Ammon nodded. He took the credit cards and began dialing.

Twenty minutes later, they reached the docks of Mutubis. Two nondescript vans awaited them. Neither was an ambulance, and Ava didn't see any paramedics, but the tough-looking men driving the vans had experience transporting wounded passengers. Ammon gave instructions and displayed the credit cards, proving this wasn't a charity case. The drivers didn't work risky jobs for free. As they loaded Sefu onto the gurney, he briefly regained consciousness. He coughed blood, gagged, and reached out blindly. Paul caught his hand and held it steady.

"Hey, kid," said Paul, "you'll be fine. We told the doctors you'd give them free *Playboy* subscriptions."

Sefu tried to laugh. Instead, a hideous wheeze escaped his chest.

"Here," Paul said, handing the teen a filthy baseball cap, "take this for luck. It's just a loan, okay? I want it back in a few days, when you're feeling better."

Sefu smiled and nodded. The driver shut the van's doors and departed for the hospital.

The travelers watched the van until it faded out of sight. Ammon returned the satphone.

Ava turned to Ammon. "What's your plan?" she said.

"Go south and hide the boat. Then sneak back to the hospital."

He helped Paul transfer the cargo and luggage from the boat to the remaining van. As they slid the twin canisters inside, Paul tried to pass Ammon a wad of banknotes, but the young Egyptian refused. Instead he patted his pocket, which held the credit cards. "I will repay," he vowed solemnly. He and Paul shook hands.

Ammon nodded respectfully to Ava, who rushed forward and kissed his cheek, causing him to blush a rich scarlet. The man watching from the van smiled in amusement. Glaring at him, Ammon retreated to his boat and disengaged it from the pier. With a wave, he started the engine and motored south.

As the Egyptian sun slipped below the horizon, Paul and Ava climbed into the second van and hid themselves under a thick blanket while the driver piled a load of heavy woven carpets atop the canisters. Its foreign passengers and cargo thus concealed, the van began the sixty-five-kilometer trek to Alexandria.

9

South of Târgovişte,
Romania, June 1462

Sultan Mehmed II sat in his tent, contemplating strategy. His method was to think three or four moves ahead of his adversary, anticipating and then neutralizing any foreseeable response. In just seven days, he'd led his army into the heart of Wallachia. Despite the enemy's unconventional maneuvers, guerrilla warfare, and scorched-earth tactics, only the walled city of Bucharest and the Snagov Fortress remained between Mehmed and the capital.

It had been a difficult, costly campaign. Destroyed bridges, traps, concealed pits, and other obstacles impeded the Turks' progress. Most peasants had evacuated to the mountains, taking along their invaluable harvests and livestock. As a consequence, the Turkish army suffered from fatigue, paranoia, and starvation. The coming days promised to be worse. Reconnaissance by trusted scouts indicated that the countryside offered no man or any significant animal, and nothing to eat or drink.

A messenger appeared at Mehmed's door. Once admitted by the bodyguards, he reported that the Ottoman navy had taken the Bulgarian ports of Brăila and Chilia, denying the enemy any hope of reinforcement by sea. "So," the sultan thought, "we can attack at dawn."

Mehmed ordered his guards to bring in a captured Wallachian soldier.

"Tell me your name," the sultan demanded.

The Christian said nothing. A guard slapped the prisoner's face with a heavy gauntlet, drawing blood, but the captive stayed mute.

Mehmed said, "This conflict is pointless. Lead me to your master and present my terms. He will surrender with honor, convert to Islam, and be named a baron in my empire. Every warrior who lays down arms and converts will be spared. For your service, you will have three thousand coins and my gratitude."

There was no response.

The sultan continued.

"Otherwise, my jailers will torture you to death. They are quite practiced in the art."

The warrior met the sultan's gaze. By way of reply, he spat. The guards fell upon the Christian with a flurry of blows, knocking him to the ground and fracturing bones.

"This fool prefers torture and death to mercy and wealth. Execute him."

Mehmed's guards dragged away the defiant Wallachian. Outwardly, the sultan acted as though such defiance was inconsequential. Secretly, he was impressed by the infidel's resolve. "With a division of such soldiers," he thought, "I could conquer the world."

Disguised as a Janissary, the Wallachian commander, called the Impaler Prince by his enemies, walked freely about the Ottoman camp. He made a study of his foe. Vastly outnumbered, the Wallachians could never defeat the Turks in open combat. His only hope for victory was the path foretold by the pope's prophecy:

that he'd capture and kill Mehmed, ending the war. To accomplish this, he must find the sultan's tent.

The camp was gigantic, bigger than most cities. The Turkish soldiers numbered more than one hundred thousand. After wandering for hours, Vlad Dracula came upon the most richly appointed tent he'd ever seen. Its exterior was covered in a dazzling geometric pattern of embroidered gold lace inlaid with precious stones. He circled the immense structure, and as a messenger entered, he stole a glimpse inside. What he saw amazed him: The sultan traveled with a harem! Nubile concubines twirled and gyrated, attired in priceless silks. Vlad inhaled the sharp aroma of incense and exotic spices. He marked the tent's location, certain it was his quarry's lair.

Some hours after sunset, Dracula launched his surprise attack. Wallachian trumpets blared and pitch torches blazed. The Turkish guards ran amok, lost in the thick smoke. Veterans of countless lightning raids, Vlad's elite cavalry attacked from several directions at once, routing the terrified Ottoman sentries.

Through the ensuing turmoil and confusion, Dracula led a disciplined commando force to the grand tent. He abducted the two inhabitants at dagger point. After lashing each captive atop a fast steed, the Wallachian horsemen sped away at a gallop.

Only later would Vlad Dracula discover that although he'd captured two fabulously wealthy grand viziers, Ishak Pasha and Mahmud Pasha, Sultan Mehmed II had escaped.

EGYPT, FEBRUARY 2013

In a turbocharged helicopter, using a pair of Swiss night-vision binoculars, Simon scanned traffic on the busy highway below.

Struggling to maintain a stationary position, the aircraft battled irregular and unpredictable winds. Occasionally a gust caused the chopper to lurch violently. Simon swore in French. His chest and shoulder ached where restraints bit into his wounds. Cairo's best doctors had provided all kinds of pills, but Simon refused narcotics. He needed his mind to be razor sharp. All he'd worked for—even his immortal soul—hung in the balance.

"Mr. DeMaj, we have them!"

"Where?"

"Near Rosetta. They're traveling with a team of local crooks."

"Change course immediately. How far?"

"We can be there in a half hour."

"Go."

The smuggler's van bounced along the pitted gravel road at a modest, inconspicuous pace. Garbed in heavy pilgrim robes and concealed under several layers of thick cloth, Ava was thankful the sun had set. The old van lacked air-conditioning, but mercifully the driver had left the rear windows ajar. From the smell, Ava guessed their route tracked an irrigation canal. They drove for ten minutes, then slowed and stopped. In an urgent whisper, the driver cautioned: "Checkpoint. Be silent."

Ava felt sweat beading on her neck. In the pitch darkness, she couldn't see Paul. Unconsciously, she reached for him. Sensing her fear, he grasped her hand and held it. A warming strength flowed into her. She relaxed, and her breathing became regular.

The driver rolled down his window and answered questions. The exchange sounded familiar, even jocular. Ava gathered that the driver knew the security team and that he'd undergone this interrogation before. She heard the glove compartment click open, yielding documents for inspection. Moments later, two raps on the van's exterior signaled a decision. The engine coughed to life, and their journey continued.

They turned west on Route 58, a coastal artery running north of Lake Idku. A half hour later, Ava detected the Mediterranean's briny aroma.

As the van reached Alexandria's outskirts, the driver invited Paul and Ava to come out of hiding. Paul immediately opened a window, and the Americans filled their lungs with invigorating air. Borrowing the driver's phone, Paul called Nick. As expected, Nick preferred to meet at a service entrance, located in an alley opposite the hotel's grand facade.

Traffic increased as they entered the city proper. The van crossed over several bridges. Ava peered down into dimly lit canals and waterways lined with scows, barges, fishing boats, and cargo rafts. The scent of dried fish reminded her of crossing the Red Sea. Was that only five days ago?

The knowledgeable driver took an indirect path into downtown, avoiding traffic jams and checkpoints. After turning onto a broad avenue tracking the coast, they beheld a glorious vista: the luminous Qaitbey Citadel, bathed in colored lights for an opera performance. Ava leaned across Paul to obtain a better view.

"Isn't it amazing?" she asked.

"Yeah," he agreed, gazing across the harbor. "Beautiful scenery, nice weather. I see why Alexander built a castle here."

Ava laughed. "The citadel isn't that old. It was constructed by the Mamelukes in 1477 to defend against Ottoman Turks. During the reign of Sultan Qaitbey—"

"Never heard of him."

"An interesting character. Ruled Egypt in the late 1400s. Although he was a dictator who imposed heavy taxes, his reign was recognized as among the best of that era. He seized power by force, but he actually cared for the people."

"Cool. I dig his crib."

Ava giggled. "You know, some of the stone for that crib was recycled from the Pharos Lighthouse. Note the huge red granite pillars in the northwest—*mmph!*"

Paul had put his hand over her mouth. "Can we save the history lesson for after supper?"

Ammon guided the skiff southward, fighting the current. He barred any thought of his brother's injuries from entering his mind. Concern would induce recklessness. If he was caught or killed, he'd be no help to Sefu. Almost an hour had passed since he'd parted company with his friends in Mutubis. Despite Ammon's youth, he was a highly disciplined captain. He longed to run at top speed, to get as far as possible from the enemy. Instead, he moved cautiously, restrained the engine, and maintained a quiet pace. He squinted in the dim light, striving to locate and dodge submerged obstacles. He knew he couldn't ignite gas lanterns without risking detection. He was uncomfortable using even his tiny flashlight. Reasoning that the authorities would seek him there, he ignored the first settlement he encountered. After he'd traveled about fifteen kilometers, he heard an unusual sound. He piloted his boat toward the bank, tied it up under some fruit trees, and killed the motor.

The sound grew louder, and soon it was unmistakable. Ammon recognized the throbbing sonic profile of a turbocharged helicopter. Seconds later, a searchlight began sweeping the river. Ammon considered his options. He could flee. There was a large settlement less than three kilometers upriver. With luck he could be there in five minutes, but five minutes was too long. He'd be spotted and shot. Even if the bullets missed, the chopper pilot could simply radio ahead, calling a swarm of cops to his location.

The patrol was almost on top of him. He reached a decision: Rather than run, he would hide. He dislodged the portable GPS from the skiff, pressed SAVE to enter the boat's coordinates, and loaded the device into his backpack. With a silent prayer, Ammon slipped onto the muddy shore and began to belly-crawl through the tangled underbrush.

The driver entered Saad Zaghloul Square and parked in a narrow alley, away from prying eyes. He helped Paul unload the canisters and bags. Paul handed him some cash as well as Nick's direct number. They shook hands, and the driver left.

"How much did you pay?" Ava asked.

"Five hundred for the ride, five hundred to keep quiet."

"Do you think he will?"

"I'm not sure. Ammon told me the driver was trustworthy. I want to believe it."

At the mention of Ammon's name, Ava's face darkened. Her mind raced back to poor Sefu, fighting for his life in God-knows-what hospital. Lost in this dismal thought, she was oblivious to the footfalls of a man approaching her from behind.

"You look like hell!" a voice boomed.

Ava almost jumped out of her shoes. She spun around to see a handsome man, blond hair *en brosse,* wearing a custom-tailored tuxedo. He looked Ava up and down.

"My apologies, *mademoiselle.* I was referring only to that fellow."

"Don't bother, Nick," said Paul, grinning. "Ava hates men."

"Just the stupid ones," she retorted.

"Then how do you tolerate this knucklehead?" Nick said, clapping Paul on the shoulder.

"Shut up and help me with the luggage."

"Whatever you say, Mr. Francona."

Taking care not to soil Nick's immaculate tux, the former ballplayers hefted the canisters onto a brass dolly and guided it through the hotel's service entrance. Ava followed them into a bustling kitchen.

Once they were inside, Nick closed and locked the door. Pointing to their bloodstained cloaks, he said, "You can't just stroll through the lobby like that. Someone will call the police."

Ava and Paul shared a glance. Obviously they were eager to avoid that experience. They took off their pilgrim clothing and Nick tossed the tattered cloaks into the incinerator.

"Better?" Paul asked.

"Much better," Nick answered, appraising Ava's tiny running shorts and bikini top, which were too chilly for the cold night air. "You look like you just came in from the beach."

She dug into her backpack, found an oversized T-shirt, and pulled it over her head.

"Can we see our room now?"

Nick led them upstairs to a beautiful suite. As the men rolled in the dolly and unloaded the canisters, Ava admired the antique furnishings. She pulled open the curtains and gasped at a panoramic view of Alexandria's Great Harbor. Directly across the water glowed the Qaitbey Fortress. Far down the corniche to the east was the modern Bibliotheca, built in 2002. To the west, minarets towered above the El-Mursi Abul Abbas Mosque complex.

"Just dial zero for anything you desire, Ava. Champagne, wine, whiskey, you name it. I told the concierge to put your charges on my comps."

"Thanks, Nick."

"My pleasure, *mademoiselle.*"

"Yeah, thanks," Paul said. He took Nick by the arm and led him from the room.

Once they were outside, Nick said, "Let me guess. Her father is in the Mafia. No, the CIA."

"It's not like that."

"Sure. First you call out of the blue using a fake name. Now you show up covered in blood, with a half-dressed teenage sexpot, and I'm not supposed to ask questions?"

"She's not a teenager. She's our age."

"Fine. Whatever. That hardly explains—"

"Nick, it's complicated. We need somewhere to hide for a day or two, just long enough to figure out everything. I'm sorry about this."

"Don't get me fired, okay? I like this job."

"*Gracias.* You're a true friend. I owe you."

"No kidding." With a wink, Nick handed over the keys, then vanished into the elevator.

Gabe previewed his post for the umpteenth time, reworded it, and struggled to avoid sounding stupid or desperate. With his mouse, he guided the cursor over the PUBLISH button and then hesitated. He rarely contributed to this forum, certainly nothing like this. His post was an admission of weakness. He anticipated the responses. Someone would flame him, he just knew it. He detested being in this position, but Gabe needed help, his reputation as a great hacker notwithstanding. If anyone could help, it would be this site's readers, who tolerated no poseurs. When posts were deemed stupid or insulting, consequences ensued. He knew of cases in which a devastating worm or virus had been inflicted on a newbie who violated protocol. For years Gabe had been a member of this insular community. He'd formed relationships of sorts with the regulars. Though he'd never met any face-to-face, he knew their tastes in music, movies, TV, books, and food. He understood their political philosophies (most were hard-core libertarians), and he'd learned to appreciate their savvy programming suggestions. After a final review, he transmitted his message.

Paul returned to the room, entered without knocking, and surprised Ava undressing for a bath.

"Sorry!" he said, retreating into the hallway. "I'll give you some privacy."

He turned to leave, then heard her voice.

"You can stay."

"Come again?"

With a shy smile: "If you don't mind, I'd like you to stay. Walking around the hotel, someone might identify you. And besides," she said, lowering her eyes, "I'll feel safer if I know you're here."

Paul was touched. Despite his stupid mistakes and all the trouble he'd caused, Ava still trusted him to protect her.

"Oh, okay. Sure. Of course I'll stay."

Ava shut the bathroom door. The antique porcelain tub was her favorite type, with little feet and an old-fashioned chain stopper. She filled the bath with piping-hot water, added aromatic salts, dropped her towel, and slipped inside. As the warmth loosened her muscles, Ava inhaled deeply and then forced all the air from her lungs. Most of her stress left with it. She reclined and for the first time in days shaved her legs. They were, she observed with satisfaction, now nicely tanned.

As Ava rested her head against the cool ceramic, her mind drifted, flowing from topic to topic until drawn back, inevitably, to the sacred relics and three unresolved questions: Where was the message? Were these the real jars? How could she be sure? Recalling the personal and professional embarrassment Dr. King suffered after presenting the dubious papyrus, Ava shivered. Counterfeit artifacts had ruined many a promising career. In 2004, authorities determined that an ivory pomegranate thought to have adorned King Solomon's Temple was phony. Ava knew well the sagas of the so-called James Ossuary and the Tablet of Solomon (a.k.a. the Jehoash Inscription), two major finds that were exposed as frauds. According to police, they'd been manufactured in a master forger's workshop, inscribed by an Egyptian craftsman, and sold through a well-known antiquities dealer. Those fakes had been sophisticated enough to fool many experts, including some at the Sorbonne. Forgers even found a way to subvert the carbon-dating process, adding bits of gold and ancient charcoal under the patina. In all three cases, archaeological provenance was lacking.

That wasn't a problem here. Paul saw the jars buried in the cave. He'd helped disinter them, but, Ava reasoned, Paul was no expert. Could he tell how long they'd been buried? What if someone buried the jars sixteen years ago, not sixteen hundred years ago? Ava closed her eyes, lost in thought.

The onyx Mercedes prowled into Rosetta just as the sun was setting, burnt orange on a cloudless horizon. Despite the windows' tint, Lieutenant Barakah was momentarily blinded by the glare reflecting off the Nile.

A name floated back to him from across the years: Aker, god of sunset and sunrise. Aker's ideogram was twin lions back-to-back, the sun hovering between them. Barakah couldn't recall the lions' names, but he knew they represented yesterday and today. No tomorrow. Interesting, he thought. At that moment, the car slowed to a stop. Sheik Ahmed commanded: "Find out what happened to the boat, then meet me at the Mahaly Mosque's front steps in two hours."

The lieutenant nodded and walked east to the riverfront. He located the moored ECG boat and requested permission to board. Barakah hailed the first officer and asked him how the Americans had escaped.

"They got away because we couldn't fire on them. It's all in my official report. Yesterday afternoon we spotted the renegade skiff heading north. We approached in a responsible manner, and we ordered the captain to power down. After he ignored our lawful command, we fired a warning burst. The skiff turned and fled south at maximum speed. Ordinarily, we would have attacked, destroying or disabling the craft, but as you know, Lieutenant, we were under strict orders not to damage the smugglers' cargo. Accordingly, we couldn't engage the fifty-caliber. We gave chase, but they outran us."

"Their skiff was faster than your patrol boat?"

"Well, we were constrained by governmental regulations to operate in a safe and responsible manner."

Meanwhile, Sheik Ahmed sat in a hospital room questioning the injured policeman.

"We intercepted the dangerous gang in the town square. Despite immense personal risk, I engaged them in direct combat and shot one of the escapees. It was a fatal wound to the chest. I may have injured others. They took the body."

Sheik Ahmed smiled politely, thanked the police officer, and commended him for exemplary service. He dropped a wad of banknotes on the table for medical expenses and left. Privately, Ahmed was disgusted. "That ignorant, lazy, incompetent swine admits he was beaten senseless by an unarmed amateur. He's a disgrace." Then Ahmed reconsidered. Perhaps he'd underestimated the American. Could he be more than he seemed?

Barakah waited near the mosque at the appointed hour. When the Mercedes arrived, he climbed in and communicated to Ahmed all he'd learned.

"I tire of this game," said the sheik.

Barakah nodded and then asked, "Where are we going now?"

"Alexandria."

"Sir?"

"Obviously, the fugitives plan to leave Egypt by sea. Why else would they come this way? Finding the river blocked, they would continue over land to Alexandria. We will do the same."

10

A shout jolted Ava awake. She sat up, hands clutching cold porcelain in fear. Then Paul's voice boomed in the adjoining room. He began laughing and talking excitedly. Soon, she heard him hang up the phone.

Ava stood up and toweled herself dry. Wrapping her long hair in another towel, she put on one of the hotel's luxurious Egyptian cotton robes. After almost slipping on the slick marble floor, she cracked open the door and peeked out. Paul was smiling. With the ivory telephone receiver wedged between his ear and shoulder, he appeared to be reading the room-service menu.

Ava cleared her throat. "What was that shouting?"

Looking up, he opened his mouth to answer. Then she heard a muffled voice from on the phone. Paul spoke into it. "Room service? Can you send us some dinner, please?"

Ava simmered with impatience. Noting her expression, Paul's eyes widened. He spoke quickly into the phone.

"Yes, thanks. Can you just—okay, hold please."

Cupping the phone in his palm, he stage-whispered, "Sefu's alive! They got through to the hospital and he's in stable condition."

Ava's shoulders relaxed and a smile blossomed. She crossed the room to Paul, sat next to him on the bed, and listened while he ordered two steak dinners and two bottles of an expensive claret. Grinning, Ava shook her head. "Nick will regret his generosity."

"The hell with it!" Paul said. "We're celebrating!"

Gabe stopped typing, stretched his arms, and took a deep breath. Several people had responded to his query. Despite his fears, no one had flamed him. No one had called him a fool or a moron. In fact, he'd received numerous sympathetic replies, but only one fellow hacker had offered actual assistance, and Gabe worried about him. He reread the IM from DURMDVL: "Let's discuss your problem directly. 919-555-3253."

DURMDVL had posted on the crypto board for years, earning a reputation for taking no prisoners. Many suspected DURMDVL of launching the viral attacks against the rude noobs. From some posts, Gabe had the impression that DURMDVL frequently raided international corporate databases, leaked documents, and even snooped on governments. Of course, it was just a hypothesis: he had no proof. All he knew for sure was that DURMDVL lived somewhere on North America's East Coast, spoke English fluently, wrote tight code, and possessed a razor-sharp sense of humor.

Gabe punched in the number. Before it rang, he noticed it was 3:08 A.M. and hung up. That call would have to wait until later in the morning. In the meantime, he decided to eat. He rued the fact that every pizza joint was closed, especially Tommy's. Leaning far back in his leather chair, he opened the mini-fridge: *nada*. Frustrated, he pushed away from the desk, rose, and checked the cabinet. Inside he found half a bag of granulated sugar, some expired pudding, and an ancient box of Pop-Tarts.

He sighed, sat again, and pulled on his shoes. CVS was open late. He could get ice cream or something. He walked out the door, then he did a quick about-face; he'd forgotten his phone. He couldn't tolerate the idea of missing a call from Ava. It had been days since he received her text. Presumably she'd deciphered his message, alerting her to potential eavesdroppers. That's why she hasn't called since, Gabe told himself, refusing to consider other explanations.

He stepped outside and stopped again. He'd forgotten his wallet.

Savoring the cool evening breeze, Ava reclined on the balcony and let her bare feet dangle over the rail. She closed her eyes and listened to the surf caress the shore. There were other sounds in the air: the rhythmic creak of moored sailboats' rigging, the cacophony of polylingual conversations along the corniche. Next to her Paul finished his steak and attacked the remnants of Ava's. Wind gusted, almost extinguishing their candles. He looked up to find her watching him eat.

"Do you remember when we met?" she asked.

"When we met? Or do you mean the first time I saw you?"

"When was the first time you saw me?"

"Freshman year. You were running."

"Why do you remember that?"

"I don't know, but I know that the first time we talked you called me an idiot."

"I did not!"

"Oh yes you did, after we discussed the game-show question in class. Don't you remember?"

"I remember perfectly. It was the Monty Hall problem. I called you ignorant, not idiotic."

"Oh, thanks," he said. "That's much nicer."

She giggled. "There's a difference."

"What?"

"Ignorance can be cured. Idiocy, I fear, is permanent."

Paul grunted, finished his drink, and reached for the bottle. Ava lifted her glass for a refill and watched as the wine refracted flickering candlelight. A halyard strummed against a mast. On the street below, frustrated drivers honked and cursed. Ava set down her wine, drew her knees up against her chest, and rested her chin on them.

"What happens now?"

Paul sighed, rubbing his eyelids. "Tomorrow I'll find us a way out of the country."

"What about the jars?"

Gazing across the ancient harbor, Paul thought for a minute. Then he shrugged. "Let's roll them into the sea."

"Ha, ha, ha. Any serious ideas?"

He shook his head. "We can't go to the police. Did you see that guy smile when he shot Sefu?"

Ava nodded. "We could take them to the Bibliotheca . . ."

"No way. Sheik Ahmed's got his hooks in the local authorities. If we turn over the jars, he'll get them. I won't let that happen, Ava. I won't let those murderers win."

"So, what then?"

"I'm meeting Nick at Monty's Bar after his shift. Maybe he knows someone who can smuggle us out of Egypt."

Ava's posture stiffened. She was silent for a moment. Then she announced: "No. For centuries, Europeans have stolen Egypt's priceless relics. I'm not going to participate in that crime. Looting antiquities is illegal and immoral."

"I don't want any loot! I'll happily give the jars to the first institute or museum you choose. Once we get out of Egypt."

"And go where? Libya? Yemen? Tunisia? Saudi Arabia? Where will they be safe from Simon?"

Paul sagged into his chair. Brilliant ideas weren't his strong suit. He had no grand strategy. He knew only that, somehow, he must keep them safe. He clung to what Father Besserion had said:

"Protect what you found." He'd accepted that charge, and his heart told him the jars would never be secure in Egypt. Suddenly Paul had a brainstorm. The more he thought about it, the more he liked it. Smiling, he sat up and turned to Ava.

"You said the jars are priceless if they're authentic, right?"

"Yes, but we can't simply assume—"

"Hear me out, please. The jars are either real artifacts or worthless junk. If they're worthless, no one cares if we take them."

"Sure, but if they're real—"

"If they're real, then they're Jesus's property! I mean, the true lost jars of Cana should belong to Christ's heir on earth, a.k.a. the Catholic Church!"

Ava opened her mouth to disagree, and then paused. It was a novel argument. If Jesus took the jars from Cana to Capernaum, presumably they belonged to him. Wouldn't the pope have a claim to Christ's property, regardless of where it was unearthed? Of course, the argument's basis, which Paul assumed as fact, was a biblical account. Not everyone accepted that version of history. Even Ava, with her Catholic upbringing, regarded most Bible stories as, in Einstein's words, "honorable, but primitive legends." She had no idea how the World Court would rule on the subject.

"Let's assume you're right. What then?"

"I propose that it's our legal and moral duty to transport the jars to a nearby Catholic country and deliver them to the appropriate bishop, archbishop, or whatever. While the cardinals are busy electing the new pope, history experts can determine the jars' authenticity. Assuming they're real, international lawyers can sort out who gets them. Maybe they belong in Egypt, maybe they go to Rome, but no matter how the court rules, we'll be okay. We never claimed ownership or sought compensation. We just relied in good faith on our plausible, albeit unorthodox, legal interpretation."

Ava smiled. "That's very clever, Paul."

His shoulders lifted, and for an instant joy sparkled in his eyes. Then he turned away and shrugged.

"Ah, well, even a blind squirrel finds acorns—"

"Anyway," she said, "what should I wear?"

"What?"

"What should I wear to Monty's? Nick burned my robe, and I presume the bikini is inappropriate."

Paul grinned. "I'll call the concierge."

Sheik Ahmed and Lieutenant Barakah arrived at the police station just after ten at night. While his underling questioned the cops, Ahmed commandeered an office and opened the telephone directory. He found the number of the local newspaper, called, and asked for the managing editor. The receptionist put him on hold. As he waited, Barakah entered the room. Seeing the sheik on the phone, Barakah apologized and turned to leave. Ahmed shook his head and motioned for the lieutenant to sit. Then someone picked up.

"Who the hell is this?" demanded the prickly editor.

"This is Sheik Ahmed."

The editor gasped and juggled the phone. Instantly his tone became obsequious. "Oh, Sheik! I'm so sorry. I had no idea! No one mentioned . . . I would never—"

"Apology accepted. Now listen carefully. I have breaking news that you'll want to publish in tomorrow's paper."

Gabe exited Lowell House and turned left onto Mt. Auburn. It was an exceptionally foggy night. Wet, snow-free asphalt glistened, reflecting streetlights. Humming, Gabe crossed the empty street, stopped at an ATM, and slid his card into the slot. At that moment, he sensed someone watching. He'd been mugged once in South Boston. He knew robbers try to catch people at bank machines. Warily, he glanced back into the mist: No one there. With a sigh of relief, he withdrew eighty dollars. Outside the CVS, he nodded to the Champ, a homeless man who frequently sought refuge there.

"Hey, bro," said the Champ. "Got any change?"

"Not yet," Gabe replied, but I'll hook you up in a sec." He went into the store and proceeded directly to the frozen section, seeking ice cream: Vermonty Python. Then he stopped, shocked. The entire freezer was empty.

"Yo!" he yelled to the long-haired clerk. "What's up with the ice cream?"

"Aw, dude! The freezer is totally wack. All that stuff melted."

"Great." Gabe sucked in a breath and pressed two fingers against the bridge of his nose. It wasn't his day. Should he go home and eat Pop-Tarts? No, that sounded gross. As he scanned aisles of junk food, he noticed a bearded man across the street, watching him through the fog. "Odd," Gabe thought. "He doesn't look like a student. He's not nearly drunk enough."

Chuckling, he grabbed a bag of Cheetos, then changed his mind. Maybe he could get a pastry at Tealuxe, just a few blocks away. He dropped the Cheetos, left, and, still lacking change, handed the Champ twenty dollars.

"Damn! Thanks, bro."

Gabe smiled. Feeling virtuous, he continued north on JFK and passed Cardullo's Gourmet Shoppe, wishing it was open. As he neared the intersection, his peripheral vision caught a flicker of movement. He looked over his shoulder. Oh, hell. The bearded man was walking behind him. Gabe wondered: "Is he following me, or am I just paranoid?"

Involuntarily, his pace quickened. He darted around the corner and turned right onto Palmer. Breathing heavily, he leaned against the brick building and waited. Moments later, the bearded man appeared. Their eyes locked. This was no coincidence. The man reached under his shirt and began to withdraw something. Gabe didn't wait to find out what. He turned and ran. The bearded man gave chase.

Gabe had a head start, but he was out of shape. He couldn't outrun anyone. Years ago he played Ultimate Frisbee, but since graduation he'd spent most afternoons and weekends working on the computer. Ava frequently invited him to run with her, but he was always too embarrassed to accept. Now he wished he had.

Heedless of traffic, he dashed across Church Street, raced past Starbucks, and turned into the adjoining parking lot where, to Gabe's horror, a tall brick wall blocked further progress. Desperate to escape, he leaped onto a car's hood, stepped onto its roof, and vaulted himself over the wall. Frightened, he tumbled into a dark churchyard. Seconds later he heard the car creak as his pursuer copied his maneuver. Gabe stood and tried to flee, but his shoe caught on a gravestone, dropping him face-first onto the cold, damp earth. He waited in terror, anticipating gunshots. Instead, rapid footfalls passed within inches of him. Holding his breath, he listened. The steps grew distant as the bearded man continued running. *In the gloom, he didn't see me fall,* Gabe realized.

He kept perfectly still. Soon he heard angry voices speaking Arabic. Two men argued and then departed. He remained motionless for a half hour, afraid to betray his position. When he could wait no longer, he rose, cautiously, and looked around. Seeing no one, he crept out of the churchyard and headed back to Lowell House. Taking a circuitous route, using backstreets and watching at every corner, it seemed to take an eternity to reach the dorm. Gabe yearned to get inside, lock the door, and strip off his wet clothes. Nearing Mt. Auburn, he inched up to the corner. He poked his head around the edge and took a peek. It was just as he feared. Two men waited outside of Lowell.

He couldn't go home.

In the elevator Paul could see that Ava was feeling her wine. Confident and relaxed, she laughed often and spoke a little louder than usual. She looked pretty in her new dress, a black Versace knockoff that hugged every curve. He struggled to keep his imagination in check.

"You look amazing, by the way."

Ava beamed. Then she rolled her eyes, feigning embarrassment.

"You must be kidding. This is so not my style. I feel like Posh Spice."

On the walk to Monty's Bar, they discussed where to take the jars. Paul favored somewhere with a large Catholic presence. Ava said, "Well, if that's the criterion, we could try Malta. It's ninety-eight percent Catholic."

"Wow. Have you been?" Paul asked.

"Not yet, but I know someone there. Professor Laurence Clarkson, from the University of Malta, taught a guest seminar at MIT last year. It was great. He's brilliant."

"We'll have to look him up."

"I will. Actually, I'm surprised you've never been to Malta."

"Why's that?"

"Because of your namesake."

"Paul Newman?"

"No, your biblical namesake."

"Uh-oh. I sense a history lesson coming."

Ava laughed. "Okay, class, now pay attention! In the year 60, St. Paul was on his way to Rome for trial before Emperor Nero. His ship was caught in a terrible storm and wrecked off the Maltese coast. At the wreck's site, known as St. Paul's Island, there's a statue of the apostle. The event is described in Acts 28:1: 'Once safely on shore, we learned that the island was called Malta. And the barbarous people showed us no little kindness; for they kindled a fire and received us.'"

"Cool. At least the locals are friendly."

"Yeah, but watch out for snakes."

"Seriously?"

"The Bible says a venomous snake bit Paul's hand in Malta. The islanders considered his survival a miracle, and legend says that they decided to convert en masse. The incident is very important to the Maltese, and it's depicted in many religious artworks. For example . . ."

Sunrise found Gabe sitting alone in the old Algiers Coffee House, nursing an espresso romano. His clothes were damp and mud-stained. His ankle hurt. He was angry. He wanted to call the police, but couldn't. If they searched his room, they'd find copious evidence of computer crime. Some hackers got off easy because they were just kids, but Gabe doubted such leniency extended to twenty-seven-year-olds. Still, he needed help. He was in exile, unable to return home and cut off from his network. Absently he scrolled through his iPhone and noticed that his last outgoing call was to a number he didn't recognize. A 919 area code? Who the hell was that? Then he remembered: DURMDVL.

Gabe hit the CALL button. As he expected, his call went directly to an anonymous voice mail.

"Hello. Sorry to call so early. My name is Gabe. I use the screen name RKNGEL. We met online and you sent me this number. You said you wanted to discuss things directly. Well, the situation has, um, intensified. I'm currently unable to access my residence and therefore have limited resources. I'll provide details via a secure mode of communication. Of course, if you don't want to get mixed up in all this, I understand."

Monty's was a tranquil lounge named after Field Marshal Bernard Montgomery. Muted, unobtrusive music kept numerous conversations private. Nick complimented Ava's dress. The men ordered whiskey; she chose a champagne cocktail.

"How is your suite?" asked Nick.

"It's great. Thanks again."

"*De nada, amigo.*"

For the next hour they went from subject to subject: U.S. politics, the Red Sox, El Alamein, Texas Hold'em strategy. Eventually, Nick smiled and said, "So, why don't you just ask me?"

Paul laughed. "Is my poker face that bad?"

"No," said Nick, then pointing at Ava, "but she's about as subtle as a bulldozer."

"Do you know someone who can fly us to Malta?"

"Sure. United Airlines? Lufthansa?"

"We're not eager to pass through airport security."

"Hmm. I suppose I could charter you a flight. It won't be cheap."

"Do you know a good pilot?"

"Several, but few I trust." He thought a moment and then went on, "Let me ask a question." Nick lowered his voice and leaned toward them. "You want to avoid airport security. Does this have to do with those two canisters we lugged into your room?"

Paul and Ava exchanged a look. "It might."

"Well, I don't need to know details, but does it involve narcotics?"

"No!" Ava shouted, eyes bright with anger. The word reverberated across the quiet bar, attracting attention from several patrons.

"Okay, okay, relax. What was I supposed to think?"

Paul apologized for Ava's outburst but corroborated her position: "It's not drugs. You have my word of honor."

"Good. Because the guy I'd recommend is an antidrug fanatic. He has a personal vendetta against Sheik Ahmed." At the mention of that name, Ava blanched. Nick caught her expression. He sank down into his chair and moaned.

"Oh, bloody hell! You didn't cross the sheik?"

Paul said, "It's a long story. I was working for DeMaj—"

"No, no, stop. I don't want to hear it. You need to be gone pronto. I was worried about getting fired? Hell, we'll be lucky if we don't get killed. I'll call Sinan right away. Maybe he can meet us first thing tomorrow. Go back to your suite and don't open the door for anyone except me."

Paul nodded. He stood, took Ava's hand, and led her toward the elevator.

Nick sat silently for a few minutes. He took a breath, finished his whiskey in one go, and opened his phone.

Gabe was halfway through a Levantine omelet when his phone chirped, indicating a new text. He keyed in his PIN and opened a message from the 919 number: "Find a public computer. Create an anonymous user account and post a message on the usual site. Create a screen name reflecting one of our common interests, something only I will get."

Gabe assumed "the usual site" meant the programming group

where he'd met DURMDVL. He entered the university computer center and followed DURMDVL's instructions. Once on the site, he posted some banal observations about process virtual machines under the screen name Pope_1000. An hour later, a reply from R.Goldberg74 appeared. The response included a line of apparent gibberish, which Gabe recognized as a code. The code revealed a symmetric algorithm. For the initialization vector, he guessed 74. That didn't work, but his second guess—1974—did, generating a string encryption key. The key enabled a secure protocol by which Gabe and DURMDVL could e-mail and IM.

Finally able to speak freely, Gabe composed a long message describing his situation. He explained that he'd installed bots on his phone to see if anyone was snooping. Yesterday, the bots had alerted him to dual traces. The first, a crude sniffer program, came from an Aden-based shipping business. The second, sleek and subtle, had been difficult to detect. After hours of investigation, Gabe tracked it back to the DeMaj Corporation.

The next part was more challenging to write. "Honestly, I'm terrified for myself and for Ava. How can I contact her? The satphone is compromised, she can't (or won't) check e-mail, and I don't even know her current location! I think she's in Egypt, but I can't confirm. Suggestions?"

DURMDVL replied: "It may be possible to communicate through the LEO phone."

Gabe snorted. "So I'm just too stupid?" He typed: "Reread previous message. If there was a way to use the LEO phone, wouldn't I have done so already? My friend's life is on the line. I told you, the satphone is subject to constant surveillance by DeMaj. You've heard of DeMaj Corp? Billion-dollar transnat w/top-notch crypto? That phone is 100% penetrated. Any incoming call or text will be intercepted, monitored, and traced."

When no reply came in a half hour, Gabe was overcome with remorse. He thought, "Why was I so abusive? Did I burn my only ally? Why don't I think before I type? I'm such an idiot!"

It wasn't the first time Gabe had dissed a friend. Gabe hated asking for help. Ever. From anyone. Asking for help was an admission of need. Whenever someone offered assistance, he became snide. He'd say mean-spirited things that he'd later regret.

"I gotta grow up," Gabe decided. "If we get through this, I swear I'll stop acting like a petty jerk. I won't insult someone who is just trying to—"

At that moment, a response appeared on the glowing screen: "G, relax and leave minor problems 2 my superior intellect. Bad guys aren't as smart as they think. After covert satphone link is established, what message 2 transmit? Require personal trivia 2 prove our message is from u & 2 confirm recipient's identity."

Back at their suite, Paul closed the door and locked the deadbolt. While unzipping her dress, Ava noticed a light flashing on the satphone. Its display indicated an unread text: "You don't know me. I'm writing on G's behalf. To prove I'm friendly, he said you mix too much Splenda in your tea. G's sorry he can't contact you directly. Bad guys are monitoring your phone, so don't use it except in emergencies. I implanted this message using a trick that (I hope) will make it invisible to them. We need to speak. Call me from a landline @ 919-555-3253. You'll get an anonymous voice mail. Code in 999. It will redirect to me."

She read the message to Paul, who then asked, "What do you think?"

"I'm nervous, but I think it's legit."

"What's the Splenda reference?"

"Gabe always says I put too much in my tea. It's an inside joke. No one else would know it."

"Then we should call."

"From here?"

"I'd prefer an anonymous pay phone, but we agreed to stay in our room until we hear back from Nick."

Ava weighed the alternatives. It was risky to call, but she was worried about Gabe. She lifted the hotel phone from its cradle and dialed the long-distance number. After one ring the call was answered and diverted to an anonymous voice mail. She keyed in 999. It clicked and then started ringing again.

"Hello?"

"Hi," said Ava. "This is Gabe's friend. Do I have the correct number?"

"Maybe. First I need to confirm your identity. Which of your friends was an extra in *Harry Potter*?"

"What? Oh, that was Jess. My friend Jessica."

"Perfect, but from now on, try to avoid proper names. We don't know who or what might be listening."

"All right, but why can't . . . why didn't my friend contact me?"

"They're after him. Men came to Lowell House. He escaped. Now he's on the run."

"Oh my God! Is he okay? How did they find him? It's my fault! He doesn't have anything to do with this! He doesn't know anything!"

"Calm down and listen. Your friend will be fine. He's smart, and we're working on the problem. I'm much more worried about you. You're in grave danger. Here are the rules: No using credit cards, cell phones, or regular e-mail. Avoid airports, train stations, embassies, or any place with security cams. Never show ID or use your real name. Don't contact family or known associates. Don't go to the police. If you follow these instructions, you'll be very hard to find."

"But we need to leave the country. How can we travel without passports?"

There was a pause. Ava heard rapid-fire taps on a keyboard.

"I show you calling from Egypt. Where do you need to go?"

"Malta."

"Are you still traveling with the same guy?"

"Yes."

"Give me his SSN."

"Paul, what's your Social Security number?"

After he gave it to her, and Ava relayed it over the phone, for several minutes Ava heard only a keyboard's clicks.

"Okay, I just dropped some awesome kung fu. You shouldn't have trouble with customs and immigration. Just go through the diplomatic line. Now, how do you plan to get there?"

"Charter a plane."

"That should work, but you'll need some real money. How can I get it to you?"

"We have a friend here. You could transfer to him, and he could give us cash."

"Perfect. Give me his name. There's no time to avoid saying it."

Ava learned Nick's full name from Paul. They didn't have his SSN, but Paul knew his birth date and former address. For DURMDVL, that was plenty.

Two minutes passed. "It's done. Nick's bank account will get a nice fat deposit."

"Thank you. We'll repay you the moment we—"

"Forget it. Now, whatever happens, don't call again from your current location. Get yourselves to Malta and keep your heads down. In a few days we'll contact you. Until then you're on your own."

Early the next morning Paul heard a discrete rap on the hotel room door. When he unlocked it, Nick entered carrying a newspaper.

"You want the good news first or the bad news?"

"Good news first, *por favor.*"

"I found a pilot to fly you to Valletta. I swore you weren't smuggling drugs or weapons and luckily he believed me. Sinan may ask more questions when we get there. Just be as honest as possible. He's got no love for the local authorities and he doesn't mind breaking some rules, but he hates liars."

"What's the bad news?"

"This."

Nick dropped the newspaper on the coffee table. On the front page were pictures of Paul and Ava. Underneath the photos, a headline in Arabic exclaimed: "American Fugitives Wanted for Murder."

"Holy Mother of God!" cried Ava. She grabbed the paper and began reading. The story claimed Paul had killed the seven men at Simon's dig and maimed a police officer in Rosetta. The two Americans were armed, dangerous, and attempting to flee the country with priceless historical artifacts. A sizable reward had been offered for information leading to their capture.

Paul exclaimed, "Nick, it's not true! We didn't kill those people. We didn't kill anyone! I did punch a cop—but only after he shot our friend. You've got to believe me!"

"I do, but it hardly matters. If you don't skip town, someone will see you and try to collect that reward."

Ava packed their bags. Meanwhile, Paul lugged the canisters

out the door, down to the elevator, through the service exit, and into Nick's '79 Jeep Renegade. Driving fast and taking shortcuts, Nick zipped his passengers through the waking city. Ava's wet hair dried quickly in the breeze. To keep it under control, she tied a scarf around her head. To conceal her identity, she added sunglasses.

When Nick stopped at an intersection, a delicious aroma engulfed the jeep. Hungrily, Paul observed several traditionally garbed Egyptian women setting freshly baked pita loaves atop garden walls to cool. His stomach rumbled.

When the jeep reached Alexandria's industrial waterfront, a friendly security guard waved Nick into harbor parking.

"I thought you found us a pilot. Aren't we going to the airport?"

Nick pointed out a pontoon plane tied to a capstan. "This is an airport," he said.

He drove up next to the pier and parked. On a dock, an impatient foreman yelled instructions to his crew. Ava inhaled a lungful of harsh diesel fumes blended with the reek of desiccating barnacles and the ozone scent of melted solder. Looking closely at the seaplane, she noticed Arabic characters printed on its fuselage. Ava spoke the name aloud: *"Zulfiqar."*

"You read Arabic?" an enormous man asked, startling her. At six foot five, with a full beard and dark, weathered skin, he presented an intimidating figure. Nick introduced his American friends to their pilot, Sinan. When Ava saw his kind eyes, she liked him instantly. About the same age as her father, he possessed the aura of one who loved life but had known unlimited sorrow. Ava greeted him in his native tongue and thanked him for accepting them as passengers. Sinan bowed slightly and smiled.

When Nick apologized for the short notice, the pilot shrugged and said, *"Mektoub."* *Zulfiqar* was Sinan's plane, a sparkling

Cessna Caravan 675 powered by a PT6A-114A Pratt and Whitney engine. It was built to seat eight, counting the pilot, but Sinan had removed some seats to create space for an additional sixty-gallon fuel tank.

As they unloaded the jeep, Sinan asked his passengers, "How much do you weigh?"

Paul replied, "Two hundred ten pounds, maybe two fifteen." Sinan nodded. Then the three men looked at Ava. She was mortified.

"How is that relevant?" she asked.

"Fully fueled, my available load is about fifteen hundred pounds," Sinan said. He pointed to the canisters. "Your mysterious cargo is a little heavier than normal suitcases. If I don't calculate the weight correctly, we could crash."

Ava told the men to weigh everything else first, add it up, and tell her what remained. Then she'd let them know if she exceeded the limit.

After they confirmed that the cargo load was not too heavy, Sinan asked Nick about money. Nick handed him a roll of hundreds, saying, "Here's four thousand dollars. I guarantee the balance when you return."

Sinan nodded and began loading the plane.

Paul pulled Nick aside and whispered, "How much is this costing you?"

"Eight thousand total. A bargain under the circumstances."

Paul winced. "Nick, I don't have much cash left, and I don't even have a credit card."

"That figures."

"We're having money transferred to your bank account," said Ava.

Paul offered to contribute his cash, but Nick waved him away, saying, "Just hold on to that. You'll need it in Malta. Pay me back once you two are safe and everything has blown over. I know you're good for it."

Handing Paul a slip of paper, he said, "This is a decent hotel. Nice rooms, but they burn their steaks."

Paul was deeply moved. "I don't know what to say, Nicky. Thank you so much."

"*De nada.*"

The two friends embraced. Paul said, "I won't forget this."

"You'd better not," said Nick, grinning. "I'm thinking World Series tickets might be an appropriate token of your appreciation."

"Done."

Once Paul and Ava were aboard the seaplane, Sinan yelled, "Prop clear!" and hit the throttle. The Pratt and Whitney engine whined, shuddered, and roared to life. Moments later, the plane taxied into the center of the bay. When Sinan radioed the harbormaster for permission to take off, Ava tensed, but the tower cleared Sinan with no questions. Paul wondered if Nick had bribed the officials.

A freshening wind kicked up a small chop upon the sea, bluer now as the sky cleared. Sinan increased speed, and *Zulfiqar* began skipping across the water. The interval between skips grew until finally they were airborne. They circled over Alexandria, gaining altitude. When they reached ten thousand feet, Sinan leveled off, increased speed to a hundred and eighty knots, and set a westerly course for Malta.

Ava dozed off after they'd been in the air for about an hour. Noticing that she was asleep, Sinan turned to Paul and said, "You have trouble with Ahmed."

It was phrased as a statement, but the pilot seemed to expect a response.

"Yes. He's our enemy."

With a curt nod, Sinan agreed. "Good. I have sworn vengeance against him and his accursed master."

"His master?" asked Paul, nervously wondering if the enormous pilot knew of his connections to DeMaj.

Ignoring the question, Sinan probed: "Why is Ahmed your enemy?"

"His thugs tried to kill us, several times. They shot our friend Sefu, a teenager who—"

Paul stopped. The pilot's face was ashen. A tempest of fury roiled behind the pilot's eyes. It was some time before he spoke again. Finally, in a cold voice, Sinan said, "Ahmed is an abomination. He has killed many innocents, many children. He belongs to the devil."

Five hours later, the pontoon plane breached a bank of clouds and the rocky isle of Malta burst into view. Sinan radioed traffic control, received clearance, and began his final approach. Before landing in the grand harbor, they beheld a stunning view: The very deep blue of the sea and sky contrasted sharply with the white and green of Valletta. Olive trees reached all the way down from Mt. Sciberras to the magnificent natural anchorage. Murmuring a prayer to Allah, Sinan executed a textbook water landing.

They rounded the bay and tied up near a customs office. Happy passengers were disembarking from a cruise ship while officials scrambled to keep them in the proper lines. Sinan exited the plane and began negotiating with dockworkers to purchase gasoline. After a few minutes, a young customs agent knocked on the cockpit window. He looked bored. Sinan said, *"Bongu!"* and provided the requisite documentation. The man glanced at the papers, gave the passengers and cargo a cursory inspection, and entered a mark on a computerized notepad. He pointed to a building and said something unintelligible to Paul. Then he handed Sinan a printed receipt and a set of colored decals. Shaking the young officer's hand, Sinan said, "*Grazzi.*" The agent smiled, nodded once, and returned to his station.

"That was easy," Paul observed.

"We have an understanding," said Sinan.

"You know him?"

"His boss, the customs supervisor, is an old friend. He knows I never allow drugs, guns, or explosives on my plane, but he understands that my passengers are particularly concerned about privacy and prefer to avoid waiting in line."

Sinan helped Paul transfer cargo from the plane onto a rolling cart. They affixed a colored decal to each item, signifying that it had been searched and okayed by the authorities.

"What now?" asked Ava.

"Inside that building is the immigration and passport checkpoint. Show them your identification and this receipt for your bags."

"Thank you, Sinan. You're a lifesaver. We're in your debt."

He shook his head. "No debt. Your enemy is my enemy. Your friend is my friend. We struck a fair bargain. I just kept up my end."

He waved good-bye to the Americans and began refueling *Zulfiqar.*

Nick wasn't surprised when, just before noon, Sheik Ahmed and his entourage entered the casino. Rather than delay the inevitable, he took the initiative. Approaching them, Nick opened his arms in greeting.

"Great Sheik, it's an honor that someone of your magnitude should grace this humble establishment. How can we make your visit more enjoyable?"

Ahmed smiled. He thought, "Here, finally, is one with style

and courage. He knows I shall likely torture and kill him, yet he greets fate with a smile, not childish tears."

The two men traveled in the same circles. Many of the sheik's contacts and business partners were Nick's upper-crust patrons. They had mutual acquaintances in the Egyptian government and military. Nick's reputation in the industry was sterling. Cairo's aristocrats considered him a reliable businessman who remained strictly neutral in matters of politics and religion. Watching the American carefully, Ahmed replied, "Regrettably, we've come for business, not pleasure."

Nick nodded. Ever since reading the morning newspaper he had known this moment would come. The sheik had informants throughout the city. Little that happened in Alexandria could be kept secret from him.

"Let's retire to my office. I shall endeavor to answer your questions in private."

He led the sheik's party away from the gaming tables, down a long hallway, and toward his door. Nick was determined not to show weakness. He knew every minute he delayed Ahmed increased Paul and Ava's odds of escaping. Yet he must not appear to be stalling. That path led quickly to a brutal death. He focused his mind and drew upon much experience playing high-stakes poker. Despite his fear, he maintained a tranquil facade. Taking keys from his pocket, Nick unlocked the office and casually invited the sheik to enter. Ahmed motioned for Barakah to accompany them. The rest of his cadre stood guard outside the door.

Nick waited for his dangerous guests to sit. Then he asked: "Gentlemen, how may I be of service?"

Barakah answered, "Last night, two Americans came to Alexandria. We have reason to believe you know their location."

Nick paused to think, buying precious seconds. He knew any

lie might begin the process of torture unto death. Ahmed surely possessed many details already, garnered from his network of spies and sycophants. Still, the fact that these men were questioning him proved that they did not yet know where his friends had gone. This chain of reasoning gave Nick a glimmer of hope. He decided on a tactic. If it worked, he might survive the meeting. With a deep breath, he began.

"I will not insult you by pretending ignorance. You are looking for my guests, Paul and Ava. As you said, they arrived yesterday. I provided a room at the hotel, and I joined them for a drink at the bar. They traveled with two heavy canisters. I presume these are your property—Paul must have stolen them. Now you seek their recovery. Correct?"

"Yes," replied Ahmed, impressed by Nick's directness. "Where are they now?"

"Because of today's headlines, they couldn't stay. I informed Paul and Ava they were no longer welcome, and I offered them a choice: I would deliver them to the airport or to the harbor. They chose the harbor. We drove out this morning. On the way, they discussed going north by sea to Greece, perhaps Crete. Of course, they might have lied, suggesting those destinations aloud for my benefit while intending to go somewhere else."

"Why did you hide them?"

"For money. When they arrived at the hotel, they were desperate. They promised me a great deal of cash for a discreet room, but after I saw the newspaper, I realized the offer wasn't enough."

"Why did you transport them to the harbor?"

Nick stiffened, pretending to be offended. "They were my guests. I owed them a certain duty of hospitality, regardless of the circumstances."

The lieutenant nodded. Then he turned to look at Ahmed, who was deep in contemplation. Barakah knew the sheik was trying to decide if Nick was lying. His story rang true and fit with every known fact. Informants had seen Nick's jeep carry the Americans and their precious canisters across town to the harbor. Soon afterward, Nick had driven an empty jeep back to the hotel. But the Egyptian sensed this dapper casino manager knew more than he let on.

Ahmed appeared to have reached a decision, but before he could speak, Nick asked:

"May I make a suggestion?"

Surprised, the sheik said, "What?"

"The fugitives must have bribed their way onboard a vessel. I don't believe they'd be stupid enough to remain here. Examine the passenger manifests of every ship that departed the eastern harbor today. Question the immigration officials. There can't be too many possibilities."

The sheik smiled. "Why would you help me?"

"All Egypt knows crossing Sheik Ahmed is suicide, but that he rewards those who aid him. You'll catch the American thieves eventually. They will die, so I'll never collect the sums they owe me. Perhaps by assisting you, I can avert a total loss on my investment."

Paul and Ava went into the immigration office and found the diplomatic line. It wasn't long before an English-speaking agent scanned their passports and asked perfunctory questions. In due course, the almighty computer beeped, granting them permission to enter Malta. A second agent inquired about their luggage. Paul handed him the printed receipt. The man read it carefully and gave Paul an appraising look. Then he returned the document and waved them through the line. The two Americans left the building and walked into the picturesque city of Valletta.

Ava spied a pay phone. She called the hotel that Nick recommended and reserved a room. Then she called Dr. Clarkson at the university. He was surprised and delighted to hear from her, insisting they meet for a drink at a tavern called the Two Gods, in the town of St. Julian's. While Ava and Clarkson chatted, Paul stepped into the Bank Ċentrali ta' Malta and traded their remaining Egyptian pounds for euros. At the Bieb il-Belt, or City Gate, they hailed a cab for Sliema. As they transferred the canisters into the vehicle, the driver muttered *"Haqq ix-xjafek"* (damn the devil). Paul didn't understand the words, but he got the gist. Grinning, he passed the cabbie an extra ten euros along with the hotel's address.

As the taxi navigated the maze of narrow streets, Paul admired the architecture.

"What's the city called again?"

Ava replied, "Valletta, named for the knight, La Valette."

In the rearview mirror she saw the cabbie nod, impressed. Paul's expression implied that the name was unfamiliar.

"Jean Parisot de La Valette, knight of St. John. He was grand master during the Great Siege."

"The Great what?"

Ava sounded surprised. "Don't you know about the siege of Malta?"

Paul leaned back. "Okay. Go ahead. I know you're dying to tell me."

"The Ottomans invaded Malta in 1565. Back then the island was held by the Christian Knights Hospitaller, a.k.a. the Knights of Malta or the Sovereign Order of St. John. The first attack was on a fortress called St. Elmo. The Turks thought Malta would fall quickly, but due to the knights' bravery and tenacity, Fort St. Elmo held out against incredible odds. The Ottomans leveled it eventually, but the fierce defense bought time for reinforcements to arrive from Italy. As a consequence, the island withstood the siege. After the battle, La Valette commissioned a new city on the site where Fort St. Elmo once stood, and lay the first stone with his own hands. He's buried here."

The taxi dropped them off at the Waterfront Hotel. They registered under aliases, paid in cash, and told the porter they'd handle their own luggage. After ensuring that both canvas covers were still securely in place, Paul loaded the canisters into the hotel's service elevator and took them up to their floor. As Ava held the door, Paul carried the canisters across the threshold and scooted them into the closet.

"That's a creative hiding place," Ava remarked dryly.

"I doubt they'd fit under the bed," Paul said.

"Whatever. You stay here and guard the jars. I'm going shopping."

A few hours later, Ava returned. In her bags were cotton slacks, sandals, a conservative silk blouse, and a white dress. Nothing too formal, but appropriate, she felt, for a meeting with important churchmen. She rode the elevator up. From outside the room she could hear the TV blasting an Italian soccer match. Ava unlocked the door, eager to show Paul her new clothes. He was snoring.

She considered waking him, then decided against it. With a sigh, she walked to the bathroom and turned on the shower. They had hours until the meeting with Dr. Clarkson. Paul could sleep.

At the Internet café, Gabe ordered an espresso from the barista, a pretty redhead with heavy black eye shadow. He carried the hot drink back to his workstation and almost spilled it when he saw the screen—an IM from DURMDVL: "Contact successful.

Transmission confirmed as secure. A is OK. Cleared Malta immigration/customs hours ago. Expects update/advice from us soon. What 2 send?"

Gusts of cool Mediterranean air swept through St. Julian's. Paul and Ava strolled past a bewildering variety of bars and nightclubs catering to the lively mix of tourists, natives, and hustlers. Moving with the crowd, Ava enjoyed a fleeting sensation of anonymity. Near the St. Rita Steps, leading from Baystreet to St. George's Road, they located the Two Gods. The peculiar tavern's exterior was bedecked with carved and painted Egyptian figures, colors and edges softened by years of weathering. Paul could tell Ava loved it already.

Inside, the comfortable smells of pipe tobacco and old mahogany welcomed them. Timeworn wooden stools, benches, and tables were distributed throughout the pub. Regular customers watched soccer on the ancient television. A stocky, middle-aged bartender introduced himself as O'Hagan and asked what they'd like to drink. His accent sounded Irish.

"I'm not sure," Paul said. "What do you recommend?"

"We've some good Maltese brews. Have you tried Blue Label or Hopleaf?"

"Both sound good."

"Or Lacto, a nice milk stout?"

Ava tried to hide her reaction, but the words *milk stout* turned her stomach. She was embarrassed to appear so narrow-minded. Grinning at her discomfort, the bartender asked, "What's your usual drink?"

"Stella Artois," Paul said. "Do you serve that?"

"Of course. Two euros for a draft."

They accepted and took their mugs to a quiet table. Paul sipped his beer.

Ava sat back. "I like this old place. The decor is interesting, and for once the bartender didn't check my ID. It must be these new clothes. I look more mature."

Tactfully, Paul refrained from mentioning that Malta's drinking age was sixteen.

She glanced up. Local TV was reporting on the Italian election. Anti-immigration marches had sparked riots in Sicily. Angry men shouted slogans at the camera, expressions of intense personal hatred masquerading as public activism. Ava shuddered.

"What's wrong?" Paul asked.

"Those guys really give me the creeps."

He scanned the bar. "Where?"

"No. On TV. The Italian right-wingers."

He twisted until he saw the screen.

"Who? Berlusconi?"

"No. The Gruppo Garibaldi."

His expression implied that additional details would be appreciated.

"Nationalists. Extremists. Reactionaries who make Berlusconi look like Bertrand Russell."

"Wow. Are they popular?"

"Somewhat. Thanks to all the recent scandals and instability, extremists will probably win a few seats in parliament."

He shook his head. "Unbelievable. You'd think the Italians would've learned from Mussolini."

"They did, mostly, but just like the disgusting skinheads and neo-Nazis back in the States, some idiots never learn."

Twenty minutes later a sharply dressed man walked through the door. His attire and manner seemed out of place in the smoky tavern, but he wore a broad smile. Paul guessed it was Laurence Clarkson. Ava jumped from her seat to greet him, shook his hand enthusiastically, and introduced Paul.

"*Bonswa!*" said Clarkson.

Paul replied, "Hey, nice to meet you. I like this place. Do you, um, come here often?"

Clarkson laughed. "Oh, heavens no, but most taverns in this town are too loud for civilized discourse. Plus, it seemed highly appropriate, given that you came from Alexandria."

Grinning, Clarkson paused, waiting for him to get the joke.

Paul didn't. In desperation, he turned to Ava. She rescued him.

"Of course! Don't you remember? The ship St. Paul took from Malta to Syracuse was Alexandrian. It was named the *Two Gods.*

"Oh. Okay," said Paul. "I get it now. Good one."

Clarkson elaborated: "The referenced gods were surely Egyptian: Osiris and Re. It's said that the *bas* of Osiris and Re met in Mendes and united. You're familiar with the stela of Ramesses IV, in Abydos?"

Ava nodded. Paul suppressed a yawn.

"The inscription establishes that the two gods 'speak with one mouth.' Furthermore, a relief in Nofretari's tomb reads, 'Re has come to rest in Osiris and Osiris has come to rest in Re.'"

Ava contributed, "And throughout the Egyptian Book of the Dead, Osiris and Re appear united. In passages, their names seem interchangeable."

"Exactly!"

Before they could continue, Paul spoke up, "Speaking of gods, we have some important business with the Catholic Church. Can you tell us who's in charge here?"

"Archbishop Cremona heads the archdiocese, but he's busy in Rome. Aren't these exciting times? All Malta is breathless with anticipation, wondering who'll be the next pope. In Cremona's absence, Bishop Garagallo has authority. I've met him. He's quite nice. Why do you need to see him, if you don't mind my asking?

"Oh, just general ecumenical questions. Nothing interesting."

Clarkson seemed puzzled. Then he smiled.

"Yes. I suspect Bishop Garagallo is extremely knowledgeable about matters such as scheduling Catholic weddings and satisfying Maltese marriage requirements." Clarkson turned to Paul and extended his hand. "I congratulate you, sir. In addition to her obvious beauty, your betrothed is an exceptional scholar, blessed with an intellect of the first rank."

"Wait, I think you misunderstood—"

Ava interrupted. "Paul, he knows already. We might as well admit it."

"Huh? Oh! Okay. Yeah. You're a tough man to fool, Professor. You saw right through our story."

Clarkson shook Paul's hand vigorously. "Call me Laurence. And there's no need for concern. Your secret is safe with me."

For some hours, Ava and Laurence discussed recent developments in archaeology and philology. The two academics covered a ragbag of topics, often finishing each other's sentences. Eventually Clarkson announced his departure. He rose, toasted their health, and finished his drink. Then he said, "I envy you two. Malta is a beautiful, romantic island. Just the place for young lovers."

He hugged Ava, gave her his mobile number, and begged her to call if she needed anything. Then he said, "*Ha pjacir!*" (enjoy yourselves), and bade the couple a good night.

"So, when's the wedding?" Paul asked.

Ava grimaced. "Obviously, he shouldn't know why we're here. So, I decided to perpetuate his misconception. Why disabuse him of a perfectly plausible explanation? It's easier than making up something."

Paul considered it. "Okay, that was smart. Of course," he reflected, "if we're on the front page of tomorrow's paper, it was all for naught."

"True, but I'm confident the media here won't be taken in by those lies."

"Hey, I'll drink to that," said Paul, finishing his beer. He rose from the table. "Want another?"

"Sure, but when you get back, let's make plans for tomorrow. I want to see the bishop as soon as possible."

Paul nodded, then walked to the bar. He flagged down O'Hagan and ordered two more beers.

"Where are you from?" asked O'Hagan, filling mugs from the tap.

"We're Americans. We met in Boston."

"Is she your girlfriend?"

"Yeah, something like that."

"Damn. You're lucky, lad. She's dead sexy."

"That she is."

The bartender set two mugs in front of Paul along with his business card.

THE TWO GODS TAVERN, ST. JULIAN'S
IMHAR O'HAGAN, PROPRIETOR

"Just call if you need anything. I can set up tours, car rental, scuba diving, you name it."

"Cool. Thanks." Paul pocketed the card, flipped O'Hagan a five-euro coin, and took off with the frothy beers.

Gabe's pride finally succumbed to his insatiable curiosity. He simply had to know how DURMDVL snuck a message through to the satphone undetected. Humbly, he sent an e-mail asking for the inside dope. A lengthy response arrived almost instantly. In it, DURMDVL reminded Gabe that his phone bots had detected reverse-transmission probes from two entities. One probe was relatively crude. Gabe's defensive software blocked it before it could access his phone's memory. The other, originating within DeMaj Corp's notorious crypto section, was a sophisticated spy program. The DeMaj probe tried to clone Gabe's phone. It would have enabled DeMaj to read new text messages (incoming and outgoing), record calls, and download anything (photos, movies, texts) saved in memory. The program monitored the target phone continuously, alerting DeMaj anytime it sent or received a call or text.

Assuming DeMaj had used similar tactics to snoop on Ava, DURMDVL simply hacked into DeMaj's computer division and used its monitoring program to access the satphone's memory. Once inside, it was easy to locate the text message Gabe sent a few days ago, rewrite it (telling Ava to call from a landline, etc.), and alter its status from "saved" to "new." It was perfect. From DeMaj's perspective, no outsider had accessed the phone. No new messages were sent or received, but from Ava's perspective, a new message appeared. She wouldn't know or care that technically it was an edited version of an old message, and as long as DeMaj's spies didn't reread the satphone's saved messages, they'd never see the altered version. Sure, it would be visible if they looked, but there was no reason to look. They'd long since downloaded and copied the saved-messages file, so they could view that data much faster by opening their in-house copy. Unless DeMaj's spies took possession of Ava's actual phone, DURMDVL reasoned, it was very unlikely they'd ever read the new text. Even if they did, all they'd get from it was a 919 phone number registered to a fictitious Panamanian limited partnership. If they tried to snoop that number, their network would acquire a virulent little file DURMDVL had nicknamed sno-krash.

Impressed, Gabe began typing a reply asking for technical specs. Then he stopped and wondered: How could DURMDVL have written such a long explanation so quickly? Seconds later, it hit him. DURMDVL was being polite! Anticipating (correctly) his forthcoming inquiry, DURMDVL had prepared a thorough response, but not wanting to bruise his ego, DURMDVL had waited to be asked before providing the details.

Gabe shook his head in disbelief. He'd met a lot of hackers. Most were very smart, some were even brilliant, but almost all were rabid egomaniacs. They lived to brag about sick hacks, and none was polite about it. For some reason, DURMDVL wanted to avoid hurting Gabe's feelings. What kind of hacker would care about that?

The casino was full to capacity. Resplendent in his white tux and tie, Nick drifted from table to table, conferring with his pit bosses. Any other night he'd have been scrutinizing the action, ensuring that no player or dealer was cheating the house. In addition, his responsibilities included congratulating big winners, welcoming regulars, and issuing comps and perks to big spenders. It was an important job. Nick's reputation for his quick wit and garrulous personality was a key reason that many whales gambled exclusively at this casino.

Tonight Nick was filled with none of his customary *joie de vivre*. Every few seconds his eyes drifted to the threatening men Ahmed had left behind, ostensibly waiting for Paul and Ava but actually watching Nick. The sheik believed Nick's story. Therefore, Ahmed refrained from killing him on the spot. Yet he didn't trust Nick completely. When Ahmed and his lieutenant departed to check the vessels' passenger manifests, they left these uniformed thugs behind to guarantee that Nick stayed put.

Thinking of the manifests, Nick grinned. The sheik would find no mention of Paul and Ava on those. Even if Ahmed had the perspicacity to demand air-transport manifests, he'd still find nothing. Sinan's flight plan listed no passengers, just cargo. Despite all the clever misdirection, though, eventually Ahmed would uncover the truth. "And when he does," Nick thought, "I'm as good as dead."

He skirted a blackjack table and congratulated a boisterous Italian on his sharp decision to split eights. The gambler made 18 and 17, the dealer busted, and the table erupted in cheers. While they celebrated, Nick watched Ahmed's men. Moments before he'd sent Jill, a popular waitress, to offer them complimentary drinks. The leggy California blond made a small fortune in tips, bringing refreshments to the casino's elite clientele. Bending low before Ahmed's goons, she coyly asked what they'd like. For a moment the two men stared, mesmerized by her décolletage. They mumbled apologies, explaining that they were forbidden to drink on duty. Flirting, the sexy waitress pouted and asked if they were allowed to drink coffee. The younger of the men smiled, stole a glance at her cleavage, and admitted that coffee would be okay. Then she knelt close to him and whispered that she could bring coffee cups filled with cognac or whiskey. He laughed thanked her for the generous offer but reluctantly insisted on actual coffee. Jill giggled, bounced to her feet, and promised that she'd be right back. After watching her sashay to the bar, the men looked toward the blackjack table.

Nick was long gone.

11

Gabe put the finishing touches on his latest long e-mail to DURMDVL. He'd written effusively of his respect for DURMDVL's inventive method of circumventing DeMaj security. He included the original code for an Internet spider he designed the previous year and recommended that they infect DeMaj's network with this information-gathering program. Gabe stopped typing, took a deep breath, and reviewed his work. It was littered with typos and other errors. He rubbed his eyes. He was dead tired. Worse, he was out of cash and couldn't afford caffeine. At the bottom of the e-mail he added another line: "Sorry for crazy typos. Need slppe. Out of money. Suggestions?"

DURMDVL quickly wrote back, suggesting he go to the nearest hotel and rack out. "Negative. Can't use a credit card or ATM. I think the bad guys are watching my accounts. If they broke into my room and penetrated my system, they can access all my info."

DURMDVL concurred with Gabe's bleak assessment and recommended that he crash with a friend, someone trustworthy. Then DURMDVL asked a shocking question: "Don't you have a girlfriend?"

Gabe's immediate reaction was: "None of your damn business!" He was flabbergasted by DURMDVL's lack of respect for his privacy. How was his relationship status relevant to the situation? Annoyed by the breach of protocol, anxiety churned inside him. Though he'd never admit it, Gabe was a hopeless romantic. He fantasized about love affairs, but in reality he had difficulty communicating with women. The objects of his affection never reciprocated his awkward advances. It wasn't easy. He and these women had little in common. Sexy girls seemed to inhabit terra incognita. Gabe questioned: "Is it my fault they like dim-witted TV shows; read idiotic gossip mags; and listen to insipid pop? DURMDVL of all people should understand," thought Gabe. "His tastes are even more rarified than mine."

Eventually Gabe calmed down. He remembered the huge risks DURMDVL was taking on Ava's behalf, and he decided everyone should be forgiven an occasional faux pas: "No GF," he wrote. "I'm not conventionally handsome."

He didn't have long to wait for a response, and when it came, he was relieved to see that the topic had been dropped: "K. Whatever. Just crash w/a friend."

Gabe's mind sorted the possibilities. When he remembered that Jess lived nearby, he felt some embarrassment. He'd been uncomfortable around her ever since she'd declined his invitation to the Silver Kingdom Renaissance Faire, but he had to go somewhere. He hadn't slept in almost two days. Plus, he rationalized, Jess deserved to know that Ava was okay. He shot a quick note to DURMDVL, logged off the computer, and headed for Jess's apartment.

The alarm rang at six in the morning. Ava dressed, went downstairs, and bought the *Malta Independent* and the *New York Times*. After determining there were no malicious stories about them in the news, Ava obtained a telephone directory and looked up the

Catholic archdiocese. She called the bishop's office but heard an answering machine. Frustrated, Ava hung up. She ordered breakfast and returned to the room. Paul was still asleep. Waking him, she said, "I called Bishop Garagallo."

Paul yawned and cleared this throat. "Super. What's up with him?"

"I got the answering machine."

"Did you leave a message?"

Ava stiffened. She wasn't his cute little secretary. "Look, why don't you call? Here's the number. I'm taking a shower." She went into the bathroom and let the door slam behind her. Paul grinned. He grabbed the remote, clicked on the TV, and found the news. The lead story concerned Pope Benedict, who'd waived the traditional fifteen-day waiting period to enable the cardinals to elect a new pontiff before Holy Week. Benedict was scheduled to hold his final public audience in St. Peter's Square on Wednesday, when he would address tens of thousands.

In local news, the Labor Party had gained several seats in parliament, three workers were hospitalized after a construction accident in Bizazza Street, and rain was expected later that night. To Paul's great relief, nobody mentioned two American murder suspects on the lam.

By eight o'clock Paul had dressed, left the hotel, and found a payphone. He called the archdiocese. The receptionist who answered understood English. Paul asked to speak to Bishop Garagallo. "The bishop is not yet in. May I take a message?" the receptionist said.

"Yes, of course you may, but I must see him today."

"Well, I'm not sure that's possible. He's very busy."

"I have to see him because we want to make a seven-figure capital contribution to the Church."

The woman paused, counting zeros. Pressing his advantage, Paul continued.

"It's imperative that we negotiate the benefaction's terms and conditions with the bishop today."

"I'll see what I can do. Would ten thirty be acceptable?"

Breakfast arrived: eggs, sausage, bacon, and toast, plus a steaming pot of coffee for Paul and a cup of hot tea for Ava. Ava finished showering and dried her hair. She left the bathroom to find Paul working the *New York Times* crossword puzzle.

"How's it going?"

"Decent. We have an appointment with the bishop at ten thirty, but I'm stuck on an obscure clue."

Ava was surprised and pleased. "How did you get the meeting?"

"Let's say American ingenuity."

Ava smiled and pointed to the crossword. "Lay it on me."

"Stately seventeenth-century French dance. Six letters."

"Hmmm. I'm not sure. It could be P-A-V-A-N-E or M-I-N-U-E-T."

Paul frowned, wadded up the paper, and dropped it in the trash.

Gabe knocked on Jess's door. He heard movement inside and a sexy voice asked, "Who is it?" Gabe envisioned Jess peering through the peephole and seeing his distorted, haggard face. "Jess? It's Ava's friend, Gabe. Sorry to bother you, but it's an emergency."

Jess flung open the door. She was wearing a short satin bathrobe. Gabe felt dizzy.

"What's the emergency?" Jess asked. "It's Ava, yes? Is she all right? Tell me she's all right!"

"Ava's fine. We contacted her. She's—" Gabe caught himself. He looked around suspiciously. Anyone could be listening. "Do you mind if I come inside?"

"Oh, of course. How rude of me. Please come in. Have a seat." Jess took in his stained clothes and unshaved chin. He also stank. "You look terrible. Have you slept recently? May I offer you something to drink?"

"Sure," replied Gabe, trying to keep his eyes on her face. "Got a Coke?"

She went into the compact kitchen and pulled a can from the fridge. Gabe sat on the comfortable sofa and watched her put on a kettle to boil. She brought his Coke and sat next to him.

"Will you tell me the whole story?"

Gabe nodded. "Yeah, okay, but it's pretty long." Involuntarily, he glanced down at her exposed thigh. "You might prefer to wear something more . . ."

Jess grinned. His face was crimson. She popped up from the sofa and went into her bedroom to change. Gabe couldn't help but notice that she'd left the door ajar.

Jess called out, "Is Ava still in Malta?"

Gabe freaked. "What? How the hell did you know she went to Malta?"

"Her parents told me. They're really worried. They called a friend with the State Department, or was it the DOJ? Anyway, they reported Ava missing, unofficially, of course. This morning they got word that Ava passed through immigration on Malta. They left a message on my voice mail."

She emerged from her bedroom in a white silk outfit to find Gabe with his head in his hands.

"What's wrong?"

"It's . . ." He sighed. "It's complicated, but if you know she's in Malta, you're probably not the only one."

After breakfast Paul asked the concierge to call them a cab. The taxi sped to the bishop's office. They arrived a few minutes early, went into the historic building, passed through extensive security, and gave their names to the grandmotherly receptionist. She invited them to wait on an antique settee. Moments later the receptionist's phone buzzed. She answered, uttered a few words in Maltese, and hung up. Then she smiled at Paul.

"Someone will be with you shortly."

Before long an assistant escorted them into an ornate private office where a surprisingly young man wearing a suit and tie sat behind an enormous ebony desk. He rose and greeted them in English.

"It's a pleasure to meet you," Ava said. "We were expecting Bishop Garagallo."

The man laughed. "Please accept my sincere apologies. I'm Zeke, the bishop's executive assistant. His Excellency had to attend to urgent matters that arose at the last minute. He's sorry, but he won't be able to meet with you today. He asked me to see you and provide any assistance or information you require. I hope you'll understand. He's a very busy man."

Ava's eyes narrowed. She detected an undercurrent of falsehood in his practiced courtesy.

"May I ask the nature of your business?"

Paul answered. "As I said on the phone, we'd like to make a substantial donation to the Church."

"Well, that's very admirable, but you don't need to see the

bishop to make a donation."

Disliking his officious manner, Ava said, "It's a donation of property, not money."

"Is that so? What type of property?"

"Unique historical artifacts," she said.

His eyes widened.

"Valuable?" he asked, leaning forward in his chair.

"Yes."

"How valuable?"

Ava smiled. Now she had his undivided attention. "The exact figure may be difficult to determine. No objects like these have ever been auctioned. Lesser artifacts of similar age were projected to fetch at least two million dollars, until they were determined to be inauthentic."

"And you believe yours are authentic?"

Ava and Paul exchanged a glance. She replied, "We think so, but we can't be positive. It would be the owner's duty to establish authenticity."

Zeke drummed his fingers on the desk, then asked, "What do you expect in return?"

"Certain guarantees," said Ava.

"Such as?"

"Should the items prove genuine, the Church must promise to display them to the public in an appropriate forum and make them available for study by the legitimate academic community. If the Church opts to sell the artifacts, which I doubt, it would convey them subject to identical terms."

"And what else?"

Ava looked at him. "Pardon me?"

"What else do you want?"

"Nothing else."

"No reward? No credit for the discovery?"

Ava was annoyed. Her look said, "What part of 'Nothing else' is confusing?"

Hoping to avert an argument, Paul jumped in. "We don't seek any reward or compensation. We'd remain anonymous."

The man was skeptical. "But that doesn't make sense. Why would you do that? Why not sell the items to a museum or a university?"

Ava was fuming. "Look, we're not here to answer your questions. We have our reasons and you have our offer. Tell your boss to take it or leave it, that is, if he can find time in his busy schedule to consider our proposal."

Ava stood, took Paul's hand, and led him out of the office.

Zeke jumped up from the desk and followed them into the hall. "Wait! Come back! Where are you staying? How can I reach you?"

Ava neither paused nor looked back.

On their way out of the building Paul detoured to the receptionist's desk. He dug the Two Gods business card out of his wallet and handed it to her, saying, "We can be reached at this number. Ask for Paul."

A moment later, the bishop's assistant walked up and snatched the card from the receptionist's hand. Ignoring her glare, he watched the Americans depart. Once he was sure they were gone, he returned to the office. He closed the door, unlocked his private cell phone, and punched in some numbers.

They arrived at the Two Gods just after noon. A jazz record played quietly on the jukebox: Sarah Vaughan singing "Lover Man." While Paul spoke to O'Hagan, Ava found an empty booth. Paul brought over a plate of deep-fried *lampuki,* some anchovy-filled *pastizzi* (puff pastry), and two frothy mugs of Stella Artois. Being careful not to spill anything, he eased their lunch onto the carved wooden table. The look on Ava's face revealed that she was still angry. Paul sat, sipped his beer, and waited. After a moment, she asked, "Has anyone called?"

"No. Looks like we have some time to kill."

A few seconds passed. Then Ava exploded: "This is unbelievable! Do they think it's a joke? We offer the Church a unique archaeological find, easily worth millions, and the bishop won't even meet us? It's unacceptable!"

"He probably does think it's a joke. Or maybe he thinks it's a scam."

"But we didn't ask for money!"

Paul took a drink from his mug and set it on the table. "What's the matter?"

Ava reddened. "Are you kidding? I'm upset because the bishop won't see us! We're in mortal danger, and he's off doing God knows what. I can't believe he'd be so inconsiderate."

"I'm sure he has a lot on his mind. Did you hear that Pope Benedict accelerated the conclave? We could have a new pope by St. Patrick's Day."

Ava rolled her eyes. "So what? The Catholic bureaucracy is hopelessly out of touch. The cardinals will just elect another stuffy European. The Church will never change!"

She was on the brink of tears. Paul reached across the table and took her trembling hand. Then, looking her in the eyes, he asked: "What's really bothering you?"

She opened her mouth to argue, then paused. He was right. "Okay, I am upset about the bishop and the Church, but I'm really angry with myself. Given the chance to crack one of the world's great mysteries, I struck out. Where's the lost prophecy? Why can't I solve the riddle?"

"Maybe there wasn't a mystery to solve," Paul said. "I'm not convinced that a hidden message exists. Would Jesus really make up a prophecy? That sounds more like something you'd get from a bogus psychic or a fortune-teller than from the Bible."

"Are you kidding? A prophecy is something uttered by a prophet. Paul, the Bible is chock-full of prophets and prophecies. Tons of folks get zapped by the Holy Spirit and start predicting the future—often in verse. Read Luke 1:67, Deuteronomy 18:18, or Acts 3:22, 'For Moses said, "The Lord your God will raise up for you a prophet like me from among your own people; you must listen to everything he tells you."' In John 13:38, Jesus himself prophesied that Peter would deny him three times before the cock crowed."

Paul waved his white napkin in surrender. "Okay, okay, I concede. You don't need to quote chapter and verse."

She blushed. "Sorry, I didn't mean to be rude. I'm just really frustrated."

He waited, giving her a chance to explain.

Ava lowered her eyes and sipped from her mug. "I've been dissatisfied for a long time, okay? I've just been too proud—or maybe too scared—to face it. The honest-to-God truth is that I'm dreading graduation. I've worked like a dog to finish my doctorate, but why? I don't want a life built around researching and debating linguistics. I'll become another Professor von Igelfeld, hermetically sealed in an academic cloister. The moment I saw the jars, I sensed this was my path, my destiny. We can't keep them, obviously, but when we surrender those artifacts, our journey ends. I'll resume my mundane existence: books, lectures, maybe the occasional pub quiz, but no adventure."

He shook his head. "No disrespect to Professor von Igelfeld, but you can do anything you want. Ava, each day offers a new adventure. With your abilities and talents you can go anywhere. What do you want to see tomorrow? Yonaguni? The Mountains of the Moon? There are no limits but those we accept. Sure, it can be risky, and sometimes it hurts, but that's real life: a thrilling spin of the wheel."

Ava smiled. She felt much better after hearing what Paul said. Then, O'Hagan made eye contact. He held a fist to his cheek, with his thumb to his ear and his pinky pointing to his lips: the universal sign for *telephone.*

Paul walked to the bar and took the receiver. "Hello?"

A gravelly voice said, "This is Bishop Garagallo. Is this Paul?"

"Yes, Excellency. Thank you for calling. Did you get our message?"

"I did. May I ask a question?"

"Of course."

"Are you the Americans who encountered some difficulty in Alexandria?"

Paul took a deep breath. "We are, but the newspaper accounts of our activities are dead wrong."

"I believe you, but I'm sure you'll understand that given the circumstances, a man in my position cannot meet publicly with . . . fugitives."

Paul was glad the man hadn't called them criminals. "Yes, Father. We understand. Nevertheless, we are eager to meet. What do you suggest?"

"Are you familiar with the Catacombs of St. Paul?"

"No."

"They're a complex of interconnected caves located in Rabat, on St. Agatha Street. The last tour begins at four thirty, but if you can meet me later, I'll arrange for the gate to remain unlocked."

"I'm sure we can find it, Excellency."

"Good. Meet me in the chapel at eight. Bring the jars. Please come alone, and tell no one of our meeting."

Paul returned to the table. Something about the telephone call bothered him, but he wasn't sure what. He told Ava the bishop was willing to meet. She was elated. Then he asked, "I assume you've heard of these catacombs?"

"Of course. St. Paul's Catacombs represent the earliest archaeological evidence of Christianity on Malta. They contain numerous tombs and important murals, the island's only surviving evidence of late-Roman and early-medieval painting. It's an important historical site as well as a tourist attraction."

"Won't it be too dark to see much at eight o'clock?" asked Paul as he tasted the fish.

"Paul, it's a cave. It's dark all the time."

He laughed. "Right. I'll bring a torch, then."

Ahmed's phone rang. He checked the caller ID and fear gripped him. It was the call he dreaded. He dismissed his entourage, closed the office door, and then picked up. "Master?"

"The Americans are in Malta. You must complete your mission. I cannot tolerate another delay. The girl is adept at solving puzzles. She may uncover the secret."

Paul and Ava walked back to the hotel and prepared for an excursion into the catacombs. Ava obtained directions from the concierge while Paul purchased a small flashlight from the gift shop. They went upstairs to change. Ava donned khakis, a T-shirt, and running shoes. Looking for his blue jeans, Paul opened the closet. He paused. The two canvas-covered canisters were still hidden inside. Noting his posture, Ava asked, "What's up?"

"Garagallo said to bring these to the meeting."

"And?"

"And . . . I don't think we should. They're much safer up here. If the bishop accepts our deal, he can send someone to collect them. Or he can come himself. Either way, I don't think we should haul them halfway across the island. It's an unnecessary risk."

"If you feel strongly, then I agree," Ava said.

They caught a cab to Rabat, an ancient settlement several kilometers inland. The taxi dropped them in the parish square outside St. Paul's Church. Less than one hundred meters down St. Agatha Street, they found the catacombs. The site was closed for the evening but, as promised, the gate was unlocked. The two Americans stepped inside. Paul turned on his flashlight. Its bright beam revealed the entrance to a sizable labyrinth. Steep steps led down into a central gallery from which passages branched off in several directions.

"Spooky!" said Paul.

Ava hit his arm. "Hush! Show some respect. These are tombs."

"Sorry," he whispered. Taking her hand, he guided her into the large chamber. Divided by a central pillar, the room opened into a bewildering series of tunnels. Immediately to their right, a wide corridor beckoned.

"Which way to the chapel?" Paul whispered. Ava shrugged. She had no idea.

"Guess we'll find out."

Paul ventured into the passage. After walking twenty-five meters, they entered a tall crypt with a raised plinth. Hewn from the natural rock were two circular tables and two semicircular benches. Ava whispered that the site must have been used for meals during the ancient festival of the dead. Then Paul stopped in his tracks. At the end of the chamber was an apse containing a variety of small amphorae and two large stone jars. Both were unsealed. Their heavy stone lids rested on an adjoining shelf. Eyes wide with wonder, Paul turned to Ava and in a hushed voice asked, "Are those what I think they are?"

His question confused her for a moment. Then Ava understood. Out of respect for the dead, she struggled to suppress her laughter. She took his wrist and redirected the flashlight's beam to a sign near the apse. In several languages, it read: EXAMPLES OF PERIOD STONEWORK AND CERAMICS.

"Honestly, you didn't think those were the other lost jars, did you? They're not even from the right century! Look at the carving style—"

"Whatever," Paul said glumly. From his tone, Ava worried that she'd really insulted him. She was relieved when his usual smile reemerged.

They continued down the passage until they reached a dead end.

"Damn. Looks like we took a wrong turn," Paul said. He led her back to the main chamber and played his flashlight over the wall signs. One indicated that the chapel was to their left. They followed the arrow and descended deeper into the catacombs. Down a few more steps was a wide room. Ava could see why it was called a chapel: A shadowy recess at its far end resembled an altar. Walking slowly in the dim light, she approached, drawing closer until a loud voice called out, "Did you come alone?"

Ava spun around. A tall, robed figure materialized out of the gloom. She tried to answer, but found she couldn't. Paul spoke for her.

"Bishop Garagallo? Hi, nice to meet you. We came alone, as you requested."

"Excellent. It's nice to meet you, too. Now Paul, I told you to bring the jars. Where are they?"

In that instant, Paul realized what had been bothering him. They'd never said the artifacts were jars! Paul needed time to think. He stalled.

"The jars? Oh, they're safe. They're in a very safe place."

"Where?"

Paul looked at Ava. She was embarrassed. His intuition told him something was very wrong. The bishop shouldn't know about the jars. He couldn't know. Unless. Paul hunted for a decent response. Then he heard Ava.

"I apologize, your Excellency. We left the jars—"

"In the other cavern," Paul finished. "We left them over in the other cavern. You see, it's my fault. I got us lost. We took a wrong turn, and, you know, those things can get very heavy. I can show you where they are. I'll lead you to them. Come this way."

Ava stared at him. She had no idea what he was doing, but she trusted him enough to play along. Paul turned and walked out of the chapel. Unsure of what to do, he tried to formulate a plan. Suddenly, he had an idea. When they reached the main chamber, he turned. "Watch your step, Father. You know Malta's reputation for poisonous snakes."

"What?" The bishop was confused. "Snakes? Certainly. I'll watch out for them."

Paul saw Ava stiffen. She knew. The real Maltese bishop would have caught the reference. She looked directly at Paul, fear written on her face. "Ava, you look a little cold. Why don't you wait for us outside? The bishop and I can carry the jars—"

"No, I don't think so." From the folds of his robe, the man

produced a pistol equipped with a silencer.

He pointed the gun at Ava. "Move away from the stairs. Stand next to him." Ava was shaking. She backed into Paul. He looped his arm around her waist and pulled her close, but for once his touch didn't calm her.

"You're not Bishop Garagallo," said Ava.

The man smiled.

"Look," said Paul, "you can have the jars. We won't make trouble. If you let her go, I'll help you carry them out."

The man smiled again. "First, show me the jars. Then we'll negotiate."

The three of them continued down the corridor until they came to the room with the stone tables and benches. Paul knew they'd both be killed as soon as the impostor had what he wanted. Playing for time, he tried to distract the man with chatter.

"So, why are you doing this? What's in it for you?"

The assassin didn't reply. Desperate, Paul began again, "It's the money, right? Of course it is. You're a professional. Can't say I blame you. For a hundred million? Who wouldn't?"

When the killer reacted to the figure, Paul knew he'd found his angle: greed. Somehow he must use that to his advantage. Praying the impostor wouldn't read the sign, Paul strode directly to the apse and turned around. Standing next to the alcove, he pointed his flashlight at the stone examples and said, "Well, here they are. The famous lost jars of Cana."

When the false bishop saw the two jars, he allowed himself a smug smile. His mission was almost complete. He raised the revolver and pointed it at Ava's face. "Go stand next to him." She complied. Grinning, the killer cocked the pistol.

This was it—now or never! "Of course, you don't really need the jars once you've seen the message," Paul said coolly.

The man paused. "What message?"

"Didn't they tell you? That's why the jars are so valuable. There's a message hidden inside. It gives the location of a buried treasure worth hundreds of millions. We uncovered it."

Paul pointed his light down into a jar. "See? It's right here. You can read it."

"Step away," the killer ordered. Paul backed up against the shelf. With one hand, he kept the flashlight on the jars. With the other, behind his back, he groped for any object he could use as a club.

With his eyes focused on Paul's face, the would-be bishop inched forward. Soon he stood directly in front of the apse. "See for yourself," said Paul. "It's written right there on the bottom, the treasure's secret location."

In the darkness Paul's fingers closed around something made of heavy stone. He watched the man's eyes. For the briefest moment, the man glanced down into the jar.

With reflexes honed by throwing out countless runners at first, Paul swung. The thick stone lid connected with the man's skull, cracking it like a ripe pumpkin. Instantly, the killer went limp and dropped to the cave floor. Ava screamed. Paul dropped the bloody stone disk, grabbed Ava's arm, and ran. He dragged her through the corridors and up the steps. As they neared the exit, Ava tripped.

She fell on top of a corpse. The dead woman's uniform identified her as a tour guide. The gunshot wound in her forehead identified her killer as a professional. Ava scrambled on all fours, desperate to escape. The cavern floor was slick with blood. Ava gagged. She felt vomit rush up her throat. Then strong hands helped her stand. A firm voice urged her to move, to run. Paul kicked open the door, and the two bolted into the street. Picking a direction at random, he dragged Ava away from the catacombs.

"No, wait! That poor woman—"

"Ava, she's dead, but her murderer might still be alive. He won't miss us again. We have to go. Now!"

12

Pope Pius II rested in the Episcopal Palace. His room offered a spectacular view of the harbor and of Monte Astagno, but the ailing pope preferred to admire St. Ciriaco Cathedral. Completed in 1189 on the site of an eighth-century church (and an even older temple of Venus), the Romanesque structure was patterned after a Greek cross. Built of gray stone, it featured a dodecagonal dome and a facade with Gothic elements. Pius II smiled, wondering if he'd be buried there.

"Holiness," said Cardinal Jacopo, "the Venetians have arrived." With difficulty, the pontiff lifted himself and turned his gaze toward the Adriatic. On the far horizon, he beheld at long last the sails of the Venetian fleet.

"Too late," he whispered, laboring for breath. "Too late."

Pius shut his eyes and fell back against his pillow. How had it come to this? Two years ago he'd been at the pinnacle of strength. Invigorated after deciphering the sacred prophecy, he'd undertaken an ambitious campaign to protect Christendom from the Turkish onslaught. Following his predecessors' instructions, the pope composed an eloquent, respectful letter to Mehmed II that revealed the prophecy's secrets and encouraged the sultan to convert to Christianity. When his invitation was ignored, Pius convened a congress of Christian princes at Mantua. He smiled, remembering that glorious day. His grand entrance to the convocation was like a triumphal procession. He stood at the dais and read the blessed prophecy to the assembled royals. Then Pius demanded a cessation of all internecine feuds and proclaimed a three-year crusade against the Ottomans. Spirits buoyed by the prophecy's guarantee of victory, the rival princes unified against their common foe and pledged unanimous support for the pope's bold strategy.

For a time it seemed the alliance formed at Mantua would succeed. Vlad Dracula led a successful resistance against Mehmed. The Wallachians attempted to assassinate the sultan. The prophecy predicted success. During the resulting turmoil the Turks would be vulnerable.

The prophecy was wrong, however: Mehmed survived the night attack. No longer convinced that victory was preordained, the fragile alliance shattered. Of course, aid promised by the duplicitous French king never materialized. Worse, France threatened Burgundy, forcing Duke Philip the Good to recall his support.

Despite suffering these setbacks and a bout of debilitating fever, the pope's faith never wavered. On June 18, Pius personally assumed the cross. He departed Rome for Ancona to lead the crusade himself. Alas, the Venetian fleet was interminably delayed. Predictably, selfish factions within the crusading army used the postponement as an excuse to pursue other interests. Milan attempted to seize Genoa. Cynical Florence recalled her forces, hoping to acquire rich lands after the Turks and Venetians weakened each other. Without Florentine participation, the crusade would fail. Rather than sacrifice themselves for nothing, even Pius's most loyal soldiers deserted. By the time the

Venetian ships arrived, the dying pope had no army with which to fill them.

Cardinal Jacopo attended his beloved pontiff, mopping sweat from his fevered brow. All their efforts were doomed. Pius had staked everything on retaking Constantinople. His failure would cripple the enlightened, humanist faction within the Holy Church. Jacopo Piccolomini-Ammannati knew he'd never sit on St. Peter's throne. Instead, the path had cleared for a weaker, less charismatic man's ascendance. Jacopo dreaded that a subsequent pope would capitulate to Spanish pressure and resurrect the Inquisition. In despair, the gifted cardinal wondered, "Is Mehmed truly the Antichrist? Or, perhaps, are we?"

Ridding his mind of such inappropriate speculation, Jacopo focused on his immediate responsibilities. He raised a chalice to his master's lips and whispered, "Please take some water, Holiness," but the pope was dead.

EGYPTIAN COAST,
MARCH 2013

Nick's jeep sped west on Highway 1. The convertible top was down. Nick wanted to leave Egypt that night, but he couldn't go without paying Sinan. To Nick, a promise was sacred. From his years in business he'd learned that if people couldn't rely on your word, you might as well pack it in. Besides, Sinan was a friend; he deserved a warning. Nick called the pilot and left a detailed voice mail explaining that Ahmed was checking passenger manifests at the harbor. "It's only a matter of time before he figures it out," Nick said. "I'm skipping until things cool. If you want your money, meet me at the Porto Marina Hotel in El Alamein. I'll wait a day. After that, I'll have to mail you a check."

Nick should have known Sinan wouldn't be the only one to hear the recording.

Paul and Ava ran through Rabat until they reached St. Paul's Church. They cut across the parish square and continued north. Every time they passed an alley Ava's heart stopped. What danger lurked there? The sheik? The police? Simon? Another assassin? Hand in hand they ran hard for an additional quarter mile. It was cathartic. The night air tasted sweet after the dank catacombs. The exercise cleared Ava's head until, with effort, she could think rationally.

They paused to rest on a stone bench beneath a statue of two lovers embracing. After catching her breath, Ava said, "Paul, some-one betrayed us, someone who knew we were in Malta."

"Right, and it's a short list. Sinan knows we're here, but I'm confident he wasn't the one. If he planned to sell us out, why fly us over from Egypt?"

Ava nodded, so Paul continued. "And we didn't get pinched at immigration, so it wasn't Gabe's hacker friend." Ava agreed with this assessment too. Then Paul asked, "Could it have been Clarkson?"

Ava's expression hardened. "That's ridiculous. I contacted him, not the other way around. What are the odds that the one person I call in Malta is an agent for Simon and Sheik Ahmed? Half a million to one? Clarkson has no idea why we're here. We never discussed the jars. Plus, he's a tenured university professor with a stellar academic reputation."

"What difference does that make? Are tenured professors morally superior to us normal people?"

"That's not what I meant."

"Are you sure?"

"Yes," she replied coldly. "I'm sure."

"Then who do you think it was?"

"Could it have been Nick?"

Paul was hurt. He stood and glared at her. "No," he said, and began walking toward Mdina.

Ava called after him. "Wait! Are you sure? How well do you know him?"

Without slowing, he shouted back, "He'd never rat us out."

"Hey! Will you just listen? It's not impossible. Think! He might have had no choice. What if they captured him? Tortured him? Injected him with drugs?"

Paul stopped. He took a deep breath and waited a few seconds. Then he faced Ava. "Okay, I admit it's possible. Every person we mentioned might have been captured, tortured, or drugged. By that standard, everyone's a suspect, but the assassin called us at the tavern. Nick couldn't have known about that. The first we heard of Two Gods was from your pal Clarkson after we landed on Malta."

Ava thought it over. He was right. She took his hand. "I'm sorry," she said quietly.

Paul lifted her hand to his lips and gently kissed it. In a warm voice he said, "Nick's a good friend. He wouldn't betray us. I know it in my heart."

Ava smiled. Then her mind buzzed with an idea. "Paul, you nailed it! The traitor was someone who knew to call us at the tavern. And the only place you gave out that number—" Her memory flashed back to the young man behind the huge black desk, the man who's ears pricked up when she mentioned historical artifacts and kept asking how much they were worth.

Paul's jaw set as he reached the same conclusion. He finished her sentence: "The only place I gave out that number was at the bishop's office. I left it for his assistant."

Fury radiated from his body like heat from a blast furnace. His fists tightened as he whispered, "That greedy little worm is going to pay."

Gabe sat on Jess's sofa, telling her all that had transpired since Ava called from Yemen. Hesitant at first, he gave only cursory details, but as Jess pressed for specifics, his explanation became increasingly elaborate. When he described helping Ava escape across the Red Sea, Jess hugged him and praised his cleverness. After that, he brimmed with confidence. His description of being chased by the bearded men took a few liberties with the truth: He neglected to mention falling on his face and implied that he'd evaded capture by stealth and cunning, but from the skeptical light dancing in Jess's eyes, Gabe suspected he'd crossed the line between poetic license and balderdash. As he recounted his conversations with DURMDVL, he paused, remembering he needed to send an e-mail as soon as possible.

"Can I borrow your computer?" he asked.

"Sure." She disappeared for a moment and then emerged from the bedroom carrying an old Dell Inspiron 1525 laptop. Gabe would have preferred something with a bit more firepower. Regardless, he booted it up and began programming the secure-communication protocol. He sent an encrypted message to DURMDVL, giving his current location, describing the limited computer hardware, and warning that others knew Ava was in Malta. He couldn't think of any way to protect her, but Ava should at least be warned that the secret was out. When he finished typing, Gabe leaned back on the sofa, yawned, and fell asleep.

On the way to El Alamein, Nick stopped at an ATM. His suite would be free of charge, but he'd need a little cash for extras. Before making a withdrawal, he decided to check his balance. He wanted to leave enough in the account to pay Sinan everything he was owed. He keyed in his PIN and hit the BALANCE INQUIRY button. Nick estimated he had about six grand saved, give or take a few hundred, but when he read the receipt, his eyes bulged in amazement. $76,427! "What the hell is going on?" he thought. Wasting no time, he withdrew the maximum allowed, hurried back to his jeep, and resumed his journey.

The Greek's Gate is a vaulted tunnel that cuts through Mdina's southern wall. As rain began to fall, Paul and Ava hurried through this dramatic stone archway and entered the noble city. By flickering lamplight they beheld conventual churches, medieval palaces and historic squares. Any other night Ava would have insisted they stop and appreciate the city's intoxicating mix of Norman and Baroque architecture, especially the magnificent Palazzo Vilhena. Instead, they rushed through, suspicious of every shadow. Inguanez Street led them to Bacchus, a popular restaurant.

"Maybe we can get a taxi here," Ava suggested.

"Good idea. Ask them to call one. I'll check that no one followed us." He started away.

"Paul!" He looked back. "Please be careful."

He returned to her, squeezed her shoulder, and nodded. Then he darted across a narrow alley and disappeared from view. Ava walked downstairs into Bacchus and signaled to an attractive hostess. Her name tag said MARIA.

"*Kif inti?*" asked Maria, smiling.

"*Ma nitkellimx tajjeb bil-Malti*" (sorry, I don't speak much Maltese). "Taxi?"

The hostess sensed that Ava was having a difficult evening. Probably fighting with the boyfriend, Maria thought. She switched to English and complimented Ava on her pronunciation. Maria explained that cars, except emergency vehicles, wedding limos, and hearses, were forbidden in Mdina, but she could call the taxi service and have a car wait just outside the gates.

Ava nodded, and Maria disappeared into the kitchen. When she returned, she said a cab was on its way. As Ava was thanking her, Paul appeared. His look communicated that he'd seen no one. Waving and saying "*Saħħa*" to Maria, the couple left. As she watched them go, Maria smiled and abandoned her initial assumption.

In St. Publius Square, a crew was busy dismantling the stage where musicians had performed an open-air concert. Warily, Ava and Paul crossed the piazza. They exited Mdina through the Notabile Gate, a massive arch festooned with elaborate sculptures and statues. After crossing a stone bridge, they spied their taxi waiting near the bus terminal.

Jogging through the first raindrops of an approaching thunderstorm, they got to the cab. The driver opened his window a crack. Paul gave him their hotel's name and address. The cabbie nodded, unlocked the doors, and invited them to enter. After his two wet passengers slid into the backseat, he put the car in gear and headed east.

They rode in silence for several kilometers. Ava was antsy. She looked at Paul: Staring intently out the foggy window, he seemed lost in contemplation. He's angry, she thought. He blames himself for everything.

In a pocket on the back of the front seat, Ava found a collection of brochures advertising island attractions. To kill time, she clicked on an interior light and began reading. One brochure described the Domus Romana, a Roman house from the first century discovered outside Mdina. The pamphlet provided a photo catalog of artifacts on display there: delicate amphorae, a beautiful Roman comb, coins, domestic utensils, richly ornamented columns, mosaics, statues, marble inscriptions, glass objects, and several stone jars identical to the ones in the catacombs. Seeing the jars, Ava went numb. She recalled how close they'd come to dying. If Paul hadn't grabbed that stone lid and bashed the impostor over the head . . .

Thunder roared.

Ava sat up, rigid, mouth open in wonder. Stone. How could she have missed that? The lid was stone. The lids were always stone. Flat disks of stone. "Of course!" Her memory flashed back to Revelation 5:2: "And the mighty angel asked, 'Who is worthy to break the seals and unlock the message?'"

Paul gazed out the window, oblivious to Ava. The storm had gained strength. Sheets of rain came drenching down. Ava grabbed his arm, demanding his attention.

"The jars were sealed when you found them, right?"

"Huh? What do—"

"Shut up and listen! In Egypt, you said the jars were sealed when you found them." She stared at him expectantly.

"Right. Yes. They were."

"And you helped Simon open them. Being super careful, you used surgical tools to unseal them, right?"

"Yes. We removed the lids. Hey! What's the matter?" Ava was shaking, her hands balled into fists.

"Driver," she yelled, "can't you go any faster?"

The cabbie grunted. He pushed the accelerator, the engine roared, and the car hurtled down the ancient Roman road.

"Ava." Paul took her shoulders and turned her body toward him. "What is it?"

"You said it yourself. Oh, why didn't I listen?" She hugged him tightly, put her lips to his ear, and whispered, "What if the message is hidden in the jars? Literally in the jars."

"But they're empty."

"No. They've never been empty."

The moment they reached the hotel Ava shot out of the cab. She raced through the lobby, startling a bell captain. Paul paid the driver, added a generous tip, and followed her upstairs. He opened the hotel room door and found her struggling to drag a titanium canister out of the closet.

"Help me!" she ordered.

"Help you how?"

"Help me open it!" They lugged the canister into the center of the room and released the latch. Air hissed. Ava washed her hands and asked Paul to remove the artifact. He spread his feet, crouched, wrapped his arms around the stone jar's lip, and hefted it clear. Hoping to facilitate her examination, he carried it directly under the light. To his surprise, Ava ignored the jar. Instead, she gently removed the disk-shaped clay lid. Holding the ancient seal under the light, she investigated both of its sides. Then she quivered. Paul saw her eyes widen in wonder.

"Look," she whispered. He stood by her and directed his gaze down where she indicated. On the inside rim the clay was cracked where he and Simon had pried it open. Beneath the dull surface he noticed a metallic glint. Paul grinned. It looked like gold.

Gabe awoke in a dark, unfamiliar room. A disturbing image loomed above him. After a moment of panic, he recognized Picasso's *Guernica*. With relief, Gabe realized he was still in Jess's apartment. He turned on the lights and scanned the room for his hostess, but she was missing. Gabe grew nervous. Did the bearded men follow him here? Did they do something to her? His heart pounded. How could he have been so thoughtless? Wracked with guilt, he scoured the room in search of a telephone. He had to call the police . . .

Just then Jess arrived with several boxes of aromatic takeout labeled SPICE THAI RESTAURANT. She'd selected Pad Thai, dancing shrimp, mango curry with chicken, a seaweed salad, and two gigantic *boba* teas. Ordinarily Gabe wasn't keen to experiment with new cuisines, but overcome with relief that Jess was all right, he scooped a heaping spoonful of each dish onto a plate. Thirty minutes later, all the food was gone and Gabe had a new favorite restaurant.

They checked e-mail. DURMDVL had replied, promising to contact Ava and convey Gabe's warning. In addition, the e-mail went on, Gabe and Jess should expect some FedEx deliveries. Jess asked, "What's that about?"

Gabe had no idea.

To create a workspace, Ava and Paul covered the hotel table with their white cotton bedsheet. Atop it sat an art deco lamp with its hot bulb exposed. Next to the lamp was the disk of ancient clay.

Ava bent over the artifact, studying it. Soon she set about widening the crack delicately, using a sharp, silver-plated letter opener. After two hours she'd made little progress. Frustrated, Ava glanced over at Paul, who was reclining on the naked mattress, struggling to stay awake. She sighed and returned to her explorations, when suddenly she noticed something interesting.

"Hey!" she said. "Come look at this."

He rolled off the mattress, joined her at the table, and examined her work. Ava had widened the crack, but only slightly.

"Great job!" he said, trying to sound supportive.

"No," she replied, exasperated. "Look at this." Her letter opener pointed to a smudge on the sheet. Paul raised his eyebrows quizzically. He couldn't imagine how that mattered, but she was the expert. "Do you need me to fetch a clean bedsheet?"

Ava laughed. "No, silly. I'm trying to show you something." With a cloth napkin, she wiped some perspiration from her brow. She daubed the artifact with the cloth and showed Paul the results. Except for a little dust and dirt, the napkin was still basically clean. Then she held the wet cloth against the seal's underside. When she removed it, the cloth was stained the clay's dark color.

"Huh!" said Paul. Then he frowned. "What's the difference?"

"The exterior is glazed, kiln-fired clay. It's waterproof, but for some reason the inside isn't. I wonder . . ."

She lifted the artifact and walked to the bathtub. Ava closed the drain, turned on the faucet, and slid the lid under the running water. Reddish clay melted away to reveal a dazzling golden disk about eighteen centimeters in diameter. With a gentle tug, Ava freed the shimmering metal from the drab exterior that had concealed it for so many centuries.

Paul was awestruck. He shook his head, "Amazing," he whispered.

"Yes," she said, "it really is."

"I was talking about you."

Too nervous to sleep, Zeke sat up late, flipping his TV from channel to channel. It was difficult to find anything to watch. At this hour, most stations ran nothing but infomercials that badgered him to buy exercise equipment. Eventually he chanced upon an actual program, a black-and-white movie. Humphrey Bogart was saying, "I hope they don't hang you, precious, by that sweet neck."

The phone rang. He jumped up.

"Hello?"

A raspy voice commanded: "We need to meet."

"Now?"

"Yes."

"Wait!" the bishop's assistant said. "Are they dead? Did you get the jars?"

"Not over the phone. Come to the parking garage behind your office. I have your reward."

The garage was dark and empty. Just a few zones were illuminated by security lights. Zeke had to suppress a shudder when the tall Italian stepped out of the gloom and set a heavy silver attaché case on the pavement. In his gravelly voice, the man whispered, "This is for you."

The younger man's body tingled with excitement. He visualized opening the case and counting the banknotes. He'd been promised more money than he could earn in thirty years working for the Church. The Italian seemed to be waiting for him to make a move. Nodding, Zeke stepped forward and smiled obsequiously. "I'm happy to be of service," he said. "Of course, now that our business is concluded, I think it's best that we never meet or speak again."

Even muffled by a silencer, the gunshots echoed in the vacant concrete building. The first bullet pierced Zeke's skinny neck. The second shattered his jaw. In agony, he fell to the wet pavement and rolled onto his back, gasping.

Roderigo advanced until he loomed over his target, covering the dying man with shadow. He raised his weapon and fired again.

"We won't."

Together, Paul and Ava opened the second titanium canister and withdrew the lid. To her delight, it too contained a golden disk. The artifacts were almost identical, although their markings weren't perfectly matched. Ava set them side by side on the table. Then she collapsed onto the bed.

"What now?" asked Paul.

Ava sighed. "I don't know. My brain is kaput. First thing tomorrow I'll go online and try to determine exactly what the heck we've discovered. I'm out of my depth. I can't process all the ramifications."

"Maybe because someone tried to murder us a few hours ago?"

"Maybe. I was so scared. That man—"

Paul interrupted. "Listen, I need to say something. I'm incredibly sorry about that. It won't happen again."

"It's not your fault!"

"Really? Let's see: I proposed going to the church. I called the bishop's office. It was my brilliant idea to give the assistant our contact number, and I'm the one who agreed to meet that bastard in private, at night, in the freaking catacombs—"

"And I'm the one who forgot to thank you for saving my life."

Paul shrugged. He glanced at the clock: four in the morning. Rubbing his eyes, he walked to the window, pulled aside the curtain, and looked out. Lights from Manoel Island Fortress reflected on the water. Everything was closed. The usually busy avenues were empty. Still, someone could be out there, watching the hotel. After a few moments, he said, "I'm very glad you're okay, but it doesn't count as saving you when it was my fault you were in danger."

When Ava didn't respond, Paul looked over at her. She was fast asleep.

He stayed awake all that night, watching over her. An hour after sunrise Ava's eyes fluttered open. She looked at Paul and smiled. Then, noting the time, her expression changed to one of annoyance. "Why did you let me sleep so long?"

"I thought—"

"Oh, never mind. Let's get moving."

They dressed and walked down to the lobby. While Paul ordered breakfast (coffee, tea, pastry, and orange juice), Ava tried to access the Internet. Unfortunately, the ISP was down. Refusing to admit defeat, she marched out to a pay phone and rang Professor Clarkson. Though surprised by her call, he agreed to meet her at the university in a few hours. She hung up, collected Paul, and led him back upstairs. Once the hotel-room door was locked, Ava removed the golden disks from their hiding place. While they ate, she reexamined the objects. Both disks had delicate, etched rings radiating from the center. Around the edge, she found on each a chain of tiny symbols. Then she noticed an interesting difference. The first disk's center was marked with a pair of symbols:

The second disk, however, was etched with:

She showed Paul.

"I recognize X and P, but what's the box thing?"

"It could be the Star of Lakshmi."

"Come again?"

"A Hindu symbol that represents Ashtalakshmi, the eight forms of wealth."

"Hmm. The disks are gold. I suppose it's appropriate."

"A better guess might be Rub el Hizb."

"What in God's name is that?"

"It's Arabic. *Rub* means 'lord,' 'nourisher,' or 'protector.' *Hizb* means 'group.'"

"I don't know anything about that, but I know X stands for ten in Roman numerals. Does P stand for anything?"

"In medieval Roman numerals, P means four hundred."

"Huh? How can there be medieval Roman numerals?"

"Don't ask. Besides, these artifacts predate that system. Forget I said it."

"I already did."

Ava laughed. "Of course, P could be *rho*. In Greek numerals, rho represents one hundred. Or it could stand for *radius*." She paused. A little bell was ringing in her subconscious, but she couldn't identify it. "Anyway, it's time to go."

As she gathered her things, Paul wrapped the two treasures in cotton cloth, concealed them inside pillowcases, and loaded them into his backpack. Surreptitiously, he grabbed his hunting knife. He suspected it was illegal to carry it here, especially on campus. Ava probably wouldn't approve, but a weapon might come in handy.

He turned to her, "Are you ready?"

Ava didn't respond. She was rooted to the floor, staring at the satphone. Its NEW MESSAGE indicator was flashing. Ava dashed across the room, snatched the phone off the windowsill, and opened the text message from DURMDVL. "Your location is not secure," it said. "Obtain a disposable cell phone and call me ASAP. 919-555-3253."

Shaded by an aluminum umbrella, Nick sipped his Bloody Mary and reclined on the chaise longue. It was ten o'clock. He'd watched the morning's gentle sun intensify. Soon it would burn fiercely. He scanned his messages: nothing yet from Sinan. He ignored all other calls. He turned off the phone and told the steward to send him a second cocktail. It promised to be a long afternoon.

Resting his head against the canvas, he opened the newspaper. Nick read for a half hour before he sensed someone approaching. He lowered the paper and scanned the beach. A teenage Egyptian was slowly making his way across the sand. The boy drew near but rather than take sanctuary beneath the umbrella, he waited at a polite distance. Nick dipped his head and regarded the visitor over his Ray-Bans. He looked harmless. Nick smiled. He motioned for the kid to approach.

"Care to have a seat?"

The courteous teenager sat and then said: "You are Mister Nick? From Alexandria?"

Nick pushed up his sunglasses again and said, "Sorry, kid. Wrong guy. I'm from Texas."

The boy made a face. "You are not the friend of Paul and Miss Ava?"

Nick's smile evaporated. "Who wants to know?"

"My boss seeks them. It's very important. He begs to ask where they've gone."

"Nope. Never heard of 'em. Y'all got me mixed up with someone else. I'm just an American tourist in for the regatta."

The boy looked suspicious.

Nick relaxed, opened his paper, and said, "Hey, there are a lot more umbrellas, kid. Keep asking around. Somebody out here must know."

Scowling, the teenager took off. Nick waited an appropriate interval before finishing his drink, pocketing his phone, and sliding his feet into his sandals. After scanning the beach in both directions, he stood and set off for the hotel at a brisk pace.

Halfway back he encountered the overworked waiter toting an enormous tray of drinks. With one smooth motion he snatched his off the tray and left two hundred-pound notes in its place. The waiter called after him, offering change. "Keep it," said Nick. "I have to run."

Paul and Ava walked to the open-air market. For a hundred and forty euros they purchased a decent world phone with a prepaid international SIM card and a rugged, waterproof case. Unfortunately, the battery required several hours of charging before it would function. Ava put it in her backpack.

The square was filling with celebrants for some kind of street festival, making it impossible to flag a cab. The university wasn't too far away, so they opted to go by foot. They traveled southwest on Triq Ix-Xatt (the Strand) for a quarter mile. To their left a magnificent eighteenth-century fortress dominated the horizon. They passed the bridge to Manoel Island, cut through the Ta' Xbiex Gardens, and veered right on Triq Imsida. After another half kilometer, they passed the Empire Sports Ground, a decaying soccer stadium unused since 1981. They turned right, then left, then passed the National Swimming Pool Complex. Finally, they crossed under the highway and were on the campus.

The university was one of Europe's oldest. Founded by Pope Clement VIII in 1592, the college had been administered by the Jesuit order for centuries. Now it enrolled more than nine thousand students. Professor Clarkson was listed in the directory under the faculty of arts, history department. He was in his office, awaiting their arrival. The professor seemed genuinely happy to see them. Paul sensed no duplicity whatsoever. The three of them chatted for several minutes before Ava came to the point.

"Dr. Clarkson, I'm sorry to ask, but could you help us with something?"

"Anything, dear."

"Would it be possible to borrow a computer?"

"Certainly." He gestured toward the silver laptop on his desk.

"Actually, our project might require several hours. I hoped to use the university's computer lab."

Clarkson thought for a minute. "Well, I don't see why not. It should be empty today because of the festival. Let's walk over, and I'll sign you in as visitors."

Just outside the door they saw Clarkson's boss, Professor Fenech, being harangued by a shrill, hawk-faced woman. The academics acknowledged each other collegially as they passed. Once they were out of earshot, Clarkson confided in Ava and Paul.

"I despise that woman. She's teaching a postmodernist contemporary history seminar: The Life and Struggle of Elisabeth Burgos-Debray. If you ask me, it really belongs in the literature department."

Sensing he'd missed another witticism, Paul smiled and nodded knowingly.

The computer lab was on the northeast corner of campus. As

predicted, it was empty. While Paul found an outlet and plugged in the phone charger, the professor logged Ava in to the LAN using his password.

"Voilà! Let me know if you have any problems. I'll be working in my office all afternoon."

Ava thanked him. After Dr. Clarkson left, Paul warned her not to check e-mail. Simon might have people monitoring it.

"Can they really watch my e-mail?"

Paul shrugged. "Honestly, I don't know. I'm not great at tech stuff. If you think it's safe, go ahead. To me, it's not worth the risk."

Despite immense temptation, Ava refrained. Rather than e-mailing, she spent several hours reading everything she could find about the secret hidden inside the lost jars of Cana. She tried to ascertain the language, origin, and meaning of the symbols etched onto the golden disks. Meanwhile, Paul poked around the empty computer lab. Finding little of interest, he returned to Ava's cubicle and sat down at the neighboring work-station. Its desktop machine was linked to a Metris LC15 Laser Probe. He inferred from the setup that an engineering student had been using the scanner to model the leading and trailing edges of microturbine blades. He toyed with the cool gadgets for an hour, then suddenly the hairs on the back of his neck stood up. Someone was watching them. He turned around and saw Clarkson standing silently in the doorway. The professor looked furious.

Without disturbing Ava, Paul rose and approached him. The normally pleasant academic was too angry to speak. Instead, he handed Paul a page printed from the *Times of Malta* website. The article said Maltese police were looking for two Americans seen in Rabat the previous night. A local woman had been murdered. The story continued: "These may be the same fugitives who fled Alexandria two days ago."

Clarkson's gaze was flinty. "We need to talk."

Nick detoured around the Puerto Marina lobby, taking a short-cut to his executive suite. He'd secured a room at the exclusive hotel through industry connections. Many wealthy guests who stayed at the Marina gambled in his casino, so naturally he had some friends on staff. The posh resort was built to emulate Venice, replete with canals. The food was stellar and the service was impeccable. Too bad he wouldn't get to enjoy either. After passing the canal bend where the gondolas were moored, Nick rounded a corner and hopped onto the elevated promenade. Then he stopped.

An elegant, middle-aged man sporting an eggshell linen suit blocked his path. Nick recognized DeMaj immediately.

"*Bonjour*," said Simon. "A pleasure to make your acquaintance."

With a taut smile, Nick estimated his odds. Simon was fit but not muscular—it had been decades since the technocapitalist had performed manual labor. Furthermore, every man's reflexes slow with age. Nick was twenty years younger with a muscular body, but his greatest asset in any fight was his intuition. He excelled at predicting his opponent's moves, thereby gaining a tactical advantage. He could read a bluff in poker and anticipate a line of attack in chess. Nick figured he could outfight DeMaj with relative ease.

As if reading Nick's mind, Simon gracefully drew open his coat, exposing a deadly firearm. The gesture wasn't aggressive, but it communicated the futility of attempting a fist fight.

Nick nodded. Message received. Simon bowed slightly and

extended his hand toward the promenade. "Come this way, *mon ami*. Let's walk and talk."

Clarkson was visibly irate. He threatened to call the police and demanded to know all that had transpired the previous evening. Ava admitted they'd visited the catacombs, but she swore they hadn't killed the tour guide. Not believing her, Clarkson asked for the murderer's identity. Ava said she didn't know and attempted to explain why, but he threw up his hands. Finding the notion of a false bishop preposterous, he insisted on a complete report. Ava apologized again for deceiving him, and tears flowed freely. At that, Clarkson's manner softened. In a gentler voice, he asked Ava what happened. She began by revealing that they weren't in Malta to marry. Rather, she explained, "We fled Alexandria to avoid false charges. They accused us of horrible crimes that we didn't commit."

Paul broke in. "It was my fault. I made some powerful enemies in Egypt when I worked for Simon DeMaj. He does business with a lot of characters: smugglers, corrupt officials, maybe even terrorists. When I learned the extent of his dealings, I quit."

"And that's why they're after you? Because you know incriminating information?"

"No. They're after us because I took something. Something very valuable."

"You stole from them?"

"Yes, but it's complicated. The items we took belong to the Church. Or Egypt. Maybe all humankind. I'm not really sure—"

Ava interrupted. "That's why we need to see the bishop. If we deliver the items to the Church, legitimate authorities can determine ownership. Professor, our methods may be questionable, but our intentions are pure. We've never claimed ownership or sought compensation. We're trying to prevent a crime, not participate in one."

Frustrated, Clarkson replied, "Pardon me for being a stickler, but before we parse the legal niceties, do you mind telling me exactly what items we're discussing?"

Paul glanced toward Ava, wordlessly asking, "Can we trust him with this?" She gave an almost imperceptible nod. Ava trusted Clarkson, but she'd defer to Paul's judgment. She'd learned to appreciate his instincts about people. Paul deliberated. His mind told him to suspect everyone, but his heart told him the professor was a good man. On the basis of that intuition, Paul decided to tell the truth.

"We stole the lost jars of Cana. They're in our hotel closet."

Clarkson almost fell over. "*Sliem Għalik Marija* (Hail Mary)," he whispered.

While the two academics discussed the jars' exalted status in archaeological history, Paul reread the newspaper report. He noted that investigators had found only one dead body in the catacombs, that of the female tour guide. The report made no mention of the impostor. This omission led Paul to an alarming conclusion: The killer had survived.

13

Someone knocked. Gabe and Jess shared a look. Walking quietly, Gabe approached the door and peered out. It was a FedEx delivery-man, and he was loaded with packages. Suspicious, Gabe's instinct was to leave the door locked. Then he remembered DURMDVL's message to expect a delivery. He signed for the shipment, and the FedEx man left. When Gabe opened the boxes, he discovered they contained thousands of dollars' worth of cutting-edge computer hardware and a new phone. Jess was floored.

"What is all this stuff? What's it doing here?"

"I have no idea. I didn't order it."

Suddenly Gabe recalled his offhand remark to DURMDVL about needing a computer upgrade. This must be DURMDVL's response. Wow, thought Gabe, the guy doesn't mess around. Refusing to consider how DURMDVL had paid for the gear, Gabe concentrated instead on getting it unpacked.

"I have to go to class."

"Okay, I'll be here."

By the time Jess returned from school, Gabe had taken over her den. Everywhere she looked an exotic computer component was humming or blinking. When he noticed her, Gabe said, "Hi, Jess. I set up everything in here. Hope you don't mind."

She sighed and forced a smile. "Of course not. How could I mind?"

With his attention focused on the computer screen, Gabe missed the sarcasm. "Great. Thanks, Jess. Oh, by the way, I finished off the rest of the Cokes. Looks like you're out of soda."

After hearing the details, Clarkson believed Ava's story. He excused himself and hurried back to his office to contact Bishop Garagallo. As he passed Professor Fenech's door, he recalled that his boss had seen him with the Americans. Clarkson swallowed. What would happen when Dominic realized they were murder suspects? Would he call the police? He turned to knock. Dominic was reasonable. If he spoke to him now, perhaps he could convince him of the truth. Then Clarkson realized it hardly mattered. Professor Xanthippe had seen the fugitives too. When that harpy connected the dots, she'd inform the authorities instantly. Time was of the essence.

He went directly to his office, closed the door, and turned the lock. A quick shuffle through his Rolodex produced a phone number for the archdiocese. He called and a polite receptionist answered. In rapid-fire Maltese, Clarkson asked to speak to Bishop Garagallo on a matter of utmost urgency. The receptionist apologized, saying the bishop was unavailable. "Where is he?" Clarkson barked.

"I'm very sorry, sir. I'm afraid I couldn't say." Then she confided, "It's been an absolute madhouse here today. Everyone's trying to follow the latest developments in Rome and then, on top of everything else, the bishop's executive assistant never showed up for work. He's gone missing. Personally, I'm not surprised. I always felt that young man was a little *wiċċ laskri* (unstable)."

"Anyway," she continued, "I'll give the bishop your message the instant he arrives."

Realizing there was nothing more she could do, Clarkson said, "Thank you very much for your help. I appreciate it. *Sahha.*"

He hung up the phone and pondered his next move.

Paul and Ava returned to the computer lab. She tried to finish her research, but after the conversation with Clarkson, she was too angry. Paul read her mood. "Come on," he said. "Let's get some fresh air."

After leaving the laboratory they crossed through the lobby, exited the building, and sat beneath a shady tree. Paul leaned against its gnarled trunk. Ava leaned against Paul.

When her words finally came, they were a torrent. She vented for a long time. Ava was both furious about and humiliated by the false allegations. Didn't the media have a responsibility to print the truth? Didn't they check their facts, research their claims? How could they be so irresponsible? She wanted to sue for libel.

Paul listened to her complaints without interrupting. When she wound down, he said: "It had to be Simon. With his money and influence, he can make them say whatever he wants. Besides, can you really blame the police for suspecting us? We were at the crime scene. Don't you watch *CSI*? Our DNA must be all over those catacombs. You touched the body, for God's sake."

Ava shivered at the memory, and Paul moved quickly to change the subject. He asked, "Did you make progress translating the symbols?"

She sighed. It had been terribly frustrating. She might have identified the language, but she still couldn't decipher the inscription. To Paul's amusement, she sounded almost as upset about the unsolved puzzle as about the trumped-up murder charges.

"Don't worry," he reassured her, "it'll come."

"I'm glad one of us is confident."

"I am."

The sun had set. Now it was getting dark. By force of habit, Paul glanced at his wrist before asking, "What time do you think it is? Let's go see if our new phone works."

The world phone wasn't fully charged, but it was operational. Leaving it plugged in, Ava dialed the 919 number from DURMDVL's text. Her first call was aborted—the signal was too weak. After unplugging the phone, Ava climbed upstairs to the roof, hoping for better reception. She redialed, and this time the call went through. After the anonymous voice mail beeped, she keyed in 999. DUR-MDVL answered, authenticated Ava's identity, and warned her that enemies might know they were in Malta.

"I'm afraid we learned that the hard way," Ava replied. She recounted the previous evening's unfortunate events. Horrified, DURMDVL urged them to leave Malta before another assassin materialized. As they discussed travel options, Ava had a brainstorm. Who better to crack a code than a hacker? With DURMDVL's assistance, she'd be able to solve the mystery much faster. On the other hand, it might be unwise to trust a mysterious computer genius whom she'd never even met in person. Ava wavered. It was risky, but as Paul often said, life is risk.

Taking a deep breath, she decided: Circumstances justified a gamble. Crossing the Rubicon, Ava told DURMDVL about the jars and the golden disks. Fascinated, DURMDVL asked Ava to send photos. "Actually, we should forward them to Gabe," DURMDVL said. "He's a superlative code breaker, much better than I am. I respect his skills. Don't tell him I said so, but he has a knack for creative, indirect thinking that just can't be replicated." Hearing

DURMDVL express admiration for Gabe's talents lifted Ava's spirits. It was about time someone appreciated him! She agreed to send the photos as soon as possible. Then, with a smile, she said good-bye to her new friend and hung up the phone. Rejuvenated, Ava walked back downstairs to the computer lab.

As they strolled along the canals, Simon said, "Nick, you have a reputation as an honorable man, one who appreciates directness. Therefore, I'll just ask: Where are your friends?"

"Sorry to disappoint you, Mr. DeMaj, but I couldn't say."

"Call me Simon."

"Okay, Simon. As I said, I don't know where they went. At the moment, I'm more concerned about myself. It's not easy to escape the long arms of Sheik Ahmed. I hear good things about McMurdo Station. Do you know if they have a casino?"

Simon stopped, turned to face Nick, and looked into his eyes. With an earnestness Nick knew was virtually impossible to fake, Simon said, "I know you're bound by loyalty. You're trying to protect your friends, but the situation has evolved. They're in greater danger than you realize. It's not hopeless. I can help them, but they won't survive unless I find them first."

"You'd help them?"

"I possess the means to rescue them and the resources to keep them safe."

"Sure, but why would you? You know Sheik Ahmed. You understand what he's capable of. Why endanger yourself?"

"I got Paul and Ava into this mess; it's my responsibility to get them out. Plus, if Ahmed gets his hands on the artifacts, there will be hell to pay—for everyone."

As they veered down the path back to the suite, Nick noticed the Egyptian boy waiting outside. Nick thought, "He's probably packing heat, too. There's no way I can take them both." Needing time to think, he temporized: "Okay, Simon. You've got a deal. Just let me collect my belongings; then I'll do what I can to help you."

Simon nodded and allowed Nick to enter. The boy followed him inside, but Simon stayed in the doorway, watching. Nick tossed his suitcase onto the bed. He folded his Paul Stuart sports coat, button-down shirts, and khaki slacks with the precision of a department-store clerk. Socks and underwear were rolled and stashed in zipper pockets; toiletries were assembled in a black dopp kit.

Then Nick stopped packing and smiled. Simon felt a pistol's cold barrel press against his occipital lobe.

"Sinan!" yelled Nick. "It's about damn time! Did you get lost, or what?"

Paul and Ava photographed each side of both disks using the world phone's built-in camera. It was a basic device, but the pictures looked all right. After transmitting the images to DURMDVL, Paul noticed that the phone was running out of juice.

"We need to leave it plugged in overnight."

He unhooked the charger and pocketed it, and they left the computer center. On the way to Clarkson's office, Paul asked, "So how much do we tell the bishop?"

Ava thought, then: "Nothing at first. Let's meet him, talk to him, and get a sense of his character. Remember that Zeke, his personal assistant, contacted the killer. I doubt the bishop was involved, but we can't be sure. Even assuming that Garagallo's innocent, having an untrustworthy employee in such an elevated position gives me reason to doubt his judgment."

Paul nodded. Ava went on: "I'll ask Clarkson to keep everything confidential for now. If after meeting Garagallo in person we decide he's legit, we'll hand over the jars."

"And the disks?"

Ava ran her fingers across the worn, nondescript backpack that held the two priceless objects. She knew it wasn't wise to keep them, but the disks were her discovery and she didn't want to surrender them before finishing her analysis. "We won't mention the disks until we're sure we can trust the bishop," she said.

When they reached the professor's office, their conversation ceased. Ava knocked. Clarkson unlocked the door and welcomed them inside. The telephone rang a moment later. It was the bishop. The professor put Garagallo on speakerphone and made the full round of introductions. Everyone exchanged pleasantries. Then Ava gave a recap of what transpired in the catacombs, excluding any mention of the artifacts. Even over the phone, the bishop's anger was unmistakable. After using surprisingly profane language to characterize his assistant's conduct, Garagallo said, "I cannot begin to express the depth of my embarrassment and rage over this incident."

"Thank you, Excellency," Ava replied. "We know this wasn't your doing."

"Be that as it may, on behalf of myself, the archdiocese of Malta, and the Holy Church, I apologize for this act of betrayal and take full responsibility. I thank Almighty God that you both survived the attack. Please accept my word that the guilty parties will meet justice forthwith."

The conversation was brief. Garagallo intended to call Chief Justice Silvio Camilleri, as well as John Rizzo, the commissioner of police. The bishop hoped to persuade them to shift the investigation's focus from Paul and Ava to Zeke. The bishop continued, "In the meantime, I can extend a formal offer of sanctuary. I hope all three of you will honor me by dining in my home tonight. We'll prepare a traditional Maltese feast."

They accepted his invitation. Clarkson wrote down the bishop's address in Valletta. Then they bade him farewell and prepared to leave.

Bishop Garagallo's palatial home occupied an entire building in the city's historic district. Ava estimated the residence to be at least two hundred and fifty years old, predating the island's Napoleonic conquest. Before the professor could ring the bell the door opened and a handsome gentleman with gray hair and a dignified bearing greeted them. Ava saw intelligence in his eyes, and Clarkson's smile of recognition reassured her that this man was the bishop, not another impostor.

Garagallo invited them to come inside and prepare for dinner in his guest rooms. Paul and Ava accepted gratefully. After receiving keys from the housekeeper, they climbed the stairs, unlocked the doors, and found two fully appointed suites. While Ava washed, Paul plugged in the phone charger. Shortly thereafter they descended the grand staircase. Spotting his American guests, Garagallo asked, "Won't you join me for an aperitif in the sitting room?"

Surprised by the offer, Paul grinned. "I thought drinking was a sin."

The bishop laughed. "No. Our Lord and Savior drank alcohol on many occasions. In fact, Christ's first public miracle was turning water into wine at the Wedding of Cana. The Church teaches us to avoid intoxication because it is a form of gluttony and because it can lead to sin, but drinking is not forbidden."

Each carrying a glass of sherry, they joined Professor Clarkson in the richly appointed sitting room. A cheery blaze crackled in the hearth, where a set of andirons, forged into miniature Dobermans, held the logs. Opposite the fire an interior wall was dominated by a striking fresco. Entranced, Ava said, "Raphael?"

"Yes. A reproduction, of course. It's *The Meeting between Leo the Great and Attila.* Do you like it?"

Ava nodded.

"I'm very pleased. It's one of my favorites."

Paul examined the wall painting. "Is that Attila?"

"Yes. Why do you ask?"

"I don't know. I guess I expected Attila the Hun to look more demonic or monstrous. Wasn't he called the Antichrist?"

"Attila was known as the *flagellum dei,* or Scourge of God. He was a powerful warrior. Countless thousands were slain at his command, but are you familiar with the particular scene Raphael has portrayed?"

Paul wasn't.

Garagallo explained: "In AD 452, Attila invaded Italy and threatened Rome. Flavius Aetius's army was vanquished; thus, no earthly power could prevent a Hunnic conquest of the Eternal City."

He approached the painting and pointed to a regal figure astride a white horse. "Pope Leo the Great, shown here with Consul Avienus and Prefect Trigetius, rode out to meet Attila in Lombardy, near the city of Mantua."

He glanced at Ava. "My dear, you are a classicist, yes? Do you know Mantua?"

"Yes, Excellency. The birthplace of the immortal Virgil."

The bishop smiled. "Correct. Mantua is also mentioned in *Romeo and Juliet.* It's where Romeo was sent after he killed Tybalt Capulet. May I refresh your glass?"

Startled, Paul looked up. He'd downed his tiny measure of Spanish sherry in one gulp.

"Sure. Thank you. It's delicious," he commented, trying to ignore Ava's disapproval. Smiling, Garagallo lifted an antique crystal decanter and refilled Paul's drink, then continued the story.

"The two leaders met privately in Attila's tent on the banks of the Mincio. When they emerged, Attila surprised the world by vowing to withdraw from Italy in peace. The Scourge of God never attacked Rome."

"Wow. Really?" asked Paul. "Pope Leo must have been a persuasive guy."

Clarkson spoke up. "Of course, not everyone believes that account. There are a host of theories regarding Attila's decision to spare Rome. His forces were greatly weakened after the Battle of Châlons. Some historians allege he was bribed. Some believe the Hunnic army was wracked with infectious diseases. Still others argue that Attila's men had grown so rich from plunder that they already possessed more gold than they could carry."

Ava interrupted. "But I sense our host favors a different explanation."

"Correct again," said Bishop Garagallo. Turning to Paul, he asked, "Do you see the figures suspended above Pope Leo?"

Paul nodded.

"Those are St. Peter and St. Paul. What do they carry?"

Paul studied the fresco. "Swords. Is that significant?"

"I find it quite significant. According to Leo's biography, during the meeting Attila received a vision of Peter and Paul dressed in priestly robes and armed with flaming swords."

Clarkson interrupted. "Flaming swords? I'm sorry, but no one buys that fanciful chronicle. It's clearly an allegory, not meant to be taken literally."

"Precisely," the bishop said. "Swords represent special knowledge, truth, or the Word. For example, Ephesians 6:17 states: '[T]he sword of the Spirit is the word of God.' Raphael uses swords to symbolize that although Pope Leo carried no weapons, he was armed with truth."

Clarkson grunted. "You make too much of it. Gibbon himself called this tale a pious fable."

"Indeed," said the bishop, "but I believe this fable is rooted in fact."

Further argument was suspended by the butler's announcement that dinner was served. The party moved from the sitting room to the formal dining room, decorated with another Raphael fresco, *The Coronation of Charlemagne.* Atop a polished African mahogany table, to ravenous Paul's great joy, sat the first course of what promised to be a feast. Garagallo's cook had prepared stuffed octopus in a piquant tomato sauce; *fenek* (rabbit) simmered as a casserole in wine; *bragoli* (parcels of chopped eggs, bread crumbs, and herbs wrapped in thin sheets of beef braised in gravy); and a crisp roasted hen served on a bed of sliced potatoes, eggplant, onions, and garlic. The symphony of flavors was intoxicating.

Between courses the good-natured historical debate resumed. Professor Clarkson and Bishop Garagallo defended their positions like master fencers, each seeming to enjoy the cerebral combat. Before long Ava joined the fray. "Didn't St. Prosper of Aquitaine describe the encounter between Attila and Leo?"

"Indeed," said the bishop. Begging their pardon, he rose and retrieved an ancient illuminated text from a bookshelf. Opening it to a page marked by a golden tassel, he read: "'Our most blessed Pope Leo, trusting in the help of God, who never fails the righteous in their trials, undertook the task. And the outcome was just as foreseen. When Attila received the embassy, he was so overwhelmed by the high priest's words that he promised peace and ordered his army to give up warfare.'"

"What does he mean when he says the outcome was 'foreseen'?" Ava asked.

"That's an excellent question, my dear," replied Garagallo, smiling. "I wondered the same thing for years, and then I unlocked the secret. Do you recall the allegorical biography's mention of flaming swords?"

She nodded.

"What do flaming swords represent?"

"As you said, a sword represents truth and flames represent the Holy Spirit. Thus, a flaming sword symbolizes a miraculous truth, or God's truth."

"Precisely. The pope came to that historic meeting armed with miraculous truth. Specifically, he carried a sacred prophecy. It foretold that if Attila showed mercy and withdrew from Italy, Leo would crown Attila's heir the rightful Roman emperor. Attila spared Rome because he believed the pope's prophecy."

For several minutes they ate in silence, pondering the bishop's words. Then Paul spoke up. "So did it come true? Did Attila's heir become emperor?"

"Not right away. Attila's greedy sons squabbled over his legacy. Divided, they were defeated and killed by the combined might of the Ostrogoths and the Gepids, but one of his daughters married the Gepid king Adaric. A child of that marriage, the beautiful Princess Austrigusa, married King Waccho of the Lombards. Waccho and Austrigusa are considered ancestors of—"

Ava gasped. Her eyes shot up to the fresco. Then she finished his sentence: "Charlemagne, emperor crowned in Rome by Pope Leo III."

Garagallo beamed.

Unwilling to surrender the field, Clarkson persisted. "That's a fine story, and I hate to be so cynical, but if the prophecy dissuaded Attila from attacking Rome, why didn't it protect the city from the Vandals in 455?"

"According to legend, the scroll on which the prophecy was written caught fire when it was read aloud. Such pyrotechnics likely had a marvelous effect on Attila, but regardless of whether it was a miracle or a parlor trick, the prophecy was consumed."

Looking up from his rabbit, Paul asked, "Couldn't they just print another copy?"

"Apparently not. The prophecy was said to come from a holy relic. Historical sources are in conflict here. Some say the relic was possessed by the Roman emperor Valentinian III; others say it was divided so that Pope Leo and Emperor Valentinian each held a piece. In any case, when the emperor was assassinated by Petronius Maximus, at least part of the relic was lost."

"And the Vandals sacked Rome shortly thereafter," marveled Professor Clarkson.

"Yes," said the bishop, "although *sacked* may be an exaggeration. Pope Leo persuaded the Vandals to refrain from violence, thus preventing Rome's destruction. The invaders remained for fourteen days, but they did not burn the city, contrary to their custom. St. Prosper reports almost no murders."

Paul asked, "Did Prospero say what the relics were?"

Ava flinched. Garagallo smiled and said, "If he did, no record survives. Predictably, it's a topic of fierce debate. Numerous scholars believe the sacred relic was the mummified head of John the Baptist."

Paul's nose wrinkled with disgust. "You're kidding! A severed head?"

"Please show some respect, Paul," Ava cautioned. "You're talking about the man who baptized Jesus."

"It took me by surprise."

"You find that hypothesis implausible?" asked Garagallo.

"Well, no, not necessarily. I'm keeping an open mind, but who would worship a rotting head—"

"Paul!"

For a moment, there was an awkward silence. Then Garagallo erupted into peals of laughter. Ava was momentarily taken aback, but then such an august churchman chuckling was irresistible. Then Paul joined, and soon all four were laughing.

When he regained his composure, Garagallo said, "For what it's worth, I tend to agree. I don't think the relic was the Baptist's preserved head."

"Good, because that would be creepy," Paul said. Ava squirmed. Ignoring her, he went on: "What relics do you think they had?"

The bishop smiled at his guests. "I believe they possessed two of the lost jars of Cana. Does anyone care for coffee?"

After dinner, Clarkson checked his messages. He'd received an urgent call from the history department chair. Apologizing profusely, he excused himself and stepped in to the garden to return the call. When he came back, he announced that he had to leave.

"What could be so important at this hour?" Garagallo asked.

Clarkson answered, "Dominic is . . . curious about the situation. He'd like to ask me a few questions."

Ava's face was ashen. "I hope you're not in trouble."

"Oh, don't worry. He's an eminently reasonable man. He won't jump to conclusions. Nevertheless, it's vital that I see him immediately."

Clarkson thanked their host for the splendid meal and made preparations to leave.

"Should we go too?" Ava asked him.

"No, that might complicate things. I'd prefer to speak with him first in private."

"Ava, I wonder if you and Paul would like to stay here awhile longer," Garagallo said. "My housekeeper prepared a variety of desserts. She'll be inconsolable if no one tastes them."

Ava glanced at Paul. He didn't seem nervous. She decided to accept the bishop's invitation. Predictably, the desserts were phenomenal. Paul's favorite was the crisp cannoli filled with sweet ricotta and chocolate. Ava preferred the warm *figolla* (soft, almond-stuffed cookies). Garagallo then invited the Americans to join him for a postprandial snifter of brandy. He led them to his private study: an interior room protected by a thick, ancient door of oak and iron. Inside, Ava noticed portraits of Shakespeare and Marlow, a statue of Democritus meditating, and a bust of Homer. Paul's attention was captured by an escutcheon mounted behind the wide desk. The heraldry featured a flaming sword and a shepherd's crook crossed above a castle with seven towers. Beneath it hung the motto GARDEZ BIEN. As Paul struggled to remember where he'd heard those words, the bishop excused himself to see about the drinks. While he was gone, Paul whispered, "Do you trust him?"

Ava sighed. "Not fully. I like him, but I sense he knows more than he's telling. Why play games with us?"

"He seems to know a lot about the jars."

"Yes but, I wonder—"

Garagallo's return interrupted her sentence. Noting her startled expression, he said, "I'm sorry. I didn't mean to intrude."

"Oh, no, Excellency. We were just discussing Shakespeare."

"Really? What play?"

215

"*The Tempest.*"

"Ah, yes." He smiled. "One of my favorites. 'We are such stuff as dreams are made on . . .'"

For several minutes they chatted about the work, Ava and the bishop quoting verses from memory. Paul's attention wandered. He resisted the temptation to gulp his brandy. Finally, Ava asked the bishop: "Something you said at dinner piqued my curiosity. You mentioned the lost jars of Cana."

"A fascinating subject, yes? You might even call it my hobby. What would you like to know?"

"You said Pope Leo and Emperor Valentinian had two jars. Weren't there six originally?"

"Yes. The Gospel of John specifies that six jars were present at the first miracle. Later, these six were split into three pairs. Each pair was hidden on a different continent to prevent destruction by the Antichrists . . ."

Paul interrupted: "Hold on. Did you just say Antichrists? There's more than one?"

"Regrettably, yes. History has withstood a seemingly endless succession."

Paul shook his head. "I'm confused. I thought Satan was the Antichrist."

Garagallo explained. "Jesus Christ epitomizes the Christian virtues, the greatest of which is love. Do you agree?"

Paul nodded. "I do."

"Thus, anyone or anything opposing those virtues is, by definition, anti-Christ. The word can describe Lucifer or any other monster who serves death, injustice, and damnation. Early Christians considered Herod and later Nero to be Antichrists. Of course, there have been others. I believe each generation must find the courage to combat this evil, embodied in some new, hideous form."

"But what use are stone jars against a monster?"

"The jars contain a prophecy. If you believe the legend, reading the prophecy aloud at the proper place and time can defeat the devil."

"Too bad it didn't work against Hitler."

Garagallo closed his eyes and anguish passed over his face. In a hollow voice, he said, "Yes. Hitler was a terrible Antichrist. Even as a little boy, I despised him. I'm proud we Maltese resisted his evil, and I grieve for all those who sacrificed their lives."

For a moment the bishop couldn't speak. Finally, he opened his eyes, gazed up at the antique crest, and went on. "As a man of faith, I believe the sacred jars' power might have stopped the Nazis. Sadly, we'll never know. At least one jar was destroyed in 455. After the fall of Rome, the surviving jars' whereabouts were lost to humanity. St. Bede believed one was given to King Osby of Northumbria in 665. He may have hidden it under Whitby Abbey or possibly Whitekirk, but the others disappeared."

Ava asked, "Were any hidden in Egypt?"

"According to legend, two jars were given to Africa. No one knows what happened to them. If I were to guess their location, Egypt and Ethiopia would be my top candidates. Why do you ask?"

Generally, Ava distrusted churchmen. She knew the Church's spotty history, and she was well aware of its recent scandals. Not all Catholic leaders had acted honorably. Yet Ava trusted Garagallo. She heard sincerity in his voice, and she shared the bottomless anger he expressed regarding the Nazis. Though she sensed he had a secret agenda, Ava concluded that the bishop was an ally, not an enemy. Having made her decision, she answered him. "Because that's where we found two of them."

Garagallo was silent. After a moment, he reclined in his chair, whispered a prayer of thanks, and said, "Please, tell me everything."

Ava told him of their journey from the monastery to Malta. She began by describing the relics' discovery and concluded by explaining how she and Paul had escaped the catacombs. For now, she omitted any mention of the disks. Garagallo listened intently. Though he nodded occasionally, he never spoke, allowing Ava to relate her story without interruption. When she finished, he asked, "What do you intend to do with the jars?"

Ava glanced at Paul. He nodded. "We want to give them to the Church," she said, "pursuant to certain conditions." She listed their terms.

For a moment, Garagallo appeared lost in thought. Then he rose, smiled, and took Ava's hands in his. With a warm voice he said, "On behalf of the Church, I thank you for your honesty, selflessness, and generosity. Naturally, in a matter of such importance, I must contact Rome. I may not receive guidance until after we've elected our new pope, but you may rest assured that we appreciate your astounding gift."

They left the study and returned to the main hallway. As they neared the stairs, the bishop said, "Friends, tonight has been a rare pleasure. Thank you for trusting me. I'm honored, and I give my word that you'll come to no harm within these walls. Please feel welcome to spend the night in my guest quarters. All are fully equipped and comfortable. Or, if you prefer to go, my butler will call a cab. Of course, none may be available right now."

At that moment, Paul heard gunshots. In an instant, he lunged for Ava, threw her to the ground, and covered her with his body. Once he was sure she was safe, he raised his head to locate the source of the attack. "Fireworks, Paul," the bishop said quickly. "Those were just fireworks. Weren't you aware of the festival? They have fireworks at midnight."

Paul glanced at his empty wrist. Then he consulted the bishop's grandfather clock. Its hands pointed straight up, and it was chiming. Embarrassed, Paul's face reddened.

"Sorry," he muttered sheepishly. "Guess I overreacted a bit." As Paul helped Ava regain her footing, Garagallo turned away from his guests and crossed the room. Heading through the doorway, the bishop turned and waved goodnight.

Outside, the street festival continued. After enjoying the dazzling fireworks, the mob of brightly costumed revelers paraded and twirled through the smoky air. The Mediterranean night echoed with the sounds of a thousand happy voices. Groups clustered to sing folk songs, play instruments, dance, and drink.

Amid the throng, two men seemed out of place. They cut through the crowd like sharks through a shoal. Ignoring catcalls and whistles from some intoxicated students, the men approached the waterfront and entered a grand structure. The elder of the two patted his pocket, ensuring that the stolen key was secure. They climbed the stairs.

When they reached Paul and Ava's room, each man drew a pistol and clicked on his night-vision goggles. Quietly, Lieutenant Barakah slipped the key into the slot. The door unlocked. Motionless, he waited, straining for the faintest sound. Hearing nothing, he eased the door open. With his accomplice covering him, Barakah launched himself through the doorway. Something flashed. Cat-quick, Barakah dropped, rolled, and came up aiming his gun. Silence. No movement. He scanned the room. The blinking light was just an old satphone charging on the nightstand. Then Barakah spotted the closet. He crept toward it. After gesturing for his confederate to enter the room, he grasped the handle and pulled. A hinge squeaked. Startled, his cohort began firing. Barakah's stomach knotted at the sound. Furious, he swung around and leveled his weapon. The younger man raised his arms and whispered an apology. For several seconds Barakah considered killing him for sheer incompetence. Then he lowered his gun and examined the damage. Bullets had shredded the room's linens and pillows, but there was no blood. The bed was empty.

At dawn the aroma of rich Ethiopian coffee lured Paul into wakefulness. He cracked open the door and spied the butler, who intimated that the bishop awaited him downstairs. After requesting a few moments to prepare, Paul washed his face, brushed his teeth, and dragged a comb through his thick mop. More than a month had passed since his last haircut, and he was starting to look like a rock star. He pulled on his dirty clothes and went to the breakfast room. Garagallo stood when Paul entered. "Did you get some rest?"

"Yes, thanks. Your guest rooms are very comfortable."

"And Ava?"

Paul grinned. "Sleeping like a baby. I didn't wake her."

"That's probably best. Unfortunately, I have disturbing news. It will be easier to tell you man to man."

They sat. Garagallo poured Paul a demitasse of steaming coffee. "Commissioner Rizzo called. There's been another attempt on your life. Last night criminals broke into your hotel room and stole the jars. Security found your bed riddled with bullet holes."

Paul sagged into his chair. Despite everything they'd endured, the jars were lost. It was simply too much. He'd been a fool to think he could protect Ava from these thieves. They'd survived thanks only to amazingly good fortune. Sooner or later, luck would run out and they'd be captured or killed. He sipped his coffee, but it had no taste. He looked at the bishop. "I'm sorry about the jars. Is there anything I can do?"

"Don't worry about that. We'll find them, but you must leave Malta. Dark forces are at work. The longer you wait, the more dangerous it will become."

"Where should we go?"

"Take Ava across the strait to Italy. The Virtu Rapid Catamaran sails from Valletta to Sicily. When I meet with the commissioner, I'll arrange tickets."

Noting Paul's expression, he asked, "Do you object?"

"No. I'm sorry, Father. That sounds fine. Italy's as good a destination as any, but it seems pointless to keep running. It's only a matter of time before they find us."

"Have faith. The tide may yet turn. There is an old German proverb: *Wo die Not am grössten ist, ist Gott am nächsten.* It means 'Where the need is greatest, God is nearest.'"

The bishop stood, walked to Paul, and handed him a small golden amulet. It was inscribed with a flaming sword and a shepherd's crook crossed above a castle. Looking into Paul's eyes, he said, "Take this. When you're in dire need, show it for protection."

Paul thanked him, looped its chain over his head, and slid the amulet under his shirt. Making the sign of the cross over his guest, Garagallo whispered, "*Gardez bien.*"

Ava was roused by the ring of the now fully charged world phone. It was Gabe, and he could hardly contain himself. "I think sound data is preserved on your artifacts!" he shouted.

221

She fell back against the pillows. Audio! Of course! That's why "no one can read it with mortal eyes." She recalled Revelation 3:6: "If you have ears, listen to what the Spirit says to the people." She laughed, then spoke aloud Jesus's admonition: "Having ears, hear ye not?"

Someone knocked at her door. It was Paul, carrying a pot of tea. He looked worried. Why was she was acting crazy?

Ava yanked him into the room and slammed the door. She set the phone to speaker and began discussing Gabe's radical hypothesis. Instantly, Paul was lost. When he couldn't stand any more technical jargon, he asked, "Excuse my skepticism, but how could ancient people record audio? Is that possible? I mean, they didn't have electricity."

Ava smiled. "Gabe, do you want to field this one?"

"You don't need electricity to record stuff," Gabe explained. "Before the advent of magnetic tape, sound was recorded mechanically. In 1877, Edison's phonograph used metal cylinders. Sound vibrations were physically printed and played back when a stylus read the impressions. You can still listen to some. There's a cool site called tinfoil dot com. Despite background noise, you can hear historical audio of President Taft, William Jennings Bryan—"

Paul stopped him. "But could they record onto a gold disk?" Ava flinched. Gabe had a reputation for intellectual arrogance. He frequently referred to techno-illiterate classmates as troglodytes and imbeciles. She feared Paul was about to be similarly flayed. Instead, Gabe answered calmly.

"Yes, of course. In fact, it's the medium NASA used. Do you remember *Voyager*?"

"The space probe?"

"Exactly. In 1977, NASA launched *Voyager 1* and *Voyager 2*. Each carried a twelve-inch gold disk containing audio recordings selected by Carl Sagan. The records were encased in protective aluminum jackets with a cartridge, stylus, and symbolic instructions on how to play them."

"I'm sure NASA could do that in 1977, but these artifacts date back to biblical times."

"That's why it's so cool. Several people have claimed to discover ancient audio recordings, but no claim has been scientifically substantiated. It was the basis for a classic *X-Files* episode—"

Ava cut him off. "Gabe, wouldn't the recorded information have deteriorated by now?"

"Maybe. It matters how often it was played and by what method. Unfortunately, playing a mechanical recording hastens its destruction. Most of Edison's recordings on tin have deteriorated, but they were played often. I suspect gold would preserve data just fine. Besides being ductile, gold is unreactive. Therefore, it resists corrosion and tarnishing."

"Enough to last millennia?"

"It'll be forty thousand years before *Voyager* approaches a planetary system. If NASA expects those recordings to last that long, then two thousand years seems possible—even on Earth."

"Can we play these disks? Obviously, a phonograph won't work. Nothing would fit, and the needle would probably destroy them, but could we reverse-engineer an ancient playback device?"

"Why do all that? Why not just capture the data to a PC running good audio software?"

"How?"

"It depends. You could use an optical scanner or a light-contact technique. Optical is easier and usually results in a better sound. Unlike bouncing a laser beam off a record, optical scanning isn't susceptible to dirt, damage, or wear. On the other hand, light contact is quicker and more authentic."

"What do you mean 'authentic'?"

"Optical-scan results require digital filtering, meaning somebody guides the process. In effect, he or she decides how the final recording will sound, but now there's some cutting-edge software incorporating precision optical metrology with slippery pattern recognition algorithms—"

"Speak English!" Paul barked.

"Okay, sorry. I'll back up. Let's say you break a wax record. Now you can't play it with a needle, right? But the information is still there—it's stored mechanically. Once upon a time, two geniuses at Lawrence Berkeley Laboratories got bored studying subatomic particles and used their scanner to optically 'read' etchings in damaged antique records. They scanned the physical objects, digitized the images, reintegrated them, and calculated what a stylus would do. The experiment turned out beautifully."

"Would that work on our disks?"

"I don't see why not. The Berkeley software is hard core. It was designed to find Higgs bosons. If we had a really good scan, I could model the artifacts' undulating grooves and extract the audio data. I can even enhance the result to remove scratches, noise, or whatever, but I don't see how any of that's helpful."

"Why not?" Ava asked.

"Because I can't do anything without scanned images. Photos won't work. We need much greater detail. Given the point density required, we'd need a high-res scanner suitable for soft, delicate surfaces—"

"Would a Metris LC15 Laser Probe suffice?" Paul asked, enjoying the silence that followed his question.

Once Ava was dressed, she and Paul took a cab to the university. As they were hurrying to the computer center, Paul told her that their hotel room had been robbed. To his surprise, she wasn't crushed. In fact, the news didn't seem to faze her. She remained enthused about their current project. After logging into the system using Clarkson's password, Ava called Gabe. Over the phone, he explained how to use the 3D scanner. She relayed the instructions to Paul, who carefully scanned both disks.

The resultant mountain of digitized information was too large to transmit by phone. Ava attempted to send it via the secure e-mail interface but the system crashed. They were stymied until Gabe suggested saving and transmitting each scanned file individually. It was tedious, but following Gabe's directions to the letter, Ava completed the task. When Gabe confirmed receipt, Ava heard excitement in his voice. She knew he couldn't wait to begin his analysis. "Okay, just one last thing," she said.

"What? What?" he asked.

"Gabe, I really miss you. It's beyond wonderful hearing your voice again. I was scared that something bad had happened. Thanks for everything you've done. You're a true and loyal friend, and I'll never forget it."

Gabe tried to reply, but the words caught in his throat. He felt tears welling up. Self-conscious, he handed the telephone to Jess and turned away, struggling for self-control.

"Hello? Gabe? Are you there?"

Grinning, Jess said, "Ava, this is Jess. Gabe will be just a moment. He got something in his eye and he's run to the loo."

They talked for a while. After bringing her friend up to speed on everything happening in Boston, Jess mentioned that Ava's parents and teachers were becoming concerned about her extended absence.

"Please tell them not to worry. I'm okay, and I'll be home soon."

"Are you sure?"

"Of course! The situation is under control. For heaven's sake, we have first-class tickets on the next catamaran to Italy. How cool is that?"

When Sheik Ahmed heard the mobile phone, he smiled. He'd been eagerly anticipating this call. Finally, he had good news to report.

Before it could ring twice, Ahmed had answered. "Master?"

"Yes."

"We have the jars. Shall I bring them to you personally?"

"No."

To Ahmed's surprise, the master did not sound pleased.

"The clever little *troia* is close to the secret. She must be exterminated immediately. Spare no expense. Utilize any resource. Stop at nothing. Kill her now."

For perhaps the first time, Ahmed detected a human emotion in the master's voice. He must be furious, thought the sheik, but then he reconsidered. Fury wasn't quite right. He'd heard something more, something hidden underneath. Was it possible? Ahmed wondered: Was the master afraid?

Embarrassed that he'd teared up during the phone call, Gabe retreated into his work. After several hours he located and downloaded the software necessary to read the scans. While the parallel processing algorithms monopolized his available computing resources, Gabe decided to eat. He pondered a momentous decision: pizza or Thai? As he vacillated between the two enticing options, he checked his inbox. It contained an urgent e-mail from DURMDVL.

"We have a problem. I've been snooping on DeMaj Corp so that if it located our friends, I'd know. As of last night, none of our spiders had detected a single usage of the term Malta, Valletta, or bishop. We know someone found Ava (and sent the assassin), but nary a word about it was uttered or typed on the DeMaj network. That doesn't scan. I've drawn 2 conclusions, both of which are scary. (A) Someone other than DeMaj sent the killer, meaning we're facing an unexpected enemy. (B) The bad guys found her in Malta almost immediately. They set up an ambush in less than 24 hours. Therefore, they have already compromised her new phone, they have a spy in the Malta police, immigration/customs, or both."

"If that's true," Gabe realized, "they'll know Ava's itinerary."

Paul and Ava strolled down Pinto Road through Valleta, then checked in at the Sea Passenger Terminal. The catamaran wouldn't depart for an hour, so they sat down on a bench to wait. Eventually Paul asked, "Would you explain something?"

"I'll try."

"How could ancient people have done all this stuff?"

"What stuff?"

"Well, for example, how could they make recordings? I understand it's physically possible, but they didn't have the necessary technology—"

"Ancient people had all kinds of technology. Thales of Miletus wrote about electrostatic phenomena in 550 BC. Heron of Alexandria invented a working steam engine in the first century."

"A steam engine? Seriously?

"He called it an *aeolipile*. The basic principle is jet propulsion. Heat up water in a sealed metal cauldron. Water boils into steam. Steam shoots out from two jets, rotating a ball."

"That's awesome!"

Ava smiled. "Do you know about the Baghdad Battery?"

"Is it the Iraqi baseball team?"

She laughed despite herself. "No. Before World War II, archaeologists discovered terra-cotta jars buried near Baghdad. Some claim they date from the Parthian era. I think the Sassanid dynasty is more likely. Regardless, they're at least fifteen hundred years old—and they're basic electric batteries."

"You mean like Duracell?"

"Pretty much. Each clay jar had a stopper. Sticking through it was an iron rod surrounded by a copper cylinder. Filled with vinegar or any other strong electrolytic solution, they produced electricity. Experts estimate each made about one volt. In 1980, Arthur C. Clarke built a reproduction, filled it with grape juice, and proved it could electroplate a statuette. The MythBusters determined it was plausible for ancient people to have used such batteries."

"That's so cool."

Gradually, as Paul and Ava talked, the terminal filled with passengers. Representatives of many nationalities and ethnicities congregated around the gate. Soon the metal building reverberated with the babble of two hundred simultaneous conversations.

Efficient security personnel appeared and organized the crowd into three lines. First, an officer reviewed identification. Second, luggage was examined by customs agents, who offered to stow heavier bags belowdecks. Finally, a smiling steward tore tickets and welcomed passengers across the gangway.

Ava and Paul waited their turn, but when the officer saw Ava's ID, he pulled them out of line and escorted them past security. In broken English, he explained that Police Commissioner Rizzo personally insisted the two Americans were to be shown every courtesy. Paul thanked the officer and helped Ava board.

Meanwhile, out on the waterfront, a diesel pump throbbed as it refueled the massive catamaran. The wharf bustled with activity. Growling, a forklift shuttled to and fro, lifting crates into the hold. Dockworkers rushed aluminum tubs of perishable food up a ramp and delivered them to the galley. Supervisors shouted instructions to burly men hefting innumerable cases of beer, liquor, wine, and soda to the ship's four bars and passenger lounges.

Amid the chaos, no one noticed a tall Italian spiriting aboard an unregistered case and hiding it in the aft engine room.

14

Mired in melancholy, Cardinal Jacopo Piccolomini-Ammannati attended the coronation of Pope Paul II. A vain, suspicious, and ineffectual man, Paul II was no elector's first choice. Rather, the self-important Venetian represented a compromise between ideologically divergent factions. To secure support in the College of Cardinals, the new pope had signed a capitulation that, among other things, required him to continue Pius's campaign against the Turks. Cardinal Jacopo was instrumental in obtaining this concession. He championed the cause not out of personal animus or ambition, but rather out of loyalty to a departed friend.

The forty-two-year-old cardinal had accomplished much in his career. He was ordained a bishop at thirty-eight. One year later he was named cardinal of Pavia. He'd served as secretary of briefs under Pope Calistus III and continued in that role until Pius II made him a member of the pontific household. Sadly, his meteoric rise would now stall. Jacopo suspected the new pope would break his political promises, arguing that preelection capitulations abridged a pope's absolute authority. By disregarding these commitments, Paul II would ignite a feud within the Vatican, weakening the Church at an inopportune time. Fraught with internal division, Rome could never check the Ottoman advance. Pius's steadfast allies, the valiant

Knights of Rhodes, would continue to fight. But it was only a matter of time until the Turks invaded Italy. Worse, Spain might persuade the isolated pope to revive the execrable Inquisition. Jacopo's humanist friends and cohorts, particularly de Volterra, Carvajal, and Roverella, feared that an anti-intellectual backlash could engulf all of Europe, strangling the nascent Renaissance in its crib and dragging Christendom back into darkness.

As soon as decorum allowed, Jacopo bade farewell to the assembled ministers, clerics, and plenipotentiaries. He had important duties to perform. On his deathbed Pius had ordered Jacopo to destroy the artifacts and the prophecy they contained. Jacopo had objected. The two men disagreed sharply on the topic. Jacopo believed the prophecy was simply mistranslated, by either accident or design. Pius thought otherwise. He insisted the prophecy was a demonic instrument, imbued with black sorcery that turned arrogant mortals away from God. To prove such speculations were illogical, Jacopo invoked the reasoning propounded by the brilliant Franciscan friar William of Ockham. Pius, however, would not be dissuaded. He ignored all arguments, endlessly repeating: *"A daemonibus docetur, de daemonibus docet, et ad daemones ducit."* (It is taught by the demons, it teaches about the demons, and it leads to the demons.)

Though he opposed the pope's decision, Cardinal Jacopo finally agreed to destroy the relics. To disobey the pontiff was an unthinkable sin, one that would expose his soul to eternal damnation. More important, Jacopo would never refuse his mentor's last request.

It was vital to act quickly, before the new pope consolidated his authority. Piccolomini-Ammannati summoned his personal secretary. While Jacopo and his fellow cardinals were locked in the papal conclave, this aide collected every extant copy of the prophecy. These Jacopo would burn. Whispering to the young priest, he revealed the ancient jars' hiding place and instructed him to throw them over the balcony. As the stunned academician turned to obey, the cardinal said, "Inside the cabinet, hidden below the jars, are two disks of pure gold. Melt them down."

The young man's eyes widened. "And what should I do with the gold?"

Jacopo smiled. "Cast it into coins. Distribute them to the poor to honor our generous new pope's election."

"Yes, Eminence."

The secretary hurried to perform his assignment. He found the secret chamber, located the hidden jars, and dragged them onto the balcony. After inspecting the courtyard below to ensure that no one would be crushed, the young priest shoved the first jar over the edge. With an ear-splitting crack, it shattered. He wiped his hands on his cassock, then repeated the process with the second jar. That task complete, he searched the cabinet and uncovered the golden disks. For a moment he was awed by the glimmering objects, but he soon regained his composure and transported them to the goldsmith.

In exchange for a modest bribe, the artisan agreed to begin work immediately. He pumped the bellows, bringing his furnace to a white heat. Inside, the disks melted rapidly. Dripping with sweat, the goldsmith removed the assembly from the fire and poured refulgent metal into a cast. While they waited for it to harden, the smith offered the priest a cup of cool water. He smiled and drank. Suddenly, the door burst open. A gang of soldiers marched into the workshop, arrested the occupants on charges of conspiracy, and seized the gold as evidence.

At trial, few were surprised to learn that the evidence had mysteriously vanished. The missing treasure, as much as Jacopo's able defense, persuaded the tribunal to dismiss the complaint.

Years later, after the death of Paul II, a group of cardinals inspected his treasure vault. They noted fifty-four silver shells filled with pearls; a collection of jewels, including several magnificent diamonds; and a cache of unfashioned gold worth at least three hundred thousand ducats. The origin of this gold remains unknown.

Though he mourned the lost artifacts, Jacopo maintained a fervent hope that the ancient secret endured. Hidden somewhere, probably in Africa, two jars still existed. The secret brotherhood would protect them. Jacopo whispered, "One alone shall be chaste. Only when two are gathered is the truth revealed." As long as two jars survived, the prophecy would survive, and the coming evil might still be defeated.

MALTA, MARCH 2013

Once clear of Valletta Harbor, the *MV Maria Dolores* throttled up its Rolls-Royce Kamewa 80 SII engines and put out to sea. Powered by six water jets, the sixty-eight-meter catamaran could make thirty-six knots running at ninety percent capacity. The Australian-built vessel's 4.6-meter clearance height (in combination with T-foil and interceptor ride control) enabled safe, year-round operation, regardless of unpredictable Mediterranean conditions. Accordingly, the experienced captain wasn't concerned by a wall of thunderclouds looming on the eastern horizon. Over the intercom he advised his passengers that the stormy forecast was no cause for alarm. The *Maria Dolores* was designed and built for rough weather. Heavy seas might slow their voyage to Sicily, but there was no danger.

Paul led Ava through the posh club-class lounge to the observation deck. They leaned against a painted metal rail and watched the evening sun dip behind Mount Sciberras. As Tommy Dorsey's orchestra warbled through the tinny loudspeaker, Paul thought how perfectly a white cotton dress complemented Ava's tanned skin. Her long hair danced in the maritime breeze, defying her efforts to tame it. With a smile, he asked, "Where are we headed?"

"Pozzallo."

"Ah, yes. Of course. I believe that was the birthplace of the immortal Homer."

She giggled. "No, just a quaint Sicilian fishing town. It has an excellent harbor, which made it an important fourteenth-century outpost. Now it's the main port for Ragusa Province." She paused, brow knitted in concentration. "Actually, it might be the only port in Ragusa Province . . ."

Amused, Paul watched Ava search her memory. After a few seconds, he said, "It's okay. We can look it up later."

"Don't patronize me," she said, then grinned.

"What should we do while we're there?"

She thought, "Hide out, stay safe, not get killed," but she said, "We might tour the Cabrera Tower. It dates back to the 1400s."

He made a sour face.

"Or there are pretty beaches."

"Yes! I vote for the beach." He knelt and opened his backpack, wondering if he'd remembered swim trunks. He nudged aside the priceless golden disks and dug through the odd laundry. He didn't see his trunks, but, happily, he found Ava's black bikini. He pulled out the bottoms and announced, "Look! We still have—"

"Put that away immediately," Ava scolded. She grabbed the backpack, zipped it closed, and hefted it over her shoulder.

Convinced that DURMDVL's suspicions were valid, Gabe didn't dare call Ava. His only hope was that their enemies hadn't yet twigged the stratagem of inserting edited text messages into the satphone. In desperation, he typed: "Current escape plan likely compromised. Strongly recommend you cancel tickets. CHANGE PLANS and find another route! G"

Moments later, in Malta, the satphone blinked. Sheik Ahmed opened the text, read Gabe's warning, and smiled. He pocketed Ava's phone and watched the doomed catamaran vanish into the distance.

The aft engine rooms were quite cramped. In fact, the challenge of squeezing three enormous water jets into each slim hull had involved some complex engineering. To create room for the intakes and drivelines, the designers chose to mount powerful boosters above and between the tandem steering jets. It was a good design, but it necessitated running all six fuel lines through the transom. To generate its 2,465 kW (roughly 3,300 HP), each jet required a generous allowance of high-octane gas. Thus, at any given moment, a surprisingly large volume of refined petroleum pumped through the nexus.

Thunder clapped as the storm began rocking the ship. In response, the captain turned the bow into the wind and gently increased the rate at which fuel coursed through the engines. Meanwhile, inside an apparently misplaced crate labeled JOHNNY WALKER SCOTCH, a digital timer counted down the final seconds until 00:00.

A raindrop hit Paul's ear. Ava was oblivious, watching waves grow into whitecaps.

"Hey," Paul said, touching her forearm, "let's get inside before all the chairs are taken."

"That sounds good."

She looked queasy. Maybe she was nervous about the weather. Or maybe she was getting seasick. They went into the lounge but couldn't find two seats together. Frustrated, Ava looked to Paul for guidance.

"Here." He directed her to an available place. "You sit. I'll see if they have hot cocoa."

Her expression implied that cocoa didn't appeal.

"What about some proper grog?" He did his best impression of a bandy-legged pirate. Ava managed a weak smile.

"Maybe bottled water?"

"Aye, aye."

He saluted, executed an about-face, and crossed the rolling deck to the bar. He spied the cocktail waitress, a slender Italian brunette in skimpy white shorts and a tube top. Paul thought she must be freezing. He estimated her age to be twenty. She watched him approach with undisguised interest. "*Ciao, bella,*" he said. "May I see your menu?"

She opened her mouth to answer, but instead the world turned upside down. Paul experienced a bizarre sensation of weightlessness until his head slammed into the unforgiving metal ceiling. Then the lights went out.

It seemed as though a long time elapsed before he regained consciousness. When Paul opened his eyes, the ship was aflame. The club lounge was a shattered waste of broken glass and twisted steel, and it was eerily silent. Through acrid smoke, he saw wrecked furniture and motionless bodies strewn about. Abruptly, his mind focused. A single, urgent need consumed him: *Find Ava.*

He tried to stand but his legs wouldn't work. Plan B: He grabbed a dented stanchion, yanked himself upright, and found the young waitress. She was in shock, holding a paper napkin against her bloody scalp and staring into space.

"Hey!" Paul tried to yell. "Get up! Get to the lifeboats!" She didn't move. It seemed his voice didn't work, either. Then the girl snapped back to reality. Bursting into tears, she grabbed Paul's hand and began mouthing words, but he heard nothing. At that point, Paul realized that he'd been deafened.

After gently extricating himself from her grasp, he climbed, hand over hand, back to where he'd left Ava. The seat no longer existed—it had been replaced by a tangle of smoldering debris. Somewhere, down in his gut, an inconceivable, poisonous, fatal query stirred: *Is she dead?* He weakened. Then, with fury, he banished the question from his mind. He had no time for it.

At this point, Paul began shouting—though he was unaware of any sound coming from his mouth. He might have screamed Ava's name or cursed fate or even roared like a lion; it was a mystery to him. All he perceived was blood pounding in his temples. He dived through the shattered window and wriggled out onto the hull, seeking a high point from which to reconnoiter. He began climbing. Soon he could survey the catastrophe's full extent.

The *Maria Dolores* was a total loss. Hundreds must be dead. Valiant crewmen were helping survivors escape, filling lifeboats and lowering them from enormous davits. An officer waved and probably shouted instructions. Paul ignored him. He prayed that Ava was safe aboard a lifeboat, but somehow he knew she wasn't. He'd climbed rather high before he realized how slick the rain made the metal hull. Paul missed a handhold and began to slide. The instinctual terror of falling generated a blast of adrenaline, shocking his leg muscles into action. Kicking and groping, he arrested his descent by snagging a cable and pushing the toe of his boot through a broken porthole. The storm had grown, and Paul guessed this precarious perch was the best vantage point he'd attain. Using his free hand to shield his eyes from the rain, he scanned left and right. He saw several corpses, including the dismembered body of a young woman. His heart stopped. For a two-second eternity, he wasn't sure. Finally, he exhaled. *Not Ava.*

The sinking ship lurched violently. Something fluttering by caught his attention. It was a woman—falling. The unexpected jolt had pitched her overboard. Clinging to the cable, Paul saw her splash into the churning sea. He concentrated on the spot, watching for any movement. When the woman finally surfaced, Paul realized with horror that she wasn't swimming. Was she dead or just unconscious? In a few minutes it wouldn't matter. Paul had to decide. *Was it Ava?* He strained for a better perspective, but in the storm, and from this distance, he'd never be sure. He closed his eyes and replayed his memory. Someone had fallen. He slowed it, trying to view the action frame by frame, like a football slo-mo. What had grabbed his attention? What had he seen? Something fluttering. What? Hair. Long hair. Beautiful long hair.

Ava.

Paul shifted his weight and gauged the distance: about fifteen meters. Taking a deep breath, he released the cable and jumped. Falling fast, he somersaulted once and extended his body. By gyrating his arms, Paul managed to stay upright and hit the surface feetfirst. He plunged and lost all sense of direction. Then, mastering his fear, he exhaled and followed the bubbles. When he broke the surface, a wave caught him in the face, blasting saltwater into his mouth. Fluid rushed up his sinus cavities. He felt as though he was drowning. Thankfully, his second inhalation was mostly air and he began to tread water.

Paul searched for Ava, but he saw nothing. Stay calm! Taking bearings from the rapidly sinking catamaran, he reckoned she was to his north. He began swimming, keeping his face above water. A monstrous wave swamped him, and briefly he was lost. Fighting off panic, he oriented himself and kicked even harder. When a second wave lifted him he used the opportunity to survey the area. There—he saw her! In that moment, though, she slipped helplessly beneath the water.

Without pausing to breathe, Paul lowered his head, and with a furious stroke propelled himself like a torpedo through the waves. It was the fastest way. At camp, when he was ten, he'd won the fifty-meter freestyle using this tactic. Push, he told himself. She's close. A few strokes more. He accepted the heat building in his lungs. By forcibly exhaling, he squeezed out some toxic CO_2, buying precious seconds, but now his respiratory system moved into rebellion, demanding oxygen. It was impossible. He wasn't fast enough. It was getting too dark to see . . .

Ava! Underwater, he caught a glimmer of a white dress. He surfaced, sucked in all the air he could hold, and dived. As he kicked down, he tried to dislodge his heavy hiking boots, but they were laced up tight. Wait. What was that? A limp body.

Ava!

He wanted to scream her name. She looked terrible. Her eyes were shut. Her skin was a ghastly green. No bubbles came from her mouth or nose. Fear beset him. This was a lost cause. He'd arrived too late. It was her time. Just let go. Couldn't he accept the obvious?

No. He kicked down and grabbed the hem of her dress. Taking a fistful of material, he pulled her toward the surface. God, she was heavy! He kicked harder and swam with his free arm, but it was no use. He felt the current dragging them down. The surface was so distant. It was getting farther, growing darker. Paul's lungs were burning, even worse than before. Then he realized—the backpack! She was wearing that damn heavy backpack! He pulled the hunting knife from his belt and dragged its sharp edge against the straps. They cut easily. As he watched the pack disappear, he thought, "If we survive, she'll kill me."

Thus lightened, he made better progress. Each kick drew him closer to the surface. His lungs were screaming now, and he'd begun to have strange thoughts. His vision was failing, as was his ability to reason. Desperate, he urged his muscles to fight. Become a machine, he commanded. No wasted motion. Just kick and pull. Kick, kick, pull! A few hard kicks. Just a few more. Pull! Ten more. Don't quit. Five more. Don't quit. Three more. Pull!

Gasping, he broke the surface. He savored one delicious breath, then, against every vital instinct, he dived back under. Swimming behind Ava, Paul wedged his hands into her armpits and kicked. When they emerged from the sea, he rolled her onto his chest, lifting her mouth and nostrils into the air. Was she breathing? He couldn't tell. He fought to keep her head above water. Fluid drained from her nose. How long had she been under? It seemed like hours, but it must have been less than a minute. Seventy seconds max. *Come on, Ava!*

His energy was failing. He hoped his head wasn't bleeding much. From the Discovery Channel, he knew the Mediterranean was home to forty-five species of shark, including the great white. Paul looked around. No dorsal fins yet, but he didn't see any flotsam either. How long could he tread water? Floating on his back, he clutched Ava to his chest. Between strokes he reached his fingers into her mouth and forced it open wide. Then he felt something. She coughed. Alive! He felt a rush of energy. He could swim for hours. Days, even! Her body wrenched with a spasm as she spat up water. Ava inhaled. Then she vomited. Her face rolled to one side and she began shuddering with dry heaves. Paul elevated her head and fought to keep it above the surface. They maintained that position for several minutes.

Ava was breathing, he was sure, but Paul was fading. He felt something stab his calf. Cramp! Jaw clenched, he battled to keep afloat. Rain fell in sheets now, as the storm whipped the sea into a frenzy. Saltwater stung his eyes and burned in his esophagus. He snorted and coughed. Ignore it! Just kick. Breathe and kick. A little longer . . .

Shrouded in silence, he saw a tunnel of light—a bright white glow shining down from the sky. It seemed to search for him. Paul was dazed. Is that God? Am I dying? He hugged Ava. If God wanted one of them, he had to take both. We're a package deal, Lord. Take it or leave it.

The light was blinding now. It centered on him, and as though the jealous sea knew salvation was nigh, enormous waves began forcing the two under. Suddenly Paul felt hands on his arms. A powerful force took hold of him. He clung tightly to Ava, refusing to be separated from her. Then, miraculously, they began to rise from the water, ascending heavenward. The light was close now, almost close enough to touch. He reached out and realized that it was a searchlight suspended from a helicopter. As a rescue harness pulled them into the cabin, Paul rejoiced. They were saved!

Every iota of his energy spent, he released Ava and collapsed. Then, just before succumbing to exhaustion, Paul saw something that filled him with dread. It was the face of their savior: Simon DeMaj.

Gabe stared at the monitor. For a moment he experienced hysterical paralysis, limbs refusing to obey his mind's instructions. Thus imprisoned, he felt compelled to reread the Associated Press wire report.

FERRY EXPLOSION DEATH TOLL NOW 513,
GOVERNMENT CONFIRMS

VALLETTA, MALTA—At most 87 passengers and crew
will survive last night's suspected terrorist attack
on the Maltese ferry *Maria Dolores*. According to
Foreign Minister Dr. George Vella, many of the
injured are being held in critical condition, including
one young woman with both legs severed. Of the 22
patients at St. Philip's Hospital, several experienced
"massive trauma" from the shipwreck. Others were
injured by falling or jumping into the water, said a
hospital spokesman. The ferry's captain, Benjamin
Briggs, survived the incident. His condition is listed
as critical.

Authorities believe the catamaran's left engine
exploded shortly after the vessel departed Valletta at
1820 GMT, with 600 souls aboard. Helicopters and
rescue boats arrived on the scene within 30 minutes.
Throughout the stormy night, emergency workers
dumped water on the burning ship and rushed the
injured to nearby hospitals. Among the survivors,
"there were numerous injuries, including fractures
and lacerations," fire department spokesman Mario
Testa told reporters. "There were a couple of people
with amputations, legs and arms." At least 10 victims
were taken to Malta University Hospital, a surgeon
there stated. Dr. Vella told a packed news conference
that investigators suspect foul play and may officially
classify the incident as an act of terrorism.

Throughout the night, recovery teams removed bodies from the restless sea, dark now save for the occasional blue flash of emergency lights. Malta's newly elected prime minister, Joseph Muscat, cut short his holiday to supervise rescue efforts. Speaking at the airport, he said: "Our government will make every effort to support the families at this difficult moment as they receive news of the tragedy."

Injured officer E. De Bono, who helped several passengers escape the sinking vessel, said it simply "exploded laterally. We heard a huge crash, and we saw a lot of smoke." An American survivor reported that the ferry was going at a "pretty good clip" when he heard an "enormous crashing sound" and "felt a sharp jolt. Everybody then began running to grab life jackets." A British passenger told the BBC: "The back end of the vessel opened like a sardine can."

A spokesperson for Virtu, which operates the Maltese ferry to Italy, said the explosion ripped out the hull steel and windows all the way along the ship's length.

No details of the deceased passengers' nationalities or identities have been released. A local emergency service told the BBC that many children were among the victims.

The Australian-built catamaran entered service in 2005 and was used for short trips across the Mediterranean, according to marine navigation expert Captain S. A. Nelson. He added that Virtu has an excellent safety record. All ferry service remains suspended to and from Malta pending completion of the investigation.

Gabe's skin broke out in a cold sweat. Overwhelming nausea stirred within him. Finally able to move, he bolted from the chair, staggered to Jess's bathroom, and vomited into the toilet. Then he rested, panting, with his forehead against the cool ceramic. Gabe felt his larynx constrict. Tears stung his eyes. He wanted to howl in anguish, but just a moan escaped his trembling lips. In shock, Gabe only gradually became aware of the telephone's ring.

Sheik Ahmed was reading a newspaper account of the bombing. Paul and Ava were listed as "missing, presumed dead." On one level, Ahmed was satisfied: He felt proud to have accomplished an important, difficult mission. On an instinctual level, though, he worried. He'd never favored this method of killing. Not for moral reasons—he had no scruples about sacrificing so-called innocent bystanders to advance his purpose. Rather, Ahmed disliked the technique's imprecision. He'd prefer to have the Americans' corpses in his trunk. Ahmed massaged his right arm as he visualized presenting the bodies to the master as trophies and as proof of the deed. Instead, he must rely on newspapers and television— notorious fabulists—for confirmation. Ahmed had loyal men watching every hospital. He'd bribed the petty bureaucrats, nurses, and clerks. By morning they'd provide a complete list of the injured. If either American had survived the shipwreck, the sheik would be happy to finish the job in person.

Paul was playing second base for the Red Sox. Jeter was at bat. He looked to his manager for a sign. Would he bunt? Something strange was afoot. Fans began singing a song Paul remembered from *Casablanca,* the one Victor Laszlo requests. The pitcher threw Jeter a hard slider. He ripped it into the gap. Then Paul was back in the water. Ava was sinking into darkness. He lunged but he couldn't reach her hand. Struggling toward her, his legs seemed paralyzed. Then he noticed Ava's eyes. They flipped open: lifeless.

"No!"

Paul woke in a clean, comfortable room. Its walls were decorated with bright Japanese prints, a dozen Technicolor waterfalls. Sunshine glowed through a window. He guessed it was about noon. Gradually, Paul remembered. Simon. He checked for his knife, but it was gone. Reaching to his chest, he felt Garagallo's amulet under his shirt. At least they'd missed that. Paul tried to stand, but his head swam. He wondered if he was still deaf. As an experiment, he mumbled, *"J'ai mal partout,"* and was relieved when he could hear it. He touched his scalp and found that his hair was shaved down to a few centimeters. Paul's face contorted with anger. What had Simon done? Confined him in a mental institution?

He wasn't restrained, so Paul decided to escape. He found his wallet in the nightstand drawer. His boots were drying on a chair by the door. Quietly, he slid off the bed. Standing, he shifted his weight from foot to foot. His legs felt sturdy, but when he took a step he grew dizzy. Fighting to stay balanced, Paul shut his eyes, then inhaled and exhaled. The spell passed.

He padded across the room and tried the door. Unlocked. This must be a nice sanitarium, Paul reasoned, not a place for criminals. That would make things easier. He grabbed his boots, opened the door, exited the room, and crept down the hall. He should find inconspicuous clothes. No—steal an orderly's uniform . . .

A door opened. Paul flattened himself against the wall, searching for a place to hide, but it was too late. Two men entered the hallway. The first wore a dirt-stained coverall and carried a sawed-off shotgun. The second was immaculate in a tropical-weight, double-breasted pinstripe. Paul recognized the man's handmade shoes. He turned to face his adversary, and when their eyes met, Simon smiled.

Paul's hands clenched into fists as he started toward his former employer, eager to repay him, in full, for his crimes. At the last second, a familiar voice begged Paul to stop. He turned toward the speaker. To Paul's amazement, it was Ammon. The teenage smuggler stood between Sinan and Nick. Paul froze, baffled. His friends hurriedly told him that Simon wasn't the real enemy. Sheik Ahmed had betrayed him too. Sensing that his old teammate wasn't convinced, Nick explained, "Look, DeMaj just saved your life. If he wanted you dead, you'd be dead."

Paul shook his head. "Even if you're right, Nick, he ordered those guards to kill seven people. Some were just children. He's a murderer."

Finally, Simon spoke. "Paul, I understand what you must be feeling. I know why you're angry, but think carefully. What exactly did you see that night in the desert?"

"You yelled and the gunmen fired on those poor people."

"Correct," Simon agreed. "But what did I yell?"

Paul searched his memory. "I don't know," he admitted. "You spoke Arabic."

DeMaj nodded. "Yes. In Arabic, I demanded that the seven men leave my camp." Recalling that moment, a somber expression crossed his face. "I thought they planned to steal the jars. I realize now they were only trying to protect them."

He swallowed, then continued, "They refused, and I became irate. I yelled. I threatened to have them arrested and . . . worse." A note of sorrow entered his voice. "I made several threats, but I swear on my mother's grave that I never gave the order to fire. When the guards started shooting, I was as surprised as you were."

Paul regarded his former boss carefully. Simon was an accomplished diplomat. He could dissemble with great skill when necessary, but he had never lied to Paul. Furthermore, Simon revered the memory of his mother. In all the time Paul had worked for him, DeMaj never invoked her name in vain. Paul began to think he might have been mistaken. Then he realized: If Simon didn't order the guards to shoot, Paul shouldn't have taken the jars, and all the horrible things that had happened since then were his fault. His shoulders sagged.

Simon read his thoughts. "No, Paul, what you did was right. After you left, I learned Ahmed had been playing me the whole time. He'd ordered his men to kill everyone, including us, rather than lose the jars. If you hadn't acted as you did, they would have won."

As he spoke, Simon unbuttoned his shirt and revealed two ugly bullet wounds. "Later that night, Ahmed shot me. He left me in the desert to die."

Confused, Paul rubbed his scalp, wondering if all he'd just seen and heard was an elaborate con. Was he hallucinating? Had he been drugged? To hell with it, he decided. Hallucinations or not, his friends trusted DeMaj and Paul trusted his friends. Nick, Sinan, and Ammon were good people. Each in his own way was smart, cagey, and perceptive. If all three believed Simon's story, it was probably true. Paul exhaled. "Okay. Where are we?"

"Capri. This is my villa."

"Where's Ava? Is she safe?"

"Yes. She's sedated. I flew a doctor, one of the best in Europe, here from Rome. He treated Ava last night and recommended she rest for a while. Her body endured a terrible shock. It was a close call."

Nick walked over to Paul and and clapped him on the shoulder. "Your lady will be fine, *hermano*. She's just sleeping."

Paul locked eyes with Ammon. "And Sefu?"

The Egyptian smiled. "Very good! He has many new girl-friends."

Paul was mystified. Nick laughed. "Look, it's complex. Why don't we explain over lunch?"

At the mention of food, Paul's stomach rumbled. He'd eaten nothing since dinner with the bishop and was beyond ravenous. The group proceeded down into the villa's kitchen.

Designed for no-nonsense cooking, the room contrasted sharply with the household's ornate aesthetic. A central island supporting an enormous hooded grill dominated the cooking area. Stainless-steel appliances glinted below cedar cabinets. When they entered, Simon's chef opened the brick oven, releasing a combination of aromas. He withdrew a sizzling cast-iron tray of *pasta 'ncasciata,* over which Paul salivated. Nick watched in amazement as his friend devoured two servings of the baked macaroni casserole filled with ground beef, eggplant, mortadella, salami, hard-boiled eggs, tomato, basil, and grated pecorino. As they ate, Paul's friends brought him up to speed on all that had transpired since they'd parted company. Ammon described how DeMaj had found him crawling through the riverbank muck, attempting to escape the corrupt authorities. Simon revealed that the cops knew Sefu's location and offered Ammon a choice: Fly to the hospital and rescue Sefu or remain in the mud and try to avoid capture. Although he suspected a trap, Ammon opted to fly. Simon had kept his promise to help Sefu, thereby earning Ammon's trust.

"Where's Sefu?"

Nick grinned. "He's recuperating on the mainland. It's an exclusive clinic, frequented by models and actresses who want confidential lipo, nose jobs, and . . . enhancements."

As Paul laughed, a tattered baseball cap appeared on the table.

"*Shokran*," said Ammon, solemnly.

Paul nodded at the earnest young Egyptian. For a moment, neither spoke. Then Paul smiled, accepted the woefully thread-bare hat, and slapped it atop his shaved head. Everyone resumed eating. Between bites, Nick told them how Simon and Ammon had tracked him down in Egypt and convinced him that Ahmed was the true threat. Over dinner, DeMaj had persuaded Nick and Sinan that joining forces against the sheik vastly increased their collective odds. Suddenly, Nick fell silent. A moment passed before Paul realized he was the only person still eating. The others were staring past him. He turned to look. There, framed in the door-way, stood Ava.

In a rapturous instant, all of Paul's doubts and pain vanished. His heart pounded in his chest and his jaw tightened. Ava shiv-ered. Jumping from his chair, Paul rushed to her. As he neared her, she began to sob. They embraced. Tears ran down her cheeks. Holding her fragile body against his chest, Paul whispered, "Ava, I'm so sorry. I didn't know what else to do. I know you're upset. I know how much they meant to you, to archaeology, to history. I'm really, really sorry. I just couldn't think of anything—"

She pressed a finger against his lips, imploring him to hush. Shaking her head, Ava tried to speak, but the words caught in her throat.

Then DeMaj stepped in. "Why are you apologizing?"

Paul weighed his options. At this point he couldn't see a reason to keep the disks' whereabouts secret. He was fairly certain that, thanks to him, the sacred artifacts were lost forever. Of course, if anyone could retrieve the disks from the sea, it was DeMaj. Perhaps Simon wanted the disks for himself. Maybe he'd sell them on the black market. Neither outcome, though, would be worse than the current situation. Then Paul looked down at the woman in his arms. No matter what else happened, Ava was alive. Simon had helped save her. For that single act, even a thousand golden disks were an insufficient reward. Paul lifted his head.

"I lost the artifacts."

"What artifacts? The jars? You lost the jars?"

"No. Ava solved the puzzle. Inside the jars she found two gold disks inscribed with symbols and ancient writing, but I lost them in the storm. They were in my backpack, and it sank to the bottom. I'm sorry."

Paul was devastated by Simon's reaction. He'd seen his boss in some tight spots, but Simon had overcome every problem and adversary. Now DeMaj's face turned pale. His usual ferocious gaze seemed infected by despair. After several seconds, he spoke in a whisper.

"We're doomed."

DeMaj turned and walked listlessly from the kitchen. Then Ava collapsed.

Nick helped Paul carry Ava back to her room. After they laid her on the bed and covered her legs with blankets, Paul asked, "What was that? Why did Simon freak out?"

"He believes in the legend of the lost jars. He says we need them to fight the Antichrist."

Paul made a face.

"Hey, you asked, I answered, okay? You know him better than I do, but I'll tell you this: It's no bluff. DeMaj takes the concept of Armageddon seriously.

Paul shook his head. "Wow. I never pegged him as religious. In fact, I thought he was an atheist."

"Apparently, he made some kind of Damascene conversion out in the desert."

Nick left, but Paul stayed with Ava. He clicked on the TV and set it to mute. After zapping through a dozen stations, he settled on Bloomberg News. The NASDAQ was way down, but the dollar was up versus the euro. The Red Sox had begun spring training. Outside the G8 Summit, in La Maddalena, activists gathered to demonstrate. Carrying signs that demanded TAX THE RICH! MAKE THEM PAY! hundreds of protesters had marched through the city, occupied a central piazza, and erected a stage. A free concert was planned under banners proclaiming: PUTTING PEOPLE BEFORE PROFIT.

He heard Ava move. Her eyes fluttered opened.

"Paul?"

"I'm here."

"Where are we?"

"Capri. You're safe."

She took his hand and smiled. Then Ava laughed.

"What's funny?" he asked.

She pointed at the TV, then kept laughing until that segued into a hoarse coughing fit. On screen, a passionate, balding middle-aged man addressed the crowd outside the G8 Summit. He shook his fist for the cameras and yelled into the microphone.

Ava croaked, "It's Bagelton!"

"What?"

Before she could explain, Simon poked his head through the doorway. After apologizing for his odd behavior in the kitchen, he asked Ava how she felt.

She looked at the infamous billionaire. He had a distinctive way of speaking. His voice, refined by years of private schools, was a practiced and accomplished instrument of his will, but his accent was unusual. Like something from the past, a rough undercurrent persisted. Each word he spoke was gauged to convey his present emotion (in this case, curiosity), but Ava sensed that the speaker was a shell, almost like a disembodied intelligence.

"I feel fine, Mr. DeMaj. Thank you for rescuing us."

"It was the least I could do. After all, it was my fault that you were in danger."

Ava gave him an appraising look. He seemed amused by what seemed to be her suspicion.

"By way of apology, I'd like to treat you all to dinner at one of my favorite restaurants. Ava, I've taken the liberty of having some outfits delivered. I hope one of them is to your taste. Paul, the clothes you left behind in Yemen are hanging in your closet."

Everyone showered and dressed. Afterward they convened in the parlor. Only Sinan and Ammon were absent—they'd hopped across the strait in *Zulfiqar* to visit the recuperating Sefu. DeMaj poured each guest a stiff cocktail and invited all to sit. A moment later, his companion de jour, the ravishing Mellania, made her entrance. Unprepared, Ava found herself gawking. She recognized the Slovakian from her ubiquitous *Vogue* covers. A few months ago Mellania's career had taken a turn for the worse. Rumors of a serious drug habit had made tabloid headlines, prompting several designers to cancel modeling contracts. Shortly thereafter, the DeMaj spin machine launched into action. Mellania held a teary press conference at which she simultaneously denied the allegations and repented her sins. Afterward she spent six well-publicized days at an exclusive Malibu rehab center. Now in recovery, Mellania was supposedly hard at work writing her memoirs, for which she'd been promised a two-million-dollar advance.

Nick and Paul stood and introduced themselves. Polite conversation ensued, then Paul said, "Simon, this afternoon you seemed really upset about the lost artifacts. I'm glad your mood has improved."

For a beat, no one spoke. Ava and Nick shared a worried look. Then DeMaj broke the silence.

"You're right. I was upset. I apologize for my reaction. That was rude."

Paul persisted. "But are you still angry?"

"I'm dismayed by the turn of events, but in the course of my long and interesting career, I've learned it's no use crying over unfortunate circumstances. Instead, we must rise to meet each challenge and make the best of tough situations. What's the quaint American saying? When life gives you lemons . . ."

"Make lemonade?"

"Precisely."

Ava's curiosity was piqued. "So you have a plan?"

"Indeed. I've spoken with the Maltese authorities and offered my assistance in the wake of the tragedy. We must determine the explosion's cause and track down the criminals responsible. Thus, it's crucial to examine and possibly raise the sunken catamaran. The Maltese have generously agreed to let me participate in the salvage effort. I've also contacted friends in Washington. I prevailed upon the director of the National Oceanographic and Atmospheric Administration to lend me a research vessel for the duration of the investigation. Are you familiar with the *Jason* ROV?"

Ava nodded.

"As we speak, it's being refitted with a powerful magnetic scanner. I intend to scour the seabed for clues, as well as for two disks of high-density metal."

Ava jumped to her feet. "But that's fundamentally dishonest! We know who's responsible for the bombing. It was Sheik Ahmed. You're concealing the truth for personal gain."

Simon's expression was stern. "First of all, my dear, we don't know it was Ahmed. He tops our suspect list, but I fear Sheik Ahmed may be just a lackey, in the service of someone even more dangerous. Of course, I don't expect the enraged citizens of Malta to accept my word for it. The victims' families deserve a thorough investigation, and I'm doing everything in my power to ensure that they get one. Prior to the inquest's completion, I'll contribute all I know about Ahmed's possible connection to the attack."

Ava rolled her eyes. "That doesn't alter the fact that you're withholding relevant information until it suits your purposes to reveal it."

"Has it occurred to you what would happen if we disclosed the artifacts' existence? Imagine the interminable delays as a horde of petty, self-interested bureaucrats bickered over who has the legal right to salvage."

"Oh, I see. You believe it's more efficient and beneficial for a self-interested capitalist to act unilaterally."

"In this case, considering what's at stake, I do."

"And I can only imagine the exorbitant bribe you must have slipped NOAA to get its equipment."

"Let's just say the boss owed me a favor."

"I'll bet."

"Ms. Fischer, I don't claim to be a saint. Yes, I'm willing to break rules when necessary. Many times I've employed tactical misdirection, subterfuge, and other tricks to accomplish my objectives. I don't shrink from doling out an occasional bribe or campaign contribution to the appropriate official, and I have conducted business with unscrupulous characters. This is the life I chose. I don't apologize for it. Condemn me if you will, but before imposing judgment, shouldn't you at least consider the people who benefit?"

"Who? Your stockholders?"

Simon laughed. "Yes, some have done very well by investing in my companies. For example, the funds that comprise the Harvard University endowment own a substantial portion of DeMaj preferred stock, but just now I was referring to the lesser-known beneficiaries. We pour hundreds of millions of dollars into the world's most impoverished regions. By transacting business with dictators and corrupt regimes, I've materially improved the lives of thousands—tens of thousands—of actual human beings. Unlike some squeaky-clean, impotent charity, I have the connections, the power, the resources, and the respect to guarantee my money is put to good use. True, a fraction is siphoned off to pay bribes, fight lawsuits, and manufacture favorable public opinion, but the lion's share generates jobs and creates infrastructure where none existed. We finance the construction of schools, hospitals, and libraries. We're building five pollution-treatment facilities in North Africa. We've endowed university chairs in Egypt and Jordan and co-funded a massive desalination center in the Sudan. In Mozambique and Zimbabwe, we gave our customers and workers free inoculations against malaria, tuberculosis, pneumonia, and meningitis, and, perhaps most important, my projects provide Internet access to millions of destitute, disenfranchised people. Knowledge is power, Ava."

"But in spite of all your noble efforts, many in Africa have a lower quality of life today than anyone had two hundred years ago."

"True," DeMaj conceded. "But is that different from South Asia in the sixties and seventies? Health outcomes are improving. Child mortality is down, and taken as a whole, the continent's standard of living is up. Not everywhere, of course, not in Congo or Mali, but in Kenya and Ghana, personal incomes have grown dramatically."

Flushed with emotion, she shot back, "At what cost? What does a man profit if he gains the world but loses his soul."

DeMaj met her stare. "When you're young and innocent, it's easy to be critical. Because you've done nothing, you've done nothing wrong. Later, as you mature, you discover innocence was never an option. The key question isn't 'How many sins have I avoided?' Instead, ask: 'What have I created? What have I improved? How much good have I accomplished?'"

Ava was silent. Paul could see that Simon's haymaker had connected. She teetered on the brink of surrender, then rallied: "I fear your argument proves too much. Without ethical principles or boundaries, all is permitted. If nothing matters except results, you can rationalize every criminal transgression and justify every selfish indulgence."

Ava continued, confident now. "For example, what social good was accomplished when you bought this ostentatious villa and rented a washed-up supermodel?"

Simon stiffened. Nick almost spat out his scotch.

"Enough!" Paul said, taking Ava's hand. "I'm starving. Let's table this discussion until after dinner, okay?" Glancing at Simon, he asked, "By the way, where are we eating?"

DeMaj swallowed his anger and smiled. "Do you know the place where the lemon trees bloom?"

The chauffeur brought Simon's gleaming silver Maybach 62 S from the garage. Paul, Ava, Simon, and Mellania rode in back; Nick sat up front with the driver. As the others socialized, Ava gazed out through the tinted glass. She was impressed by the island's beauty and tranquillity, but Simon's argument reverberated in her mind. Though she hated to admit it, DeMaj had a point. Notwithstanding all her talents and abilities and despite her world-class education, she'd accomplished nothing that actually mattered, nothing that improved people's lives. As the sun dissolved into the horizon, she wondered if she'd chosen the right path.

Ava's thoughts were interrupted by the already-intoxicated Mellania braying that everyone must have another drink. The car's tiny wet bar featured a variety of miniature bottles. Giggling, the Slovakian bent over the seat, popped a piccolo of champagne, and filled two foaming glasses. Leering, she offered Paul a flute, allowing her arm to graze his chest as she moved. When he accepted, Ava felt a flicker in her abdomen. Nodding to the model, Paul said, "Thanks, Mel, but I prefer something less bubbly," and with a conspiratorial wink, he handed the drink to Ava. She felt dizzy.

Minutes later the car arrived at Da Paolino, a restaurant on the Marina Grande known for its Caprese cuisine. The owner met Simon at the door and led them to a table on the patio within a grove of delightful lemon trees. Ava smiled, noting that several menu items incorporated fresh lemon. Music played in the kitchen. Edith Piaf sang and an accordion bellowed. When the wine arrived, Simon raised his glass.

"*Cento di questi giorni!*"

They drank the toast and began to eat. Ava started with a salad of sliced mozzarella, vine-ripened tomatoes, and basil. Sautéed ravioli stuffed with fresh *cacciotta* (a soft-textured, mild-flavored cheese) was her main course. Between bites, Ava looked at Paul. If his freshly shorn head made him self-conscious, it certainly didn't inhibit his appetite. He demolished a titan's portion of spicy *pirciati* (pasta with anchovies, lemon, onion, garlic, capers, black olives, basil, tomato, and pepper), a spinach salad, and three glasses of Sancerre.

When Simon had finished off his rigatoni with sautéed pumpkin flowers, he leaned back, smiled, and turned to Ava. "How was your supper, Ms. Fischer?"

"Marvelous, Mr. DeMaj. Thank you. You're a generous host."

"My pleasure."

"As much as I've enjoyed this sumptuous meal, though, I can't impose further on your hospitality. How soon can we leave your home?"

He took her question in stride.

"What's the rush? Officially, you're still considered lost at sea. You never had legal permission to enter Italy, so it might be tricky to depart. Furthermore, I believe the Egyptian government has taken an interest in your whereabouts."

Paul met his eyes. "We're innocent of those charges and you know it."

"Of course, of course. It's just a technicality. My lawyers are working diligently to resolve the situation. In the meantime, may I suggest you try to enjoy a brief vacation on Capri?"

Ava began to argue but then stopped. "I suppose we can tolerate a few days here."

DeMaj smiled. "You like the island?"

"I agree with Emperor Tiberius's opinion. It's spectacular."

"Yes, Tiberius loved Capri. He spent the final ten years of his reign enjoying its serenity. Did you know he founded the first archaeological museum here?"

She nodded.

"Of course, Tiberius wasn't the only emperor to appreciate Capri's delights."

"Didn't Augustus vacation here?"

"Yes. And Caligula. Each built a villa on the island."

Nick laughed. "I've heard some crazy things about Caligula."

Ava adroitly changed the subject. "Did you know," she asked everyone at the table, "that Capri wasn't always an island?"

"How's that?" Paul said. "The strait must be five kilometers wide. Did the Romans build a giant causeway or something?"

Ava smiled. "No. According to Strabo, Capri was part of

mainland Italy. When the sea level rose, it became an island."

"Well, I think Strabo is full of it," Paul joked.

"Yeah," Mellania giggled, beaming at Paul across the table. "Me too."

Ava's face colored. Her lips thinned into an expression of disgust. Under the table she clenched her napkin and thought about strangling the empty-headed tramp.

"Regardless," said Simon, watching Ava closely, "it's an island now, and for that I'm thankful."

She turned to look at him. "Yes, I'm sure you prefer it this way. Keeps out the proletariat."

He lifted his hands in a supplicant's gesture. "If Mother Nature saw fit to provide a moat, who am I to object?"

"Of course, it's no impediment for the right kind of visitors, meaning those with private yachts."

"I don't own a yacht, *mademoiselle*."

"Oh, right. I forgot. You don't need one. You own a helicopter. Or do you have two?"

"I own twenty."

Ava gasped. "Twenty?"

"Simon collects helicopters," Paul said, hoping to defuse the situation. "It's one of his passions."

Despite herself, Ava was impressed. "You collect helicopters?"

DeMaj angled his head to one side and shrugged as only a Frenchman can—an expression of modest pride with a hint of carelessness.

"Would you care to see my collection?"

After dessert they thanked the restaurant's owner for a splendid meal. Simon's driver was outside, flirting with a hostess. Spotting DeMaj, the chauffeur ended his conversation and hurried to start the car. Ava took Paul's arm, casually ensuring that Mellania couldn't sidle in between them. The car sped back to the villa. After clearing the security gate the driver veered away from the house and approached a large, windowless structure built into the hillside. Simon typed a code into a recessed keypad and the automatic door opened. They entered a cavernous hangar full of helicopters.

With obvious pride, Simon jumped from the car and led his guests toward a Bell 47 Sioux AH1, his first purchase. Powered by a six-cylinder turbocharged engine, the Sioux had flown in Cyprus with the United Nations. Adjacent was a Sud-Ouest SO.1221 Djinn, built at Rochefort for the French army. Simon found the retired '59 Djinn in a storage facility at Versailles-Satory and restored it to glory. Nearby were two German helicopters: a Bölkow Bo.102, the first helicopter built in the Federal Republic after World War II, and an MBB Bo.105M, designed by Messerchmitt-Bölkow-Blohm for police and air ambulance.

"The 105 was a light-attack helicopter," Simon said, enthusiasm apparent in his tone. "This one was operated by the West German army."

Mellania stifled a yawn; Simon ignored it.

As he went on and on, extolling the technical merits of his '56 Bell 47H (one of only thirty-four built), Ava noted her companions' glazed expressions and experienced a moment of clarity. Is this how she sounded when talking about history? In the future, Ava resolved, she'd pay more attention to her audience and avoid smothering them with extraneous detail.

Meanwhile, Simon had directed attention to his modern exhibits. Conspicuous was an Aérospatiale SA-330 Puma that had participated in Opération Daguet.

"And this is my sentimental favorite." He gestured toward a helicopter displayed on a concrete riser: "The AS 565 Panther."

Stepping up, he placed a loving hand on the craft's fuselage. "In eighty-two, I commanded one in Lebanon. We survived some tight scrapes." For a moment, Simon was lost in reverie.

Ava whispered, "Is he for real?"

Paul nodded. "Simon loves helicopters. They're his children."

"Does he still fly?"

"Hell, yeah! He's a legit ace. He keeps all these birds in top condition, and occasionally he takes one for a spin. Whatever else you think of him, never doubt his piloting skills. Simon can really fly."

Noticing a locked doorway, Nick asked, "What's in there?"

DeMaj cocked an eyebrow. With a sly grin, he whispered, "Nothing that's included on the public tour." He pulled an electronic passkey from his jacket, swiped the door, and ushered his guests into a dark antechamber. When Simon flipped on the lights, they beheld a jet-black aerodynamic machine.

Impressed, Nick whistled. "Is that what I think it is?"

"May I present the RAH-66 Comanche prototype. Assembled in Boeing-Sikorsky's Stratford, Connecticut, facility, it first flew on January 4, 1996. Only four were completed before the U.S. Congress canceled the program."

"It must be worth a fortune!"

Pleased to have an appreciative listener, Simon expounded on the topic. "Well, the Comanche is state of the art. The LHTEC engines are shielded against infrared. Its composite airframe incorporates several antidetection features: silent running, stealth faceting, energy-absorbent materials. It's effectively invisible to radar."

"And, I presume, illegal for a private citizen to own," said Ava.

"Officially, this helicopter does not exist." Simon smiled. "But I have friends in the industry."

"I'd love to see it fly," Nick said.

Simon beamed. "I'm free tomorrow after five o'clock. Why don't we pop over to Naples for some pizza?"

"Are you serious?"

"Of course. I can accommodate two passengers, provided you don't mind getting cozy. Care to join us, Mellania?"

She demurred.

"But wouldn't that be an act of war or something? A Comanche has to be loaded with classified missiles and technology," said Nick.

"Oh, no. We'll have no problems. True, some design elements are classified, but the U.S. military removed all armaments, countermeasures, and combat equipment long before I took possession. Despite what you may have heard, I'm not in the munitions business."

Ava and Paul left the hangar together and strolled toward the villa. The main house, perched atop a high precipice, had been constructed to take advantage of the view. Hand in hand, the Americans walked to the cliff and peered over the edge. It was a stunning drop. Hundreds of feet below, waves battered ancient boulders. A boreal wind gusted in from the sea. Ava shivered, visualizing slaves thrown to their death by a sadistic emperor.

"Can we go back?" she asked. "It's getting chilly."

Paul took off his coat and draped it over her shoulders. "Follow me."

He led her through a sliding door into an airy gallery decorated with Hokusai prints. Ava relaxed. It was much warmer inside. She stopped to admire a striking Shirabyŏshi dancer. Something about the woman's attire sparked a question in Ava's mind.

"Paul, did you come up with that anagram: hat bag?"

He looked sheepish. "No. I can't take credit for that. Hatbag was Simon's code name for our dig in Israel. I had no idea what it meant until he explained. I figured you'd love it because you're both . . ."

Her voice turned cool. "We're both what?"

"Look, don't take this the wrong way . . ."

Her eyes narrowed.

"But you remind me of him sometimes."

Ava scoffed. "I hope you don't expect me to be flattered."

"No. I mean, I know you think he's an evil capitalist."

"I'm hardly alone in that judgment."

"Right, and I don't mean to offend. Obviously, you're a much better person. I'm just saying you're alike in some ways. I bet you have a lot of common interests."

Disgusted, Ava stomped off to bed. Paul started to follow, but another print, one depicting a clumsy chess player, reminded him of Sefu. Out of habit, Paul glanced at his wrist. Was it too late to call the clinic? As Ava vanished into the adjoining chamber, Paul exhaled. Someday she'd get to know Simon. The two of them would probably while away countless hours discussing Tintoretto, Sobek, Charlemagne, and Thales. Then maybe she'd understand.

Midnight found Simon and Nick seated across a chessboard. DeMaj opened with the King's Gambit, sacrificing a pawn to gain a commanding position. Sipping his single malt, Nick mounted a vigorous counterattack, but on the twenty-seventh move, he faced a dilemma: whether to exchange his active knight for a defensive bishop. After some thought, Nick passed on the exchange and retreated his piece. Pouncing, Simon advanced his queen. "Mate in six," he announced.

Nick slumped. Then, straightening his back, he began to reset the board. Glancing up, he caught his opponent in a smirk.

"Don't get cocky, DeMaj. I play better after I take my first lick."

Simon laughed. "Like Masséna."

"Who?"

"Marshal Masséna was a brilliant tactician, perhaps Napoleon's best field commander. Bonaparte said Masséna was useless until the first cannons fired, then he became a lion."

"Sounds like my kind of guy."

"Mine too," Simon agreed. "Nick, you play well, but withdrawing your knight was a mistake."

"I felt vulnerable."

"Conquer that fear. Use it to your advantage. Weak players shy away from open, complex positions because they dread the unknown. They tie themselves in knots to avoid exposing their king, afraid the essential piece will be caught in the crossfire, and to be sure, common sense supports this habit. Superlative players, on the other hand, embrace complexity, seizing opportunities to attack from unexpected angles. Create confusion, then let your opponent's aggression work against him. Tempt him into rash moves by risking something precious. In my experience, a queen standing brazenly undefended often lures the enemy into a fatal error."

Nick pushed himself back from the table and gave Simon a long, appraising look. After a moment, DeMaj inclined his head and said, "Shall we play again?"

15

The sheik's call woke Barakah at two in the morning.

"Meet me at the harbor immediately."

A half hour later four men were cruising north aboard the *Saracen,* a Riva 63 Vertigo. The glassy Mediterranean shimmered under the full moon's glow. Ahmed took a long drag from his cigarette. Tossing it overboard, he directed Barakah to follow him belowdecks and shut the door. The cabin's dark hardwood floor contrasted with its pale oak, leather-bound bulkheads. In this private setting, Ahmed revealed some information gleaned from his spy within the DeMaj household.

Both targets had survived the shipwreck. Consequently, the master had directed Ahmed to eliminate the troublesome Americans before they interfered with his *Piano di Rinascita* (Plan of Rebirth). Ahmed didn't appear angry or frustrated by this turn of events. In fact, he seemed elated. Emboldened by the sheik's high spirits, Barakah pressed a question.

"What is the Plan of Rebirth?"

Ahmed eyed his assistant. "Be patient. Soon, all will be revealed. The time is near. With one bold stroke, our master's grand vision will be realized. I cannot disclose details, but take comfort in the knowledge that you will play an important role."

Barakah nodded, apparently satisfied.

They reached Marsala in less than three hours. Ahmed throttled down the twenty-four-cylinder shaft drive and steered into Don VeMeli's secluded harbor, where a team of dockworkers waited. Each man wore a red Gruppo Garibaldi armband. Refueling was conducted in silence and with efficiency. As dawn broke over Sicily, Barakah cleaned and loaded his automatic pistol. He reclined into the comfortable leather seat, mouthed a prayer, then slept. Spiritually, he was at peace and ready to perform his sworn duty.

The next morning everyone except Mellania, who claimed illness, met for breakfast. Ava was the last to arrive.

"*Buon giorno,* Ms. Fischer. Did you sleep well?"

"Quite well, Mr. DeMaj, thank you."

"I heard a nasty rumor that you prefer tea to coffee."

"I'm afraid so."

Shaking his head with exaggerated disdain, Simon muttered, "*De gustibus non disputandum est*" (there is no disputing tastes). Then he signaled to the cook, who brought forth a sky-blue porcelain tea service. Ava was struck by how lovely it was. The delicate china was almost translucent.

Feigning nonchalance, she inquired, "Tang dynasty?"

Simon inverted a bowl to reveal its inscription. "Can you translate?"

"'Made on the sixteenth day of the seventh month of the second year of the reign of Emperor Yingsong,'" Ava whispered.

DeMaj filled a cup with fragrant *keemun hao ya* and presented the steaming tea to Ava. She inhaled its bouquet, and immediately her shoulder muscles relaxed. All her anxiety faded. She drank. The complex black brew conveyed a pastoral sweetness accented with a hint of rose. She raised her eyes to Simon's. "This is sublime," she said.

He acknowledged her compliment with a small bow. While his guests finished eating, DeMaj left the room. He returned a moment later and handed Ava a thin black rectangle linked to a plastic cord.

"Thank you?" she said, confused.

"It's a digital encryption scrambler. Plug it into the headset jack on your world phone, enter a sixteen-digit code, and it'll roll the scrambling up several thousand times, giving you hours before the pattern recycles. My team estimated the fastest computer on earth would need twelve hours to derive the sequence. Provided you change your code reasonably often, conversations are secure. I presume you have some calls to make. Your parents, in particular, will be happy to hear from you."

Ava arched an eyebrow. "You spoke to them?"

"Your mother is a bright, charming lady. We contacted your friend Gabriel too, but when I assured him you were safe, he seemed . . . skeptical."

Ava's eyes widened as she realized that the shipwreck would have been international news. Her parents, Gabe, and Jess must be worried sick! Excusing herself, she grabbed the scrambler and rushed upstairs.

Paul asked then: "What about DURMDVL? Does he know we survived?"

Simon chuckled. "Your DURMDVL has proved difficult to locate. The whole crypto team is impressed by his security. At one point we thought we had him. Instead, the rabbit trail led us to a horrible Rick Astley video."

"What the hell is that?"

"DURMDVL's idea of a joke, apparently."

Ava found that the world phone they'd purchased in Malta was still functional thanks to its waterproof casing.

A female voice answered Ava's dialing.

"Hello?"

"Mom? It's Ava."

"Oh, thank God you're safe!"

"Yes, I'm fine. It's wonderful to hear your voice. I thought it would go straight to voice mail."

"No, no. I've been waiting by the phone all day. Mr. DeMaj told me to expect your call."

"I'm not sure we can trust him."

"Well, he saved my baby's life. That makes him a friend until I have reason to believe otherwise." Ava thought she heard a tremble in her mother's voice. Embarrassed, she changed the subject. Besides, switching to small talk might erase some of her mother's worry.

"So, why are you home on a school day?"

Her mother laughed. She taught music at Sidwell Friends, an elite private school. When the headmaster learned Ava had been aboard the *Maria Dolores,* he gave her the week off.

"You're right. I should go back, now that I know you're safe, but honestly, I'm enjoying my mini-vacation. Anything to avoid those overprivileged kids and office politics."

Ava knew her mother was joking. She had never wanted to teach. She took the job so Ava could attend Sidwell without paying the astronomical tuition. But Ava's mother had grown to enjoy her work. Every so often she connected with a particularly gifted child. Such moments made the tedious hours of babysitting and bureaucracy worthwhile.

Ava and her mother chatted for a while. They laughed and exchanged stories, relishing the joy of conversation, but when Ava mentioned Paul, her mother became intensely curious.

"Paul? Paul who? Not the same Paul you liked in college?"

Blood rushed to Ava's cheeks and she shifted uncomfortably. "Yes, I guess so. Anyway, Jess and Gabe are waiting to hear from me . . ."

"So, when will you be coming home?"

"Soon. There are a few things I need to finish here."

Ava's mother caught the tone of her daughter's reply and decided not to argue—they'd been down that path before. "Okay, sweetheart. Keep in touch, and please try to be careful. We want you home in one piece!"

Ava said good-bye to her mother, then dialed Jess's number. A British voice answered. Once Jess realized it was Ava, she covered the receiver and called out, "Gabe, pick up. It's Ava!" Then: "Darling, are you safe? We've been so worried!"

Happy to speak to each other again, Ava and Jess chatted and giggled like children. Their reunion was interrupted by Gabe's rush of questions about the shipwreck. Eventually, he said, "Ava, I don't know how to tell you this. The disks—"

"What? Tell me!"

He sighed. "The audio from the disks is, well, it's garbage. I isolated the two recordings. They were roughly identical. Unfortunately, both have been corrupted. Too many years in the desert. Maybe the grooves degraded over the centuries. All that remains is a weird clamor and some incomprehensible moans. I'm sorry. I tried to clarify, but there isn't enough there."

"Both disks?"

"I'm afraid so." He sounded despondent.

"Just send me whatever you've got."

"Ava, you don't understand. The data's ruined. It's gibberish."

"I want to listen, okay? Even if it's gibberish, it's two-thousand-year-old gibberish. I almost died for this stuff, Gabe. I need to hear it for myself."

"Of course," he said. "I'll e-mail the files ASAP."

After she finished her phone calls, Ava slipped down to the study, where Simon kept a few computers available for guests' use. She logged on to the Internet, and for the first time in weeks she opened her e-mail. Naturally, the inbox was jammed with messages. Ignoring dozens, she identified Gabe's most recent. Two files were attached. Each contained the audio captured from a golden disk. She downloaded both attachments onto a flash drive. Then, holding her breath, she opened and played the first file. It was just as Gabe described: harsh, atonal sounds with bizarre moans in the background.

Ava realized someone was knocking. She clicked PAUSE and called out, "Who is it?"

"It's Paul. Are you all right? I heard creepy noises."

Hurrying him in, she explained what Gabe had discovered and unpaused the recording. Surprised at first, Paul wrinkled his nose at the howls and creaks. He could see Ava was disappointed. On the brink of tears, she said, "It's ruined. Whatever was on those disks is lost. Maybe the audio data degraded after so many years. Maybe we screwed up the scan. Or maybe you were right: Ancient peoples never had the necessary technology . . ."

He touched her arm. "Hey, let's get out of here. Just us. Want to go for a hike around the island?"

"That sounds nice."

They decided to explore Punta Cerena by way of the Sentiero dei Fortini (Footpath of the Fortifications). Ava returned to her room, donned a navy blue minidress, slid her feet into sandals, and tied her hair with a silk ribbon; she would meet Paul outside.

The afternoon was glorious. Gulls called and wheeled, riding thermals up the cliff wall. Ava let Capri's light and crisp blue sky revive her spirits. She found Paul in the garden, wearing his lucky cap, sharing cashews with an appreciative red squirrel. Simon's loyal groundskeeper and bodyguard, Tomás, was stationed atop the garden wall, brandishing a lupara. He raised a hand in greeting, looking like an extra from *The Godfather*. Under Tomás's watchful gaze, the Americans passed through the pergola, crossed the outer courtyard, and departed.

They took a bus part of the way, then enjoyed a quiet stroll along the island's southwest coast. Hand in hand they sauntered past the Orrico, Pino, and Mesola, French forts used when Capri was part of the Napoleonic empire. Flowers perfumed the Mediterranean air. The footpath terminated at the Lido del Faro, a popular swimming spot, with boats for rent and rusted iron steps leading down into the sea. At the poolside café, Paul found a table with a lighthouse view. The bartender served Paul a glass of cold Forst beer; Ava asked for pinot grigio. Relaxed and happy, they sat on the sun-kissed terrace. Ava leaned back in her chair and closed her eyes. Paul sipped beer and smiled. He could stay here forever.

Nick met Simon at the hangar just before sunset. The two men climbed into the Comanche's futuristic-looking cockpit and initiated its prelaunch sequence. Moments later, they were aloft.

Nick marveled at the chopper's silence. "How can it run so quietly?"

"Amazing, yes? Honeycombed dampers and vibration mounts muffle the engine, and an ingenious configuration of airfoils, blades, and tips diminishes rotor sound. All that goes only so far, of course: The real sorcery is ANC."

"Antsy?"

DeMaj laughed. "Active Noise Cancellation."

"Which means?"

"Sound-field modification by electroacoustical means."

"Oh, right. Obviously."

"It's simple, really." Simon tapped a box above his head. "The master control 'listens' and responds to unwanted noise by driving a speaker to produce an opposite sound field. Opposite fields cancel each other, and the result is silence."

Nick shook his head. "That's wild."

Simon grinned. "That's nothing. Wait till you see her move!"

In the graying twilight Barakah yawned, then rose. He took night-vision binoculars from his equipment bag and examined the rocky shore. Soft spray blew in loose clouds above blackened stones. He glassed up to the commanding escarpment and studied the view. There was no sign of the house, but segments of well-paved road descended between the ancient trees. By instinct more than training, he scanned for movement. Detecting none, Barakah lowered the glasses, took a deep breath, and wiped his nose on the back of his sleeve. Resuming his vigil, he watched as dusk turned to dark.

Ava opened her eyes. Content, she watched Paul, who watched the sea. Then she noticed something around his neck.

"Is that necklace new?" She'd never seen him wear jewelry.

"Necklace? Oh, wait. You mean this?" He reached under his shirt and withdrew the golden amulet. "Bishop Garagallo said it would protect us."

272

"Why didn't you show me?"

"I was afraid you'd call it superstitious nonsense.'"

Ava laughed. "May I?" He handed it over. As she examined the markings, her brow furrowed.

"The symbols match the shield behind his desk."

"Yeah, you're right. Do they mean something?"

"I'm not sure," she replied, returning the amulet. "But I've seen it somewhere . . ."

"Think food would help your memory?"

"Absolutely!"

Instead of getting a menu, Paul let the waiter choose for them. As an appetizer he brought a loaf of Apulian-style scanata bread covered with sesame seeds. Paul dragged a slice through olive oil, balsamic vinegar, and fresh herbs and popped it into his mouth. Dinner was octopus *a strascinasali* (boiled octopus dressed in olive oil and fresh lemon), sardines *a beccafico* (rolled sardines stuffed with sautéed bread crumbs, pine nuts, and anchovies), and *patati cunsati* (seasoned potatoes), washed down with another round of drinks.

Later, the soothing sound of waves against rocks was pierced by a squeal of electronic feedback. A ska band had taken the stage and was tuning up. The waiter explained that the restaurant sometimes offered live music and occasionally fireworks. At the mention of pyrotechnics, Paul blushed, recalling his embarrassment at Bishop Garagallo's. He promised not to throw Ava on the floor again. She gave him a noncommittal smile, moistened her middle finger, and rescued a fallen sesame seed from the table linen. Paul wondered what she was thinking.

That night the two Americans strolled toward the Orrico bus stop under a gigantic moon. Paul studied his companion's face.

She seemed lost in contemplation. To ease her mind, he said, "Suppose you have two buckets and a water hose. One bucket holds five gallons, the other holds three. How can you measure four gallons?"

For a nanosecond, Ava seemed annoyed. Then, with a grin, she said, "Use the hose to fill the larger bucket. Pour water into the smaller one until it's full. Dump out the small bucket. Pour the remaining contents of the large bucket into the small bucket. Refill the large one. Pour water from the larger bucket into the smaller. When the small bucket is full, the larger one will contain four gallons."

Paul laughed. "Wow! I guess that was easier than I thought."

"It's a classic. I've heard it before."

"Oh, sorry. Want another?"

"Bring it."

"A prisoner is trapped in a cell. On the wall are two buttons, one directly above the other. The correct button opens his cell. The other button opens an adjoining cell. He doesn't know which button to push. Because he has just one chance to escape—by throwing his food bowl at the proper button—should he aim for the top or bottom?"

Another smile: Ava's mood was improving. "Is that it? Do you want the answer?"

"No, there's more. I forgot to say that the prison is on that crazy island."

"What island?"

"The one where every man acts rationally but also cheats on his spouse."

"What difference does that make?"

"It keeps the divorce lawyers busy."

She laughed, not so much at the lame joke, but at Paul's

attempts to lift her spirits. In a flash she realized why he'd always been so popular. It wasn't just because he was handsome, athletic, and from a prominent family. Rather, people gravitated to Paul because he cared. When he saw someone hurting, Paul's instinct was to give comfort and cheer. Ava loved that about him.

"So, what's your final answer?"

Leaning close, she whispered. "He should aim to hit both buttons."

"Nice," said Paul. "Most people don't think of trying both at once."

Ava froze. She recalled something Clarkson had said: "The two gods speak with one mouth." An idea went through her mind. Invigorated, she surprised Paul with a peck on the cheek.

"Let's go home. I want to check something."

Simon landed the Comanche on a private helipad just outside Naples. They transferred to a waiting car, which then brought them deep into the city. Minutes later they were seated in the downstairs section of Pizzeria Brandi. A waiter appeared.

"Do you like Margherita?" Simon asked Nick.

"Sure. Just like Mama used to make."

"*Due, per favore, e vino.*"

While they waited, Nick noticed that his companion's mood had changed. "Is something wrong?"

Simon rubbed his temple. "Sorry. Today's the anniversary of my mother's death. She passed when I was six."

"That must have been hard, but if it's any consolation, I'm sure she'd be very proud of you."

Simon lifted his head. "You think so?"

"Absolutely."

"I hope so. I know she'd want me to resist the coming evil. She'd urge me to fight until the bitter end. That really would make her proud."

Before Nick could say something else, Simon lifted a hand for silence. Several boisterous customers were watching the television and applauding. Nick recognized their red armbands. The reporter spoke.

"Following this afternoon's emergency session, a Gruppo Garibaldi spokesman blamed Islamic extremists for the terror attack. 'This is mass murder,' said Galeazzo Grandi, who himself survived a car bombing in 1995. 'The time for negotiations has passed. More than half the victims were Italian citizens. What will those people do next?'

"Maltese Minister B. C. Pisani, who has repeatedly urged his government to hunt down the attackers, was pleased by the Italians' support. 'I agree that negotiation is undesirable and impossible with these assassins, who so many times have sown death,' he said, reading from a prepared statement.

"In Washington, the State Department pledged solidarity: 'The United States stands resolutely with our European allies in the fight against terrorism in all its forms. No political pretext can justify premeditated murder.'

"A confidential source close to the investigation has revealed that the bombers used titadine, a type of compressed dynamite. The Islamist group Hamas recently purchased eight tons of titadine, according to Spain's *El Mundo* newspaper. Nevertheless, a U.S. intelligence official, speaking on condition of anonymity, questioned whether the bombers were Islamic terrorists. 'It's too early to tell who is responsible. We're not ruling out anyone yet.'

"Deputy Grandi disagreed. 'We all know who did this. As usual, liberal appeasers and fifth columnists oppose any appropriate response, insisting nothing be done until the investigation is complete, but we can't afford the luxury of certitude. We must act now before the terrorists perpetrate an even greater tragedy.'"

Simon rose from his seat. "It's time to go."

Sheik Ahmed was not a real sheik; he'd appropriated the title, just as he had seized everything else he possessed. Ahmed's parents, Arab peasants, had died in Egypt's Six Day War against Israel. The penniless orphan was then "adopted" by a Cairo brothel catering to wealthy Europeans with perverted sexual tastes. Trapped in this hell, Ahmed learned the power of fear. As he fought to survive, he began to value strength and cunning above all other attributes.

A bright, attractive child, by his tenth birthday he'd perfected a means of enriching himself while avoiding degradation. After charming an intoxicated pedophile, Ahmed would slip narcotic powder into the john's drink, preventing him from acting on his lust. The potent drug rendered a victim unconscious for several hours. During this period, Ahmed helped himself to currency from the slumbering European's wallet or purse. He learned to pocket no more than a few bills, sums that would be overlooked in the morning stupor. He reinvested the stolen funds, purchasing ever bigger parcels of narcotics. Within two years the local dealer was complaining that little Ahmed had cut into his profits.

On a moonless night Ahmed ambushed and garroted his competitor, supplanting him as the brothel's main supplier. This aggressive move brought Ahmed to the attention of the local Mafia, who dispatched a pitiless Italian thug nicknamed La Belva (the Beast) to untangle the situation.

La Belva captured the scrawny twelve-year-old brat who'd dared to commit murder and administered a savage beating, but when little Ahmed accepted the blows without a single tear or a whimper, the Beast smiled. Soon, Ahmed was his favored protégé. The hardened child followed his Italian master everywhere, absorbing innumerable lessons in cruelty and violence. Ahmed never blamed his idol for beating him senseless. Instead, he came to believe that he deserved it.

The Beast was fearless, bloodthirsty, and dynamic. Ahmed worshipped him. As the thin boy matured into a solid teen, he became the Italian's trusted subordinate and most merciless enforcer. At twenty-five, Ahmed assumed full responsibility for the network's operations in Egypt. By then the Beast, who'd become Don VeMeli, had branched into politics. Ahmed provided invaluable support. The rising capo was continually awed by his master's ingenious schemes. Year by year their power, wealth, and influence grew. Consequently, Ahmed's faith in Don VeMeli was limitless. He'd rather die than disappoint him.

Ahmed sat in the darkness and smoked. His very existence was proof that he'd never failed his master. He massaged the arm Don VeMeli had broken all those years ago. Unaware that he was speaking aloud, Ahmed promised: "I will kill them for you, master. We cannot fail. I will slice their privileged little throats. I will cut out their arrogant, disrespectful hearts."

Paul and Ava rushed back to Simon's villa. As they hustled through the back gate, Paul glanced around for Tomás. Curiously, he was nowhere in sight. Paul slowed, scanning the courtyard. Impatient, Ava grabbed his hand and dragged him into the house and to the study. She turned on a computer. She located the memory stick containing the encrypted wave files Gabe had transmitted and began saving them to the hard drive. Meanwhile, she asked Paul to power up another laptop. Though he didn't know her purpose, he complied. A few minutes later, both computers were operative.

"What now?"

Instead of answering, Ava uploaded the data onto the second computer. On the first, she opened the recording Gabe had captured from the artifact marked CHI. On the second, she opened the file he'd derived from the RHO disk.

"When I count to three, hit play," she ordered. "Ready? One, two, three, play!"

They clicked the two buttons simultaneously. After a brief pause, the eerie noises began, just as before. Ava held her breath. Then the clamor changed. Instead of discordant noise, actual music emerged.

Ava shook her head. "Gabe guessed it right off the bat: mutually interdependent sequences." The two recordings contained a common set of sounds but they were out of phase. Played sequentially, the disks produced jarring nonsense; played simultaneously, they harmonized. And when the libretto began, it wasn't alien gibberish. Rather, it resembled a Gregorian chant. Paul watched Ava listen, enthralled by the otherworldly voices she'd discovered. Then she began to quiver.

Touching her shoulder, he whispered, "What's the matter?"

She turned. He saw fear in her eyes.

"I . . . I think I can understand it."

He took her hands. "What are they saying?"

"Something horrible."

NEAR CALA D'INFERNO, ITALY

The master reclined in his private study, watching the news

on television. NBC reported that on Monday, the College of Cardinals would meet for the first time since the pope's resignation. "Under the supervision of Cardinal Angelo Sodano, the college will convene to deal with important ecclesiastical business, but Vaticanologists say some of the most significant discussions will unfold at private apartments, in restaurant backrooms, and around the coffee urn as cardinals meet in small groups to suss out who among them will become the next pope. After the congregations, the caucusing continues in informal, intimate settings. 'All the real business takes place at night over anisette and grappa,' said Christopher Bellitto, associate professor of history at Kean University.

"Modern conclaves have not lasted more than a few days—not surprising, as the whole point is to decide quickly. Nevertheless, it's a tedious and time-consuming process. There are as many as two ballots every morning and two ballots every evening. Each cardinal takes an oath before casting a vote and the totals are tallied three times. It all happens in the Sistine Chapel, where silence is mandatory. The modern procedure was created by Pope Gregory X after a papal election that dragged on from 1268 to 1271, infuriating the people.

"Some speculate that the 2013 conclave will be the longest of the past one hundred years, but Vatican expert George Weigel disagrees. 'Although it's true that there are many possible candidates, there's also a sense that this is a critical moment in the Church's history.' With the eyes of the world focused on Rome, the cardinals are under intense pressure to elect a new pope within three days."

The master laughed. "'How poor are they that have not patience.'" He glanced at the clock, dizzy with excitement. So few hours remained! After years of planning and preparation, the day of reckoning had arrived.

Ava reset the files and prepared to listen again to the otherworldly recording. She reviewed her notes: scribbles of words and bits of sentences on a yellow legal pad. She felt compelled to translate the message, but it wouldn't be easy. Looking up, she saw that Paul was staring out the window. He seemed nervous.

"What's outside?" she asked.

"Oh, nothing. I'm just surprised Tomás isn't here."

"Maybe Simon gave him the night off. Or maybe he went with them to the mainland. Who knows?"

"Yeah, I guess. Anyway, are you about done?"

She made a face. "You must be joking. Consider the problem's complexity. I don't speak the base language. I'm not sure anyone does. It resembles Old Syriac, but it's funky. I'm speculating, but I think the vowel sounds may have shifted over the millennia. I recognize some basic structures, a few terms might be correlates, but I can't just wave a magic wand, shout Eureka! and knock out a transcript."

"But I thought—"

"Language is idiomatic, Paul. Grammar matters. For example—" she looked down at a sequence in her notes and said—"this word is repeated throughout. I suspect it means 'pilgrim,' but it could just as easily mean 'journey' or 'travel.' It could also be a verb, as the word *voyage* can be a noun or a verb, and it might mean different things at different times, *capisce?*"

He looked hurt. "Of course. I didn't mean—"

She softened. "I know. You didn't mean to be impatient or

disrespectful, but I'm trying to decipher a message that's at least two thousand years old and written in an obscure dead language. The process takes time. Plus, I don't even have the crucial reference materials."

Paul nodded, chastened. "Okay. So let's get the hell out of here and go to a library. Let's call Gabe and Professor Clarkson."

"No. Before we tell anyone, we need an idea of what it says. Someone murdered hundreds of people to prevent us from decoding this message. I won't put our friends in jeopardy again until we know why."

"Wait till we tell Simon! He'll call in favors with the NSA, hire a team of Nobel Prize–winners, and you two can write a comprehensive, scholarly article for *Scientific American*."

Ava wasn't amused. Rather, she looked frightened.

"What's wrong?"

Her eyes dropped to the notebook. "Paul, I'm pretty sure this sequence means 'rising demon' or 'new devil.' Frankly, there's a lot in here about the devil. Remember what Garagallo said about Antichrists? I think this is some kind of warning."

"What's the point of that? Everybody knows the Antichrist is bad news."

Ava didn't laugh. "This says: 'He is here.'"

Gabe woke from a pleasant dream. He yawned, stretched, and scratched his neck. The wall clock indicated that it was almost suppertime. Gabe rolled off the couch and when he stood, his knees protested audibly. Surveying the small apartment, he thought: What a mess!

Jess was back from class; he could hear her singing in the tub. Thirsty, he staggered to the fridge. When he peered inside, he chuckled. The bottom shelf held thirty-six cans of Coke, organized into six neat rows of six cans each. She must have hit the grocery while he was napping. He grabbed a can, popped the top, and closed the door. Just then, his computer beeped. Taking a swig, he walked over to the desk: He'd received an encrypted message from DURMDVL. While waiting for it to unscramble, he blew his nose, swallowed a Sudafed, and chased it with another gulp of Coke.

He settled into the comfy chair and began to read: "GET OUT OF THE APARTMENT. THEY'RE COMING."

The message sent his body into maximum alert. He began breathing faster and deeper. His adrenal glands spewed epinephrine, causing his heart to pound. Gabe stumbled to the apartment's front window and separated the blinds. As he looked out, a white van entered the lot below. Its doors opened, and two armed men emerged. His stomach clenched. They'd found him.

16

Regal Constantine rode through his camp near Prima Porta. He dismounted, went into his tent, and allowed a valet to remove his armor. Then, exhausted, he collapsed and ordered a bath. The strategist reclined his head and reflected. It had been an interesting year: Only seven months ago, he gathered this army, crossed the Cottian Alps, and conquered northern and central Italy. Beloved by the people, Constantine advanced slowly along the Via Flaminia, watching the opposition's morale deteriorate and achieving many victories without bloodshed.

Now he faced a true challenge. His enemy, Maxentius, controlled Rome and the Praetorian Guards. Though the populace despised Maxentius, the city was well fortified, stocked with African grain, and protected by the almost impregnable Aurelian Walls. Constantine's advisers expected Maxentius to sit tight, as he had during the invasion of Severus in 307 and of Galerius in 308. Constantine knew the city's defenses were formidable and that they could withstand any siege. A new stratagem was required.

A guard shouted: "Augustus! A message!"

Constantine accepted the letter and, recognizing his mother's seal, ripped it open. Flavia Iulia Helena was a remarkable woman. Born a stable maid, she had used her wits and charm to rise in society, eventually marrying the governor of Dalmatia. Since his death she'd spent most of her time unearthing relics in Jerusalem.

"Beloved Son," he read, "I write today from Palestine, near the site of Christ's tomb. Please accept Bishop Macarius as my emissary and grant him an audience. He brings an offer of certain victory over the forces of evil."

Constantine raised an eyebrow. Certain victory?

"Macarius carries relics of astonishing power," she continued. "They can render your army invincible, if its cause is just. Son, I know you believe the Empire should tolerate all religions. To prove your sincerity, swear two things: First, promise to extend the religious freedom you granted Gaul, Spain, and Britain to the entire Empire. Second, promise to honor the Christian God by razing the vulgar temple Hadrian built near Calvary and constructing a grand cathedral in its stead. May divine favor preserve your successes together with the good of the state. May God grant you victory!"

He pondered the unusual offer. His first thought was to disregard it as mere superstition, but he'd learned to value his mother's counsel. She'd advised his father and helped him achieve great things. He understood her appeal for religious freedom. Helena was a devout Christian, a follower of a faith that was illegal throughout most of the empire. Politically, it would be difficult to legalize Christianity, but if the offer was legitimate . . .

"Summon the emissary," Constantine ordered. The guards ushered in Bishop Macarius, who bowed respectfully.

"I'm told you bring powerful relics. Show me."

Constantine gazed in wonder at the shining disks, each golden as the sun, and listened to angelic voices. Two scribes, one Greek, one Roman, translated the message. When Constantine heard "In this sign, you will conquer," he knew just what to do. That night, as his troops prepared for battle, Constantine commanded them to paint a new sigil on their shields: chi (**X**) crossed by rho (**P**).

Wicked Maxentius brooded in his palace. His situation was dire. The populace was beginning to support that son of a harlot Constantine. Citizens cheered for him, shouting acclamations during circus games. At the afternoon chariot races, spectators taunted Maxentius, chanting that Constantine was invincible. Maxentius knew Rome's defenses could withstand a long siege, but if the people turned against him, he might not survive.

A messenger approached.

"What news?"

"Master, the keepers of the Sibylline Books have seen a prophecy. It foretells that the enemy of Rome will die tomorrow, on the anniversary of your accession."

Maxentius was elated. He believed his anniversary to be a lucky day. Confident of victory, he issued bold new orders: "Prepare the army. Tomorrow we march north to defeat Constantine in open battle. We'll see who is invincible."

Maxentius crossed the Milvian Bridge, a stone structure carrying the Via Flaminia across the Tiber. Holding the bridge was crucial to defending Rome. He organized his force, which was twice the size of Constantine's, into long lines with their backs to the river.

Soon, Constantine's soldiers appeared. Instead of traditional standards, their shields displayed the mysterious new insignia. The army deployed along the length of Maxentius's line and attacked. It was not a long battle: Constantine's cavalry routed that of

Maxentius. Constantine then sent his infantry, who pushed the rest of Maxentius's troops into the Tiber. Many were slaughtered or drowned. The disciplined praetorians at first held, but under relentless assault they finally broke. Fearing defeat, Maxentius ordered a retreat. Only one escape route remained: the bridge. Then, miraculously, the bridge collapsed. All of Maxentius's soldiers were killed or taken prisoner. Maxentius himself drowned in an attempt to swim across the river.

Constantine entered the city in triumph. Jubilant that the enemy of Rome had finally been defeated, crowds celebrated their new emperor's grand entrance, parading Maxentius's severed head through the streets. Constantine returned seized property, recalled exiles, released political prisoners, and offered the Senate a role in his government. He forgave Maxentius's supporters and vowed to extend religious tolerance throughout the empire. In response, the Senate proclaimed him "the greatest Augustus."

For almost thirty years Constantine traveled with the golden disks and marched under the CHI-RHO symbol, which came to be known as the Labarum. Thus armed, he achieved victories at Cibalae, Adrianople, the Hellespont, and Chrysopolis. After Constantine's death, the sacred relics remained in Rome, protecting the Eternal City from evil.

BOSTON, MARCH 2013

Gabe burst into Jess's bedroom. She grabbed a towel and covered herself. Gabe hadn't even noticed that she was naked. He locked the door behind him. "How high is the balcony?"

"What? Why do you—"

"Those men are outside! Can we climb down?"

She shook her head. "I don't think so."

Furious, Gabe ran his hands through his hair, trying to think. Jess pointed to her bathroom. "How about that window?"

He raced into the tiny room. Its tiled floor was covered with dirty laundry and towels. Just outside the window was a big swamp oak. One branch looked close enough to reach. Standing on the toilet, he unlatched the window and tried to lift it, but several coats of paint had sealed it shut. After quickly donning jeans and a sweatshirt, Jess rushed to help. She locked the door as Gabe drew a Swiss Army knife from his pocket, flipped it open, and began gouging into cracks. Seconds later the two of them heaved against the pane. Wood split with a loud crack. Holding the window open, Gabe kicked the mesh screen. It bent, snapped off, and dropped. Involuntarily, Jess gulped.

Someone was now rapping on the apartment door.

"Hurry!"

Taking Jess's hand, Gabe helped her up. Nervously, she poked her bare feet through the opening, then, with a dancer's grace, eased herself out. Balanced on the sill, she let her heels glide across the dry stucco ledge until they wedged against a decorative corner piece. Gripping tightly, Jess looked down. She'd be lucky to survive, she thought. She studied the oak. Its closest branch was four feet away though it seemed miles. Jess glanced back at Gabe, eyes asking if this evacuation was absolutely necessary. As if in reply, the apartment door crashed open.

"Go, you'll make it," Gabe said urgently.

Jess took a breath and jumped.

She hit the branch hard, scraping her cheek and biting her tongue. Rough bark bit into her skin. Terrified, she hugged the tree and tasted warm blood. With supreme effort, Jess overcame her fear and began inching down the trunk. She found a solid foothold and descended the next stage with relative ease, moving from branch to branch. Ten feet aboveground she chose a sturdy limb, let herself hang from it, and then dropped to the ground.

After determining that no bones had broken, Jess watched her heavyset friend try to replicate her actions. Feeling helpless, she stage-whispered encouragement, but it was useless. He'd snagged a belt loop on the latch. The bathroom door gave way and angry voices shouted in Arabic. Desperate, Gabe leaped headlong through the opening, clawed the nearest branch, swung, and tried to wrap his legs around the trunk. Unable to bear his weight, the limb snapped, and Gabe fell three stories.

Inside Simon's villa Paul strode back and forth, occasionally peering over Ava's shoulder or out the window.

She raised her eyes from the notebook. "Will you please stop pacing? You're driving me crazy."

"What? Oh, sorry. Are you almost done?"

"I told you!"

"I know, I know. Horribly complex, two thousand years old, et cetera, but are you at a stopping place? I really want to go."

"Not now. Let me finish this stanza."

He swore. "Will you please just indulge me?"

She looked at him.

"Maybe I'm getting paranoid, but I haven't seen any security guards around. That feels wrong. Even if Tomás went to Naples, Simon would have left someone."

Ava opened her mouth to argue. Paul was jumping to conclusions. Then she reconsidered. Paul's intuition was usually on target. Maybe he was right.

"What do you have in mind?"

"I bet the Piccolo Bar is still open. Can you finish the translation there?"

Ava gave in. She gathered her papers and they made for the gatehouse. As they rounded the final corner, Ava froze. Two men, armed with identical SPAS-12s, patrolled the driveway. She recognized one immediately: He'd followed her in Yemen, and she'd never forget his frightening face. Like a specter from her nightmares, he opened his mouth to reveal sharp, wolfish teeth.

As the man raised his weapon, Paul reacted with lightning speed. Gripping Ava's arm, he yanked her back behind the building. "Follow me," he said. "Run!"

Concealed by a retaining wall, they hurried uphill on a narrow path that tracked the cliff's edge. Far below, waves thundered against crags. Not far behind, the pursuers' footfalls pounded closer. Paul raced ahead, rounded the final corner, and cut toward the main house, but as he broached the illuminated portico, two silhouettes appeared. Soon he could distinguish their features. The first man, dark-skinned and lean, was a stranger. The second was Sheik Ahmed.

Paul skidded to a stop. Unprepared, Ava slammed into him but Paul barely noticed. Rather, shielding her with his broad body, he backed away from Ahmed. The sheik advanced.

The Americans retreated to the cliff, hoping to escape the way they'd come. Unfortunately, their path was blocked by the men with guns. Backed up against the precipice, they were trapped.

Keeping Ava behind him, Paul lifted his arms and announced, "Okay, Ahmed. You win. Let her go and I'll surrender."

The sheik smiled. "How gallant. Sadly, you're in no position to negotiate."

"I stole the jars. I'm the one you want. She had nothing to do with it."

Pleasure radiated from Ahmed's eyes. He raised his weapon.

Paul's mind raced. "Wait!" he said. "What about the disks? I know where they're hidden. I'll lead you to them."

Ahmed shook his head. "You're a miserable liar, Mr. Grant." Glancing over his right shoulder, he continued: "Besides, my spy confirms that the artifacts were lost at sea."

Slowly, a third figure materialized out of the shadows to stand beside the sheik. Her posture proud, Mellania gave them a cold smile.

"Surprised?" she asked.

Realizing how thoroughly they had been betrayed, Paul's shoulders sagged.

The sheik laughed, enjoying Paul's despair. "You see, Barakah? Never trust a woman. It's her nature to deceive."

The wind howled and the surf hammered the rocky shore. Ahmed clicked the safety off his pistol.

Suddenly, Ava shouted. "Wait!"

Paul turned. A vision of courage, she was balanced on the ledge. Long hair blowing in the gale, eyes bright with defiance, she extended an arm to dangle her notebook over the edge.

"I know why your master covets the jars. I know why he forbade you to destroy them. He has a secret. The jars hid that secret for two thousand years, but I deciphered it. Shoot now, and his prize is lost."

The sheik's smile dissolved into a sneer. "Insolent girl. You think a schoolgirl's scribbles matter to him? Our victory is preordained."

"You know I'm right, Ahmed. He's vulnerable. He's scared. Why else send his best agent? Lose the secret, and you fail him. Tell me, what's the Beast's penalty for failure?"

Fear showed in the sheik's eyes. For a second Paul thought

Ava's gambit would succeed. Instead, their enemy regained his composure. "No. We cannot fail. Victory is certain. Kill them. Kill them both."

As he issued the command, a powerful voice roared in challenge. "Ahmed!"

From the darkness, Sinan attacked. He took the first gunman by surprise and shoved him off the cliff. The Yemeni reacted faster. He dodged Sinan's blow, pivoted, and raised his gun, but an instant before it fired Sinan grabbed the barrel, diverting his aim. Sinan ripped the weapon from his opponent's hands. Like Ariosto's Orlando in fury, he raised the gun above his head, reared, and clubbed his adversary's face. Unconscious or dead, the man dropped. Sinan turned. Eyes burning with rage, he charged.

Ahmed fired. His first bullet clipped Sinan's thigh. The second shot flew wide, but the third shattered Sinan's wrist and the fourth opened his stomach. He collapsed. With a sadistic smile, Ahmed continued firing, emptying the clip. When the gunshots finally stopped, he ejected the spent magazine. "Finish them, Barakah."

The lieutenant aimed. Desperate to save Ava, Paul played his final card. Whispering a prayer, he pulled the bishop's amulet from his neck and held it before them like a shield. The talisman had no effect on the sheik, but when Barakah saw it, he paused. Then, to Paul's shock, he pointed his weapon at Ahmed. Though Barakah's mission was incomplete, the sacred amulet signified that it was time to reveal his true allegiance.

Sheik Ahmed's jaw dropped in disbelief. Then he erupted in a paroxysm of grotesque laughter. Spittle flew from his lips as he raved, "You fool! You weakling! You've damned yourself! Can't you see that the master's triumph is inevitable?"

Barakah shook his head. In a calm, confident voice, he said, "No. Your master will fall. It is written."

Fury blazed in Ahmed's eyes. Nostrils flaring, he said, "You're blind. Nothing that happens here matters. The infidel leaders have already gathered. Three hours after sunrise, the master will touch a button and blast them all to hell."

Barakah was unmoved. "There's still time for you to save yourself. Reveal the master's plan. Renounce Satan, and your life can be redeemed."

The wind gusted savagely now, tearing at their clothes. Sheik Ahmed seemed to consider the offer. Then, quick as an asp, he dropped the Ruger, pulled a knife, and whipped his arm around Mellania's thin neck. Pressing the blade to her jugular, he began to back away.

Barakah raised his weapon. "It's no use, Ahmed. I'll kill her. I won't let you escape. Surrender is your only option."

The sheik grinned. "Sorry, friend, but that's a lie. You're not strong enough to sacrifice her. Your spirit is crippled by mercy."

Barakah hesitated. Ava was sure he'd pull the trigger. Instead, he lowered the pistol.

Smiling victoriously, Ahmed backed his hostage down the narrow walk. "Prepare yourselves, cowards. Tomorrow, in the bloody aftermath, humanity will crave a strong leader. When the world sees a mushroom cloud, people will beg for safety and security at any cost. Then he shall rise in glory. Then he shall reign!"

As he spoke, a massive shadow rose from behind the cliff, obscuring the stars and casting all into darkness. Mellania screamed in horror. Startled, Ahmed released his captive and turned. He took only a second to comprehend the threat, but that hesitation was fatal. Barakah fired twice. Both bullets slammed home, shattering Ahmed's rib cage and spinning him around. Barakah fired a third round. It caught Ahmed's throat, which sprayed dark blood. Gasping, the sheik staggered. He lost his footing, slipped over the edge, and plummeted three hundred feet into the Tyrrhenian Sea.

At Boston Police Headquarters, a uniformed officer carrying a stack of papers entered the dispatch center and announced, "Here's another fifteen."

"No kidding."

He snorted. "How many is that?"

"Faxes? About a hundred."

"Hell! All alike?"

"Basically. Each hails from a different phone number, but they contain the same warning."

"Terrorists are attacking Cambridge?"

"Yep. With machine guns. It's got to be a hoax."

"Who'd send a hundred faxes as a hoax?"

"Stupid college kids. Some are still angry about the Lite-Brite deal, some just love to prank the police. Did you know they put a squad car on top of MIT's Great Dome? Here, look at this." He opened the departmental e-mail. "In the last quarter hour, we've received scores of messages with the same subject line. Plus one crazy nine-one-one call."

"What do we do?"

"I still say it's a hoax, but we can't take chances. Call the sergeant detective. If she says roll, we roll."

The second he knew Ava was safe, Paul ran to help their fallen comrade. He knelt, cradled Sinan's head in his hands, and tried to administer some aid. Ava watched and then the silent helicopter landed just behind them. A door snapped open. Nick leaped out to assist Paul. Moments later, Simon emerged. Weeping and wailing, Mellania ran to embrace him. Ignoring her, DeMaj hurried to check on Ava. His face livid with concern, he took her hand and asked, "Are you hurt? Did they touch you?"

She shook her head, then pointed at Mellania. "She betrayed us."

Simon's jaw clenched. He threw an arctic glance at the Slovakian, his expression revealing infinite contempt. Terrified, Mellania fell back, turned, and tried to run off, but Barakah was on her instantly. He twisted her wrist, lowered his sobbing prisoner to the ground, and secured her arms behind her back.

Once Barakah had her under control, DeMaj directed his attention to Sinan. "How bad is it, Paul?"

"Critical. Call an ambulance!"

Simon was already dialing. He connected with the A.S.L. Anacarpi via a private number and advised them to prep for an emergency patient. Gore flowed from numerous wounds. His ruptured femoral vein and artery fed a bloody pool so deep that it reflected scarlet-tainted moonlight. Paul removed his shirt and began ripping it into strips. He used some cotton to stanch the bleeding and wrapped an improvised tourniquet around Sinan's leg. Then, using a branch Nick had broken from a sapling, Paul twisted it tight.

"Where'd you learn that?"

"Boy Scouts."

Just then Sinan coughed blood. Wheezing, he drew a shallow breath. His eyelids fluttered open. Catching sight of Paul, he whispered, "Ahmed?"

"Dead."

Despite the pain, the Arab smiled. Whispering *mektoub,* he relaxed his muscles and let his eyes slip shut.

Nick went white. "Is he gone?"

Paul checked Sinan's vitals. "Just unconscious, but his pulse is very weak. I wouldn't expect—"

Nick shook his head. "Don't say it."

Rather than wait for an ambulance, Simon ordered his chauffeur to bring the Maybach, and they then loaded Sinan into its plush backseat. Nick insisted on riding along, blaming himself for the Arab's involvement. After impressing the circumstances' urgency upon his driver, DeMaj passed Nick a roll of five-hundred-euro notes to ensure that the doctors gave Sinan their undivided attention. Wishing the passengers good luck and Godspeed, he watched the car disappear down the road.

With all her might Jess struggled to pull her injured friend upright. "Gabe, please!" she begged. "Try to walk! Help me!"

His reply was a howl. Shards of pink bone protruded from his shin. Jess gagged and fought the urge to vomit. Succumbing to panic, she shivered. Stupid! If only she'd grabbed a phone! In her mind's eye she envisioned her mobile resting uselessly on the bed table. Then taking a deep breath, Jess cleared her mind of doubt and steeled her will to the task at hand.

"Get up right now, Gabriel," she ordered. "I will not tolerate this display of weakness. On your feet!" To her surprise, he obeyed. Moaning, Gabe pushed up from the blood-soaked ground, balanced on his good leg, and tried to walk. Seizing the opportunity, Jess wedged herself under his meaty arm, letting him use her body as a crutch.

"Come on now, Gabriel, move! One, two, step! One, two, step! One, two, step!"

It worked. They eased from the slippery ground and onto the pavement. With each stride Jess shouted, insulted, harassed, and cajoled Gabe into going farther. She intuited that if he rested, even for a second, he'd pass out. One, two, step! Her goal was in sight: a tall hedgerow. He could flop down behind it, concealed from view, while she ran for help. It was only twenty feet. If they could reach it before—

Someone yelled. Jess understood enough Arabic to know that she'd been ordered to halt. She turned her head. A bearded man stood on her balcony, aiming an automatic rifle.

Having received Simon's permission to interrogate Mellania privately, Barakah handcuffed her and led her into the main house. After they were gone, Ava asked, "Is that wise?"

"The lieutenant promised to share any information he obtains," DeMaj said.

"And you're sure he'll keep his word?"

"Why? You suspect Barakah's a triple agent?"

Squeezing in next to Paul on the loveseat, Ava thought about the question. "No, I trust him. He saved our lives, but Mellania might be able to manipulate him. Ahmed indicated that Barakah has a certain . . . sensitivity toward women. The interrogation might be more effective if we all participate."

DeMaj shrugged. "Question her if you want, but I'll never speak to her again. Besides, she won't know anything useful."

"Why not?"

Simon crossed the room to adjust a wall-mounted shoji board autographed by Habu. Once it was level, he said, "Because she's a traitor. Our adversary would never reveal plans to a traitor, no matter how lovely her exterior. I'd wager that only Ahmed and the master knew the details. The former is gone and I doubt," he said, gazing at Ava, "that the latter has a weakness for women."

For Jess, the decision was clear: She wouldn't cooperate. If a machine gun was fired in the middle of Cambridge, it would summon the police faster than any phone call. Ignoring the man's orders, she forced Gabe to continue, step by bloody, agonizing step, toward the relative safety of the hedge. Gritting her teeth, Jess cringed, expecting gunshots. None came.

Her spirit soared. "Come on, Gabe. Don't quit now. Keep moving. One, two, step!" Stealing a glance behind her, she observed the gunman. Instead of aiming his rifle, he was waving furiously. For a moment, Jess was confused. Then something dreadful dawned. He was signaling an accomplice. Her peripheral vision detected movement. Rounding the building's far corner, a second gunman approached.

Standing behind the wet bar, DeMaj set up three glasses and opened a leaded-crystal ship's decanter. While Simon poured each of them a double brandy, Paul called Nick. Sinan's prognosis was bleak; the doctors gave him little chance of survival.

Dispirited, Paul let the telephone drop. Simon gave him a glass and put a comforting hand on his shoulder. "Chin up, Paul. If he's meant to live, he'll live. If not, *mektoub*. It was God's will."

Ava frowned. Noting her reaction, Simon said, "Ms. Fischer, have you contemplated the sacred jars' true significance?"

"Of course. Historically, their importance was immense."

"No, I'm speaking of their theological significance. Why was the prophecy placed in these artifacts?"

She began to think. A powerful notion entered her mind. Before it crystalized, Simon spoke again.

"In the Gospel of John, Christ utters a remark that at first glance seems out of character. He asks his beloved mother: 'Woman, why do you involve me? You know it's not my time!' Why would Jesus say that?"

The question hung in the air.

"Was it because with Christ's gift of foresight, he knows the brutal manner in which his human life will end? Perhaps the mortal part of Jesus is afraid." said Simon.

Paul nodded.

"So, Jesus wants to put off his fate for a bit longer, but that's not God's plan. Instead, Christ pushes aside selfish desires and performs his first miracle, initiating a ministry that will transform the world. The miracle at Cana is the moment when Jesus accepts his destiny."

"How is that relevant?"

"We too have a destiny. We can embrace our fate with courage or we can flee from it in terror. Either way, inexorably, destiny will find us."

Paul looked at his former boss.

DeMaj sighed. "I know. I know. I've always been a skeptical empiricist. Now I'm preaching. Recent events have caused me to, shall we say, reconsider. I'm sure of one thing: Sinan believes in destiny. If he passes tonight, he'll die content. He kept his vow."

"What vow?" Ava asked.

"Years ago, he swore to defeat his blood enemy and avenge his child's death."

She gasped. "Ahmed killed his child?"

"Sinan's teenage son was a heroin addict. In 1998 he injected a hot dose. The sheik was his dealer."

Tears pooled in Ava's eyes. Paul took her hand. Then he raised his glass. "To Sinan: His friend is my friend, his enemy is my enemy."

NEAR CALA D'INFERNO, ITALY

The master rose before the sun. He stood in the dark room and stretched. This would be a day to be remembered. Years of planning and millions invested would finally bear fruit. Today's bold action would be the capstone to the decades-long strategy of tension he'd helped orchestrate. By tonight, his ultimate goal and birthright would be within reach. Father would be proud!

Though he'd never actually served in the armed forces, the master dressed in a crisp military uniform. He left his private chambers and went out to mingle with the troops. He saw excitement and anticipation written on their young faces. Many suspected the Gruppo's fabled Plan of Rebirth would begin today, although none knew exactly what that entailed. Smiling, he shook hands with some officers and saluted others. So many fierce patriots! So many beautiful martyrs!

A bit later, Lieutenant Barakah returned. Simon offered him brandy, but the devout Muslim took only water. After he'd quenched his thirst, Ava asked, "What news?"

The Egyptian rubbed his face, visibly exhausted. "Mellania doesn't know anything."

"And Tomás?" Simon asked icily. "Did she kill him?"

"No. She slipped GHB into his drink. Your man's been unconscious for hours, but he'll recover."

"What will happen to her?"

Barakah glanced at DeMaj. "With your permission, sir, I'll turn her over to the *carabinieri*. She'll be charged with assault, conspiracy to murder, and violating parole."

Simon nodded. "Did she say anything about the master?"

"No. She's never met or even spoken to him. Almost nobody has, except Ahmed. That's a major source of the master's power: He's invisible. My mission was to infiltrate the organization, ascertain his whereabouts, and investigate something he called the Plan of Rebirth. Unfortunately—"

Paul interrupted. "Hold on. Just who, or what, is the master?"

"We're not sure," Barakah answered. "Our prime suspect is a shadowy figure some call Don VeMeli, but he's better known as La Belva.

"Who?"

Simon stood up. "I have a thorough file." He walked to his desk and tapped keys on his computer until a page emerged from the printer. Ava took it.

"'Salvatore T. VeMeli, a.k.a. La Belva, born November 16, 1953. Sardinian. A violent drug lord who rose to great prominence in the 1990s, VeMeli is alleged to have killed at least thirty people by his own hand and ordered the deaths of several hundred . . .

"'As a teenager, VeMeli began committing murder for hire. After killing a popular athlete, he was forced into hiding. When VeMeli was arrested and tried for that murder, he manufactured an acquittal by intimidating the jurors and witnesses. Later, he worked in heroin refining and export. An efficient, ruthless criminal, he became a major player in narcotics. The profits were vast, and young VeMeli grew tremendously rich.

"'In 1976, an omen caused La Belva to believe himself destined for greater things, and he began plotting war against his rivals. Throughout the 1980s, he expanded his drug-trafficking network into South America, Greece, and Asia. He invested millions of drug profits in international banks and newspapers. He affiliated himself with Propaganda Due, a right-wing political cabal. In the 1990s, VeMeli's faction waged a campaign for underworld control. At that time, most dons protected themselves with bribes rather than violence. They were highly visible in their communities, rubbing shoulders with numerous politicians. Don VeMeli's strategy relied on the "law of misdirection." He remained hidden and was rarely seen, even by fellow Mafiosi. He orchestrated the murders of high-profile law-enforcement officials on other mobsters' turf. Whenever a policeman or a well-known judge was killed, more criminals were blamed. In January 1993, he framed a rival for the car-bomb assassination of two respected prosecutors. This act caused widespread condemnation and led to a major anti-Mafia crackdown, resulting in the capture and imprisonment of La Belva's primary competitors. Consequently, Don VeMeli seized control. In 1994, he entered the political arena. He's rumored to have bankrolled the extremist Gruppo Garibaldi—'"

Paul interrupted. "Okay, he's evil and dangerous, but is he the Antichrist?"

Barakah finished his water. "Possibly." He nodded to Simon. "Obviously, Mr. DeMaj suspects it. I believe it, and my organization has amassed significant evidence that Don VeMeli himself agrees, but could I prove it?" He shrugged.

Ava shook her head. "That's immaterial. Stay focused on the facts. He's a terrorist, he has no scruples about committing mass murder, and he's been plotting a major attack for years."

Paul had a brainstorm. "Hey! If he thinks he's the Antichrist, he'd want to attack the Church, right? The cardinals are gathered in Rome. They're a perfect target!"

"That was our initial assumption too," Barakah said. "When Benedict announced his resignation, we anticipated that Don VeMeli would be tempted to move against the Vatican. My superiors communicated with the Swiss Guard. Security for the conclave will be the finest on earth. I don't believe an attack there will succeed."

Paul smiled with satisfaction until he saw Ava's face.

"What?" he asked. "What did I get wrong?"

Before she could answer, Simon spoke. "Ms. Fischer picked up on something in the dossier: the law of misdirection. Our foe's modus operandi is to attack from unexpected directions. Hence, Rome is too obvious. When you wage asymmetrical warfare . . ."

Something in the way Simon talked reminded Ava of her father. She flashed back to a sunny afternoon in Washington when he'd spent hours helping his precocious five-year-old daughter memorize the periodic table. At one point she erupted in frustration, insisting that the elements should be organized differently. Patiently, Dr. Fischer explained the various considerations and historical precedents. He'd spoken with clarity and care, just as Simon was doing now.

". . . and in the current, hypervigilant atmosphere, smuggling a bomb into Vatican City would be virtually impossible."

"Yeah, that makes sense, but if not Rome," said Paul, "where? I mean, it could be any place—Jerusalem, Boston, Paris, New York . . ."

Silence filled the room as everyone imagined the worst.

Paul slammed his fist on the table. "Damnit!"

"I share your frustration. I wish Ahmed had said more," Barakah said, "but frankly, I'm surprised he disclosed as much as he did. I've been working to uncover his agenda for months. This was the only time the sheik revealed any details."

Anxiously, Ava looked out a window. The morning sun was cresting Mount Solaro. She cracked her knuckles. "Ahmed implied the bombing was imminent. We've got to hurry."

DeMaj agreed. "What else did he say about the attack?"

She searched her memory. "He said it would be bloody. He said people would be afraid and demand a strong, decisive ruler. He said the infidel leaders had already gathered."

Ava met Simon's stare. As one, they said: "La Maddalena!"

17

Jess's mind was searching for options. There must be a loophole, some clever way to escape, but despite her determined exterior, she'd begun to sense it was hopeless. Even if they reached the hedge, the gunmen would follow. Forcing Gabe onward was simply cruel, and the thugs would be on them in seconds. Distracted by despair, Jess misjudged a step. Gabe's fractured leg brushed the curb and she felt him shudder in pain. With a growl she demanded he keep moving. They took one giant step, then another. The hedge was only six feet away now, but what could they accomplish by struggling? This was absurd. She should ease him down, let him rest. Instead, she elbowed his ribs.

"Two more steps, Gabriel. Don't surrender! One, two, step!" Her voice had grown hoarse. She doubted Gabe could even hear it. He tottered, smothering her body under his bulk. With a final effort, she braced her legs, shouldered all his weight, and heaved him forward. Falling, Jess's knee spiked on the gravel. Gabe's weight forced her to the ground and pain tore through her. Sobbing, she rolled him off her and into the hedges.

She turned onto her back and looked up at the sky. When one of the machine gun–wielding men stepped into view, Jess laughed. "Go ahead and shoot," she said.

He aimed, then his expression went from pleasure, to confusion, to rage. A second before he fled, her ears registered the welcome wail of police sirens.

It took an hour to refuel the Comanche. Barakah spent the time on the phone with his contacts to alert them to the threat. Ava sat in the study, translating the prophecy. After changing into clean clothes, Paul used Simon's secure line to contact Ammon and Sefu at the Segev Clinic. He explained Mellania's betrayal and urged the boys to be cautious. When a confident Ammon announced "I shall protect him," Paul couldn't help but grin. Next, he called Jess's apartment. No one answered, and Paul grew nervous. Then he glanced at the clock and did the math. It was suppertime in Boston, and they'd probably stepped out for pizza. He left a long voice mail explaining the situation and warning that Mellania might have compromised their location. Just as he hung up, Ava came in. Paul considered sharing his concerns but decided against it. She'd be paralyzed with worry, even though there was nothing more to do.

Reading the shadows on his face, she asked, "What's wrong?"

"Nothing, except that I've never heard of La Maddalena. Who's she?"

Ava sighed. "It's not a person. It's an island."

Paul's expression was blank.

"Napoleon conquered it. Admiral Nelson used it as a base. Mussolini was held prisoner there, before being rescued by—"

He signaled for silence. "Is it far?"

From the doorway, DeMaj said, "About four hundred kilometers. Just north of Sardinia. Come quickly. We don't have a second to lose."

NEAR CALA D'INFERNO, ITALY

Pacing behind the command desk, Don VeMeli was waiting. He despised waiting. Departure had been delayed too long already. His personal conveyance, an attack helicopter on loan from the army, sat fueled and ready. They could be more than one hundred fifty kilometers away within an hour but, infuriatingly, he couldn't leave. All morning he'd occupied himself with the trivial tasks that were the lot of a diplomatic division supervisor, his official position. Standing in the background, carefully off camera, he watched his military sycophants and legislative factotums welcome dignitaries, representatives, and the world press. Maintaining a broad smile, Don VeMeli appeared calm and serene, but an ember of concern smoldered within him. Ahmed had not reported. Surely the mission was complete. Why didn't he call?

Dozens of phones seemed to ring simultaneously. As a buzz of panic spread throughout the communications center, the master realized that Ahmed had failed. Two servicemen sprang from their desks and burst into the office, each jostling for priority. They informed him that numerous security organizations were on the line reporting a possible terrorist threat. Deflecting these calls to his nominal superior, Don VeMeli contacted the Gruppo's vast network of informants. His spies confirmed the reports, adding that DeMaj and the Americans were flying to La Maddalena by helicopter.

If they're coming here, he thought, it could mean only one thing: The girl had unlocked the secret. Cursing Ahmed's incompetence, the Beast barked to his staff: "Contact the air force. Islamic terrorists just hijacked a military helicopter. They must not approach the island!"

Terrified aides backed away from Don VeMeli. None had ever seen him so angry, but after his outburst, La Belva quickly regained his composure. There was still time, he reasoned. The glorious plan would still succeed. He commanded a team of pilots to prepare for action. He knew from Mellania that DeMaj's helicopter didn't carry weapons. A heavily armed squadron would intercept DeMaj over Isola Caprera and eliminate him.

Roderigo came into the command center. Confused by all the activity, he sent his master a questioning glance.

"Demand nothing from me," Don VeMeli said. "What you know, you know."

The sleek black Comanche hurtled northwest. Simon redlined its twin LHTEC T800-801 engines, pushing the helicopter to exceed one hundred seventy-five knots. Below, the sea churned. DeMaj looked back at his passengers. Ava's eyes were shut, her face a study in concentration. She was replaying the mashed-up audio file on her headphones. All her energy was focused on completing the translation. Paul drummed his fingers against the radar display. He looked nervous.

"Worried?" DeMaj asked him.

Paul smiled. "Nah. We'll be fine. Ahmed was bluffing. They can't have a nuke."

"Why do you say that?"

"Terrorists have never built one. It's too complex, too expensive."

"Yes, but they might have bought a rogue device on the black market."

"If it's that easy, why didn't bin Laden acquire one? He had plenty of money."

"The main problem isn't acquiring a warhead; it's moving it. Years ago, a Soviet airbase commander sold part of his arsenal to the Russian mob, which then resold the WMDs to terrorists. They were caught trying to smuggle the bombs out of the country. It's difficult to transport fissionable material across an international border. U.S. Customs pioneered a variety of effective techniques to prevent it."

"Then how could Don VeMeli sneak a bomb into Italy? And how could he get it onto the island?"

Simon looked thoughtful. "Perhaps it was already there."

"What do you mean?"

"During the Cold War the U.S. Navy established a nuclear submarine base at Santo Stefano. They ran boomers out of there for decades."

"Boomers?"

"Ballistic missile subs. Ohio class. In 2008 I heard a rumor about a missing warhead."

"How could that happen?"

"To cut costs, the Navy replaced obsolete sub components by leveraging commercial, off-the-shelf hardware. In 2007 they contracted with Lockheed Martin to complete the D5 Life Extension Program, which included missile reentry vehicles. Supposedly, when they upgraded the subs' Trident D5 warheads from W76s to W88s, one W76 disappeared."

"How powerful is a W76?"

"Six times Hiroshima," Simon said quietly.

After a long silence, Paul spoke up. "Are you sure? I never heard a word about it."

"The Bush administration kept it quiet, and I can't blame them. If the story broke during the presidential campaign—"

"The press would have accused Bush of using scare tactics to swing the election."

DeMaj nodded. "And the 2008 financial crisis was spinning out of control too. News like that might have crashed the system."

"So what happened to the bomb?" Paul asked.

"No one knows, but after the incident, the Navy closed its base. The American commander lowered the flag and transferred custody to the mayor of La Maddalena."

Ava closed her notebook, pulled off her headphones, and stretched.

"Finished?" Paul asked.

She nodded. "I've done what I can. Will we make it in time?"

"We'll make it," said Simon. "The moment we arrive, I'll drop you at the summit or as close as possible. Then I'll set down at the nearest pad and come meet you."

"What do we do?"

"Fulfill the prophecy. Thwart the Antichrist."

Paul's eyes narrowed. "What the hell does that mean?"

"Any ideas, Ms. Fischer?"

"Maybe." She opened her notebook and pointed to a quatrain. Touching Paul's arm, she said, "Read this passage."

> *"Unless the prophecy is proclaimed*
> *Where the great leaders gather,*
> *A new devil rises: invincible deceiver!*
> *Evil and terror consume the world of man."*

He looked up. "I don't follow."

"Garagallo said Pope Leo stopped Attila by reading a prophecy at their meeting."

"So?"

"So maybe we're supposed to read the prophecy at the G8 Summit."

"What good will that do?"

Ava dropped her eyes, deflated. "I don't know. Probably nothing. It doesn't make much sense. Frankly, all of this stuff seems like—"

"Superstitious nonsense?"

A sad smile flickered. "Exactly."

"Well, I don't give a damn if you believe it," said Simon. "We've got to try. It may be the only way to prevent Armageddon."

"But it's ridiculous. How can a prophecy stop a bomb?"

"I admit that it requires an extraordinary leap of faith, but what other options are thre? Should we run away? Just quit? Right now my people are communicating with the security services of each nation involved in the summit. We're providing the intel we learned on Capri and we're doing everything possible to raise the alarm, but no one's likely to take immediate action. People often call in false threats. They did in London. Furthermore—" DeMaj checked his watch—"even assuming the authorities believe us, I doubt they can evacuate everyone on such short notice. La Maddalena isn't connected to the mainland by road, and unless Ahmed was lying, the deadline is less than fifty-five minutes from now. They might clear a few critical buildings or hotels, but not the whole city."

Ava slumped. It seemed hopeless.

Simon went on: "They can't evacuate everyone, so we must do everything in our power to prevent the attack. Through his organization, Barakah is spreading the word that we're en route to La Maddalena. With luck, some of their people will arrive before we do. Fritz and my crypto team are hacking the Beast's network, searching for something useful. Honestly, I doubt they'll find anything, but—"

"But at least they're trying," Ava finished his thought.

"Precisely. And the same goes for us. Even if the prophecy is just superstitious nonsense, even if we're on a fool's errand, we must try. We must fight until the final bell."

That made sense to Paul. "Okay. Just tell me what you need. If we go down, at least we'll go down swinging."

"I'm in too," Ava said. "If you think it might help, I'll proclaim the prophecy to anyone who'll listen, but first, please answer one question."

"Go ahead, Ms. Fischer," said Simon.

"If your people are screaming bloody murder to eight national intelligence services, warning them of the attack and telling them we're on our way, isn't La Belva going to hear about it? If he knows we're coming, won't he try to stop us?"

Simon looked at her with approval. "Yes. I anticipate he'll try to stop us. In fact, I'm counting on it."

The cockpit radio crackled to life. It was Fritz. "Mr. DeMaj, I regret to report that you've been denied permission to enter La Maddalena's airspace. It's now a restricted security zone. Unauthorized aircraft will be intercepted and if necessary destroyed."

"Message received." Simon looked over at his two passengers, gauging their emotions. Neither American spoke as the helicopter continued west.

"Would the Italians actually shoot us down?" Paul asked.

"They might try, but it's hard to shoot what you can't see."

Simon took the chopper into a steep dive, leveling out less than three meters above the waves, close enough to see schools of fish darting just below the surface. Paul's stomach did somersaults. He knew the Comanche was responsive and agile. It could fly sideways and even backward at sixty-five knots, but reading flight characteristics off a printed page was nothing like experiencing them live. He glanced at Ava, expecting to see her quaking.

Instead, she was leaning forward into the restraints. Her eyes were bright, and her posture indicated confidence. Paul marveled at her courage.

Beneath them whitecaps navigated around and between the heavy maritime traffic originating from the Strait of Bonifacio. Out of necessity Simon buzzed directly over one small ship. Its alarmed sailors hit the deck. As the morning fog lifted, a granite archipelago materialized. They drew closer, until Ava could perceive the ruins of ancient fortifications atop the easternmost promontory.

"Is that La Maddalena?" she asked.

"No. That's Isola Caprera. La Maddalena is a bit farther."

Paul nodded. "So once we get there, how do we proclaim the prophecy? Just shout it from the nearest street corner?"

Simon shrugged. "We'll deal with that when we get there."

Ava's eyes sparkled. "I've got an idea."

She opened her phone, attached the digital scrambler, and called DURMDVL. "I need a favor. Can you get me an unlisted phone number, and pronto?"

"Sure."

"Find the private cell-phone number for Dr. Ron Bagelton."

Just a few seconds passed and they had the number. Ava thanked DURMDVL, then hung up and dialed. After several rings a man answered. Ava recognized his voice. She put the call on speaker. Then, taking a deep breath, she began.

"Professor Bagelton? My name is Ava Fischer. I caught your lecture at Harvard and I saw you speak at the G8 protest yesterday." She bit her lip, forcing herself to continue. "You're a brilliant man and a mesmerizing, passionate speaker."

"Why, thank you, my dear. Thank you very much indeed, but I'm afraid you have me at a disadvantage. How did you—"

"I'm a huge fan of your work. Your creative scholarship is amazing."

She could actually hear him smile as he replied, "That's very kind of you to say."

Encouraged, Ava pressed on. "So would you do me a favor? I'm in the area, and it's urgent that I make an announcement at this morning's protest. I'm sure a man of your importance can get my brief statement broadcast over the loudspeakers."

"Well, I—"

"It'll be very quick and—" she put some huskiness into her voice—"I'll be incredibly grateful."

Paul made a face.

Bagelton didn't reply immediately, but when he did, she knew he wasn't convinced.

"Yes, that sounds like an interesting proposal, but I'm sorry to disappoint you. Unfortunately, I don't wield quite the influence you presume. On the other hand, I do know all the members of the organizing committee. I'd be happy to speak with them on your behalf. Perhaps we should discuss your urgent needs over dinner?"

Ava rolled her eyes in frustration. She was about to hang up when Simon spoke up. "May I try?" She handed him the phone. "Professor, this is Simon DeMaj."

Bagelton gasped. "Mr. DeMaj, it's an honor. To what do I—"

Simon cut him off. "Ms. Fischer is traveling with me. I enthusiastically support this project, and I want her announcement to air live from the protest. It should be easy to arrange. Now, Dr. Bagelton, you probably know my reputation. I control a great deal of money, and I'm not afraid to spend it. If I get what I want, I'll endow a generous archaeological research foundation, with you and Ms. Fischer codirectors."

The professor was silent for several seconds, then: "By 'generous,' what exactly do you—"

"Shall we say five million? No, make it six. I'll pledge six million to underwrite your invaluable historical research. Naturally, you'll exercise complete discretion over the funds' disbursal. My lawyers can write up the formal proposal this afternoon."

Even over the phone they could hear Bagelton suck in a breath. He coughed, then cleared his throat. "Yes, that is quite generous. No question about it. Thank you, sir. I don't know what to say. I'm honored."

"Splendid. Just remember, the endowment is conditional on Ava speaking at today's demonstration. Is that clear?"

"Oh yes sir. Crystal clear. Just let me—"

"No need to explain. I know you can handle it. We'll call back in—" he glanced at his watch—"fifteen minutes to confirm. Don't let us down. We're counting on you."

Grinning, DeMaj hung up and returned the phone to Ava. "Paul, see if you can get in touch with Kevin in Houston," he said. "Have him draft the necessary documents."

Paul laughed. "Wait, were you serious? Six million?"

"Of course. If it gets Ava on the air, it's money well spent."

After watching the attack squadron depart, Don VeMeli boarded his helicopter. He carried only one item of luggage: an expensive silver attaché case. His pilot powered up the chopper's engines. The aircraft lifted off the ground, circled the camp, and began its journey south. Out the port-side window, VeMeli looked at the quaint seaside village of La Maddalena. Soon, he knew, it would be a smoking ruin. No, he corrected himself—not a ruin, a radioactive testament to his strength. Of course, for the first few years no one could know he was the bombing's architect. Appropriate enemies would be blamed, causing the world's so-called free nations to scream for vengeance. Don VeMeli's minions within the Gruppo Garibaldi and similar organizations worldwide had been anticipating such an attack for years. After the atomic detonation they'd be validated and lionized by the public for issuing warnings. The master's handpicked candidates were perfectly positioned to capitalize on the attack, vastly increasing his global power and influence. The subsequent world war would generate even greater opportunities for expansion. Someday, Don VeMeli dreamed, when his hypocritical and sanctimonious enemies groveled beneath his merciless boot, he'd reveal the truth. He was certain that future historians would perceive the wisdom, even the necessity, of his action. They'd call him a great leader endowed with matchless courage and vision. Someday, the world would thank him.

In fifteen minutes they called back Bagelton and received mixed news: He'd convinced the committee to broadcast Ava's message, but the sound system wasn't sophisticated enough to patch through a mobile signal. Frustration evident in his voice, Simon said, "No problem. I'll bring her to you. Where's the main stage?"

"Piazza Umberto."

"How do we find it?"

"On Via Garibaldi," the professor said, "between the port and City Hall."

"Roger that. We won't have any problems."

"Sorry to contradict, boss," said Paul. He tapped the radar display. Its flashing screen indicated several helicopters nearby. One had shifted to an intercept course.

Simon swore. "We've been spotted."

He lowered his visor, rolled his shoulders, inhaled, and took a firm grim on the controls. He turned north, reduced speed, and scanned the horizon. "I've got him!" he said. "AW129 Mongoose."

"Dangerous?"

"Lethal, but in this fight he's limited to his twenty-millimeter cannon. Missiles won't lock on us."

Now they were passing over Caprera. Keeping the sun to his back, DeMaj descended until they flew between treetops. As the incoming Mongoose tried to match his altitude, Simon increased velocity and performed a series of banks and turns, using the terrain to his advantage. The Comanche's advanced engines and streamlined airframe gave it a significant speed edge over the attacker. The outclassed Mongoose simply couldn't bring its gun to bear. Unfortunately, at that moment three more helicopters joined the pursuit.

"Hold on!"

Throttle maxed, DeMaj altered course. He charged directly at the choppers, assuming an attack posture. The Italians reacted instinctively, banking to avoid his line of fire. Then Simon pitched into an almost vertical climb. Squeezing every drop of power from the Comanche's twin turbos, the aircraft shot up twenty meters, hopping right over the attackers. Paul watched in shock as three sets of deadly blades passed harmlessly below them.

The Italians, taken aback by the exotic maneuver, faded into the distance. With a satisfied smile, DeMaj executed a snap turn that left Paul holding on to his safety harness for dear life. Moments later, they topped a rocky escarpment and beheld La Maddalena.

"We don't have much time," Simon cautioned. "Find Piazza Umberto."

They tracked Via Garibaldi, a busy coastal thoroughfare lined with shops, restaurants, and bars. As they neared the marina, Ava gave a shout. "There!" she said.

She pointed to a crowded piazza dotted with palm trees. DeMaj slowed, circled tightly, and landed near a rickety wooden structure festooned with political banners. Paul saw numerous placards emblazoned with the slogans OCCUPY THE SUMMIT and JOBS NOT BOMBS. A large contingent from the Stop the War Coalition was in attendance, as were many Friends of the Earth. Surprised activists scattered as the helicopter came in to land.

While Paul disconnected the safety harness, DeMaj looked over at Ava. He gestured toward the protesters' makeshift stage and its mismatched microphones.

"You know what to do?"

Holding her notebook tight, she said yes, but her quavering voice betrayed her fear. Meeting Ava's eyes, Simon smiled. "Don't be afraid. Trust fate."

Then something caught his attention. Approaching rapidly from the southeast were the four Italian choppers.

"Go!" he shouted. "I'll distract them!"

Paul jumped out, helped Ava down, and slammed the door. Crouching, the Americans ran through a maelstrom of stinging sand and dust. When they cleared the prop wash, Paul gave Simon the signal. Raising a hand in farewell, DeMaj increased his vertical thrust and rocketed skyward.

The master's phone rang. It was Roderigo. "DeMaj eluded the squadron," he said. "He's trying to land at Piazza Umberto."

"What? How is that possible?"

"Their helicopter is invisible to radar. Plus, he's a superb pilot, much better than anticipated." Don VeMeli heard another man in the background. Roderigo continued, "Apparently, they've touched down. A woman is exiting the helicopter."

Don VeMeli grabbed his pilot's arm. "Reverse course immediately. Head north, toward Piazza Umberto. I'll finish her myself." The pilot nodded.

Roderigo asked, "Master, are you sure that's wise? You'll be exposed. Hundreds will witness the killing."

"Obey your orders and leave the rest to me." Smiling, Don VeMeli glanced down at his attaché case. Unbeknownst to even his closest staff, it contained a powerful shortwave radio transmitter. Once his chopper cleared the area, a simple keystroke would eradicate every living creature within twenty kilometers of the city. The only witnesses to his crime would be piles of irradiated ash.

Speeding past two security guards, Paul and Ava rushed up a flight of stairs and emerged onto the wooden stage, where they surprised four elaborately costumed musicians.

"Who the hell are you?" the guitarist demanded.

"Security!" yelled the drummer.

Just then Bagelton arrived. When he saw Ava, a spark of recognition showed in his eyes. He addressed the band: "Guys, guys, these two are the performers I told you about. The committee invited them to make a brief statement. Why don't you take five and get some grappa?"

Regarding Ava with interest, the vocalist smiled. "So, baby, what's your gig?"

Before she erupted, Paul stepped in.

"It's an avant-garde piece. Spoken word."

The musician nodded in approval.

Ava ventured toward the stage, but the bass player blocked her path.

"Wait!" he said, breath reeking of marijuana. "What are your politics? This is a grassroots gathering, not a platform for corporate shills."

Her mind raced. "We're trying to prevent global warming," she said.

"And promote nuclear disarmament," Paul said.

Appeased, the musician moved aside. "Fight the power!"

Once Ava's path was clear, Paul positioned himself atop the stairwell to prevent anyone from interfering with her performance. He appropriated a microphone stand, inverted it, and balanced it on his shoulder. With a heavy club, recently shaved head, and grim expression, Paul presented an intimidating figure.

Ava took a breath, then marched across the platform to the microphones. Nervous, she tapped one. It was active. Standing alone, center stage, she felt utterly exposed. Seconds passed. The crowd, distracted for a moment by her dramatic entrance, began to grow restless. Someone whistled. Others murmured. Sound techs flashed her the thumbs-up, urging her to speak. Ava's throat constricted. Her heart pounded. She stole a backward glance. The musicians were loitering nearby, smoking and passing a bottle. Bagelton's face betrayed equal parts greed and curiosity. And there, standing guard, was loyal Paul. His warm eyes met hers, and he smiled. All her fears vanished. At that moment, Ava realized she was hopelessly in love.

She opened her notebook, cleared her throat, and began to speak.

Simon remembered his mother. He was four and she was teaching him to read. He saw her long, elegant finger glide across the yellowed pages of a paperback filched from the used bookstore. When prompted, he tried to pronounce the magical words. She helped him sound out the most difficult. Together they consumed all types of books, but he loved adventure tales the most: *The Song of Roland, The Death of Arthur, Robinson Crusoe, Huckleberry Finn;* Dumas, Stevenson, Kipling, Tolkien, H. G. Wells, Jules Verne. Often, his exhausted mother fell asleep before a story's conclusion, leaving her precocious son to finish it alone. As she dozed, he would read each word aloud, sure she was dreaming about the characters and desperate to know each story's end.

Simon took this precious memory, locked it back deep within his heart, and refocused his mind on the present. His cockpit radio was tuned to a live broadcast from the protest. Over the air Ava's confident voice began to proclaim the prophecy. He smiled: such a brave, brilliant young woman. He coaxed the Comanche into a steep bank, flew low behind a granite hillock, hovered, and scanned the radar. Four blinking icons represented the Italian helicopters he'd eluded. The Comanche's advanced tactical avionics provided a detailed description of each Mongoose's position, bearing, speed, and weapon status. His adversaries had separated into a standard military search pattern. DeMaj calculated he had forty seconds, perhaps a minute, until they pinpointed his location.

Then, a fifth icon appeared. It wasn't searching for him; rather, it was flying directly toward Ava, and it was armed with a heat-seeking missile.

"Fire!" Don VeMeli shouted at his subordinates. "Why don't you fire?"

"A moment longer," said the copilot. "It's difficult to attain missile lock on such a weak heat source. These weapons were designed for antitank combat."

At starboard, the sun was a disk of burnished gold. Wincing from the glare, the master shielded his eyes. "I don't care if it locks. Precision is unnecessary. Destroy the whole stage."

"Sir, you don't understand. If the missile won't lock, it won't arm. It wouldn't detonate."

Don VeMeli bristled with rage. "Imbecile! Use the guns then. Do whatever it takes!"

"Right away, sir." Flicking a switch, the pilot aborted the missile launch, swooped down into cannon range, and reduced speed. Below them, a young woman was shouting strange words into a microphone. As the helicopter maneuvered for a clear shot, Don VeMeli whispered, "We have you now."

Then the copilot screamed. Don VeMeli looked east, and for a second saw his doom.

Almost silent, invisible to radar, and hidden by the brilliant sun, DeMaj had advanced with impunity. Achieving tactical surprise, he flashed out of the morning sky and bore down upon his target. One final time he urged the Comanche's engines to maximum thrust and then attacked his enemy's flank, rushing forward like a divine wind. He hoped his mother would be proud. With a joyful heart, he looked forward to seeing her again. Just before impact, he caught the devil's eye. Smiling, Simon whispered, "*Shah mat.*"

Paul moved the instant he saw the helicopter. It was painted military green and was fully armed. As it circled, Paul dropped his makeshift club and rushed forward. He didn't dive. He didn't jump. He ran directly at Ava and tackled her from behind. The impact knocked her off her feet, scattering her papers. Paul and Ava flew three rows into the crowd, where a cluster of astonished protesters broke their fall. Despite the collision, Paul heard no complaint, because at that moment, the sky exploded from a massive detonation. He felt searing heat on his back. If a piece of shrapnel found them, it would be fatal. Keeping Ava's body underneath him, he held his breath, clasped his hands, and prayed.

18

The helicopter's impact had created an enormous fireball, and the flaming debris demolished the makeshift stage. Like a bonfire, it blazed for hours. Several protesters were injured, hit by shrapnel or doused with burning gasoline. Many more were hurt in the rush to escape, as terrified activists and concertgoers stampeded away from the flames. A young boy's shoulder was shattered. An Italian girl, trampled by the hysterical crowd, required surgery and a middle-aged man from California suffered a stroke. Nevertheless, not a single bystander died. The press dubbed it the "miracle at La Maddalena," and Ava couldn't really disagree.

Despite this good fortune, the Italian government remained embarrassed by the incident, which became a political hot potato. Galeazzo Grandi and the reactionaries blamed "foreign elements" and "outside agitators." In a press conference, Grandi stressed Simon's North African roots and his connections to the Arab world. Other right-wing politicians lamented that military security had been hamstrung by bleeding-heart peaceniks and civil libertarians; the Left characterized the episode as "yet another example of capitalist oligarchs stifling political speech and repressing the right to free assembly." Newspaper editorialists demanded greater restrictions of citizens' ability to purchase military hardware.

Paul and Ava were detained by the U.S. Secret Service. Held

for a week and denied access to legal counsel, they were questioned separately at first, then jointly. Ava was furious about the gross infringement of her constitutional rights. Paul was so thankful to see Ava alive that he would have signed any confession they offered.

At first no interrogator credited their story. As time passed, however, each new fact tended to corroborate the Americans' account. At that point the character witnesses began their campaign. On behalf of the Church, the indefatigable bishop Garagallo championed the couple's cause with vigor. Professor Clarkson organized a candlelight vigil, while Gabe and DURMDVL flooded every congressional office with texts, tweets, and e-mails. Nick pulled strings, utilizing his network of wealthy business connections. Ava's father called in favors, as did Paul's many influential relatives. Jess, eyes blazing with indignation, made a particularly forceful appearance on MSNBC. But it was the discovery of the missing warhead, hidden in the basement of a luxury hotel, that finally turned the tide. Paul and Ava were perfunctorily thanked, released, and reminded in the most severe terms of their binding legal and moral obligations to keep silent about the matter.

BUENOS AIRES, MARCH 13, 2013

On a late-summer afternoon in the Argentine capital, the sun was just setting when the news broke: Catholic leaders had astounded the world by selecting Jorge Mario Bergoglio, former archbishop of Buenos Aires, to be the next pope. In the city's many bars and cafés, joyful crowds gathered to toast and cheer. A happy chaos filled the streets, as the overwhelmingly Catholic population celebrated—some praying, some pointing at screens showing live broadcasts from Rome.

The new pope wasted no time in breaking with tradition, taking the name Francis. According to Church spokesman Thomas Rosica, the pontiff selected this name to reflect the "special place in his heart for the poor, for the disenfranchised, for those living on the fringes and facing injustice." The new pope's choice also represented his opposition to violence because "Francis loved peace."

Later, Pope Francis delivered an inspiring message: "When we don't walk, we are stuck. All of us must find the courage to walk in the presence of God. Only in this way can the Church move forward." He extended his blessing to everyone, including non-Catholics, saying, "You are of different religions, but you are all children of God."

ROME, MARCH 19, 2013

Ava ran hard, and as she ran she wept. She'd left the hotel in the morning, jogged out into the Piazza della Rotunda, and circled the ageless Pantheon. Passing Bernini's *Elephant and Obelisk* in the Piazza della Minerva, she took the Via del Piè di Marmo east to the Collegio Romano. She kept up a spirited pace, hoping strenuous exercise would dispel the tempest roiling within her. Instead, Ava's mind replayed an endless loop of frightful images: a man chasing her in Yemen; a policeman smiling as he shot Sefu; the throng of anti-immigrant rioters intoxicated by rage; and Sheik Ahmed's madness. She relived the terror she experienced when La Belva's helicopter exploded and the dizzying blend of guilt and gratitude she felt on learning of Simon's final sacrifice. With a cringe, Ava recalled her litany of petty insults. By what right had she judged him? Who was she to judge anyone?

Cutting north, she ran toward the Piazza di Sant' Ignazio.

There, in the shadow of the baroque Jesuit church, Ava paused, winded. Reaching for her feet, she stretched. Rays of sunshine reflected off the rooftops. Dappled Italian light began to warm the street. A dog barked as the first wave of shopkeepers emerged, readying their quaint stores and cafés for a busy day, the Feast of St. Joseph. Ava smiled. Her sadness finally ebbed and was replaced by a sense of purpose.

She resumed her course, pushing to complete another circuit. What's done is done, she realized, and can't be undone. Mistakes cannot be erased, but perhaps they can be redeemed. Rather than hiding in academe, Ava vowed to embrace life, utilizing her gifts and abilities to make a better world. Inspired, she felt better—good enough to attempt one more lap.

A sweaty, exhausted Ava flashed her room key to the hotel doorman. She crossed the lobby, smiling again at its graceful arched ceiling, red tile floor, and clean, whitewashed walls. In the room she found Paul stuck on the phone, just as she'd left him. With his free hand, he waved a greeting, then pantomimed a mouth yammering endlessly. Simon's death had generated a host of complications. His will named Paul as the executor, tasking him with distributing DeMaj assets to a select group of charities. In addition, by a quirk of Italian law, Paul had become Mellania's guardian. A nonresident alien, she'd been paroled into Simon's custody after her previous arrest, and upon his death she'd become a ward of his estate. Thus, despite Paul's duty to testify for the prosecution at Mellania's trial, he'd begun the arduous process of finding her a good criminal lawyer. Ava recommended hiring the cheapest attorney in the phone book.

Covering the mouthpiece with his palm, Paul stage-whispered,

"I'm sorry. It shouldn't be much longer." Ava shrugged, removed her new pink Reeboks, and retreated into the marble bathroom. She stripped away her sweat-soaked clothes and stepped into a relaxing shower.

An hour later she reappeared looking clean and pretty. Paul sat slumped behind the desk, still holding the phone to his ear. He'd ordered brunch: A platter of *salame di Aant'Olcese* (coarse-ground, aged Genoa salami mixed with salt, black pepper, garlic, and white wine), a brioche, butter, fresh fruit, and sliced tomato sat untouched on the marble-topped table. Ava lifted a bottle of fruit juice from a silver bucket and poured herself a glass. After waiting a suitable interval, she crossed the room, took the phone from Paul's hand, and hung it up.

"Time to eat," she announced. He smiled at her.

Halfway through the meal, Paul said, "I spoke to Nick last night. Sinan's recovering. He'll be okay. Nick will stay with him until he's out of the hospital."

"What a relief!"

Paul gestured toward a nicely wrapped parcel resting on the nightstand. "That's for you."

Her eyes widened. "Why, Mr. Grant! How generous! Thank you. I don't—"

He raised a hand for silence. "It's something he wanted you to have."

Hands shaking, Ava opened the package. Inside was the priceless blue porcelain tea service. A handwritten card read: IN CASE YOU NEVER LEARN TO ENJOY COFFEE —S.D.

To celebrate the new pontiff's official inauguration, more than one million visitors from around the world had gathered in Rome, infusing the city with optimism. As the flags of numerous nations waved in the bright sunshine, Pope Francis addressed the crowd. He urged his listeners to become protectors: "The vocation of being a 'protector' . . . is not just something involving us Christians alone; it also has a prior dimension which is simply human, involving everyone. It means protecting all creation, the beauty of the created world. . . . Whenever human beings fail to live up to this responsibility, whenever we fail to care for creation and for our brothers and sisters, the way is opened to destruction and hearts are hardened. Tragically, in every period of history, there are 'Herods' who plot death, wreak havoc, and mar the countenance of men and women. Please, I would like to ask all those . . . of goodwill: let us be protectors of creation, protectors of God's plan inscribed in nature, 'protectors' of one another and of the environment. Let us not allow omens of destruction and death to accompany the advance of this world!"

Hours later the Americans were strolling along Via Condotti. Hoping to arrive on time at the historic Caffé Greco, Paul took Ava's hand and helped her cut through the crowd.

Open since 1760, the establishment had hosted Stendhal, Goethe, Keats, and Baudelaire. Casanova sipped drinks there, as did Mark Twain and Lord Byron. Gogol wrote *Dead Souls* in the same room in which Wagner and Liszt met for pastries. Rossini composed on the rear parlor piano. The painter de Chirico called it "the place to sit and await the end."

Paul and Ava waited in the foyer for a table. Eventually a tail-coated *cameriere* escorted them beyond a carved wooden bar, past tourists resting on red velvet sofas, and into a labyrinth of private salons. Mendelssohn's "Violin Concerto in E Minor" played in the background. Rooms were adorned with gilt antique mirrors, faded photos of the café's illustrious habitués, and romantic paintings set against a backdrop of gold and red damask. The *cameriere* seated them on richly upholstered chairs before a table of Napoleonic design. Paul ordered *granita di caffè;* Ava asked for a *cioccolata calda* with extra whipped cream.

After the waiter left, Ava excused herself to visit the rest room. As she stood, Paul's eyes involuntarily tracked her thigh-high stockings, right up to the point where they disappeared beneath a pleated miniskirt. Feeling his eyes on her, she suppressed a grin. Paul began stammering an apology but then the world phone rang. Ava scanned the caller ID and answered. Waving adieu to Paul, she walked off engrossed in conversation.

When she returned, Paul asked, "Who was that?"

"DURMDVL."

He tensed. "What's wrong?"

"Not a thing. We're getting together when I'm back in the States."

"Okay," he said, eyes clouding.

She looked at him. "Is that a problem?"

"No, of course not. That guy saved our bacon. I owe him big time."

Ava giggled. "DURMDVL's not a guy. She's a sophomore at Duke."

He brightened. "Seriously?"

Before Ava could explain the illogic of his sexist assumptions, Barakah arrived. Paul stood to greet him, and Ava invited the officer to sit. He presented the couple with notarized confirmation that Egypt had dropped its extradition demands and dismissed the criminal charges against them. Ava was relieved.

"And may I add that the Order of the Shepherd sends its compliments. You've earned our eternal gratitude."

"Awesome," said Paul. "I have no idea what you're talking about."

A smiling Barakah said, "We're a secret brotherhood, sworn to protect humanity. Garagallo's amulet bears our crest. Some claim the order was founded by Joachim of Flora in the twelfth century, others say it's much older."

"Joachim the what?"

"Joachim of Flora was an influential mystic theologian, a contemporary of Richard the Lionheart," Ava explained. "Joachim visited Jerusalem during the Crusades and foretold the dawning of a new age in which rigid Church hierarchy would be obsolete and Christians could unite with non-Christians. He was too radical to be canonized, but the Franciscan monks considered him a prophet."

Barakah nodded. "Brother Joachim understood the true message. He taught that Antichrists threaten all humanity, not just Christians. Accordingly, our brotherhood welcomes any who oppose hatred and evil. Regardless of faith, we are all children of God. Catholic Bishop Garagallo and Coptic Father Bessarion are my brothers, as were the seven brave Egyptians who fell defending the jars."

Recalling that moment, Paul's face darkened. "I'm not sure I deserve any gratitude. "

"You played a critical role. But for you, Ava would have perished."

"But for me, she would never have been in danger."

"Perhaps, but who else could have unlocked the prophecy? If she'd remained in Boston—"

"I'm not exactly sold on my contribution either," Ava said. "A helicopter crash stopped La Belva. Simon DeMaj sacrificed his life. All I did was shout into a microphone. Anyone could have done that."

Barakah shrugged. "The fact remains that you read the prophecy aloud and the devil was vanquished. Whether this was coincidence or predestination is unclear. I don't believe in coincidences, but then I'm just a policeman, not a philosopher."

Paul smiled. Barakah stood. "I respect Simon's decision. He died a hero, but we each played a role. Both of you faced destiny with valor. You put others' lives before your own, and when darkness threatened, you found the courage to fight. For that, we're forever in your debt."

He replaced his chair, bowed formally to Ava, and took Paul's outstretched hand.

"*Gardez bien.*"

Ava and Paul left the café. Hand in hand, they walked to the Spanish Steps, where artists, students, and backpackers had gathered to drink wine and socialize. An olive-skinned lad strummed a familiar melody and sang, "Each day I pray for evening, just to be with you."

While Paul went looking for a good place to sit, Ava dropped a coin in the musician's guitar case.

Resting on the ancient masonry, she crossed her ankles and leaned back against Paul. Together they watched the Roman sun disappear behind Michelangelo's dome. Daylight dimmed. Then, for an instant, Ava beheld a bright emerald gleam. "Paul, have you ever seen anything so beautiful?" she marveled.

He didn't respond. Curious, she turned to find him looking at her. Their eyes locked and he whispered: "Yes."

Ava couldn't breathe. Her pulse thundered. He pulled her toward him. Her lips parted. She shut her eyes, opened her heart, and surrendered herself to his kiss.

EPILOGUE

Catherine de Médicis knows secret paths through the palace. Though born in Florence, she'd lived in Paris all her adult life. It has been twenty-two years since her uncle Pope Clement VII had arranged her marriage to King Francis's second son, Henry of Orleans. She pauses a moment, remembering the innocent child she'd once been.

Her arrival in France had caused quite a stir. To enter grandly, the diminutive Catherine employed a Florentine artisan who, on her behalf, created Europe's first pair of high-heeled shoes. After the wedding Catherine toured the country. The king found his new daughter-in-law a wonderful traveling companion, but King Francis aside, Catherine had few allies at court. She was generally disliked by the French. Jealous nobles referred to her as "the Italian woman." Many suspected foul play when Francis's eldest son died, making Henry heir to the throne. When Francis died, in 1547, Catherine became queen.

Despite producing seven children (three of whom became kings of France), Queen Catherine has retained her youthful figure. She is an attractive, regal woman with fair hair and the enchanting eyes of a Medici. Nevertheless, her marriage is a loveless farce. Catherine's husband is openly besotted with his domineering mistress, Diane de Poitiers, who controls the weak-minded king.

Francis had been an enlightened monarch. Under his rule, in 1534 seven gifted university students formed the Jesuit order. Now de Poitiers is pressuring Henry to reverse his father's humanist policies; to stifle the dissemination of knowledge by banning the sale or import of all unapproved texts; and to persecute the Huguenots, many of whom Henry now orders burned at the stake. These radical decisions infuriate Catherine. She thinks it unwise to punish men who worship in private and never take up arms against France. The queen conceals her political opinions, however, and focuses her considerable energy and attention on maternal duties.

To serve as tutors, she'd beckoned a variety of intellectual luminaries to Paris, eminent scientists, authors, and doctors. One provincial healer, who had protected her family from the plague, made a particularly strong impression. Catherine had him designated royal counselor and physician. It is this man whom she seeks now.

Catherine passes through the majestic library that King Francis had so greatly expanded. In 1537, his Ordonnance de Montpellier required that the royal collection receive one copy of every book sold in France. Francis appointed the noted humanist Guillaume Budé his chief librarian and summoned the Italian master Leonardo da Vinci from Rome to serve as Paintre du Roi. At Francis's request, French agents had scoured the monasteries of Europe and amassed a wealth of rare books and manuscripts. Later, Francis shocked Parisian society by opening his library to scholars of all nationalities, facilitating the general diffusion of knowledge.

Catherine exits the main gallery via a concealed doorway. She enters a musty, forgotten chamber that had once housed the king's personal library. As a younger woman she'd often escaped here. In this hidden room she was free to explore, read forbidden books, and avoid the disagreeable courtiers' incessant barbs. Peeking around a bookshelf, the queen observes Michel at his labors. The doctor is seated at a writing desk, not far from a mechanical lion Leonardo gave King Francis in 1515. Classical volumes by Livy, Suetonius, and Plutarch as well as the medieval chroniclers Villehardouin and Froissart are arrayed around him. Scribbling diligently by candlelight, the doctor appears to be translating the ancient writings into French.

"What wicked secrets have you unveiled?" she whispers to him.

The physician, startled, jumps to his feet, bumping a candlestick and almost scorching an irreplaceable manuscript.

"Oh, your Highness! My manners are unforgivable. I sincerely apologize. I did not hear you enter, I was so immersed in my research."

She smiles. "You are forgiven. What are you reading? Galen again? Hippocrates?"

"No, my lady. Today I'm translating prophetic works of great antiquity."

"What manner of prophecy?"

"Just . . . arcane eschatological matters, nothing of practical significance," he says.

Intrigued, by his obvious embarrassment, the queen commands, "Doctor, read aloud what you have translated."

Michel gulps.

"'At that time the prince of iniquity, who will be called Antichrist, shall arise from the tribe of Dan. He will be the son of perdition, the head of pride, the master of error, the fullness of malice who will overturn the world through dissimulation. He will delude many by magic art, and fire will seem to come down from heaven. When the Roman city is attacked, the Antichrist is revealed.'"

"The Antichrist?"

"Yes, Highness. He is an evil force or being who threatens humanity's future. This volume describes the invasion of Gog and Magog and the tribulations that precede the end of days."

She nods thoughtfully. "I have something that might interest you," she says.

The queen crosses the chamber and pulls a tattered portfolio from the alcove where she found it, quite by accident, more than a decade earlier. It must have sat undisturbed for years. The reign of Louis XI ended long before Catherine's time. Befouled by a century's accumulated dust and rat droppings, and with the Spider King's royal seal broken, the packet appeared worthless, but its contents were intact. Opening the folder, Catherine withdraws seven sheets of fragile vellum and passed them to the curious doctor. He is amazed to behold a bizarre ancient apocalypse. Someone had translated the prophetic text from Old Syriac into Latin and organized it into quatrains. As Catherine has anticipated, the physician is enraptured. Eagerly, Michel de Nostradamus spread the vellum across his desk and begins to read.

> *The enemy of Romans killed*
> *On the anniversary of his accession.*
> *The stable maid's constant son*
> *in this sign shall conquer!*

> *The new city contemplates damnation,*
> *Birds of prey circle the heavens.*
> *After victory, pardon to the captives,*
> *Cremona and Mantua witness great evils.*

Allies repel invaders eastern,
Flaming swords across the river,
The scourge is merciful before death,
A lion crowns his heir.

Cities twin of seven hills,
The younger stands one thousand years,
Before the desert army cheers,
Never again under Rome!

The wise vicar defends the Tiber,
One walks barefoot to the white kirk
After him, the papal vessel is lost,
Shattered to its great detriment.

Here the crusader lies—death at Ancona,
Venetian sails too late, too late,
The sultan survives a night attack,
The dragon's son twelve years in chains.

Though Colossus's island falls,
The Christian city is retaken,
After the great invader's death,
Italy again defended.

By the hermitage—a lost castle found,
Do pilgrims arrive too late?
Surprised by night, seven guards attacked,
Can the last act be done?

David Beckett

Winds howl against the travelers,
Letters intercepted on their way,
Great disaster near, combat very bitter,
Even the bravest heart trembles.

Without succor from the devil,
Pilgrims cannot pass from Egypt,
Pursued by a wicked African heart,
Who terrifies the heir of Romulus.

One leads divisions against the shepherds,
Where veins open, food for the dead,
Cries, tears at Malta,
Combat by night, valiant captain victorious!

The infamous man, who gathers gold,
Raised from low to high estate,
Reverses course, takes up the cross,
Under the pyramids' shadow.

Sons of England sent from France,
By grapes, goose, and stag,
Now come great floods and storms,
Flags! Shipwreck! An ocean fleet defeated.

The spider stings the fisherman,
An opening to the Mahometans,
Dreadful horrors and vengeance,
Malta sold for a falcon.

As for the light, led thus by its angel,
The princes draw near to judgment,
Famine and war beyond cease in Persia,
Heaven's arrow stikes the northern kingdom.

From the fifth celestial light
A lion speaks in riddles.
The Bishop of Rome resigns his throne
The lady cannot answer.

Mankind misled by a false prophet,
Foolish lords wage ignorant war,
Witness the rapacious, bloodthirsty demon
Evil laughter and rejoicing.

A crafty one avoids the snares.
Enemies assail from three sides,
Strange travelers concealed by hoods,
The translator's grandeur must not fail.

Unless the prophecy is proclaimed
Where the great leaders gather
A new devil rises: invincible deceiver!
Rage and terror consume the world of man.

Behold your Antichrist: He is here.
How much blood must flow, valiant, and be gone?
The demon stokes the furnace of war,
And burns the last Golden Age from Earth!

2012 TUSCANY PRIZE FOR CATHOLIC FICTION

NOVEL

Wild Spirits
By Pita Okute

NOVELLA

The Book of Jotham
By Arthur Powers

2012 Tuscany Prize for Catholic Fiction – Selected Short Stories
Edited by Joseph O'Brien

OTHER TITLES BY TUSCANY PRESS

NOVEL

A Hunger in the Heart
By Kaye Park Hinckley

CPSIA information can be obtained at www.ICGtesting.com
Printed in the USA
LVOW12*1559210414

382583LV00010B/120/P